Opeki

Quentin Black

Copyright © 2025 Quentin Black All rights reserved

The characters and events portrayed in this book are fictitious. Any similarity to real persons, living or dead, is coincidental and not intended by the author.

No part of this book may be reproduced, stored in a retrieval system, or transmitted in any form or by any means, electronic, mechanical, photocopying, recording, or otherwise, without the express written permission of the publisher.

Cover design by: Golden-Rivet

https://golden-rivet.com/

DEDICATION

To Gary & Fiona Mew

AUTHOR'S NOTES

Though set in 1997, some historical events might have received the artistic licensed brush stroke regarding chronological fluidity.

Definitions of specific terms and phrases are italicised and emboldened and can be found in the glossary.

DEDICATION

To Gary & Fiona Mew

AUTHOR'S NOTES

Though set in 1997, some historical events might have received the artistic licensed brush stroke regarding chronological fluidity.

Definitions of specific terms and phrases are italicised and emboldened and can be found in the glossary.

PROLOGUE

Until death, all defeats are psychological.

—attributed to Robert Greene,
derived from the teachings of Carl von
Clausewitz.

ACKNOWLEDGEMENTS

Holly Mew, for your constant support.

Golden-Rivet, for the cover design and promotional video.

Alun Denbigh-White, for your pre-proofing and plot critiques.

Daniel 'Farno' Holmes, for your editorial input.

1

1995. Late Spring.

PRAGUE CITY CENTRE — CZECH REPUBLIC — MORNING

Frank Carlsmith squeezed his fist in relief as the radio announcer in his right ear screeched that Denis Irwin had scored in the eightieth minute against Southampton

He sat alone in a Škoda 1203 van, its white and blue paint dulled by the sun and soot, reminding him of a second-hand Scooby Doo Mystery Machine.

It clung to a kerb within the clattering bustle of Prague's city centre

"Yeh, fuck off, Blackburn," he whispered to himself as the goal kept Manchester United's title hopes alive over their Lancashire rivals.

He took a drag of a Cleopatra grape-flavour cigarette; a half-finished pack had been left in the van.

Frank didn't have an allegiance to a particular brand and enjoyed the taste.

Through the windshield, across the blurred reflection of passing trams and trailing headlights, he watched the restaurant.

He caught his reflection in the shop window opposite, the crown of once purely ginger hair seeming to turn greyer by the day.

Stop your whinging, he told himself. *You were lucky to hang on to the colour this long—at least you've still got the lot.*

Born in the late forties, Frank remembered that when he was around ten years old, his usually fiscally responsible father purchased a television set.

Everyone in the family knew his United-mad dad had done so to watch the European Cup semi-final versus Real Madrid.

They lost.

However, it was the first time an English club had entered the European Cup after United had won the First Division title by eleven points.

They all remained hopeful of future success—until the Munich Air Disaster.

His father had pessimistically declared, *'That's fucked it.'*

Still, out of the literal and metaphorical ashes, Sir Matt Busby's efforts to evolve the team over time culminated in winning the European Cup.

Took a decade, though, mind, thought Frank, who wondered if the nation of Russia would make a similar resurgence.

Despite the modern, urban Wild West the major cities of Russia and the former Soviet Bloc countries currently resembled, Frank's **SIS** handler had stated, *'…a confused, wounded bear can be just as dangerous as a healthy, predatory one. Besides, it won't be confused and wounded forever.'*

His blue electrician's overalls, worn at the elbows and smelling faintly of tobacco and engine oil, bore the same logo as the van. They concealed a physique that, despite his approaching fifty, remained tightly corded with hard muscle.

Not that his current work required the same level of fitness and physicality as his **SBS** days. Frank remembered that, back in his short Royal Marine career, one of the corporals had a folded piece of paper slid into the square of clear plastic that protected the size label of his green beret.

When Frank had asked him about it, the corporal replied, *'I write down the most challenging thing I've ever done in the Corps—training doesn't count. So, when I am going through hard times, I can look at it and think, "Well, this is not as hard as that," or I get to change it for whatever I am going through and feel good about myself.'*

Frank had copied the corporal's lead, and it surprised him that despite the numerous Special Forces operations, it was the SBS exercises simulating the retaking of North Sea oil rigs from terrorists in the late seventies that remained beneath his old beret.

Arduous swims from miles out after release from the submarine, followed by brutal climbs up the installations' legs using magnets while burdened by all the necessary kit. After this, clearances using **simunition** while maintaining the delicate balance between aggression and control, only taking out the 'terrorists', not the civilians.

At the time, Frank remembered a footballer in a telly interview justifying a bad tackle with *'…I got caught in the moment and couldn't stop…'* to which Frank had thought, *If we said the same, an innocent person could die.* Once he returned to Poole and **deserviced and reserviced** his kit, Frank thought, *Now then, there is fuck all I can't accomplish.*

The yellow brickwork of the U Holubů restaurant caught the morning sun. Situated at an intersection in the city centre, Frank noted a complete lack of graffiti distinguished it from the surrounding buildings.

He took a swig of bottled water. When

operating in certain countries, a decision had to be made whether to drink the tap water and risk illness or use bottled water, potentially drawing attention to the fact that you weren't a local.

Fortunately, many locals in Prague drank bottled water due to concerns about the old pipework.

The horn 'pip' of a blue Opel Kadett alerted him to Tomáš Koukal's arrival.

Frank knew the haggard restaurant owner would have had the wolves of both fear and hope fighting within his psyche for the past two weeks.

The Mancunian had begun developing Koukal as an asset more than six months ago.

The fifty-one-year-old transplanted German, originally from Leipzig, had found himself ensnared via gambling debts to what he thought was the Russian mob—technically accurate, but Frank and SIS had discovered it to be specifically the Mogilevich group.

The Ukrainian-born Russian organised crime boss, Semion Mogilevich, not much older than Frank, had been an economics graduate from the University of Lviv.

Although Mogilevich's crimes could involve violence, it had been impressed upon Frank that the crime lord's astuteness regarding the global monetary system made him particularly dangerous.

Frank pulled the Škoda out and drove to a parking spot just outside the restaurant.

He got out, opened the back doors and took out a red mechanic's service cart, placing a large toolbox on it.

Metallic rattling sounded as he pushed,

dragged and lifted it through the restaurant's entrance to meet a pale Koukal, who informed him in English, "The big boss and whatever gorilla he has with him will be less than fifteen minutes."

Frank nodded. "Lead the way."

Koukal looked at him for a moment before turning and walking down the hallway.

A long, narrow runner stretched along the floor, woven in rich burgundy and gold, hushing their steps.

The dining room looked as big as some of the ***galleys*** and cookhouses Frank had been in.

Golden morning light crept in through tall, drape-framed windows, casting long, elegant shadows across the parquet floor. The chandeliers, comprising opulent blooms of crystal and brass shaped like the crowns of kings, glimmered faintly in the natural light.

The gold covings contrasted with the pastoral green of the floral-patterned wallpaper.

"OK," said Frank, looking around. "I will set up facing the stag head ornament light in the corner."

"Will he not be suspicious that you are not in the control room?"

"Yes, and he'll come up to confront me," said Frank. "Which is where I want him."

"His bodyguard is very professional," said Koukal, his nerves jumping out of his mouth.

"Good," said Frank. "Then he won't be a hair-trigger."

Koukal fidgeted for a moment. "What happens to me if you fail?"

"It's my people you are going to meet to extract you, Tomáš. You and your money are safe, even if I am not."

Frank took out a scrap of paper and handed it to him. "All the details are on that. I suggest you ***scarper*** while you still can."

Tomáš Koukal whirled around and left.

Frank moved the hexagonal wood stand on which the stag head rested to expose the plug socket behind it and donned the headphones of the Walkman attached to his hip—not that anything played through them.

Tomáš's German sense of timing could be relied upon as minutes later Frank heard the outer door bang open with a voice calling in Russian, "Tomáš! Gde ty?!"—*Tomáš! Where are you?*

Frank's hand reached into the toolbox to pull out what he needed.

The dining room door slammed open as Frank knelt, feigning fixing the plug socket behind the stand.

"Ey. Gde Tomáš?"—*Hey. Where is Tomáš?*—called out the voice behind him.

Frank bopped his head a little to the imaginary music.

The steps thumped closer, and the voice roared, "Gde Tomáš?!"

Frank spun around, pulling the pin of the M52 grenade.

2

TWO YEARS LATER

KASTAMONU FOREST — NORTHERN TURKEY — DAWN

In the dawn twilight, the wind whispered through the skeletal branches of the Kastamonu Forest. The kind of wind that watched, curling through the trees in long, measured breaths, mimicking the way Genrikh Bezmenov now breathed while watching the crepuscular Anatolian deer through the Leupold Vari II scope of his German bolt-action Mauser 98 hunting rifle.

The tall Bezmenov remembered his first hunt in the dead of winter within the Bryansk Forest of Russia, close to Belarus.

That had been over four decades ago, when the Russian was shy of a teenager. His uncle on his mother's side had been a party historian and a decorated tank commander during the Great Patriotic War.

He'd taken a quasi-father-figure role to Genrikh in the wake of his father's death.

The square-jawed, salt-and-pepper Bezmenov was currently around two decades older than his uncle had been back then.

'If there is a mother with her fawn, then shoot the fawn,' his uncle had said.

'Why?'

'Because a mother can survive without her fawn. The

opposite is not true—the fawn will die a brutal, prolonged death,' came the reply. *'Most of the time, the mother will hang around her dead offspring, and you can shoot them both anyway.'*

His first kill had been clean, tracking the crosshair up the back of the mother's front leg and stilling it just above and behind the shoulder.

The stag he stalked now walked a more magnificent creature than the European roebucks he had encountered back in those days; much heavier, longer, thicker-necked, taller and this one having twelve points on its antlers, whereas the most he had seen on a European roe had been six.

Given the way its coat of rich, earthen red, almost bronze under the pale sun, constantly shifted position, Bezmenov wondered if the deer knew his presence and intent and chose to engage the ***SVR***—Foreign Intelligence Service of the Russian Federation—colonel in a death game of dare.

His uncle had also told him, *'A day hunting that does not result in a kill is still a good day. The day you shoot an animal without killing it cleanly is more than a bad day—it is sacrilege.'*

This stag would teasingly present itself broadside-on for a second, only to turn and face Bezmenov's direction or away.

He had not hunted for a long time and didn't wish to risk a neck shot.

Patience, he told himself. *You will get him.*

He relaxed, floating the crosshairs in tandem with the bull's movements.

It ate. Raised its head. Broadside.

The crack of the Mauser's report thundered through the valley.

The electrical signals in the stag's already dead body made it take several bounds before its collapse.

"Seventy metres," came the voice from behind. "Fine shot."

Bezmenov turned to face a tall, black-haired man with gloved hands in the pockets of an olive-waxed overcoat.

Ravil Yelchin stood as a rising star within the ***Solntsevskaya Bratva***—the organised crime element that had established itself as the most powerful to emerge from the chaos of the USSR's collapse.

Ravil, already one of its leading figures and not yet forty, had established himself as that rarity within organised crime—a leading money maker and a brave soldier.

The two spoke in Russian.

"Thank you for allowing me the privilege," replied Bezmenov, slinging the Mauser over his shoulder and moving towards the deer.

They reached the carcass together.

The younger man said, "Hunting is not a rarity for me, though less so now. Seemed only right for you to rediscover your affection. Maybe you can do more in retirement—though that might be a while."

The SVR colonel wondered if the crime boss might have guessed the nature of their meeting.

Standing over the bull, Bezmenov touched the stag's eye to ensure a lack of blink reflex.

He felt a vague satisfaction on seeing it indeed a clean kill—not only did this reduce the animal's suffering but the risk of the meat being contaminated by damaged innards.

The two men talked as they went through ***gralloching*** the stag.

His uncle had recommended simply washing his hands, but the adult Bezmenov donned a pair of plastic gloves, as did Ravil. They manoeuvred the animal to face down the gentle slope, and Bezmenov checked for any obvious disease.

"I was a little surprised with regards to the invite," said Ravil. "Out in the middle of nowhere. Rifles. I thought maybe my relationship with the SVR had expired. But then I thought that if the colonel wanted me to disappear, perhaps he wouldn't risk himself."

Bezmenov used his old *ladon'*—around six inches—hunting knife to bleed the animal, inserting it sideways an inch or two above the sternum, pushing it towards the heart, severing the blood vessels.

As the two men gripped and manoeuvred the beast to speed the bleeding, the older man answered, "Perhaps I invited you because I knew it was the only way to get you out into the open."

Bezmenov opened the animal's throat and grabbed hold of the food pipe, cutting and then pulling it, scraping away the excess red flesh to reveal the white tacky surface before severing and tying it in a balloon knot.

He also cut the trachea, which always reminded him of a rubber chicken's leg, to allow for the lungs to be pulled out.

"We both know my death would be as simple as you ordering Makar to assassinate me."

Two years prior, Bezmenov had sent the twenty-two-year-old Makar Gorokhov to see Ravil regarding fifty-two million roubles that Ravil had extorted from various Moscow officials following the collapse of the Soviet Union.

Typically, a fully-fledged deep-cover agent of the SVR would be no younger than twenty-five; only university graduates were eligible, meaning they did not enter training until at least after their twenty-first birthday, and the training for an 'illegal'—deep cover—took three to four years, as opposed to the two or three for officers with official diplomatic cover.

However, following an exodus of KGB—the SVR's Soviet predecessor—agents in the wake of the collapse, desperate measures had been taken and compromises made.

Makar had been identified as a prodigy, as his high school grades had been exceptional, despite his standing as a nationally-rated Sambist—a practitioner of Sambo.

Plucked from high school, Makar had been sent to the Andropov Red Banner Institute (KGB/SVR training academy).

After passing the screening, spycraft and intelligence training and a year of advanced specialisation, Bezmenov took a personal interest in his probationary period of field training and trial missions.

Following Makar's first trial mission, Bezmenov summoned the fearsome young agent to his office to give him his orders to recover the money Yelchin had stolen.

Placing his index finger over the point of the outward facing blade, Bezmenov completed a long, shallow incision along the deer's belly, being mindful to avoid cutting into the body to prevent the blunting of the blade and hair entering the carcass.

Steam rose in waves from the cavity.

"You're correct there," admitted the SVR colonel. "I never asked you about young Gorokhov's performance that day. Our arrangement being established confirmed its success, but I lack knowledge of the details."

Ravil chuckled. "As you know, I was residing in a hotel in Prague. Later that evening, I was to attend a party for one of the other members of the brotherhood. I had ordered room service. In walks the waiter with the tray. My security goes to pat him down, only to find their consciousness unceremoniously stripped from them during a very brief fight. I grab my Röhm RG Series revolver—I like the extra reliability over automatics—and point it at the man, only for him to show a complete lack of fear. Told me to dismiss the security as they came around. I initially refused, stating that since I had a gun, he was in no position to be giving orders. He then turned, knelt, interlaced his fingers and told me to check the bullets in the revolver. I did to see they were star-crimped."

This information indeed surprised Bezmenov; blank rounds were usually crimped at the end—either roll or star—for several reasons, including holding the propellant powder in place. Makar must have ascertained that Ravil had been armed and somehow switched out the ammunition beforehand.

Bezmenov began to gently pull the guts out while using his knife to free them from the surrounding tissue.

"Any ideas how he achieved that?"

"No, and I have asked."

"What then?" asked Bezmenov, laying them on a nearby rock.

"Well, seeing the weakness of my hand, I heard his proposal," said Ravil. "Or, I might say, your proposal—to pay back part of the money I had allegedly extorted and take Makar on as an adviser of sorts. Or… what were the words… I could suffer a fever."

The colonel busied himself removing the penis and testes and said, "I am glad you accepted his first suggestion. I am sure you'd agree it has been advantageous for all parties."

"Accepting his proposal not to attend the U Holubů restaurant for Semion Mogilevich's birthday that night was especially advantageous to me. The Czech police raided it. But then Semion never arrived either. However, thirty of the Bratva were arrested."

"Yes," said the colonel. "Rumours abound that the Solntsevskaya Bratva were due to assassinate Semion Mogilevich that night. Luckily, your boss Sergei Mikhailov did not attend either."

"Yes, luckily," said Ravil.

Bezmenov set about removing the pluck—the heart, lungs, kidneys and liver—placing it with the guts. Though these were undamaged due to the clean shot and thus edible, he wanted to lighten the weight and mess for the hike back.

He had no doubt that not only had Ravil warned his Bratva boss off, but he had also done the same for Mogilevich.

The colonel said, "I have a proposition for you. Highly lucrative but highly dangerous."

"Intriguing," answered Ravil. "So… you have a proposition, not the SVR."

Bezmenov's heart beat harder as he prepared to pass the point of no return.

"That is correct," said the foreign intelligence colonel. "And if they did know, it would mean both our deaths—yours perhaps quicker."

"We should talk money before specifics."

"You will pay me three million US dollars."

A moment of quiet fell as Bezmenov went through the process of removing the buck's rectum.

"Pay you three million for what?"

Bezmenov inhaled through his nose.

"The location of three man-portable atomic demolition munitions."

Another quiet moment ensued.

The Mafioso said, "I was told that these 'suitcase nukes' were the stuff of Western spy novels?"

"They are not," said the SVR colonel.

A hush floated down as they set about sectioning the carcass and dividing the parts between their respective backpacks.

"You will have to elaborate further, Colonel."

"Are you interested?" he asked, and they both stood to begin the hike back.

"There might be certain parties willing to pay a lot of money for such items," stated Ravil. "But despite my faith in your professionalism, I need to know that this is not a speculative adventure. Not as the English would say, 'A wild goose chase.'"

Bezmenov nodded his acquiescence. "Not only are 'suitcase' nukes real, but we built over one hundred and thirty of them. Most are the model RA-115S, and a minority are the model RA-115-01S, which can be submersible."

"They can fit into an actual suitcase? Or was that hyperbole?"

The SVR colonel nodded. "Thirty centimetres in length and width and eighteen centimetres thick. Designed so that the radio receiver port and charger would have room in the same suitcase."

"As simple as leaving it somewhere it won't be found and walking away?"

"Not exactly. They need to be detonated by a radio trigger. Very powerful and can be triggered outside the blast radius."

"Good to know for the potential trigger man."

"Yes," Bezmenov said cautiously. "However, the closer the detonator to the radio receiver, the more reliable the signal."

"You mean the more determined the triggerman, the more likely the bomb will explode."

"Yes, though I have no reason to doubt its reliability," said Bezmenov before quickly moving on. "The United States and Israel have developed their versions. Each RA-115S has a yield of around one kiloton. For perspective, the atomic bomb dropped on Hiroshima had a yield of approximately fifteen."

"Can you describe the effects of it?"

"In the open, a hundred and fifty metres of vapourisation. Severe structural damage and likely lethal radiation dose up to five hundred metres. Flash blindness occurs when looked at directly. Glass shatters for two to three kilometres. The fallout could spread several kilometres if taken by wind, but it takes many minutes to build. All this is mitigated if detonated within a structurally strong building or underground."

"And there are over one hundred and thirty of them," exclaimed the usually calm Ravil.

"Not anymore. During the Dissolution of the Soviet Union, the Kremlin ordered them to be removed from the arsenals of the individual Eastern Bloc militaries for decommissioning and their assigned target plans destroyed. They were under the control of the ***GRU***'s 12th Main Directorate. However, the politicians—rightly—sensed dissension amongst certain senior GRU officers, and so a KGB detachment was sent to oversee the decommissioning."

"And you were on that detachment," said Ravil, more as a statement than a question.

"I was tasked to lead it, with some vague oversight. It was all very chaotic at the time," said Bezmenov. "A former GRU operative named Stanislav Yablokov and his cohorts stole three of them. In late 1991, he attempted to sell them to the Chechen militia. He had arranged a meeting with one of their leaders. An assembly I also attended with a Spetsnaz team—a brief firefight ensued where some of the Chechens escaped but the other attendees killed. I killed Yablokov after he revealed that the three munitions lay in his vehicle."

"Not that your official report stated that."

"No."

They walked on, and after a few moments, Ravil said, "The agents you paid me to have killed in Europe were your co-conspirators."

"Some," admitted Bezmenov.

"You're a sly fox, Bezmenov," said Ravil with almost admiration in his voice. "Can you give me a rough idea of their location?"

"Northern Ukraine."

"Of course," said Ravil. "Chernobyl. Any hint of radiation signature would be masked there."

"A good guess, but the cases are designed to delete radiation emissions, though minute amounts might still escape," said Bezmenov. "However, the specific area is heavily restricted yet largely unmonitored."

"Here is another guess—the area is due for a modification, repair or demolition, and you are now considering your current age to be a good one to retire."

Though he'd had dealings with the cunning Bratva boss for years now, the speed and accuracy of Ravil's mind could still occasionally surprise him.

"The specific area will naturally not be made known to you until the transfer of funds into escrow, but yes, the structure is set for… refurbishment."

Ravil asked, "Outline the dangers of obtaining these weapons."

"There is only a danger if things go wrong," said Bezmenov, who instantly recognised the stupidity of the statement and quickly said, "Whoever retrieves them will have to pass an armed guard. However, they are unaware that the devices are present at the installation they are protecting."

"I run a team of criminals, not paramilitaries capable of taking on armed Ukrainian security."

"You will not have to," said Bezmenov. "Though under Ukrainian jurisdiction, we still have an indirect involvement regarding the handling of Soviet-era infrastructure. I can issue you and your men the relevant permits to perform an inspection and an information pack to feign suitable knowledge."

Ravil said, "So, my part is to enter Chernobyl. Fake my knowledge of nuclear material disposal. Load three atomic devices. Escape. Hold said devices before organising their sale and pray the KGB—my mistake—the SVR never discover my organisation's involvement? And for the location, a fake permit and a 'How to be a nuclear scientist' book, you want three million American dollars?"

"I want three million dollars for the initial risk I took in stealing and hiding them in the first instance. For the risk of aiding you. And to have enough to escape Russia and live a comfortable life, which means oiling the hands of certain government officials in a certain country," countered the spy master. "Considering I know that Yablokov and the Chechens had agreed on a price of eighteen million US dollars back then, you see how lucrative it can be for you."

"What parties do you imagine would buy?"

Bezmenov glanced at Ravil. "You already stated that there were certain parties who might be interested."

"Not many that I have contacts with," said Ravil. "You, however, will have many."

"I am not—"

"Here is the deal," interrupted the younger man. "We will pay you three point two million and carry out the… procurement of these devices."

"What is the extra two hundred thousand for?"

"We both know that the organisations I might have contact with and which have that sort of money, namely the Colombian cartels, the **FARC** and our Japanese, Chinese and Italian counterparts, have no need or wish to explode nuclear devices," said the Mafioso. "But you do have contacts—however tenuous—with the sort of organisations with both the funds and intent. Groups like Hezbollah, Al Qaeda, **Aum Shinrikyo** or perhaps even the IRA could scrape together the money for one. The extra two hundred thousand dollars is your fixer and auctioneer fee. Because once we have them in our possession, I do not want anyone apart from you to know we have touched them. Besides, those groups are more likely to trust a highly placed SVR colonel than a street criminal like me."

As the two walked, the distinctive contact call—***dvui***—of a nuthatch echoed through the forest.

Bezmenov considered his options.

He had assumed that Ravil might have sold them himself via proxies to the said organisations. But he could see his point; overtures by a criminal organisation—even one as powerful and rich as the Solntsevskaya Bratva—might not be taken seriously.

However, even though the extra two hundred thousand dollars had a strong attraction, what Ravil proposed increased his exposure almost exponentially.

But I will be on the run anyway, thought Bezmenov.

Then it came to him.

"I will organise the auction. Whatever the total sale value, I get half. It was my idea, my execution in the first instance. And I am the one exposed—like you said, no one would know of your involvement."

There was barely a moment's silence before Ravil countered, "Sixty-forty in my favour. I have to distribute the money amongst my team, who will be doing the heavy lifting. Your team no longer exists."

Bezmenov had already considered the price they might fetch on the black market.

He knew he couldn't reach out to state-level actors like North Korea or Iran—at least not directly—so he'd have to sell them to a terrorist network with less liquidity and therefore fiscal bargaining power.

The fact that they had Soviet serials and radioactive fingerprinting lessened their value due to their age and—if the buyer cared—their potential traceability over a reverse-engineered mock-up.

He reckoned only two groups had instant access to the funds to afford all the devices.

Al Qaeda's leader was Osama Bin Laden. Though allegedly estranged from his family and therefore their purported five-billion-dollar fortune, the SVR's last report put Osama's personal fortune at around thirty million dollars, but he would have access to wealthy Islamic donors.

Hezbollah had the backing of Iran, a nation that had expressed an interest in developing a nuclear capability during the rule of Shah Mohammad Reza Pahlavi back in the 1950s.

Maybe they would express interest in having one of the small, portable tactical nuclear weapons reverse-engineered.

He knew the relationship between Hezbollah and Al Qaeda was complex; though both shared common enemies in Israel and the United States and thus shared some limited logistical support and training, the Sunni extremists often looked upon the Shi'a Hezbollah as heretics.

Neither would want to cede the weapons to the other.

Throw in maybe a negotiator from Aum Shinrikyo or maybe the IRA, and the price could be driven higher.

Though accepting he was a former Soviet-era spy and perhaps the antithesis of a capitalist businessman, he felt confident he could facilitate a sale upwards of thirty million if he could initiate a bidding war.

Four times his original asking price just to arrange and oversee an auction.

Bezmenov switched to English, "You have a

deal."

SOUTHERN END OF MACGILLYCUDDY'S REEKS MOUNTAIN RANGE — IRELAND — AFTER MIDNIGHT

The Black Valley lives up to its name, thought Eddie O'Neil as he admired the brightness of God's sky jewels.

Only the thin silver blade of moonlight caught the glisten of damp rock and sodden moss on the floor of the County Kerry valley—one of Ireland's more secluded places and therefore ideal to take possession of weapons.

At this hour, the silence wasn't peaceful—it was watchful. An ancient, brooding quiet, broken only by the distant trickle of water and the steady wind that moved like breath through the pines.

Eddie O'Neil stood alone beneath a gnarled hawthorn, his breath misting out in short, sharp plumes, his hands buried in the heavy pockets of a waxed Barbour jacket. He had worn this coat for years. Like him, it bore the signs of prolonged use—creased at the elbows, a small tear at the shoulder stitched with dental floss.

O'Neil knew the end was coming—last year, the Docklands bombing in London had ended the 1994 ceasefire. Though Eddie had turned down more than one opportunity to become one of **The Seven** and sit on the IRA Army Council, he was generally privy to what was discussed through two of the members.

In the coming months, a ceasefire would be called and, maybe next year, a permanent agreement negotiated.

His father, originally from Dublin, had been an ordinary nationalist who had attended some civil rights protests—he had never even attended a meeting of **_the Stickies_**, let alone the Provisionals.

And still they lifted his old man off the street in West Belfast as if he were a dangerous dog. They kept him for nine days as O'Neil's mam figuratively tore her hair out trying to find out what was going on.

With most of the **_provos_** interned, the Loyalists had gone on a rampage of intimidation against the Catholic families in the city.

Eddie O'Neil, the middle child of five brothers and two sisters, was around sixteen years old at the time and had been lauded as a theatre actor prodigy. Upon his release, his father made him swear not to get involved in **_The Troubles_**.

O'Neil discovered years later that the Brits had put his father through at least two of their infamous 'five techniques' of interrogation, which consisted of wall-standing in a stress position, hooding, subjection to noise and deprivation of sleep, food and drink.

His elder brother, Iain, had not heeded their father's advice and had been recruited at the age of nineteen.

Within a couple of years, Iain was dead.

A light appeared in the distance, and O'Neil knew it to be Ernie McVoy, Eddie's recruiter all those years ago.

He checked his watch; it was ten minutes past the agreed time.

He'd told Ernie not to be late.

The lights came closer and closer until O'Neil

could make out the red Ford Transit he had been expecting.

The van turned into and trundled down the track leading off the main road to the rough parking alcove behind O'Neil's own dark purple Vauxhall Cavalier that he used as an inconspicuous work car.

The van's lights cut out, and both the passenger and driver's doors opened.

Out of the passenger's side alighted Tayeb al-Sarraj. Though O'Neil had never met the man, he knew the diminutive Libyan; Eddie had seen him in blurred surveillance photos—dark eyes and hair, olive skin and buzzard nose. And one of the more influential arms brokers this side of the Atlantic.

He wore an oversized fur-lined leather jacket not dissimilar to the one Rocky wore out in Russia in preparation to face Ivan Drago.

The other man stood well over half a foot taller than al-Sarraj and ten years older than O'Neil's thirty-nine.

Silver tongue, soft hands, eyes like muddy water. Once a father figure. Perhaps once a patriot.

Perhaps not.

Ernie McVoy had recruited him back in the seventies, three weeks after the execution of Iain.

Though McVoy's beard had grown thicker as his hairline thinned, he still stood with an assuredly straight posture and a wide grin.

"Aon scéal, a chara?" he said—*Any story, friend?*

Eddie knew that McVoy liked to alternate the handful of Irish phrases he knew to convey fluency.

O'Neil replied, "Grand, yerself?"

"I am good," said Ernie before he half turned

to the Libyan. "Tayeb, meet the legend that is Eddie O'Neil."

McVoy had told Eddie he would be stepping back from liaising with arms suppliers, as switching the PIRA's contacts would keep the Brits guessing.

However, Eddie knew the real reason.

Eddie took a step and held out his left hand. Tayeb paused before stepping forward and grasping his hand.

The Libyan's head jerked sideways with a metallic thunk as brain matter, blood and bones vacuumed from the side.

As Eddie's left hand released the collapsing Libyan's, his right hand whipped out the Taurus PT92 pistol from the waistband of his jeans.

He pointed it directly at McVoy, who spluttered, "What the fuck are you doing, Edward?"

"You should have asked yourself that two decades ago when you had my brother murdered."

A pause.

"What are you talking about?" said McVoy, desperation riveting his voice.

"I heard a tape recording of you admitting to ordering Willie Doak to kill our Iain. I wonder if anyone else suspects you were a Brit informant for all those years. The irony of you torturing suspected **touts** while you might be the biggest of them all. You agreed to give me up to the Brits, too. In return, they'd shack you up in some town like Oban after a plastic surgeon gave you a new face."

"I am no tout. And whoever supplied you with that tape had it doctored—are you an **Amadán**? This is their chance to take us both off the table—me in the ground and you in the **gaol**."

The PT92 did not waver, and Eddie replied, "That was my first thought, Ernie. So I went to see Doak on his deathbed. I was expecting a protest to the accusation, but then, I couldn't do much worse than stage four cancer. The thing is, I never mentioned your name, but he confirmed it."

Eddie caught Ernie's hands beginning to shake, his eyes darting around.

He continued, "And all over a ***beour*** who didn't want you anyway."

Anger laced McVoy's reply, "She wasn't just a girl. She was mine. I had the ring and was going to propose—and yer fuckin' Iain knew that. Of all the girls in Belfast, he had to… meet her?"

Eddie nodded. "No a beating, no a kneecapping? No, you had him kelled—couldn't even do it yourself."

After a moment, Ernie pleaded, "Please, Eddie, we go way back. On my mother's—"

The PT92's 9mm round punched McVoy through the face, turning it into a hideous hole of bloody teeth, mandible and pulp.

Eddie stood in the silence for a while as the weight from his chest lifted. However, though he had avenged his brother, he couldn't help but mourn the life he had given away.

The steps broke his reverie as the tall, dark, hawkish Scotsman with a face of angles and a body of edges appeared wrapped in a ***ghillie suit,*** holding an Accuracy International Arctic Warfare sniper rifle.

"Let's get them in the Transit," said the moustached man around his late twenties who went by the name 'Lewis', at least on this side of the water. "The bodies won't ever be found."

As the Scotsman stripped off the ghillie suit, Eddie said, "Tell me why you're doing this again?"

"Because we didn't want it coming out years down the line that we gave asylum to IRA torturers. We didn't want al-Sarraj supplying weapons. Two birds with one stone."

"That's not what I meant," said Eddie. "Why did you tell me the details of those murdering Loyalist bastards? Was that your superior's idea or yours?"

"Bloodthirsty Loyalists aren't conducive to a peace agreement, Mister O'Neil. I am sure—"

"That's not what I asked."

The two killers' eyes met, and Lewis said, "I am giving you a gift, Mister O'Neil. Don't look the gift horse in the mouth."

"Even if it means getting me fucked over down the road? Let's not pretend the Brits haven't got form for that."

"Men fucking men over is a trait of humanity, not of a specific nation or organisation. The man whose face you've just made a skull cave should be proof of that," said the black-haired soldier. "Now, I suggest we continue this philosophising when we're not standing directly over a pair of corpses."

Eddie admired how the younger man put his point across with logic instead of denial.

He returned the PT92 to his waistband and, after opening one of the Transit's back doors, helped the Scotsman rest the bodies' heels on the scuff plate. They set about stamping on the legs to break them.

Upon climbing into the back of the van, Lewis said aloud, "How the fuck did a Libyan manage to get one of these? The Russians have not long unveiled this to the public. A bag full of detachable cartridge boxes, too."

With that, the Scotsman lifted out the thirteen-kilo V-94 Anti-materiel rifle.

"Hard to hide from a twelve-point-seven millimetre round. Hard to catch a shooter from a mile away."

"My thoughts exactly," said Lewis, placing the huge rifle back in. "Let's get them in."

The two men heaved and folded the two bodies—now more malleable due to the broken limbs—into the boot.

Next, they scooped up the chunks of brain matter and bone before pouring bottles of cola over any obvious blood splashes.

The scene would remain 'forensically dirty' but would prevent the suspicions of a dog walker or hiker.

Before departing, the two stood between the cars.

"I guess this is it," said Eddie. "Obviously, Lewis isn't your only name."

"Obviously."

"Do you get to choose it?"

"I did."

"Why did you pick that one?"

"You won't like it."

"Tell me anyway."

"I watched *Who Dares Wins* as a starry-eyed fourteen-year-old—Lewis Collins seemed cool."

"Let me guess," said Eddie. "You permed your hair, bought a Ford Capri and joined the Paras after watching *The Professionals*."

Lewis smiled. "If there isn't a next time, Mister O'Neil, then good luck in your future endeavours."

After a cordial handshake, Eddie returned to his Vauxhall Cavalier and Lewis to the Transit, and both disappeared into the night.

3

PERIMETER OF THE CHERNOBYL
EXCLUSION ZONE — UKRAINE — MORNING

The UAZ-469 off-road military light utility vehicle passed the triangular sign of yellow and red warning of the area being affected by radiation.

Makar Gorokhov hoped that, of all the missions he had been on, this one would not deviate from the plan he and Ravil Yelchin had painstakingly worked on.

If it did, it meant he might have to kill Ukrainians, an act the Russian in him would consider bordering on familicide.

The relationship between Ukraine and Russia had been fractious since the collapse of the Soviet Union. Though Makar had begun his training in foreign intelligence in the post-Soviet era, he still felt it an affront that certain sections of the Ukrainian population and political system would strive to disassociate from Russia in her hour of need.

A source of anger for Makar, and indeed a lot of Russians, had been Ukraine's entitlement over the Crimea—a transfer under the Presidium of the Supreme Soviet in 1954—to the point where Russia was on the precipice of capitulating to an agreement to lease Crimean naval facilities from the Ukrainians to maintain its Black Sea Fleet.

However, with both peoples originating from the Kyivan Rus' and sharing many linguistic, familial and social similarities, Makar considered them, if not cultural brothers, then at least cousins.

Not that the men with him cared that much for such politics—the four men of Ravil's organised crime brigade cared only for their reputation within the brotherhood.

Luckily for the intelligence officer, Ravil had fostered a culture where professionalism was held to a higher ideal than elsewhere within the Solntsevskaya Bratva.

Throughout his young life, Makar had, in addition to his diligent training in Sambo, followed the Soviet protocols for strength training, namely programmes centred on multi-joint, compound exercises using heavy weights, low reps, with long rests between sets.

As a result, his six-feet-one-inch frame—though stocky—belied a musculature of high-tension muscle fibres.

Indeed, he had proven his ability to ragdoll larger men around on more than one occasion.

He knew, though, that despite the open hostility displayed by members of Ravil's Bratva receding over the past two years, a shallow pool of suspicion remained. However, he also sensed their grudging admiration for him due to several incidents where he proved not only courageous and nerveless under danger-pressure but that his skills in armed and unarmed combat, surveillance, counter-surveillance and operational planning exceeded those of anyone they had ever met or indeed knew of.

Makar would have been the youngest of the group but for Lev, a curly-haired blond who could border on hyperactive.

Evengi, the eldest at thirty-four, drove steadily in tandem with his nature.

Stanislav and Igor, two dark-haired Belarusians, both around thirty, sat in the back, humouring Lev's stories.

The security at the Chernobyl Nuclear Power Plant had its responsibilities split between four elements: the Ukrainian Ministry of Internal Affairs (MVS) provided the generic law enforcement and guarded the thirty-kilometre Exclusion Zone, Military and National Guard units were stationed to help restrict access, and the Chernobyl Exclusion Zone Administration (CEZA) managed the permits that Makar and the four Bratva soldiers now possessed.

The Security Service of Ukraine (SBU) handled the counterintelligence and protection against the type of activity Makar was about to attempt; indeed, if he and his Bratva unit were ambushed, it would be the SBU behind it.

Makar guessed the first checkpoint would be over the brow of the small hill, a standard tactic to compress the thought time on first seeing it.

His guess proved correct.

On the right side of the road stood a simple concrete bunker, which Makar assumed housed the telephone and provided a rest station for the sentries.

To the left sat a circular machine gun nest built from a mix of white and bottle green sandbags. The SVR agent assumed a stone or wood surface within it, as the soldier stood with his upper torso exposed over the 7.62 mm calibre PKS.

The machine gun had the capability of firing eight hundred rounds per minute and appeared to have a two-hundred-and-fifty-round ammunition box attached—in short, it might have only taken a single long burst to shred through the UAZ-469, Makar, and his men.

"Get your documents ready," said Makar as the driver slowed the vehicle to come into line with the MVS policeman, who, in most other European countries, would be mistaken for a military officer.

Makar wound down the window, and the policeman asked, "How many occupants?"

"Five, including me."

"What is the purpose of your visit?"

Makar knew the question and therefore the answer redundant, as the Chernobyl Exclusion Zone Administration would have forewarned the policeman. Still, he knew the practice necessary to keep out ***stalkers***—illegal tourists or scavengers.

"We are here to offer our assistance on the deteriorating sarcophagus covering Reactor 4."

The sarcophagus referred to the massive steel and concrete shelter built after the disaster to limit radioactive contamination to the environment.

"Documents, please."

The papers slid from Makar's hand into the policeman's as his colleague skirted around the vehicle like a badger around a tortoise in its shell.

Makar asked, "Could you please inform your relief-in-place that dosimeter scans will not be necessary as we are removing some of the components in boxes for further testing. It is there in the accompanying letter."

The SVR agent knew it to be paramount that they pass checkpoints on the way out without the use of radiation detectors. Though the intelligence stated that each device had its signature reduced by means of borated rubber and cadmium-doped polyethene panelling, if a keen-eyed guard started inspecting closely, they might encounter trouble.

"I will pass the information on," the policeman stated. "Though we never know who the relief-in-place will be. The checkpoints have been doubled to keep the fucking journalists out."

"Western?"

"Yes," said the policeman. "Ukrainian and Russian-speaking journalists must be able to name their price now."

"I think perhaps I am of the wrong profession," said Makar before lowering his voice conspiratorially. "Perhaps in the wrong country, too."

The policeman laughed, seemingly appreciating the dangerous joke. He handed back the documents. "You will drive five kilometres down this road without deviation until you reach a converted hangar. You and your team will be fitted with your protective suits there before driving on. OK?"

"Yes," answered Makar.

The policeman signalled to his colleagues to let them through.

Soon, the UAZ-469 rolled up to a distinctly less militaristic checkpoint just outside a rusted half cylinder made of sheet steel—like a giant had half buried an empty can and left it there.

Makar had expected the men manning this one to have full respirators; alas, they simply wore cloth masks without goggles, the hoods of their all-in-one green suits raised.

The Russian guessed that the discomfort of standing all day in full protective gear was traded in for the risk of radiation poisoning that might not manifest for years.

Indeed, there had been a mass evacuation of

some 116,000 people from the thirty-kilometre exclusion zone in the immediate aftermath of the May 1986 explosion, but by late 1987, the **samosely**—self-settlers—made up of elderly villagers and farmers, had settled, whose return had been tolerated by the Soviet and then Ukrainian governments.

The driver wound the window and leant back to make it clear to the sentry that Makar was the one to address.

"Sir, drive into the hangar, but do not get out until we have closed the shutters. You will then be issued your protective clothing."

Makar simply nodded, and the driver followed the directive.

The SVR agent surmised that if he were an SBU officer in command of taking down Makar and his men, he would pick the hangar they had just entered to stage the ambush; far enough into the exclusion zone to form a tight perimeter but with the reactors away from any small-arms fire.

They had also boxed themselves in.

His hand dropped to the side of his car seat base, his fingers delving into the folded slit to slide out the MSS "Vul" silent pistol.

The Vul's length just pipped a US dollar bill and fired 7.62MM calibre rounds. Its magazine held six.

Developed for assassination, not combat, Makar figured it better than nothing.

Men similarly dressed to those outside, except wearing what reminded Makar of a shortened chef's hat, stood in and around the steel box frames supporting the structure.

Hung on one of the horizontal units were

three sections of green all-in-one protective suits—Makar assumed they were small, medium or large.

Once the vehicle had stilled, Makar said quietly, "Just wait a minute."

However, there were no commando-types flooding in with assault rifles; instead, one of the men gesticulated to the suits like an irate Parisian shop assistant.

Makar slipped the Vul into his pocket and said, "Let us get out."

They did so and donned their suits as a clipboard man noted the shoulder numbers using an industrial marker.

Another man issued their respirators, and after they tightened them, he held up a spray and said, "I will spray your hoods, and when I tap your shoulder, pull them over your heads. Then I will come around to each in turn. Thumbs up if you cannot smell any sweetness. Thumb down if you can. I repeat, thumb up if you cannot smell a sweetness. Thumb down if you can."

The team passed the respirators' integrity tests first time, and the tester said to Makar, "Look, it's another seven kilometres through the city to the reactors. If you do not wear them for the journey down, at least keep the windows up and pull them on before entering the site."

"OK," said Makar, appreciating the man's practicality.

The team got back in and drove out.

Makar had not been within the Exclusion Zone before, let alone seen the abandoned city of Pripyat.

A sensation of surrealism pulsed within as he

observed the yellow and red triangular signs growing like wildflowers amongst the derelict buildings, abandoned cars and deserted parks.

Everything chipped, tinged, rusted and overgrown, like the entire place lived in a hospice of landscapes.

Soon, he could see the yellow gondolas of the twenty-six-metre Ferris wheel peering out over the trees.

Next, the road took them through the crumbling high-rises with unkempt trees crawling up them like starfish on a ship's hull.

He imagined zombies creeping in the ruins once the moon came out.

Lev, one of the more comedic of Ravil's Bratva, said, "Disappointing."

"What was you expecting?" exclaimed Igor, one of the older, more serious soldiers. "Vienna? New York? Paris?"

"No," said Lev. "It has been over ten years, and there are still no superheroes. Where are you, Mister Radioactive Man?"

They all laughed, including Makar.

It took fifteen minutes for the tower resembling a striped rolling pin to appear on the horizon.

"Everyone, put your respirators on," ordered Makar.

Ten minutes later, they arrived at the site of several huge buildings listing like broken ships.

Stopping at the first of two barriers spaced thirty metres apart, a white-suited figure approached the UAZ-469 on Makar's side.

The white figure simply asked, "Unit One?"

"Yes," Makar replied. "Specifically, the turbine hall."

"How many of our workers do you need?"

"None," said Makar. "We have enough men. We just need to remove certain debris, take pictures and measurements, and we'll be on our way back."

Makar willed the figure to accept—if he was insistent on Makar's team requiring a chaperone, then the former SVR agent might be forced to eliminate whoever it would be, and a host of challenges would arise as a result.

The white respirator walked away without response, and the barrier remained firmly down.

"What is he doing?" asked Lev edgily.

When Makar observed him heading back, he relaxed a little.

The white respirator appeared at the window and handed him a Motorola Saber—a handheld radio—and said, "For any obstacles you cannot solve or any information, contact me on that."

"Thank you," replied Makar.

"I will marshal you around to the site."

The barriers came up simultaneously, and they followed the marshal on a torturously slow route around.

When led inside, the team alighted.

At eight hundred and five metres in length, the turbine hall might have been one of the longest single-space buildings in the world.

To the right, the elevated perimeter walkways looked down on the main floor, and on the left side, five massive pipes hung, running the entire length.

The giant half-cylinder structures, not unlike the suit-fitting hangar, covered turbines lying along the centre like the spine of a giant mythological oceanic creature.

The marshal said, "How long do you expect to be?"

"Not long, hopefully," said Makar truthfully. "If it starts to go beyond two hours, I will let you know."

"OK." The marshal nodded. "Let me know at least ten minutes ahead of your leaving time."

Once the marshal had disappeared, Makar ordered the team to take out their tools and follow him.

The tools came in a shelved polymer box with wheels, which trundled behind Makar.

Though he had a map, Makar had memorised the layout.

A crew of white and beige suits could be heard on the far side of the turbine hall talking and clanging. Various clanks, hisses and beeps of varying decibels permeated the room.

Makar led them over to where the pipework curved into an alcove on the left side.

The intelligence he had received did indeed look accurate—left corner, four-centimetre steel panelling riveted by six hexagonal bolts.

"Igor, Stanislav, take clipboards and a tape measure and position yourselves twenty metres on either side. Look like you know what you are doing and call out if anyone approaches," commanded Makar.

The pair departed.

When Makar gestured with his fingers, Lev stepped forward with an EI-1M Soviet Electric Impact wrench.

Makar could sense Lev's nerves even through his suit and respirator and said, "Lev, remember what I told you—you could hit them with sledgehammers, set them on fire or explode a grenade next to them, and they will not go off without the radio receiver being attached and the trigger sending the signal."

Lev nodded. "Yes, Makar."

"Comfort yourself with the fact that if I am wrong, not only does this place already have an Exclusion Zone, but our deaths will not be prolonged."

The SVR agent could not tell the genuineness of the team's laughter through their respirators.

Lev set to work.

Makar had travelled through Central and Western Europe enough to witness the positive correlation between a market-driven economy and the superiority of manufactured goods.

Some of the soviet products did indeed benefit from a simplicity of construction that could equal reliability—the Kalashnikov being a good example—but Makar's suspicions that power tools did not come under that category were confirmed when the EI-1M began to splutter on the fourth bolt.

"*Ye-bat*'," whispered Makar venomously, using the rough Russian equivalent to 'fuck'.

He watched Lev and Evengi change the battery, but to no avail.

The two respirators faced him, and he hid his concern with a shrug. "Evengi, tell Igor and Stanislav to get the manual wrench."

The older man did so as Lev fiddled with the EI-1M. Though futile, Makar guessed it to be more out of nerves than expectation.

The trio returned carrying what resembled a steel crucifix.

After seeing the bolts burn out the motor on the impact wrench, Makar could only imagine the torque necessary to release the bolts.

Makar took a few paces back to keep watch.

Slipping the wrench over, the four men—two on either side—pulled and pushed in opposite directions to spin the bolt off.

Barely a centimetre of movement.

They heaved again; still no significant movement.

He quickly deduced that they might exhaust themselves before they could get them out.

He stepped forward. "Igor, Lev, Stanislav, take one side. Evengi and I will take the other."

Makar took 'the slack' out of the handle as he tensed his entire musculature for the exertion. Keeping his core tight, he repeatedly spat the word "pull" like a coxswain.

The bolt began its creaking acceptance of its fate, and within less than a minute, it came out. The final bolt took but a little longer.

Next, they selected their hammers and crowbars and set about the edges.

Makar knew this part would be noisy and decided that if all hands were on deck, it would be quicker.

They hammered the straight claws in, lifted in unison and shifted it over the opposite edge a hand span's width.

Their banging and scraping echoed, and they eventually switched from levering using the crowbar's straight edge to pulling with its bent claw.

Eventually, the gap became large enough to fit a man down. Makar, recognising that despite what he had said, any of the others might find themselves crippled by nerves, ventured, "I will go down. Take up sentry positions and do not let them come close without warning me."

He could almost see the relief through their respirators.

Makar took an FOS-3 Miners' head torch from one of the tool shelves, donned it awkwardly over his respirator, picked up his crowbar and began down the rusted ladder.

It reminded him of a vast industrial chimney, but he reached the floor around the depth the intelligence said he would.

He turned on the torch to find the brickwork remarkably well preserved after a decade.

Makar had heard myths of a construction crew post-disaster installing this secret compartment during the investigation but had considered it just another Russian conspiracy tale.

And yet, here he stood.

The intelligence report stated that the suitcases were concealed behind the opposite wall.

Makar counted five bricks from the left and seven up before prodding hard with the crowbar.

Movement.

He hit it harder.

He climbed the ladder a few rungs and called up, "Mallet."

A sledgehammer, which would not be out of place in a western museum, lowered itself into his hand.

Within two minutes, Makar had smashed a

hole large enough to reveal the suitcases.

The SVR agent took a moment, considering his situation, on the precipice of stealing weapons of mass destruction.

And not in pursuit of any ideological ideal.

He shook himself from his reverie and lifted out the top case, finding it just as heavy as he imagined.

Reportedly, each case contained all necessary components: the bomb itself, the radio-receiving unit and the detonator, despite them all being disconnected. He did not check, as exposing himself to even trace amounts of radiation seemed pointless. If all the components were not there, then Ravil could still demand payment due to faulty intel.

He climbed the rungs again and called up, "Evengi."

The older Russian's face appeared, and Makar simply handed him the case, then another, before bringing the final case up.

For the sake of speed, he took the risk of enlisting the rest of the team, except Evengi, to replace the panelling.

"Evengi, keep watch until it's time to put the bolts back."

After a few minutes of heaving, the panelling clunked into place.

"Evengi," said Makar, "close in."

Makar knew that though the bolts only needed to be hand tight as opposed to fully torqued, they still needed to crank on all six.

As Evengi stepped forward, his head snapped to his right before hissing, "Someone is approaching."

Makar soon heard soft steps turn into nerve-stretching clicks as Evengi held up a halting hand.

The SVR agent commanded the remaining trio, "Stack the suitcases and congregate around them," before joining Evengi.

As the white-suited figure strode up to them, Makar said to Evengi, "Do not physically impede him."

The accusing voice rasped through the respirator, "What are you doing? I was told you were to be taking out some of the defunct equipment? That is further up the hall."

"We will be."

As the white-suited figure closed in, he said, "Why have you not approached us? My lads are on their break now."

"For how long?"

"Sixty minutes. It takes fifteen either side to get to the cafeteria."

The figure shunted past the pair and rounded on the trio that even to Makar's eyes screamed suspicion.

He made his decision.

Taking a long step, he snatched up the sledgehammer.

The white-suited figure turned. "What have you—"

Five kilograms of flattened steel pulverised through the respirator, throwing its twitching victim onto his back.

"We do not have much time," commanded Makar. "Let's get the panel back off."

The men sprang into action.

With the panel open, they dragged the white figure to the edge under Makar's instruction, who grabbed a screwdriver and a hammer.

"Throw him in."

They did so, and Makar followed him down.

The figure lay like a crumpled crash test dummy.

Makar had not killed a man before—despite Western propaganda, the vast majority of KGB and now SVR agents never did.

He flipped over the white-suit and braved himself like a child about to receive an injection.

He tore open the suit and placed the tip of the screwdriver over the sternum, angled into the left pectoral.

A pair of hammer blows ensured the supervisor's death.

Makar wiped the screwdriver clean of his victim's blood and looked up to see Evengi peering in.

Good, he thought. *He can bear witness.*

Makar climbed out, not needing to see their faces to sense their shock.

He addressed them, "We need to get the panelling on as quickly as possible. Who knows how long it will be before his absence is noticed."

They scrambled to carry out his orders.

Makar pushed the talk button on the Motorola Saber. "Ready to depart."

A short crackle. "Understood. Ten minutes."

As Makar watched the panelling clank back into place, he hoped the supervisor had enough autonomy not to be missed for a while.

4

PORTSMOUTH — ENGLAND — MID MORNING

Miles Parker sat in the turquoise Jaguar XJ in an underground car park of Gunwharf Quays.

Usually, he would never have come this far out of London for a meeting with a covert operative, even back when he was a case officer.

Now recently promoted to senior officer, the tall and imposing Parker had made an exception for a one Frank Daniel Carlsmith.

Though technically his boss, Parker couldn't in good conscience consider the former special forces and current black operations operative an underling, despite Carlsmith's working-class origins.

The former SBS rating, in addition to being fourteen years Parker's senior, had more successful operations behind him than any soldier from what was colloquially known as *__the increment__*.

Both the SAS and SBS provided cream-of-the-crop soldiers with the requisite experience to work directly with SIS.

In almost all cases, the men provided had acquired the rank of sergeant, however as the fame of *__the regiment__* had grown, first with the Iranian Embassy siege and next with various memoirs published post-Gulf War, every Saudi prince, Colombian warlord, Hollywood director, Private Military Company executive and oil and gas CEO wanted former British Special Forces soldiers on their payroll.

This had caused a temporary drying up of the talent pool, and certain high-up civil servants, in their infinite wisdom, had issued a directive to the SAS's Revolutionary Warfare Wing (RWW) and the SBS's Maritime Counter Terrorism Wing (MCTW) to give some of their less experienced members a chance.

Additionally, there had been rumours that soldiers with ancestral roots in South Asia or the Middle East should be given heavy consideration.

Parker watched Carlsmith's maroon Ford Mondeo crawl past him, despite there being spaces. Frank would wait several minutes, and if Parker observed a suspicious shadow, he was to call Frank on the Motorola StarTAC they both possessed.

The mobile phone could fit in one's pocket, whereas a couple of years ago, Parker had only seen some of the city yuppies with brick phones.

After a few minutes, the passenger door of Parker's Jaguar opened, and Frank got in.

"Christ," exclaimed Parker. "How did you approach without my seeing you?"

"You would have been more alert had you been cruising on Clapham Common."

Parker, indignant, rasped, "I have never been to Clap—"

"Relax, Miles," laughed Frank, slapping Parker's thigh. "Though a word to the wise—an overly strong denial could suggest guilt."

Parker could smell alcohol on him, which was a rarity. If it were anyone else, it would explain the Mancunian's exuberance, but Frank had always been like this.

Parker, seeing as it was Saturday, asked, "I take it Manchester won?"

"United, yeah. Remember there's Manchester City Football Club, too," said Frank. "This Solskjær, what a striker."

Parker reached into the back for his briefcase and disengaged the rotary lock before handing Frank a file.

"His name is Bruce McQuillan. Former Parachute Regiment and B Squadron SAS. He's been seconded to ***The Det*** for the past six months."

Parker referred to the covert surveillance and intelligence-gathering unit, known as 14 Intelligence Company, also referred to as ***14 INT*** or The Det, which operated *almost* exclusively in Northern Ireland.

Candidates underwent a gruelling selection course, with a heavy emphasis on surveillance tradecraft, urban disguise, surveillance driving (including pursuit and counter-surveillance tactics), counterintelligence awareness and advanced weapons handling and unarmed combat.

Such was its success that Parker had been told that the 14 Intelligence Company would continue in some guise even if a lasting peace were brokered.

"How's he gotten on?" asked Frank, despite reading the file.

"On the face of it, remarkably well. Exemplary marks on the selection course. Slid into the surveillance role with an ability rarely seen from someone of his direct-action background."

"Meaning he showed a restraint sometimes lacking in some of the more trigger happy types who wear the maroon and beige berets?"

"Precisely," admitted Parker. "Seemed that the RUC and Five were having a little trouble ascertaining if a certain property was a safe house for

Raymond 'Razor' McKibben, wanted for the Newry Community Centre bombing. McQuillan, operating under the name Bruce Lewis, had been working as a joiner in the area. The van had armoured panelling, and he had a Browning Hi-Power, but that was it. And as a part of his cover, he—not his handlers—decided to join the local Kingdom Hall. And so, he—not his handlers—decided to knock on said door with a copy of the New World Translation of the Holy Scriptures. When McKibben answered, it seemed that McQuillan did his best to convince 'Razor' that Jehovah is the one true God. Seemed that he was sanctimoniously asked to leave, but not before the security services got their photographs—and permission to arrest McKibben, which they did less than two hours later."

"So he's a bit of a maverick who gets results," said Frank. "What's the problem?"

"As you're aware, stringent background checks are carried out. He hails from Glasgow, his Protestant Scottish father married his Northern Irish Catholic mother. Arthur Donald McQuillan was an aid worker out in Lebanon in 1975 when the Lebanese Civil War broke out. He was found dead with a shot to the back of the head—inconclusive as to who pulled the trigger, and the subsequent police report is technically a 'wrong place, wrong time'. His mother's background causes but a minor concern, there was nothing denoting support for republicanism or that she even returned to Northern Ireland regularly, if at all. I guess it is assumed that if she married a Protestant, then she couldn't have sympathies, certainly none that would be passed on to her son, who joined the Paras of all regiments."

Parker referred to the fact that, certainly in the wake of **_Bloody Sunday_**, the Parachute Regiment stood as easily the most hated of all British infantry regiments by Northern Irish Catholics.

"His mum still alive?"

"No, killed herself not long after Bruce joined the army. Manic-depressive. Never remarried after the father's death."

"And so?"

"And so, he's put forward for an attempt to turn one Edward Jack O'Neil under the threat of a trial without jury under the Northern Ireland Acts. Word on the street was that he was getting disillusioned with both the political and paramilitary leadership. The idea was to send this Bruce McQuillan out to contact him, with some spurious evidence of O'Neil being the mastermind behind several high-end bank robberies to fund the cause."

"Eddie O'Neil, the man whose nickname is 'The Nun' because he can't get dirty?"

It mildly embarrassed Parker that, until that moment, he hadn't known why the Northern Irish bank robber had acquired the sobriquet.

"Yes, quite," said Parker. "However, MI5 had information that they had been sitting on for over a decade—that Ernest McVoy, O'Neil's original recruiter, had been the one to order the death of O'Neil's brother, Iain. Except, he told O'Neil it had been the work of Loyalists backed by the British Security Services."

Frank laughed. "I can see what's coming now. The reason MI5 sat on it was because McVoy worked for them."

The deduction surprised Parker, who

confirmed, "That is correct."

"Christ almighty, the IRA's most infamous interrogator of touts is one himself?"

"Well, 'is' might not be the operative word since his last check-in was meant to be two weeks ago after a preliminary 'meet and greet' he was to oversee between O'Neil and Syrian arms dealer Tayeb al-Sarraj. It seems Mr. al-Sarraj has gone missing too."

"And al-Sarraj works for you? For us?"

"Not exactly. He has a favourite mistress who is one of ours, and al-Sarraj was very loose-lipped, so to speak, with her. A trove of information—likely gone."

"Well, that's no good."

"An internal investigation has been conducted. No definitive conclusions, but it's highly likely that not only has Bruce McQuillan leaked classified information to a known terrorist, but he's been actively aiding him in the assassination of more than one Loyalist paramilitary."

"On what basis did they come to that conclusion?"

"The belief is that we are approaching a deal with some permanence, and as a result, surveillance on some of the more ardent and talented paramilitary members has been stepped up. It seems—"

"I bet ya a tenner the level of surveillance hasn't been quite so heavy with regards to the Loyalist paramilitaries," Frank interrupted

Parker shrugged. "Even the crown's resources are finite, Frank."

"I am sure."

"Last year, O'Neil managed to temporarily dump his surveillance twice for three days at a time, once in May and once in December. And Bru—"

"—And Bruce McQuillan took his leave periods around these times?"

"Yes," admitted Parker. "It isn't the evidence we have that concerns us. It's the evidence we don't. McQuillan stated to his handlers that he was taking his leave in Glasgow. Discreet inquiries could not corroborate this. And we couldn't speak to him directly as it would spook him before we knew the facts."

"So, why have you pulled me out the boozer then?"

"The higher-ups want him gone, Frank."

Silence for a few moments, and the northerner replied, "And a former SBS rating was more plausible than anyone from Hereford who might have a soft spot for him?"

"Yes."

"Is that what we are now, Miles? Murderers of our own people?"

"The enemy within, Frank."

"If the suspicions are true, not one British serviceman, intelligence officer or civilian has been harmed by his actions," sneered Frank before adding, "I'd hold off calling him a traitor."

"Then what would you call him? One of our more prized assets is now missing, not to mention the two Loyalists."

"McVoy's usefulness was coming to an end. He was disassociating himself from the stalwart, fight-to-the-death republicans. If he has been killed, then he's received a deserved retribution instead of riding off into the sunset of the Mediterranean. Ditto the two Loyalists."

Parker could feel an exasperation rise in his throat. "Then what do you suggest? Just letting him go?"

"No," said the killer of many men. "I did not say that."

PERIMETER OF THE CHERNOBYL EXCLUSION ZONE — UKRAINE — MORNING

Makar had often marvelled at how time could seem to change speed.

He understood the neuroscience behind it: the fewer novel experiences one encountered with age, the more the routine bled days into an indistinguishable haze, and the sharper recollections of youth—compressed with vivid detail—seemed longer in contrast. It was why, to someone like Bezmenov, the collapse of the Soviet Union seven years prior felt like yesterday, while to a twenty-four-year-old conscript, it might as well have happened in the era of the czars.

But now, here, in the belly of the decommissioned power facility, Makar experienced the physical sensation of time slowing. The marshal's pace seemed almost calculated to provoke madness, every footstep an insult to urgency. It was like watching an ice floe drift across a frozen ocean while knowing you were bleeding out beneath it.

Not that their operation was in immediate jeopardy. The turbine hall—long, dormant and resonant with echoes—mercifully had no security cameras. And if the marshal were missed, it would take hours, possibly longer, for his absence to spark concern. Still, the risk loomed like a phantom just out of reach.

When they finally reached the exterior access gate—a journey that felt geological in length—Makar handed back the Motorola Saber radio with a firm nod, face composed into its default posture of dignified boredom. They were waved through.

But the moment the UAZ-469 left the line of sight from the access point, the tempo of reality snapped back like the twang of a stretched elastic band. The vehicle lurched forward.

"Slow down, Evengi," Makar snapped, his voice low but edged with steel. "They have security cameras around the area. Let us avoid unwanted suspicions."

The older driver complied instantly, lifting his foot from the accelerator as though chastened by a father.

Makar turned to the rest of the team, his voice firm but even. "Remember, at the next station, they will spray both us and the vehicle down. Intelligence suggests they have no recourse to check the vehicle."

He didn't believe that entirely. The intelligence report could be outdated. Or flawed. Or compromised. But to assign a sentry to the back of the UAZ—especially now—would invite a layer of scrutiny they couldn't afford.

As they pulled into the checkpoint facility, a long half cylinder of ribbed concrete and corrugated steel, Makar scanned for signs—nervous eyes, a shift in posture, a glance too long. *Nothing.*

A lone checkpoint guard emerged from the inner threshold and met them near the access door. He was young, his face raw from the wind, and his uniform slightly too big for his narrow frame. To Makar's relief, the guards ushered the men into the spray-down chambers one by one instead of herding them in together—standard protocol, but not always adhered to. By the time the last man entered, Stanislav and Lev had already exited, towelling off behind the blast-proof glass while the UAZ-469 underwent decontamination behind a transparent polymer barrier.

So far, so good.

But Makar did not allow himself the luxury of relief. The final checkpoint loomed—the bottleneck.

And the most heavily armed.

He forced his breathing into a measured rhythm, watching the steel-panelled buildings and skeletal gantries recede behind them. The hulking shape of a PKS heavy machine gun rotated—slowly, deliberately—until its barrel faced *inwards*. It was manned.

His heartbeat spiked. Just slightly.

The guards stationed at the gate didn't look relaxed. There were no casual salutes. No lazy wave-throughs. Instead, they stood taut, glancing between the vehicle and their commander with a tension Makar didn't like. Something had shifted.

A different commander approached the driver's window and knocked with the flat of his knuckles.

Makar lowered it slowly.

"Yes?" he said, his tone curt, impatient, every inch the scientist, too burdened by duty for pleasantries.

"We need everyone out. And to scan the inside with a dosimeter."

The words carried the weight of finality. Makar's mouth dried. His brain ran calculus at speed—distances, weapons, exposure times.

"Did you not receive a handover brief?" he asked, injecting frost into his tone.

The man blinked. "We're elected—"

"We have been given authorisation from the CEZA to remove certain materials for off-site testing," Makar interrupted, each word crisp, authoritative. "If that box is opened, you risk exposing yourself and everyone else to radiological contaminants. I suggest you go and read your handover brief—that is what it is there for. Because if you don't, your post here will end—and a new one as a liquidator will begin."

That word hung in the air like fallout.

Liquidator. The ones who cleaned up the disasters. Who scraped molten graphite from reactor roofs and buried comrades in lead-lined coffins. The ones who glowed in the dark.

The guard commander faltered. His gaze shifted slightly—uncertain now, but not yet folding.

"I do need to check the handover brief," he said cautiously.

Makar's fingers, just beneath the seat edge, touched the smooth grip of the MSS 'Vul' silent pistol, hidden in a slit in the upholstery. Cold steel met the pads of his fingertips.

The guard commander continued, "The previous commander *did* brief me. I did not recognise the vehicle. Apologies, sir."

Makar stared at him. Blank. Arrogant. Aloof.

Then he simply rolled the window back up without reply.

"Drive," he ordered.

And the UAZ crept forward, its tyres crunching over the gravel, carrying death in its belly towards the free world.

NORTHEAST OF THE BLACK SEA — MORNING

Genrikh Bezmenov stood on the Stenka-class patrol boat's deck watching the sun's molten disc bleeding into the blue swells of the Black Sea.

Three days ago, Ravil had contacted him: the RA-115S 'suitcase nukes', complete with the radio receiver units and detonators, had been successfully recovered.

Now, the SVR colonel was allowing himself to truly absorb each passing moment.

In a few weeks, he would either be basking under the Central American sun in anonymity or rotting inside Penal Colony Number Six in Nizhny Tagil.

Bezmenov had lived the past five years under a persistent hum of low-level anxiety. But now, the blue-eyed Muscovite sensed it—his moment. He had been patient. Daring. The time had come to cash in on both.

He knew how the Kremlin would handle the aftermath: should a device be detonated and a terrorist group claim credit, Moscow would point fingers at Iran or North Korea. With Russia having been led by recent weaklings like Gorbachev and Yeltsin, the Americans would believe it. And once Washington declared war on whichever nation they chose to blame, perhaps Russia—his Russia—could begin to rebuild from the chaos.

He narrowed his gaze. A speck moved across the horizon.

After a few minutes, the outline of the approaching Azimut AZ 40 luxury speedboat confirmed itself.

> Aboard were three prospective buyers for the nuclear devices:
> —Aum Shinrikyo, the Japanese doomsday cult bent on Armageddon.
> —Hezbollah, the Iranian-backed Shi'a Islamist militia.
> —And Al Qaeda, the rising Sunni terror group under Osama Bin Laden.

Bezmenov knew Aum Shinrikyo lacked the financial weight to compete, but their presence was tactical—it would inflate the bidding atmosphere, stir paranoia. The illusion of competition was often enough to double the price.

As the AZ 40 throttled down and pulled alongside, Bezmenov's nervous system flared—despite extensive vetting, the possibility of a sting operation by his own people could never be entirely ruled out.

He heard footsteps behind him and said flatly, "Oleg, take your men. Cross-decks. Ensure there are no threats."

"Yes, sir," replied the square-jawed Siberian ex-Spetsnaz.

Oleg boarded with two similarly built men, each armed with a PP-90M1 submachine gun. The civilian crew of the speedboat looked confused—unnerved. *Good,* Bezmenov thought.

Ten long minutes passed before Oleg

reappeared and bellowed across the deck, "Clear of threat!"

Bezmenov crossed the gangway. Oleg leant in. "They are waiting in the cabin."

Inside, the air-conditioned space reeked of pine cleaner and leather polish. The cream upholstery glowed under recessed lights, the tawny cushions lending warmth to the sterile lines of the seating alcove.

"Anatoly. Maxim. Return to deck," he instructed.

His bodyguards brushed past him, sealing the door shut behind them.

Four men sat across from one another, paired on opposite benches.

Nezu Shiota of Aum Shinrikyo wore a leather pork-pie hat, a green-checked coat over a white shirt and a bubblegum-pink tie—an outfit as bizarre as the cult he represented. Beside him sat Ali Shukr of Hezbollah, a younger, stockier, thick-bearded, black-haired man with a stony expression.

Opposite sat the tall, slim Ramzi al-Wahishi of Al Qaeda, bespectacled and composed, next to the dour, heavy-browed Viktor Szombati, the Hungarian fixer long wanted by Interpol for facilitating some of the world's darkest arms deals and disappearances.

Viktor stood at once. "Your men searching us was not necessary."

Bezmenov replied coolly, "Do not be unintelligent—it is never necessary until it is."

"I don't—"

"The colonel is correct," al-Wahishi interrupted in English—the only language shared by all present.

"Thank you," Bezmenov said, then turned to Szombati. "You may wait outside. Or on my vessel, if you prefer."

The Hungarian glared, clearly unused to dismissal. Most players in Middle Eastern and European underworlds knew that maintaining Szombati's favour was considered *wise business*.

Bezmenov, however, had no intention of doing further business with him.

Szombati left in silence.

Good. Let him think the cargo involved RPO-A thermobaric launchers, remote-controlled IEDs, and other Soviet-era ordnance, thought the Russian.

Only the other three would know the truth: they were bidding on three RA-115S portable nuclear devices.

Once alone, Bezmenov said, "Gentlemen, what I am about to disclose is classified to the strictest degree of 'need-to-know'."

His nerves jangled. This was the moment—the widening of the circle. Once two parties were outbid, they might not keep the secret. He had contingencies for that, too.

Al-Wahishi broke the silence. "How can we be sure this isn't an extortion attempt by a desperate Russia?"

"You know the amount you're authorised to offer wouldn't so much as plaster over my dying nation," said Bezmenov. "But it's enough to vanish. To change my face. And the last thing I—or Russia—need is a vendetta with the likes of you. Besides, you may bring your own experts to verify the devices at the point of exchange."

Al-Wahishi nodded. "Tell me about these

munitions. The yield."

The phrasing struck Bezmenov—'*Tell me*,' not '*Tell us*.' The Saudi had already written off the others.

Bezmenov had assumed Hezbollah's Shukr would be the dominant force. He was state-backed.

The Russian realised he might have underestimated al-Wahishi's ambition and monetary access.

"Each has a five-hundred-metre blast radius," he began, deciding to exaggerate the effects a touch. "Thermal radiation capable of third-degree burns. Severe structural damage and lethal radiation exposure within a kilometre. Flash blindness up to ten kilometres. Tens of thousands dead or crippled if used in an urban environment."

"How are they detonated?"

"Radio remote-controlled. The triggerman can stand outside the kill radius, though proximity improves reliability. If the receiver is disconnected, no amount of jostling—no fall from a rooftop—will cause a detonation."

"How old are they?"

"Manufactured in 1981," said Bezmenov. "Brezhnev was still in power. Their cases remain sealed, the components inert and uncorroded. No oxygen, no moisture. You can run pre-checks on the receivers."

Hezbollah's Shukr finally spoke. "Do your people know they're missing?"

"They do not know these three *exist*. They were off-ledger. Moscow believes all ADMs were decommissioned in 1991."

Shiota cleared his throat. "So… how does this work?"

Bezmenov straightened. "Each of you will write down your offer—one figure. No negotiation. The highest bidder wins. Funds will be transferred to Mr Szombati, who will serve as escrow agent."

Al-Wahishi raised an eyebrow. "Strange, you dismissed him, yet you trust him with millions?"

"I said, 'Need-to-know.'"

The Yemeni raised his hands in silent assent.

Shiota asked, "Must the bid be for all three?"

"Yes. But options can be had for one. If another wishes to outbid you for all three, they must triple what you offer for one."

Bezmenov suspected Al Qaeda and Hezbollah would compete for the complete set. Hezbollah might even attempt to reverse-engineer one in Iran.

Ali Shukr asked, "You expect our offers tonight? I could pay more for devices than for ordinary munitions."

"If you offer and cannot pay, I will default to the next highest. I have other potential buyers. I will not be left holding these once you disembark."

That was a lie. There were no other auctions. But they didn't know that.

Bezmenov pulled a notepad and three pens from his briefcase. He tore out three blank pages and placed them with envelopes on the table.

"Mark your initials. Seal your envelope. Hand them to Viktor. I will contact him tomorrow to declare the winner."

He let silence settle over the room.

"There is a lower limit," he added.

No one asked the amount.

With that, he turned and exited, the heavy door sealing behind him like a tomb.

5

KASPAROV TEXTILE PLANT — IAŞI — ROMANIA — 1:42 A.M.

The summer day had left a cold night that seeped into Ravil Yelchin's bones as he stood with his hands deep in the pockets of his overcoat, his breath ghosting faintly in the broken light spilling from the factory's overhead bulb.

The abandoned textile plant, a relic of Romanian communism, had crumbled into disrepair, perfect for a transaction that no man would ever speak of.

At a battered steel table under the lone light, Kasper Bálint worked in silence. The Romanian-Hungarian technician moved with the assurance of a surgeon, methodically installing the last of the GPS transmitters into the modified casings of the three black suitcases laid open before him.

Each battered case housed what would soon be traded as Soviet RA-115S tactical nuclear devices—suitcase bombs.

To all but the keenest eye trained in Soviet engineering, the devices looked unchanged. The modifications—the carefully shaped cavities, the embedded antennas disguised as structural wiring—were seamless.

Behind Ravil, Makar Gorokhov stood in still silence, a heavy, immovable presence. His eyes never left Kasper's hands, and Ravil knew his mind would already be ticking through contingencies for betrayal.

Ravil turned slightly towards him, keeping his

voice low in the pair's native Russian.

"We would be hunted to the ends of the earth if they ever went off," he said. His breath barely stirred the cold air.

Makar's reply was quiet, even.

"There is a better than average chance the buyer's authenticator will not decipher the difference. How can he? These devices are not meant to exist."

The younger man's logic gave him some comfort, but he hedged his bets with the traditional Russian phrase of, "If it is God's will."

He let his gaze drift back to the working technician.

"We need the handover to be completed," he murmured. "We'll notify the relevant agency when we get our Bratva's money."

For the last few years, Ravil had been cultivating a fortress mentality within his own Brigade. He did not aspire to be the Moscow **Pakhan**—Boss—essentially the Russian Bratva's equivalent to an Italian Mafia's 'Don of Dons'.

What he wanted was for his Bratva (Brigade) to have much more autonomy and thus greater money making capability without the headache of managing all the other Bratvas.

"Surely if 'The Great' discovers our hand in this, his apparent fondness for you will disappear along with our existence."

His young right-hand man spoke the truth. Konstantin 'Kostya' Volodin was the current Head of the Moscow **Obshchak**—the communal criminal treasury—and therefore the current and all-powerful Moscow Pakhan.

His moniker of 'Kostya Velikiy'—*Kostya the*

Great—had been given to him long before he ascended the top position, and he did indeed seem like a loving father to an errant son to let Ravil get away with certain actions that he wouldn't any other Pakhan.

Ravil played his part in insulating himself by kicking up exceedingly generous amounts of his ill-got gains. Though that helped the old man—who loved his custom-tailored Brioni suits and huge Black Sea **Dacha**—Ravil suspected Volodin saw something of himself in Ravil—or maybe something he missed.

Ravil had been one of the first to dare bring up to the council that to attract new, and better, members, they had to relax the stipulation that to be made a fully-fledged ***Vor v zakone,*** you needed to have served prison time.

He also expressed his distaste for the traditional tattoos given as part of the ceremony, as he pointed out that they were simply identifiers for Western law authorities, which seemed less susceptible to corruption.

In truth, neither expression had been revelatory amongst the street guys, but to utter them before a council still heavy with older Vory v Zakone, most of whom were now off the street, had been a dangerous gamble.

It had helped that Ravil had spoken to Volodin in private regarding his public proposals before the council. At the meeting, they proceeded to act out the prearranged script.

Volodin's sonorous voice had announced, *'Ravil, you may forgo the rituals in your Brigade only. As an experiment. If it succeeds, the council might vote on their future eradication. If it fails, then you will fall on your sword.'*

Still, Makar was correct—the stealing of suitcase nukes and their subsequent detonation would see Ravil's Bratva killed to a man.

"And Viktor's trust," Ravil added, his voice like polished stone. He smiled thinly.

Trust from the international fixer Viktor Szombati was not easily won, nor easily discarded.

A man like Szombati was the kind of business partner who could sink you simply by refusing to deal with you again.

As always, they were operating on a knife's edge between survival, profit and damnation—he looked forward to one day tasting the rarified and clean, cold air of being untouchable.

Across the room, Kasper Bálint straightened, wiping his gloved hands on a cloth. He picked up a small black device—no larger than a pack of cigarettes—and crossed towards them.

He stopped a metre away, offering the device to Ravil.

"It's done," Kasper said, his English crisp and accented but clear. "All three transmitters are active."

Ravil took the receiver from him and turned it over in his gloved hand. It was heavier than it looked, solid and straightforward: a toggle switch, two small LEDs, and an extendable antenna tucked flush to the body.

"The battery life for the transmitters?" Ravil asked without looking up.

"A week, maximum," Kasper replied. "Normally, it would be two. I widened the location radius to stretch the signal life… as you requested."

Ravil nodded once. It was a compromise they had agreed upon: '*Sacrifice precise location data for more time.'*

Four days to complete the exchange, alert the SVR and disappear.

Kasper gestured briefly towards the cases still lying open on the table.

"I reworked the internal framing," he said. "The antennas look like part of the structural support wiring. Even if they inspect the devices… they'll find what they expect to find."

Ravil allowed himself a flicker of approval.

The man might be worth the exorbitant fee.

Besides, Bezmenov was the only man alive who had seen the original devices, and he would not be seeing them again.

Satisfied, Ravil stepped to the second duffel bag lying at his feet. He bent, unzipped it and lifted out a heavy metal case. He set it on the table, popped the locks and opened it to reveal neat stacks of U.S. currency, arranged in two precise columns.

Kasper's eyes flicked to the money—a professional's gaze, clinical rather than greedy.

"May I verify?" asked Kasper rhetorically.

Ravil inclined his head and took a step back. "We do not take offence at thoroughness."

Kasper produced a portable banknote scanner from his jacket, methodically sampling random bills.

Two minutes later, he clicked the case shut and relocked it.

"Thank you," he said.

Before Kasper could reply, Makar stepped forward.

He didn't raise his voice, but the menace in his tone was unmistakable.

"It would be… unfortunate," Makar said, "if

anyone were to remember this night."

Kasper gave a slow nod. "I will forget."

Ravil offered him a thin, cold smile. "Good."

Without another word, Kasper packed his tools, hefted the money case and disappeared into the night beyond the shattered doorway.

The factory swallowed the noise of his departure.

Ravil lingered a moment longer, feeling the weight of the receiver in his pocket.

The game was now set in motion.

The only question was whether they could survive playing it

EAST DET — BELFAST — EARLY MORNING

The sky was beginning to pale; that strange, blue-grey softness before dawn had taken hold properly. Bruce McQuillan stood on the cracked concrete outside a shuttered café in East Belfast, collar turned up against the early morning chill. The streets were empty save for a few milk floats and a newspaper van rumbling past.

He had returned from leave just two days ago and lamented on how he should have taken a holiday to Spain when he had the chance instead of burying bodies in the Republic.

A nondescript Cortina rolled up quietly and parked. Out stepped Commander Vincent Keegan, head of East Det, wearing a flat cap and an old raincoat that made him look more like a pensioner out for a stroll than the man who'd run covert surveillance teams for two decades.

Keegan didn't offer a handshake, just gave

Bruce a once-over.

"How was your leave?" Keegan asked.

"Good, sir, did the rounds with the family."

Keenan jerked his head towards the car. "Let's walk."

They moved side by side down the street, their footsteps echoing on the damp pavement.

"You are to meet a contact at the 'Elliot Bottle Factory' on Old Kent Road tonight at twenty-two hundred hours."

"London?" asked Bruce, feeling silly as he said it.

Keegan nodded. "The order came from above my boss. Not Hereford either. If I were to guess, I reckon it came from *Legoland*."

The Det commander used one of the nicknames for the SIS Headquarters, Vauxhall Cross, so called due to its 'blocky' design.

And Bruce knew that Keenan was insinuating that he had been selected for what was known in hushed tones as *the increment*. However, Bruce wasn't so sure—the vast majority of the lads selected were members of *the wing*, the SAS's Revolutionary Warfare Wing (RWW) or the SBS's Maritime Counter Terrorism Wing (MCTW), which Bruce wasn't.

Then again, he had been aware of the manpower shortages they had been experiencing lately.

"Am I arranging my own transport?"

"I've got a ferry booked for you," Keegan said. "Larne to Stranraer. Leaves in three hours."

Bruce nodded silently.

"You'll take the green Mondeo from the lock-up on Ravenhill. It's fuelled, unregistered, and the plates will hold up."

They turned a corner. The air was sharper here, the kind that made your lungs feel like they'd been wiped clean.

Bruce's eyes flicked towards the awakening city.

"If I don't come back, then it has been a pleasure, sir," he said sincerely.

Keegan gave a dry smile. "I am aggrieved to be losing someone with such a talent for this type of work. You should come to the other side."

"Like when Eunice Huthart went from contestant to *Gladiator*."

"I am not that well-versed in the intricacies of Roman history, I am afraid."

Bruce chose not to embarrass Keegan as the officer handed him an envelope. Ferry ticket. Cash.

Bruce nodded once, tucked the bundle into his inside coat pocket and walked away without another word.

ROMANIA — PORT OF CONSTANȚA — EARLY MORNING

Viktor Szombati stood overlooking the strange juxtaposition of the flat metropolis of the Romanian Port of Constanța and the Black Sea.

The vehicle fumes mixed with the salt air as he waited in a communications building, currently amid renovations.

Over many years, Viktor had identified 'greasers' from many a port, particularly those around the Black Sea—their Atlantic and Mediterranean counterparts proving only mildly more challenging.

Despite himself, he felt a pinch of guilt as the operations manager for this part of the port had no idea exactly what he had allowed in or the type of exchange he was providing security and privacy for.

Neither did Viktor—however, the fee that Bezmenov had deposited into his bank account far exceeded his usual amount for overseeing handovers.

Perturbing to him was that he had made enough transfers to know what ammunition and weapons crates looked like.

And these boxes were not that.

He doubted they contained drugs—large shipments of narcotics came out of places like Romania and Turkey, not into them.

If he had to guess, given who he was handing off the container to, he reckoned on some kind of commercial or military grade explosives using either plastic blocks of Semtex, or more probably, M112 Demolition Charges made up of US military blocks of C-4.

If Viktor had to guess, the wily KGB—or SVR, or whatever name they were using now—colonel would ensure that not only could the ordnance not be traced back to Russia but also be blamed on another state.

The thought sent a chill through Viktor, knowing he was one of the few to hold that knowledge. However, Viktor knew that Bezmenov knew that he always kept insurance in the event of a seemingly untimely death.

The static burst on his walkie-talkie with the words, "They are here."

Viktor redundantly said, "No more than three."

He watched a blue Dacia 1310 being stopped by his armed men in a mostly empty car park a few fence lines down.

Three men alighted.

Ramzi al-Wahishi, the original negotiator, and imposing, handsome Adam Umar.

Umar had not long returned from the front line of the Bosnian War. He had served with the *El Mudžahid*—Bosnian mujahideen—and made a name for himself, accumulating in his involvement in the recent Mostar car bombing.

Though the presence of such an intimidating man might have seemed redundant, given that an earlier search ensured Umar was unarmed and that Viktor had five armed men around him, the fixer knew that the Al Qaeda fighter's presence implied future violence if any thievery was to be attempted.

Indeed, forty million United States dollars now sat in an account controlled by Viktor, thirty-six million of which awaited transfer to an account of Bezmenov's choice after the bomb had been transferred into Al Qaeda's hands.

Viktor didn't know the bespectacled man with grey hair and a white goatee carrying a large briefcase.

He addressed al-Wahishi, who stood in the centre, "The items are around the corner. You will check, and once satisfied, your transport will be allowed access. We will guarantee your security within a five-kilometre radius from the port. Anything out of that is not our responsibility."

"That will not work. A man like you might have struck an immunity deal with Interpol for our arrest and—"

"And then I would have swapped looking

over my shoulder for law enforcement to looking over my shoulder for towelheads who would blow themselves up. Now, do you want the munitions or your money back?"

Though Al Qaeda's use of suicide bombings had been inconclusive, Viktor, who had ears everywhere, knew they would be making increasing use of the tactic.

Al-Wahishi and Umar stared at him for a few moments while the white goatee looked mildly embarrassed.

Al-Wahishi made a gesture of capitulation, and Viktor signalled his men that they be taken around.

Viktor joined them, keeping on the opposite side of Umar.

After a five-minute walk through some turns, they arrived at the unit.

Two more of Viktor's guards stood on either side holding Puşcă Automată model 1986 assault rifles.

Viktor gave them the nod, and one peeled inward to release the trio of salt-licked bulldog locks before setting about pulling open the hinge doors.

The Hungarian fixer could see the nervous fidgeting of all except the white goatee, who stepped forward and entered after uttering a couple of phrases in Arabic, a language Viktor had only an embryonic grasp of.

The group simply marinated in the awkward silence as time seemed to stretch.

Finally, the white goatee reappeared, and relief flooded Viktor's system as he nodded. The Hungarian issued instructions through his walkie-talkie, allowing the transport to proceed.

Al-Wahishi nodded at Viktor with a look of subtle satisfaction.

"You have helped change the course of history, Viktor."

"There are many more steps from here to then, al-Wahishi."

"These bombs will purify our enemies." The Al Qaeda agent smiled. "The great Satan's sins of Hiroshima and Nagasaki have returned to punish them—or at least their allies."

A dark pool swirled in Viktor's stomach, threatening to pull his heart into it.

No wonder the deposit in his account remained so high—had he just helped smuggle the myth of Russian 'suitcase nuclear devices'?

Part of him wanted to order his men to gun them down and simply steal the money.

Alas, he said, "Unless you plan on detonating it in Romania, I suggest we get this going."

With the opening of the gates, the bright red and blue DAC 6135 truck appeared. It looked conspicuous to him, but then he guessed that might have been the point.

Three of al-Wahishi's men jumped out of the truck and, with Viktor's men and a forklift, loaded the heavy steel compartment onto it.

Once loaded, al-Wahishi stepped up to him. "Maybe you should keep all the money."

"Why do you say that?"

"What is the communist going to do? Tell his boss to send Russian commandos after you? He will have to tell his boss why and sign his own death warrant."

"Do you know why I have survived all these years, Mister al-Wahishi?"

"Why?"

"Because I do what I say I am going to do. My word is my greatest shield."

The Yemeni's eyes lingered on his face for a few moments. "I understand."

SOUTH-EAST LONDON — ELLIOT BOTTLE FACTORY — LATE EVENING

Bruce briefly wondered if he had the correct address on Old Kent Road.

The clean metallic signage of 'Elliot Bottle Factory' glinted in the waning amber light of late afternoon, casting a faint golden sheen over the drab brickwork, momentarily transforming the grime-streaked façade into something almost elegant. The factory's industrial blue cladding contrasted sharply with the warm hues spilling from the upper windows, like sapphires bleeding into flames.

He eased the aqua-green Ford Mondeo into a narrow parking bay to the left of a short stairwell leading to the main entrance. His eyes tracked the brushed aluminium panel beside the doorway, confirming he'd come to the right place.

Then the man stepped out.

Broad, compact, wearing a turquoise polo shirt stretched taut across shoulders that spoke of decades under resistance. The fabric did little to disguise the muscle beneath—dense, utilitarian strength.

Only the cropped salt-and-pepper hair and a beard caught in the indecision between grey and white hinted at his age—maybe fifty.

Bruce's pulse quickened.

He knew this man.

Glasgow in the late 1970s still wore its old epithet: "No Mean City." The phrase, inherited from the razor gang era of the 1930s, still held weight, sharpened by territorial vendettas and the constant crackle of sectarian tension.

Back then, Bruce's father was away in the Middle East, his mother scraping by with two jobs. The nine-year-old boy found surrogate family in the street gang scene, running with the Govan Young Team—the juvenile wing of the adult Govan Firm.

He'd gotten his kicks from ***Skelp Runs***—quick hit-and-run raids across hostile territory, especially against the Govanhill lads.

But one incident changed his life forever.

An arranged mass brawl outside Queen Street Station saw Bruce backing up the senior Govan boys against the Gorbals Fleet. The chaos had been electric—shouting, bottle shards, fists smacking flesh.

He got stuck in.

But at some point, Bruce had gone down. Pinned beneath a heavier lad, a shattered bottle raised to carve up his face. The glass caught the light. He remembered the sound of his own breath, shallow with panic.

And then—the sirens.

The police swept in. His attacker fled. Bruce tried to get up, but his ribs screamed. A shadow loomed over him. Thick arms grabbed him like scaffolding.

The officer wasn't just any copper.

Martin Dunn—a revered name within

Scottish judo circles and beyond. He dumped Bruce in the back of a Panda car, not the 'Black Maria' van, and drove him home.

Bruce could still recall Dunn's voice as he told Kathleen McQuillan on the doorstep, too: *'Send him down to the dojo at Bellahouston tomorrow at six. Don't skelp him so bad he can't train.'*

Kathleen sent him with belt stripes on his back.

In one of the old colour photos Bruce remembered, Martin Dunn stood on the third-place podium of the 1971 BJA National Championships. Gold had gone to Brian Jacks, a judo prodigy who'd soon take Olympic bronze and become a household name through the TV show *Superstars*.

Second place—ginger-haired and built like a bulldozer—was a Royal Marine named Frank Carlsmith.

Dunn had once said of him: *'Fuckin' unit he was and could fight like a poacher's dog. Was a Royal Marine. Never saw 'im again after that.'*

That was the man he was looking at now. Forearms like steel rods. A cigarette dangling from two calloused fingers. He raised his chin, beckoning Bruce out of the car.

Bruce stepped out, locking down any expression that might give away his recognition.

But to his surprise, Carlsmith's face crinkled into a broad smile, creasing deep lines across weather-beaten skin.

"I've heard good things," he said. "You can call me Frank."

Bruce offered a neutral smile. "You can call me Bruce."

A man like Carlsmith could call him anything he wanted.

Frank chuckled like he got the joke.

"You smoke?"

"No."

"Health freak?"

"Not really. But they'll keep taxing the hell out of them. By the time I hit your age, they'll cost five times as much."

Frank nodded, seemingly approving. "A forward thinker. I like it."

He stubbed the cigarette out on the wall with deliberate force, then flicked the butt neatly into a bin below the stairs.

"Let's cut the suspense, shall we?"

Inside, men in white coats moved about with professional detachment—hairnets and beard covers secured tight. Their movements were swift but practiced.

"Bottled water line," Frank said as they passed through. "Need the gear to stop contamination."

He bounded up a steel industrial staircase as if it were a country path, punching a code into a keypad and swinging open the Portakabin door.

Plastic sheeting covered the carpet like a disposable skin.

A large white plastic table dominated the centre. Sitting on top was a black, blocky device that resembled a VCR without a telly. But with the manual pull-down screen on the wall, Bruce guessed it was one of those new digital projectors.

"No flip chart or blackboard? I must be moving up in the world."

"Cost about as much as that Mondeo

outside," Frank quipped before gesturing to the rear. "Coffee's back there. Make us one—Julie Andrews."

Bruce clocked the lack of slang.

No "brew". Not even "wet". Frank wasn't using any military patois.

He took note.

However, a ***Julie Andrews*** preference for hot drinks had morphed in the military. When Bruce was a ***crow*** Para, he had been summoned to the sergeant major's office for a misdemeanour and ordered to make the **SNCO** a Julie Andrews coffee. Bruce had assumed that to mean one with 'a spoonful of sugar'.

However, the subsequent spitting out of the beverage, punch to Bruce's gut with the verbal lashing of *'Julie Andrews, as in white nun…white, no sugar—get it? You fuckin' Full Mong Jacket'* had educated him to the contrary.

Their coffee preferences matched, so he turned to make two cups before turning back once they had been made.

Then he froze.

Frank Carlsmith was now holding a Heckler & Koch P9S pistol fitted with a suppressor.

"So, that's why the plastic sheeting," Bruce said calmly.

As Frank stepped sideways and locked the door behind him, Bruce remained still. He was unarmed. Frank wouldn't miss.

But if this had been a straight kill, he'd already be dead.

"Place one cup north, one south of the table," Frank instructed, the pistol never wavering. "And don't try the coffee-to-the-face Bond trick—it'll be your last."

Bruce complied, believing him.

They sat across from each other. Frank's trigger finger rested lightly, but the barrel still pointed squarely at Bruce.

"Seems you've landed yourself in a bit of bother across the water," Frank began. "And I bet you're thinking, '*They don't know for sure.*' Thing is, you'd only be half right."

He sipped.

"They've got circumstantial stuff—Eddie O'Neil, Ernie McVoy, the Syrian arms dealer, the topped Loyalists… It all adds up funny. But they don't need proof, Bruce. They just need you… gone."

"I understand," Bruce said quietly.

"Good. Don't waste the coffee. There are decaffeinated kids in Africa."

They both drank.

"They sanctioned me to murder ya," Frank said, like he was telling him the weather. "You know why they came to me?"

"Because you're the best they have?"

"Flattery'll get you everywhere." Frank grinned. "But what else?"

"I'd guess you're Poole-based. Bit of detachment."

Bruce didn't bother explaining how he deduced it—he knew bootnecks of Frank's era went SBS rather than SAS more often than not. Though he didn't think now was the time to tell Frank how he knew he was, or had been, a Marine.

He was reminded of the acronym and saying they had: OARMAARM—*Once A Royal Marine, Always A Royal Marine.*

"Fuck me, bang on," exclaimed Frank. "SIS is

just the extension of the old boy, public school network. Do you know why they call them public schools when they are actually private, fee-paying schools?"

Bruce shook his head.

"'Cos back in medieval England, education was limited to tutors to the aristocracy and church schools, but by the sixteenth to the eighteenth century, these schools like Eton, Westminster and that started accepting students outside of the area as long as they could pay. Hence were open to the 'public'—well, members of the public who could cough up the ***brass***. Funny that."

Bruce nodded, not understanding why it was relevant, especially when being held at gunpoint.

Frank continued, "Anyway, they want people like us to do the dirty work—but we'll always be one of the help."

"I see that," Bruce replied.

"You follow football? Celtic? Rangers?"

"Never really got into it."

"Aye, probably complicated growing up with a Catholic mam and Protestant da."

Frank leant back.

"You could support United—Ferguson's from your neck of the woods. Protestant, but wife's Catholic. Like your parents. Or… like, they were."

Bruce didn't expect this. Frank was… voluble. Not the silent killer stereotype. Charismatic. Charming, even.

"I thought you had to be raised into football," Bruce said.

"Come on now. Born-again Christians are the most zealous of all. They've got less time to prove themselves."

"They've got more to prove," Bruce agreed.

Frank gestured theatrically.

"Exactly. And you're about to be born again. Only, this time—I'm your God."

"How?"

"You mean how or why? Can't tell with you Jocks."

"Both."

"You know Cantona? Walked into Old Trafford like he owned it. Genius and a liability. But the gaffer stuck with him because he could help him win. That's the game, Bruce. You've got bottle. But I need to know why you helped Eddie O'Neil."

Bruce inhaled. The gun was still there. The room still quiet. Lying would be pointless.

"They don't need my confession."

"No. But I do. I need to know why—before I go out to bat for you."

Bruce exhaled.

"My grandad was a riveter. Died in a works accident, leaving my gran and mum. You can imagine that times were hard for a widow with a child, but my gran was apparently a good-looking woman and soon remarried. The husband was all sweetness and light at first, then the physical abuse of my mother began—stress positions, cold baths, hand over the mouth and pinching her nose 'til she thought she'd die—things that wouldn't leave marks. I discovered later that one of the reasons this Peter Murray 'turned' was because during the marriage to my gran, he discovered, or at least guessed, he couldn't have his own kids. My gran was too reliant on the stepdad's wage and was too drunk to help herself, let alone her child."

Bruce watched Frank nod and continued, "My great-aunt, the youngest of my gran's six sisters, had sent around her husband with new furniture and a television. Back door was open, as was the norm back then. Except Murray had *Rock around the Clock* by Bill Haley & His Comets blaring on the new electric record player he had given the family two weeks before. That was why Murray didn't notice him standing there as he performed his old 'hand over the mouth, nose pinching' routine on my eight-year-old mum. Luckily, the music also drowned out his beating Murray to within an inch of his life."

He saw Frank's lips part. "Eddie O'Neil is your great-uncle?"

"He doesn't even know."

"Fuck me," murmured Frank.

"The O'Neils knew that one battering wouldn't be enough to keep Murray and my mum apart. So, they sent her to Scotland to live with relatives on my grandad's side. They gave my gran the concocted story that she wanted to get my mum away from the border campaign and that the employment prospects were better. Whether people guessed or not was neither here nor there, but it got her away—good thing, too, as The Troubles really did begin years later. I always reckoned my maternal, Northern Irish Catholic genealogy might have been too complex for even the background checkers."

Frank was silent for a moment longer, then said, "I called Martin, your old judo sensei. Luckily for you, he said you were a good lad."

Bruce felt a wash of hope, confirmed by Frank's following words of, "You work under me now. For the foreseeable. You do what I say. When I say it. How I say it. Do you understand?"

"I understand."

Frank lifted the P9S.

"Not for nothing, but if it ever does come to me killing you, you'll never see the weapon."

6

HOTEL SOKOLNIKI PALACE — MOSCOW — EVENING

Genrikh Bezmenov's heartbeat quickened with each phone call he ended. He stood in a terrycloth bathrobe, peering down from the window of his mid-tier suite, watching the crowds below surge in time with a Scottish pipe band marching through the avenue. The keening of the bagpipes nearly drowned out the hiss of the en-suite shower.

The room smelled of old tobacco and stale fabric softener. It was not the most expensive suite in Moscow, though he could have afforded it. Caution had overridden comfort—visibility came at a risk. He'd opted for discretion, not decadence.

Bezmenov tapped the ash from his *Belomorkanal* cigarette into a chipped, green glass ashtray perched precariously on the windowsill. The acrid smell clung to the curtains. He had always smoked *Belomorkanals*, like his uncle before him. Unlike the rising tide of Russians switching to Marlboros—a Western contagion he found more offensive than the McDonald's billboard now towering over the heads of the crowd—Genrikh remained loyal to his own slow death.

Below, the people had gathered by the hundreds of thousands for the 850th anniversary of Moscow. What appeared to be a celebration was, to Bezmenov, a mass hallucination—a desperate population seeking escape from the poverty, corruption and chaos of Yeltsin's Russia.

The country was no longer run by the Party. Thieves ran it in tailored suits—oligarchs who'd bought the bones of the USSR for kopeks on the rouble. And yet, even now, Bezmenov couldn't quite decide whether he despised or envied them.

The final of four secure phone calls confirmed the transfer: his millions had landed across the offshore accounts he'd cultivated for over a decade.

He had already greased the right palms in Nicaragua, offering regular political "donations" to President Arnoldo Alemán. It was a trivial price to pay for what the country offered in return—a legally grey, politically ambivalent refuge. Not forever, no. But long enough. Long enough to vanish before the SVR recovered from its decay.

Once they regained their bite, he'd be long gone. His face surgically altered. His identity retired like an agent's pistol. Paris, Tokyo or New York had their draws, but in Nicaragua, he could live like a king, off the grid, off the radar.

The safe house he'd purchased through a now-dead cousin years ago would be his first stop. No one in his current circle knew about it. Not the SVR. Not even Olga.

Tomorrow, he would board a nine-hour, nearly seven-thousand-kilometre flight from Vnukovo to Vladivostok under a name he had not used since 1989. From there, a freighter bound for the Philippines. Once at sea, he would disappear.

The SVR would, predictably, turn their attention west—Belarus, Ukraine, the Baltic states. Routes traditionally favoured by defectors. *Let them.* Bezmenov wasn't defecting. He couldn't, not after what he'd done. Not after handing over a nuclear device to Islamist extremists.

No. He wasn't changing sides.

He was leaving the board entirely.

The shower ceased. Steam continued to billow beneath the bathroom door. A few moments passed before Olga Danilova emerged, wrapped in the feminine twin of his bathrobe.

"Thank you for waiting until after the sex to smoke," she said, half reproachful, half affectionate. "You no longer have the excuse of ignorance, Genrikh. They are bad for you."

She had been his mistress since her assignment—as his wife's carer.

Marina Bezmenov had suffered from Huntington's disease, a drawn-out tragedy that slowly robbed her of dignity and movement. Olga had been her second nurse, the first having left suddenly after several years without explanation. Ten years his junior, Olga had proven to be more than a caregiver. Gradually, she assumed the domestic space—eventually, his bed.

Even now, Bezmenov often wondered whether Marina knew before she died last year. Twelve years after diagnosis. Quietly, painfully.

And when Marina passed, he had chosen silence over transparency. Not to protect his reputation. He could've survived being called a monster. But he feared what exposure would do to his career—a career he no longer intended to keep.

He waved a dismissive hand, exhaling smoke.

"A Western fallacy. They blame tobacco instead of their processed filth."

He didn't believe it. But he wasn't prepared to

stop.

"I will keep trying," Olga said, stepping closer. "Perhaps I'll wear you down one day."

"Given the difference in our ages," he said dryly, "I suspect you will succeed. Eventually."

"Hopefully not too late."

He stubbed out the cigarette and, for a moment, hesitated.

"Olga, there is something I must tell you… and ask of you."

He gestured towards the bed, pulling a chair from the dresser. They sat facing one another.

"If I were to go away," he said, locking eyes with her, "would you come with me?"

She blinked. "Away? Like a vacation?"

"No. Permanently."

"Where? How?"

"Somewhere hot. Money will not be a problem. Yes or no?"

"My God, Genrikh. What have you done?"

He stood, already retreating into silence. "I understand."

"Sit down," she said sharply. "Of course I will come. Don't act like a child."

He obeyed.

"I assume if I do this," she said, voice steadier now, "I won't be able to speak to my family again?"

He nodded.

"And we'll be hunted? By your… employers?"

"Yes."

"Are we to defect? If that still exists."

"No," said Bezmenov, then he realised she deserved something. "I have made a sale of… munitions to a party outside of Russia. The sale has proven lucrative."

"How lucrative?"

"Enough that we can live comfortably for the rest of our days."

"Even with them hunting us?"

"Yes. We will be in a safe place. I might have to… change my face?"

When her hand went to her mouth, he quickly said, "You can just change the colour and style of your hair."

"I am not worried about my face, you fool. I like your face. It is one I fell in love with."

"All faces change with time."

She nodded. "When do we leave?"

"I go tomorrow night. You'll meet me. But you must move within a day or not at all. After forty-eight hours, my absence becomes an unauthorised departure. They'll look for you."

"Will they come for my sister?"

"Does she know about me?"

"Only that you exist. Not who you are."

"Then she'll be fine," he said smoothly to veil his lack of confidence in his words. "They may question her, but she won't face… advanced methods."

"Where am I going?"

"I'll deposit the funds. You'll receive instructions. You cannot fly directly—they'll track it."

Guilt tightened his chest. He should never have involved her. She deserved a clean escape, not a life of shadows.

He desperately wished she could come, but he wouldn't send any instructions.

She stared at him as he buttoned his shirt. He

stood over her.

"A week from now," he said, "we will be away from this crumbling state."

RIZE PROVINCE — TURKEY — MORNING

Ramzi al-Wahishi stood before a semicircle of young men, all of whom were cross-legged on a faded red-and-gold carpet, their eyes burning with reverence. The air was warm, cloying with the scent of sweat and citrus.

Sunlight pierced the thin blinds, striping the floor with light. Outside, tea fields stretched across the hills—green waves owned by the Great Eastern Islamic Raiders' Front, who had granted al-Wahishi and his men haven in the workers' quarters.

Today's sermon was different. Today, he preached ***Istishhad***—the exalted concept of martyrdom.

He spoke softly in Arabic, the rhythm of his voice commanding.

"When the Prophet faced the Quraysh at Badr, he had little—just over three hundred men and two horses. The enemy had over 1,100 horses. And yet, the cry went out: *'O thou whom God hath made victorious—slay!'* And Allah struck fear into the hearts of the disbelievers."

Murmurs of awe rippled through the gathering.

"Victory does not lie in numbers. It lies in intention. The Muslim warriors at Badr were prepared to die in the name of Allah. That is Istishhad."

He paused. Let the weight settle.

"We have procured a gift. A fist of Allah. It

will kill thousands of disbelievers. But it will also claim the lives of those chosen for this mission."

He scanned their expressions. No fear. Only eagerness. And one man's reaction in particular pleased him.

Zubayr al-Adel sat at the rear, his eyes fixed, his nod slow but sure.

Al-Adel, the twenty-seven-year-old with a suspiciously acquired O-1 visa. The others had questioned him—until he led from the front in the truck bombings in Riyadh. Eight Americans had died. Doubt had been killed with them.

"To be chosen," Ramzi continued, "you must pass a gauntlet of trials. Not only in faith but in action."

He saw Zubayr lean forward slightly.
And in that moment, Ramzi knew.
The chosen was ready.

7

SOUTH-EAST LONDON — THE KING'S WATCH PUB — EARLY EVENING

The low hum of conversation filled the pub like background static—pint glasses clinking, fruit machines singing, a distant whiff of vinegar from a forgotten basket of chips on the bar.

Frank Carlsmith leant on one elbow, his pint of bitter half drained in front of him. The air was tinged with the tang of disinfectant and old smoke. Football scarves hung limp above the bar. The King's Watch was the kind of place that had survived Thatcher, the miners' strike and three World Cups without ever changing the carpet.

Behind the bar stood Len Ford, fiftyish, soft around the middle now but still sporting a boxer's shoulders and a busted knuckle or two. He wiped glasses with the same rag he'd been using since before Sky Sports was a thing.

They both stared at the TV, mounted high in the corner. The sound was faint but recognisable—*ITN Evening News* presented by Dermot Murnaghan.

"I like that black newscaster with the beehive," Frank said, sipping his pint.

"Trevor McDonald?"

Frank twisted his head to stare at him. "Fuck off, *Moira Stuart*, you plank."

Len barked a laugh, shaking his head as he plonked another glass onto the bar rack.

"Classy bird, that. Used to fancy her, didn't

ya?"

"Still do." Frank grinned. "I remember getting a semi listening to her read the death toll in Rwanda."

Len smirked, flipping a bar mat. "You and your—look here, she's a proper sort."

The news faded into a promo for an upcoming film. A split-second image of Cameron Diaz appeared, all legs, red dress and that megawatt grin.

"She was something in that film, *The Mask*," Len said, nodding with admiration.

Frank said without hesitation, "She's tidy, but she ain't no Salma Hayek in *Dusk Till Dawn*. Snake dance. Fuck me running."

Len whistled low. "Fair. That scene. That snake. That… whatever it was."

"Religion, mate," Frank said. "I'd have converted to Aztec on the spot."

Len laughed again, this time quieter. He looked down as he dried his hands, then back up at Frank with a more subdued expression. "Anyway. What's up with ya?"

Frank took a moment. The joviality cooled slightly as he watched a bus bomb story start to roll across the headline banner on screen. "I am just upset that there aren't more strong male ginger role models on the box."

Len sniggered but said, "OK, you don't want to talk about it. Fair enough."

Frank scratched his jaw with the back of a thick hand. "Nothing, really," he said. "Just… taken on someone at work I maybe shouldn't've. Young lad. Got talent, loads. But he's a wild card."

Len raised an eyebrow, leaning over the bar.

"You can always sack him."

Frank gave a dry chuckle. "That's the plan, if he fucks up."

Len paused. "Or are you worried he'll take your job one day?"

Frank looked at him. "I *want* him to. That's the point."

Len nodded slowly, rested his arms on the counter and said, "All you can do is what you can do."

The front door opened with a squeal. A draught swept in.

Len nudged Frank, nodding discreetly towards the entrance.

A man had stepped inside—a tall, narrow figure with a long black coat and slicked-back hair. His cheekbones looked carved from flint, and his expression conveyed the polite wariness of someone who never quite relaxed in public.

He moved like someone used to the streets—but not these ones.

Eastern European, though softened by years in London. His accent wouldn't be obvious unless he spoke. Even then, it would carry that strange neutrality shared by old spies and waiters in Soho.

Frank didn't need a name. He just gave a slight nod.

"Right," he said. "Time to work."

He downed the rest of his pint. "'Ere ya, Len, could you get us two more of those?"

"I'll bring 'em, Frank."

The Mancunian stood up, rolled his shoulders and crossed the floor to the far corner booth, where the shadows were thick and the noise thin.

The man was already sitting. Waiting.

VNUKOVO INTERNATIONAL AIRPORT — RUSSIA — MID-MORNING

Bezmenov's heart exhaled its first true breath of relief as the Tupolev Tu-134 thundered down the runway and lifted into the air.

He knew this was only the beginning of his escape to freedom. But experience had taught him one brutal truth—*if* the SVR, or any of Russia's other long-armed agencies, had caught even a whisper of his intentions, this plane would never have left the tarmac.

He had left behind a carefully worded message for his superior, claiming he had received an urgent lead from an informant in Tula and would call that evening. A ruse. Thin, but plausible enough to buy him hours.

The interior of the Tu-134 was a spartan affair compared to the Western airliners he had occasionally flown on in recent years. The difference in luxury and comfort was stark. Still, he was grateful—grateful to be seated near the rear engine and more so to have secured a window seat.

Bezmenov reached into the inner pocket of his blazer and withdrew a blister pack. He popped a single pink tablet and washed it down with a hard gulp from a lukewarm bottle of water.

Under any other circumstances, he would never dull his awareness. However, the tactic of taking *Relanium*—or diazepam, as it was known in the West—had proven effective in managing jet lag. Better to be sluggish during the stopovers and groggy for a few hours than arrive in Vladivostok sleep-deprived and vulnerable.

As the aircraft climbed higher, the grey sprawl of Moscow gave way to majestic stretches of birch forests and patchwork fields, the vast, aching beauty of the Russian landscape unfurling beneath him.

He realised, with a sudden twist in his chest, that this would be the last time he gazed upon the Motherland from the air.

Whenever he had travelled before, returning home always brought a rekindled appreciation for all that was uniquely Russian:

—The impromptu gatherings around crowded kitchen tables with vodka and song.
—The cultural humour, woven into sarcasm and soul.
—The ease of speaking Russian without needing to dip into other tongues.
—The thick, satisfying *Borodinsky* black bread, steaming dumpling dishes.
—The riotous cheer of *Maslenitsa*—Butter Week—festivals marking winter's retreat.
—The lively chatter of open-air markets, the small talk at bustling street kiosks.
—Even the subterranean ballet of Moscow's metro system, with its chandeliers and statues.
All of it now… *behind him.*

He knew the Russian communities in Nicaragua had thinned since the fall of the Soviet Union. Those that remained had mostly gathered around Managua, isolated and outnumbered.

For a fleeting moment, Bezmenov considered doing the right thing. Alerting someone—the SVR, the CIA, Mossad—that *Al Qaeda now possessed a nuclear device*. That perhaps they could stop it. Perhaps thousands of lives could be spared.

Then the moment passed.

He didn't want them to stop it.

If there were anyone he despised more than his own countrymen, it was the Americans. And if anyone on this earth hated Americans more than he did, it was these Islamic fanatics.

He guessed New York would be the target. It had to be.

And in that realisation, he saw the grim, poetic irony: the mujahideen, once armed by the Americans to bleed the Soviets dry, would now detonate a bomb to kill tens of thousands of Americans.

And Bezmenov, once a sentinel of the Soviet empire, would be far away—watching, waiting. Smiling.

KING'S WATCH PUB — CORNER BOOTH — EVENING

Frank slid into the corner booth, his back instinctively against the wall, eyes scanning the room without moving his head. The other man was already seated—tall, razor-featured, his black coat folded neatly beside him like a shed skin.

Dmitri Chernov. A man who wore the quiet the way others wore a Rolex—effortlessly, with a hint of menace.

Frank nodded a greeting. "Dmitri."

"Frank."

The table between them bore old scars—cigarette burns, carved initials, a sticky patch someone had given up trying to clean.

Neither of them shook hands. They never had.

"He wants to see you," Dmitri said, straight to the point. His English was near flawless but clipped—like every word had been vetted first.

Frank arched an eyebrow. "And this couldn't be delivered with a phone call?"

Dmitri gave a slight shrug. "He said it was important. Told me to tell you personally."

"So, what's so bloody important he couldn't just tell *you* and let you pass it on?"

Dmitri's expression barely shifted. "I don't know." A pause. "All I know is it is to do with The Wahhabi Club."

"Which one?"

"I can't—"

"Throw me a bone 'ere, Dmitri. I'll act like it's new news when he tells me, but I could do with prepping. Is it Al-Gama'a al-Islamiyya, Lashkar-e-Taiba—"

"It is Binny's Boys."

"Fucksake," sighed Frank on confirmation of Osama Bin Laden's Al Qaeda. "I've been telling our people for years that this fucking Saudi prince is going to be the new news. What is it exactly?"

"I honestly do not know. But I will say this—whatever it is, it has made the big guy very nervous. Hence him reaching out to you. Says you will thank him, too."

Frank stared at him for a beat. The guy wasn't given to exaggeration.

"Alright," Frank said, exhaling through his nose. "Give me a couple of days."

Dmitri tilted his head slightly. "He would prefer sooner."

"Yeah, well, I'd prefer to wake up without any grey in my hair and a back that doesn't sound like bubble wrap."

A faint trace of a smile ghosted across Dmitri's lips. He relented with a nod.

They sat in silence for a moment as Len approached with two fresh pints. Frank gave him a nod of thanks, then turned back to his guest.

Dmitri leant in slightly, his voice quieter. "Is it true? What they say—about how you met the boss?"

Frank gave a slow blink and leant back in his seat. "Certain stories have a way of growing arms and legs."

They said nothing for a while after that.

Frank looked over Dmitri's shoulder at the flickering telly above the bar. Football highlights now. Something lower-league and scrappy. Just how he liked it.

He reached into his coat, pulled out a crumpled cigarette packet and tapped it against the table.

"Tell him I'll be bringing someone over."

"Who?"

"A protégé."

Dmitri nodded. "OK."

"And tell him I want looking after," said Frank. "I'll be travelling over a thousand bastard miles, after all, and missing episodes of ***The Bill***."

"Considering that you seem to be one of his favourite people, I believe that will be the least he will do."

8

SIS HEADQUARTERS — DIRECTOR'S OFFICE — MORNING

The office of the Chief of the Secret Intelligence Service, deep within the fortress-like modernist expanse of Vauxhall Cross, was elegant but austere. Mahogany bookshelves lined one wall, filled with leather-bound volumes and folders marked only with coloured tabs. The room was shadowed in tasteful earth tones—olive carpet, walnut desk, cream-panelled walls—and the faint tang of pipe smoke still lingered in the air, a ghost of a habit Sir Andrew Maremount had finally broken during the Thatcher years.

A framed portrait, *The Death of Nelson*, by Arthur William Devis, hung above a bust of Mansfield Smith-Cumming, SIS's first chief, who famously signed his dispatches with the letter *C* in green ink.

Despite ***the Circus*** not being a military institution, Miles Parker felt the urge to snap to attention. Old habits died hard—especially when standing before a man like Sir Andrew Maremount, similarly known internally and throughout Whitehall simply as *C*.

Parker was a tall, formidable presence, all angular lines and well-suppressed tension, but next to Maremount—who stood a half-foot shorter and easily two decades older—he still felt an almost adolescent unease. Maremount had a way of dressing you down that made you feel less like a subordinate officer and more like a clever schoolboy who'd written a brilliant essay on the wrong subject.

Today was such a moment.

"We protect democracy, Miles," Maremount snapped. "We do *not* practice it."

His voice had the sharp edge of an Oxford don who'd run out of patience. Parker kept his expression neutral, hands folded behind his back. Maremount continued, pacing slightly behind his desk, a vein twitching in his temple.

"Much thought—and courage—went into making this decision. And you're telling me the asset won't carry it out?"

Parker remained steady. "Sir, he didn't say he wouldn't. He requested a deferral to bring the miscreant into line with our objective. I thought he deserved the chance. If you disagree, then he'll proceed with the original directive."

There was a pause. Maremount's eyes narrowed, evaluating.

Then, slowly, he lifted his hands from the desk, exhaled through his nose and adjusted the cufflinks of his shirt with mechanical precision.

"Sit down, Miles."

Both men mirrored each other as they sank into the chairs opposite one another. The tension didn't vanish—it just sank deeper into the carpet.

Maremount leant back, fingers interlocked across his waistcoat.

"Imagine spinning plates, Miles… except they're intrinsically connected. One falls, and the rest follow."

Parker gave a slight nod. He understood the metaphor, if not yet the warning.

"You admire Frank Carlsmith," Maremount said—not as a question but as a declaration.

"Yes," Parker replied without hesitation.

"As do I," Maremount added. "As does the Service. The man's record speaks for itself. But admiration doesn't equal carte blanche. There's a ranking structure for a reason."

"I understand, sir."

Maremount gave a slight nod, then changed tack. "Do you know why the Israelis won in '67 and '73?"

"Superior intelligence. Rapid mobilisation. Poor coordination among the Arab coalition—"

Maremount cut him off. "Not just poor coordination. The command structure of those armies was a shambles. Nepotism wasn't just common—it was expected. Every officer was someone's cousin, brother-in-law or nephew. No accountability. Orders passed over more hurdles than a poodle at Crufts. Meanwhile, the Israeli model empowered what they called ***strategic corporals***—men who could make real-time battlefield decisions. Clarity of hierarchy, trust in the competent, ruthless execution."

He paused.

"Do you understand?"

Parker considered. Then answered honestly. "No. Not fully."

Maremount allowed a thin smile—part approval, part warning.

"I'll give you this latitude, Miles. But remember—the tail does not wag the dog."

"I understand," Parker said, more grounded.

They sat in silence a moment longer. Outside the office window, the Thames moved in slow, silted loops beneath a grey London sky.

The Circus turned slowly, but it never stopped.

RUSSIA — IRKUTSK INTERNATIONAL AIRPORT — LATE MORNING

Bezmenov forced his rolling pupils to still as he opened his heavy lids.

He guessed that the bounce of the Tupolev's wheel on the airstrip had awoken him from his Relanium-induced stupor.

The SVR officer peered out the window to confirm they had landed at Irkutsk International Airport for a refuelling stop that could last for over an hour.

He let his leaden eyelids slide back down.

Time floated past before a whoosh of cool air swirled, and the percussion of heavy boots banged his diaphragm.

His eyelids came up—much lighter this time—to see three men wearing black jackets, their Makarov PM pistols on display, and each with a Tonfa-style baton in their hands.

He briefly wondered if the aghast passengers and crew could hear his cold heartbeat.

Nestled in the centre of their **ushankas**, the double-headed eagle on a shield emblem of the newly-formed **FSB** stared at him like a demon's eye.

The shortest, in the centre, ordered him, "Colonel Genrikh Bezmenov. Follow us. Immediately, so there are not any disturbances."

Even through the effect of the Relanium, Bezmenov knew that '…*any disturbances*' meant '*the three of us beating you with our batons before dragging you off.'*

Briefly, he thought of protesting his innocence, for no other reason than this would be relayed to his eventual interrogators and plant a seed of doubt.

However, he knew by observing the twitching of the baton hands that any defiance would result in a physically and mentally impairing beating, of which he could not afford.

He stood with as much dignity as he could muster.

The centre officer said slyly, "Do not be troubled, Colonel. The flight to Krasnoyarsk is just two hours. The plane is waiting for you."

Krasnoyarsk was home to several penitentiary camps—and the facilities to interrogate the prisoners.

RIZE PROVINCE — TURKEY — EARLY MORNING

Ramzi al-Wahishi allowed himself a thin smile as he watched Zubayr al-Adel lead the others through the endurance course.

Before the candidates' arrival, he had ordered their hosts—the men of the Great Eastern Islamic Raiders' Front—to construct a proper assault circuit. Burak Sangu, ever eager to impress, had beamed with pride as he unveiled the finished product: an imposing gauntlet sprawled across the wooded outskirts of Rize Province.

Al-Wahishi had shown no outward reaction, but privately, he approved. It was well-built: rope walls, monkey bars, cargo nets both horizontal and vertical, balance logs, trench jumps, mud tunnels, sandbag carries, agility stones, and finally, a firing station armed with three well-maintained Browning Hi-Power pistols. Primitive but effective. It would do.

For the past two days, al-Wahishi had conducted a private evaluation of each of the seven candidates. He made them quote Qur'anic verses by heart, justify their understanding of *istishhad*—the theology of martyrdom—and field-strip and reassemble AKs under pressure. Now, starved of food, sunburnt and blistered, they faced their final test.

The shooting drill at the end was deliberately less meaningful—by the time they reached it, the least fit joined the end of the queue to fire and so were the most rested. What mattered to al-Wahishi was not aim but will.

By dusk, the seven stood before him, forming a sweaty, dust-caked semicircle, breathing heavily, bodies trembling with fatigue. But it was the eyes he read—the flickers of hunger, doubt, devotion and something darker.

Some of them were ready.

Some of them were not.

"You've shown strength," he said, his voice cutting the still air like a blade. "To complete this course after two days without food shows commitment. But not all of you adhered to the fast."

A ripple of unease passed through the group.

"There were violations."

Their heads turned, each searching the next for a flicker of guilt.

"The truth," al-Wahishi said coldly, "can save a man."

Silence.

He took a few slow paces away, then turned sharply.

"Zubayr. Ayman. Hamza. Step forward."

They did so.

"There are cameras in the pantry," he said simply. "That alone I would have forgiven. Hunger is a test. But lying? The Quran is clear."

He stared at them, one by one.

"'The believers are those who are truthful, steadfast, and obedient.' Surah 3:17. You all know this."

Nods.

"A thief can have his hand cut off. But what can be done with a liar?"

He lifted his tunic, revealing one of the Browning Hi-Powers holstered at his hip. He drew it slowly, released the magazine to show it was loaded, then clicked it back into place with a metallic snap. Chambered a round. Safety off.

Then, with chilling composure, he offered the pistol, grip-first.

"Who among you is ready to do what must be done?"

The question hadn't finished leaving his lips before Zubayr al-Adel moved.

Like a cobra uncoiled, he snatched the pistol from al-Wahishi's hand with startling speed. He didn't speak. He didn't hesitate. He tucked the weapon into the waistband of his fatigues, turned, and began walking back down the hill towards the others.

They scattered on the first shot.

Men from the Great Eastern Islamic Raiders' Front, already stationed at the perimeter, began to close ranks—but they weren't needed.

Zubayr moved with silent, terrifying purpose.

He dropped the first man with a round to the head. Then he ran, pursued, closed the gap and dispatched the rest with cold, mechanical efficiency.

When it was over, four bodies lay sprawled, the dust slowly settling around them.

Zubayr walked back up the incline, shoulders square, his pace unhurried, the weapon still in his hand. He said nothing. The look in his eyes made words unnecessary.

Al-Wahishi did not smile.

But inside, he knew. They had their team leader.

9

INTERROGATION CELL — KRASTEK FACILITY — NIGHT

The light buzzed above like a dying insect. Not flickering. Just persistent. Oppressive.

Bezmenov sat on the hard metal chair, spine ramrod straight, though he was exhausted. The walls were a pale institutional green, the kind of colour chosen not to calm but to wear you down slowly. There was a camera in the corner boxed, old, analogue, probably recording to tape. He made no effort to hide the calculation in his eyes.

They had taken his belt, shoes and watch. Left the uniform. Not out of courtesy but ritual. SVR men from the KGB era were still afforded a certain theatre of treatment.

He had been processed with the quiet efficiency of a system that had outlived six governments and would outlive six more. Strip-searched, photographed, questions barked more for formality than answers. He noted the rank and mannerisms of the guards—young, precise, scared of what they might not know. That told him everything. This wasn't a rogue faction. This was high clearance.

Now he waited, the fog of Relanium long since burned off by adrenaline and dread. He ran through the deceptions he might tell—each variation weighed and tested.

Rogue elements in the Ministry.
Coercion.
Operation within parameters not understood.

Fabricated defection under deep cover.
A leak from an unsanctioned section.
None would hold.

The steel door unlatched with a metallic groan and opened with surprising softness. Into the room stepped Major Andrei Arkadievich Sokolova.

Bezmenov's heart slowed.

The name preceded the man—field operative turned counterintelligence star. Young, by GRU standards. Dangerous, by SVR ones.

His early years in the service had been marred with suspicion due to his father being a *fartsovshchiki*—black market dealer. No doubt contributing to Sokolova's impressive professional drive.

The file had said 'precise'. The rumours had said 'patient'. He looked the part: greying at the temples prematurely, uniform sharp without looking vain, eyes like razors. The kind of man destined to outlive the reformers and become a legend of the next regime.

Sokolova did not sit. He merely closed the door behind him and leant against it—casual, unimpressed.

"Colonel Bezmenov," he said, his voice mild but edged, "I appreciate your punctuality. Few men arrive at their interrogations by military aircraft anymore."

Bezmenov exhaled through his nose.

"I was told Krasnoyarsk has a beautiful cathedral. I assume this is not the tour route?"

A faint smirk tugged at Sokolova's lips.

"Not for dissidents, no."

Bezmenov steepled his fingers in front of

him.

"Major, there was a time, not long ago, when your kind saluted mine."

Sokolova's expression didn't change.

"Yes, and there was a time the Romanovs ruled. We all outlive someone."

Bezmenov weighed the man again. Then he made his first attempt.

"I was running a long operation on Middle Eastern extremist channels. I made contact with assets that needed… oblique handling. Everything I did was for the long-term gain of the state."

Sokolova blinked. Once. Then turned from the door and walked in a slow arc behind the chair opposite.

"You're referring to the handover of a nuclear device to Al Qaeda?"

Bezmenov didn't flinch. "I do not recognise that phrasing."

"Genrikh, we still have our agents and informants throughout the world," said Sokolova. "You should have known how talkative both the carpet barons and the Sake snakes can be when they have lost a bid and have nothing to lose. Given how remarkably similar the intelligence from each source was, despite the eight-thousand-kilometre distance."

"Perhaps a joint misinformation operation against us," said Bezmenov, feeling that silence would be tantamount to confession.

However, he could hear how weak and hollow it sounded aloud—the Iranian Ministry of Intelligence and the Japanese Public Security Intelligence Agency had no formal intel alliance due to Japan's alliance with the US and the Iranians being seen as a state sponsor of terrorism against the Americans.

Sokolova stopped behind the chair.

"Tell me about your left-hand wife," said the major, using the Russian term for 'mistress'.

"Who?"

"You have more than one? You are a strong man, Colonel." Sokolova smiled. "Tell me about Olga Danilova."

Something shifted in Bezmenov's chest. His face froze, but a tremor crept through his hands before he could will it still.

"What about her?" he asked, too carefully.

"She is… resourceful. Convincing. Her report on your activities goes back nearly two years."

Bezmenov scoffed, a brittle laugh. *He's lying*, he thought.

"I believe your phrasing was, *'She would wear me down eventually.'*" Sokolova stepped to the side. "It seems you were correct."

The door opened again. Bezmenov's breath hitched.

Olga.

She stepped in slowly, arms tucked to her sides, gaze not quite meeting his.

She looked… different. Not scared. Not proud. Just resigned.

He said nothing.

And she said nothing.

Her silence broke him far more efficiently than any screaming denial. After a beat, Sokolova dismissed her with a nod. She left without looking back.

The door clicked closed.

The silence that followed was bone-deep.

Bezmenov stared at his fingernails.

Finally, he spoke. "I will tell you everything."

Sokolova didn't interrupt.

"You may question me for as long as you wish. I will give you names. Times. Accounts. Locations."

He looked up, and his eyes were steady now.

"But… I ask for one thing."

Sokolova raised an eyebrow.

"The dignity of ending my own life. When this is over."

There was a long pause. Then the major nodded slowly, almost imperceptibly.

"You know the state, and therefore I cannot sanction it."

A shrug. "Then you begin the process of deciphering the truth from the lies of my words—when you do finally get me to talk."

Sokolova stepped forward, calm as a priest. "Perhaps a clever officer of the old KGB—like you—had the foresight to hide something in the seam of his trousers."

He set the paper gently on the desk.

"Something very small. Easy to overlook. But… conclusive."

Their eyes met.

Bezmenov saw it then. The line. The rare, invisible thread between enemies who understand each other too well.

Sokolova turned without another word and walked to the door.

GLASGOW — THE COPPER STAG PUB — MIDDAY

Bruce sat behind the upper balustrade, his eyes flicking to the door every time a patron creaked it open with a gust of cool, wet wind. The dense fug of the pub seemed to suck it in like a yawn.

Scotland must have already had its two-week summer, he thought.

The air inside held the years of smoke, spilt Tennent's and Saturday night songs, all baked into the wood-panelled walls and faded tartan carpet that had once been red but now lived somewhere between maroon and surrender.

Three days had passed since his meeting with Frank Carlsmith, and the euphoria of being alive had taken this long to simmer into mere gratefulness.

Bruce hadn't doubted that orders from above had been given to assassinate him, hadn't doubted Carlsmith's ability to do so, and hadn't doubted Frank's supposedly seeing something in him as being the reason he still lived.

Frank had ordered Bruce to return to his home city and not to set foot out of it until he contacted him, and if he did, then he might find his death reprieve rescinded.

Bruce knew that despite feeling constricted, if he stayed for any appreciable amount of time, he would always feel a warmth towards his native city.

The nostalgia of misty childhood memories of his buoyed up father occupied him; on one particular occasion in their living room, his mother had looked up from the paper to ask his dad, *"Don, if you had the choice between winching the most beautiful woman in the world for a million pounds or me for free, which would you choose?"*

Winching, pronounced 'wenching', being Scottish slang for kissing passionately, and his father—as quick as a flash—had answered, *"Silly question, Kathleen, my darling, because you are the bonniest lass in the world."*

His father had motioned an arms' width circle with his hands as he said *world,* causing Bruce and his sister Sandra to giggle and their mum to fail to hide a smile that appeared as a smirk.

Donald McQuillan had been a humanitarian aid worker, and in 1975, he failed to return from the last of several trips to Lebanon.

The details of his death remained as hazy as Bruce's recollections of his father's life, but the hardships that afflicted the family afterwards remained all too clear.

He did know this had been his father's local, and he doubted it looked much different.

A dim yellow light spilt from brass sconces that might not have been polished since Thatcher first came to power. A haze of cigarette smoke curled lazily in the air, like it had nowhere better to be. Every surface gleamed with the dampness of beer—not wet exactly, but sticky with the ghosts of a thousand pints clinked and sloshed in celebration, consolation or nothing.

At the back, a battered fruit machine blinked and hummed its siren song to no one in particular, its fluorescent buttons sticky with grease and hope. In the corner, two old boys sat under a cloud of John Player Special smoke, arguing in thick Glaswegian over a Partick Thistle result from '82 like it had just happened last week. One had a flat cap permanently welded to his skull; the other wore a Celtic scarf despite the warmth, nursing a half pint of heavy like it was the last one he'd ever see.

Bruce perused the copy of the Daily Record left on the table beside him, with the headline:

TIME FOR A FRESH START
Blair Promises Jobs, Hope and Change for Scotland.

Exclusive: Labour leader tells the Record why it's time to boot out the Tories after 18 years, with the sidebar of **'I BEAT CANCER – THEN WON £50K ON THE LOTTO!'** A Glasgow mum's miracle week.

The handsome middle-aged landlady climbed the stairs balancing the tray of his steak, chips and peas with the aplomb of an English butler.

Hair dyed a deep auburn, piled high in a no-nonsense beehive held together with a lifetime of hairspray and sheer willpower.

She arrived at his table in a cloud of Charlie Red perfume before deftly sliding his meal and swapping his empty glass for a full one of McEwan's Lager.

"Thank you," he said.

Straightening her padded shoulders, she stood long enough for him to look up at her, keeping the travel of his eyes off her ample cleavage.

Before he could get a word in, she cut across him in that voice of hers—like sandpaper soaked in honey and twenty Regal Kings.

"Wait a minute… I've been wrackin' ma brain tryin' tae place ye. You're no' Don McQuillan's boy, are ye?"

He looked up again, caught off guard.

"Aye... that's me."

She grinned, eyes narrowing like she'd just won a bet.

"Thought so. No many fellas wi' a face like that. Ye've got yer faither's jawline. Lucky sod."

"Cheers," he said. "Did ye know him well?"

"No as well as ah wanted tae!" She laughed. "Could ***rip yer knitting*** sometimes but a proper charmer, so he was—but aye, daft in love wi' yer mam. Lovely woman. Ah was sorry tae hear about her passin', son."

Bruce just gave a quiet nod. "What's your name?" he asked.

"Caroline," she said. "An' yours is Robert, aye?"

"Bruce."

She clicked her tongue and laughed. "Course it is. When he told me, I just thought of Robert the Bruce."

He smiled.

She squinted at him. "You still in the army?"

"For now."

She leant in just a wee bit, lowering her voice with a nod.

"Well, listen, you're welcome in here any time, hen. And you're no payin'. Don did a lot for folk round here, includin' helpin' keep this place afloat more than once. This is the least I can dae."

He smirked. "In that case, I'll be in every night."

She rolled her eyes and gave him a gentle clout on the cheek with the back of her hand.

"Ye're no the type to waste yer life sittin' in here wi' the rest of these reprobates. Yer scran's goin' cold," she said as she left.

As he tucked in, Bruce felt a sense that he should have more of a yearning to stay in the city in the face of such friendliness.

He remembered a dog trainer coming onto Stirling Lines to give elements of B Squadron a display of the capabilities of Belgian Malinois and their superiority to the more widely used Alsatian.

Lean, muscle-bound and dark-furred like a shadow cut loose from a man's heels, the Belgian Malinois trotted into the centre of the field beside his handler.

It had sat without command, ears twitching, scanning the onlookers like it was weighing each for intent. You could feel it—the hum beneath the stillness, the tension wound tight like a tripwire.

The handler stepped back and lifted one fist.

In a flash, the dog exploded forward. Not ran—launched. Legs coiled and uncoiled like pistons, his body flat to the ground, a guided missile of fur and fury. Across the field, a man in a padded bite suit braced himself, just in time to be hit full force in the chest. The sound was full and deep, like a rugby tackle in a cathedral.

The Malinois had clamped on—with savage precision. No thrashing, no wasted movement. Just unrelenting, controlled pressure. The decoy fell backwards with a grunt, pinned under fifty-five pounds of pure intent.

'Out,' came the handler's steel-flat voice.

The dog instantly released and backed off two paces, eyes never leaving the man on the ground, ears up, body trembling with discipline.

Everyone appeared suitably impressed, perhaps seeing the display as an idealisation of their own profession in canine form.

Towards the back end of the questions session, the handler—a pre-eminent expert on working dogs in general—had been asked, *What sheep dog has the hardest job?'*

*'Ahh, if I had to pick, I'd say the Kangal from Turkey. They have to protect the flocks high in the mountains from wolves. The Ovcharka from the Caucasus has to do that too, but Kangals have been known to go up against the **Boz Ayı**—the brown bears. The thing is, though, doesn't matter how old or how much they have fought, those Kangals can only stomach so much time at home before they are bursting to get out again. It's in them.'*

As if tracking his thoughts, Bruce's pager vibrated and beeped. He immediately trotted down the stairs and fixed eyes with Caroline.

"Can I use the pub's phone?"

"Of course, hen, come around the bar. It's underneath the corner." She smiled.

Bruce dialled the number, and Frank's voice answered, "492983 188837 tomorrow for 13.00. Call me on the mobile when you get there and I'll direct you. Bring your ***quiet tour*** kit, enough to sustain you for the foreseeable. Got that?"

"Got it."

SAFE HOUSE PRAYER ROOM — DUKHAN — NORTHWEST QATAR — NIGHT

The air in the room was heavy with heat and paraffin. Candlelight flickered from each corner and the centre of the floor, forming a crude pentagon of flame. The five candles represented the Five Pillars of Islam, their slow-burning wax casting long, devout shadows across the woven rugs and bare stone walls.

Despite the late hour, sunlight was banished entirely by a billowing white flag draped across the only window—a great sheet bearing the black crescent and star of Al Qaeda's provisional seal. Outside, the safe house masqueraded as a disused oil workers' station. Men in stained overalls sat lounging on crates and broken stools, rifles beneath newspapers or tarpaulins, eyes constantly flicking down the quiet roads of Dukhan's outskirts.

Ramzi al-Wahishi stood before Zubayr al-Adel, the younger man's head bowed in reverent silence. For four days, Ramzi had drilled him relentlessly on theology, martyrdom, tactics, behaviour, cover stories and improvisation. This moment was to be Zubayr's consecration. But then a message had come: Khalid Sheikh Mohammed himself would be arriving. He wanted to meet the martyr before striking his blow against the Great Satan.

That gave Ramzi reason to pause.

KSM—now Al Qaeda's principal operational strategist—was no longer just a conduit between Bin Laden and the cells. With Osama confined to Afghanistan and the Pakistan borderlands and Zawahiri focused on Egypt's revolutionary axis, it was KSM who shaped the global game board. Ramzi had begun to suspect that Khalid Sheikh Mohammed was not only the most dangerous man in the network but possibly its true architect.

There came a knock on the door.

"Yes," Ramzi said calmly.

A guard leant in, his beard trimmed short, eyes sharp. "He is coming, Sayyid."

Ramzi inclined his head in acknowledgement. He cast a final glance at al-Adel, who remained still, composed, and terrifyingly serene.

Outside, the low growl of an engine ceased. Doors opened. Heavy footsteps approached.

The door opened. Three guards entered first, broad men in white thawbs cinched tight over Kevlar. The bulges at their hips were noticeable to his eyes—pistols, likely Makarovs, well-maintained and easy to conceal. They took their places in the corners of the room, saying nothing.

Then he arrived.

Khalid Sheikh Mohammed walked in with the fluid poise of a man who believed history bent towards him. He wore a pristine white thawb robe, his black-and-white keffiyeh secured by a thick agal. His beard was lustrous and shaped like a hanging bib of authority, and his pink-lensed glasses gave him the faint appearance of a genial professor. Only his eyes betrayed him—piercing, calculating, sovereign.

"Salam alaikum, brother Ramzi," KSM said in fluent, faintly accented English.

"Wa alaykum as-salam, brother Khalid."

KSM scanned the room. "Leave us."

The guards began filing out. KSM touched Zubayr's forearm.

"Not you." He smiled. "You are the reason for my arrival."

Now alone, KSM turned to Zubayr and placed his hands reverently on the younger man's shoulders.

"After this," he said, "your name will echo through Islam for generations. You will be one of the chosen few who began the global jihad that drove the Satans of America and Israel into the dust."

"I am honoured that you and Sayyid al-Wahishi have chosen me."

KSM chuckled deeply. "You think we chose you? No, Allah chose you. Before your bones formed in the womb, it was written."

Zubayr's lips twitched. "Let us pray the Americans and Israelis have not read what's written."

For a heartbeat, the room froze.

Then KSM broke into laughter—deep, delighted. The others joined him in its wake.

"It is written in the divine," KSM said. "No cross-worshipper or Zionist could even comprehend it."

"Good to know, Sayyid."

"Do not call me that," said KSM with a smile. "You are the one above us now."

Ramzi caught the edge in his voice. Was that irritation? A veiled slight at Ramzi's own use of the title?

Zubayr replied, "Thank you, but we are all equal in the eyes of Allah."

KSM raised his brows, then nodded slowly. "True. Then allow me to say—you are above me in mine. What you are about to do cannot be overstated."

"Thank you… Sayyid."

KSM's eyes gleamed with amusement. "Brother Ramzi tells me you've been well-prepared."

"I have."

"Then let me ask you, why are you taking a Holland America Line cruise ship?"

"Because airport inspections are thorough, especially for men who look like me. Boarding a cruise ship, I can bring luggage aboard without it having to pass through the same rigorous protocols. The Queen Elizabeth II departs from Southampton, but getting there means passing through the Eurotunnel, with a chance of customs checks. Why double the risk?"

"Your cover identity?"

"Rami Dewan. An American-based outreach consultant in internet services and e-commerce."

KSM smiled faintly. "Tell me something about e-commerce."

"It's young but destined to explode. As secure payment systems develop, consumers will shed their hesitation. People worship convenience even above quality. They'll type their credit card details with the same ease they light a cigarette. That's why they'll invest in 'CyberCart Express'. I hand them a brochure and pitch. Most will flee before I finish."

KSM grinned. "And if someone insists on inspecting your bag?"

"I martyr myself. Right then."

KSM's face darkened, serious now. "I have more questions."

What followed was a one-hour interrogation, clinical and relentless. KSM's delivery was calm, methodical, almost tender. He fired questions in multiple ways, circling back to the same scenarios to test for inconsistency. He probed the mission—timing, detonation fail-safes and reaction contingencies.

They moved on to Zubayr's fabricated history—his upbringing in Sacramento, his estranged mother, his distant cousin in Nevada, his early fascination with computing. KSM interrogated his cover until it felt real.

Then came the religious tests. Detailed questions on Christianity, its denominations, its theological rifts, as Zubayr was meant to be a culturally Christian convert—an identity that would help explain his Americanised inflexion and distance from ritual.

Through it all, Zubayr never faltered.

Ramzi observed silently, his chest tight with pride and something darker.

At last, KSM stood.

He turned to Ramzi, but his eyes remained fixed on Zubayr.

"He is ready."

Then he looked at Zubayr.

"And when it is done, the world will change. Perhaps not today. Not this year. But we will be remembered as the men who pulled the first pin on the collapse of the West."

Zubayr's voice was even.

"Inshallah."

10

SVR DIRECTOR'S OFFICE — YASENOVO — MORNING

The mahogany doors stood like the gates of judgement—high, polished and weighty with unspoken consequence.

Major Andrei Arkadievich Sokolova adjusted the collar of his uniform and knocked once, sharply. A pause, then the low voice from within:

"Enter."

The Director of the Foreign Intelligence Service—Director Valentin Viktorovich Rutko—sat behind an expansive desk of lacquered walnut, angled perfectly so the morning light from the tall windows could fall across it like a blessing.

Behind him, the SVR crest hung like a crown. There were no photos. No clutter. Just a globe on a bronze stand, a set of red telephones and a neat stack of folders that were likely older than some nations.

Rutko himself was a man carved from winter: thin, still and faintly frostbitten around the eyes. His presence made Sokolova think of those rare Siberian wolves who chose stillness over barking—a man who spoke softly and only when it mattered and whose silences said even more.

Sokolova stepped in, heels striking the hardwood floor like punctuation. He stopped two paces from the desk and saluted. Rutko gestured with a slight nod.

"Major Sokolova. Sit."

The chair across from him had the same

posture as its occupant: upright, formal, unforgiving.

Rutko picked up a sheet of thin, grey paper and held it between two fingers. "Bezmenov confessed. Every detail corroborated."

Sokolova inclined his head once.

"You broke him well."

"Thank you, Director."

A flick of Rutko's eyes up to meet his.

"A shame about the… oversight during his initial processing. One would expect the search team to detect a potassium cyanide capsule, especially if it had been sewn into the inner seam of his trousers."

The silence that followed was not pregnant but surgical.

Sokolova remained composed.

"Perhaps it was old tradecraft. He was, after all, an officer of the Cold War."

Rutko's lips pressed into something not quite a smile.

"Strange, though. That he waited until his debriefing was complete before using it. One might say… convenient. For us."

A long pause.

"Yes, sir," Sokolova said evenly.

There was a hum from one of the red phones. Rutko ignored it.

"Once again, you have demonstrated your efficiency, Major."

Sokolova said nothing.

"Do you want my job?"

A flicker of surprise. Sokolova allowed it to show. Slightly.

"With respect, sir… you'll likely be retired before I'm eligible."

Rutko gave a rare, brief laugh. "True. But certain achievements… accelerate eligibility."

He tapped a dossier in front of him—a thick one, marked in red.

"Three man-portable RA-115S atomic munitions. Disappeared during the collapse. Bezmenov admitted to hiding them. He also sold them."

Sokolova nodded once, his face like granite.

"Your task," Rutko said, sliding the dossier across the desk, "is to recover or destroy those devices. You will have full reach—SVR, GRU, FSB. This threat is transnational, and it demands an imperial response."

Sokolova did not hesitate.

"I accept."

"Good." Rutko leant forward, voice lowering. "If you succeed, you may be sitting on this side of the desk in less time than your previous ambition. If you fail…"

A long pause. Then a soft exhale through the director's nose.

"Well, let's just say failure would be bad for everyone involved."

Sokolova stood, accepted the file and saluted.

"Yes, Director."

He turned, stepped through the door and let it click shut behind him.

The hunt had begun.

DENTON — MANCHESTER — MORNING

Bruce sat in the ash-grey Nissan Primera, a car that fit the priority characteristics of covert vehicles—

reliable, inconspicuous and economical.

He had an unobstructed view of this Denton bodybuilding gym that sat just over half a football pitch away, like a battered old pit bull on the corner of a row of brick-faced terraces, its sign slightly askew, one letter constantly flickering, even in daylight.

The street seemed alive with the grit of a town that worked hard, drank harder and never pretended to be anything it wasn't.

The Scotsman recognised that in his immediate elation on not being killed by Frank, he hadn't considered that the older operative might have wanted to spare him so that he could use him as a fall guy.

The entrance door opened with a metallic groan.

Out rolled Carlsmith like a boulder carved from old discipline in a chunky, green wool knitted sweater, jeans and dark trainers.

With a grey and red leather *Head* holdall slung over one shoulder, his legs, thick and unhurried, floated him towards the Primera, and Bruce knew the eyes would be scanning, even in this environment, for ***dickers***.

Bruce watched him approach and started the engine to hum low.

Frank opened the back door, shoved his holdall in and joined him in the front.

"Straight down the road. Take a left at the T-junction."

As Bruce pulled the Primera off the kerb, Frank declared, "'E's got some birds in there training for what's called 'Fitness and Figure' competitions.

You heard of 'em?"

"Like bodybuilding?"

"Nah," said Frank. "I asked the owner, and he said it's a new thing that's just taking off—it's not extreme muscularity, he says they'll get judged on *'aesthetics, tone and athleticism.'* It's niche at the moment, 'specially here, but he reckons it'll take off. Think more like Sharron Davies in her heyday or those lasses off *Gladiators*. But he's got them on the weights—squats and deads too."

"Can only be a good thing," said Bruce.

"Continue up to the roundabout, take the third turn off," instructed Frank. "Hey, guess what a girl will say to you when you have a big cock?"

Bruce, indulging him, asked, "What?"

"I didn't think you'd know." Frank smirked. "Second left after the zebra crossing."

The roads were speckled with puddles, rimmed with oil rainbows. Traffic lights blinked their cycle in a tired rhythm.

Bruce admired a mural of Oasis's Gallagher brothers on the side of a record shop.

Eventually, the Primera rolled down Stockport Road, past terraced rows of red-brick houses with sagging satellite dishes and front gardens half-heartedly fenced in. Washing lines flapped with damp jumpers and toddler-sized jeans.

Frank gestured to a parade square of vehicle lock-ups, the colours of each garage door alternating between red and blue—maybe a nod to the city's football divide.

"Pull up and park about six feet off the red one at the top left corner," said Frank.

The Nissan ground to a halt in front of the

red panelling and both alighted.

Frank underarmed a set of keys to him. "I'm having a tab. Set up the table, projector and screen. Through the side door."

Inside, the garage smelled faintly of old metal and chalky sweat. On the opposite side hung a heavy red and white Manchester United flag from the wall like a battle standard, slightly sun-faded but ironed with reverence.

A portrait of a young Jigoro Kano, founder of judo, watched from the back like a ghost of discipline from above a utilitarian sink.

A white judogi, yellowing with age but still crisp at the collar, hung on a hook like it was waiting for the next round.

A bearded dragon sat basking under a UV light, unmoved by the clutter and the hum of the fan. In another tank, a royal python lay coiled in its hide, eyes like glinting beads. Crickets chirped from a tub on a shelf, a soft, rhythmic background noise that somehow made the space feel more alive.

Bruce carried out Frank's orders, pulling down the screen before setting the Electrohome EPS800 Conference Room Projector on top of the fold-out rustic pine table with turquoise legs.

The pair of chairs matched the table, and he set one facing the screen and another just off to the side.

Frank bounded in soon after with the scent of smoke trying to cling to him, carrying a black vinyl snooker cue case.

"Good, good," said Frank. "You met Denis and George?"

"Hard to miss," said Bruce. "Who looks after

them when you're away?"

"An old boy across the street. Works part-time at the pet store. I keep him in beer tokens and go around for a natter every so often."

As if reading Bruce's mind regarding the security of the place, Frank pulled out what looked like a metal detector from the case.

Bruce had seen an **_NLJD_**—Non-Linear Junction Detector—only once before and knew it could detect electronic devices and eavesdropping equipment even if they were switched off.

"'Ere ya are, get the kettle on while I do this. Stuff is in the cupboard," chirped Frank.

Bruce, noticing that Frank hadn't reminded him of his preference, felt glad he remembered it.

Despite his experience as an SF operator, Bruce accepted the unspoken rule of **_crow culture_**. Junior always makes the brews.

Both finished their tasks around the same time and sat in their respective chairs, Bruce facing the screen and the older man off to a flank.

A slide clicked into place showing four different images of a stone-faced, moustached suit, one a very old mugshot and the others taken with a long-lens camera.

"Now then," began Frank after a sip of his coffee. "Tell me what you know about Al Qaeda?"

"Its leader is Osama Bin Laden. Fought in Afghanistan against the Soviets back in the eighties. Has a bee in his bonnet regarding the Saudi royal family. Hates the West."

"Anything else? Any details?"

Bruce, despite his AO being Northern Ireland, felt a worm of unease as he shook his head.

"No."

Frank's cheery demeanour vanished. "You are now assigned under the remit of going anywhere at a moment's notice. Your knowledge of organisations and their players has to be much broader and deeper. I suggest you pull your ***Salfords*** up and set aside time every day to absorb this."

Bruce masked his embarrassment. "I will."

"The Bin Laden family aren't rich—they are wealthy. Construction empire. Ties to the Saudi royal family. So large that they are grouped in accordance with the nationality of the wives—'Saudi Group', 'Lebanese Group', 'Syrian Group', 'Egyptian Group', you get the picture."

"Is Osama Bin Laden in the Saudi Group?"

"No, Syrian mum," said Frank as the slide changed to show various images of men in white robes, cloaks and head coverings. "But he is born in Saudi—Interpol and the FBI list his birthplace as Jeddah, but my sources indicate Riyadh. Like I said, the family has access to billions. The best schools—Al-Thager Model School when he is a lad, an English-language course in Oxford after that—probably where he becomes an Arsenal fan."

Bruce detected a hint of disdain in Frank's voice and remembered a tabloid article stating the London club had acquired some kind of French maestro as manager, heating the United rivalry.

Frank continued, "Then he studies business and economics at the King Abdulaziz University. While there, he becomes a student of Palestinian-Jordanian Islamist jihadist and theologian Abdullah Yusuf Azzam—he was the man who issued the fatwa backing a Jihad against the Ruskies when they invaded

Afghanistan. Osama essentially follows him to the Pakistan-Afghanistan region to help in the war effort. It doesn't go well at first."

Bruce said, "Which is when you took a hiatus from the British military."

It was now an open secret that some of the more talented members of the SAS had 'resigned' to work for a private military contractor named *Keenie Meanie Services*, or KMS Ltd, a UK government front used to conduct deniable operations.

After the Soviet-Afghan War was over, many of the members were not only welcomed back to Hereford with open arms but also found themselves fast-tracked for promotion.

Except that Bruce knew that Frank Carlsmith did not return.

Frank afforded him a smile. "The Mi-24s gunships or Hinds as we called them were murder. Could pop up and rinse the mujahideen wherever they were—you've seen *Rambo III*."

"Yeh." Bruce nodded.

"We supplied and trained the **mujis** with Blowpipes. The top brass were rightly shitting themselves that if we gave them anything too hi-tech, it would find itself in Iran being reverse-engineered. But these Blowpipes weren't getting the job done— you had to track the target visually and guide it with a joystick, hard enough when you've had hours and hours on it, fuckin' ninja for an Afghani farmer for whom the phrase 'technologically advanced' was hooking the wife up to a plough, 'specially when a dragon that could fly two hundred miles per hour spitting thirty millimetre cannons, rockets and missiles. You needed balls of steel, let me tell ya."

Bruce appreciated the subtlety of Frank telling him he was on the ground against the Soviets without actually saying it.

"But the West got wind that the Russians wanted to invade Pakistan after Afghanistan."

"Why? Surely they knew they wouldn't be able to hold it?"

"'Cos the Ruskies have always wanted a warm water port, and the Pakistani coastal city of Gwadar would have been suitable. So, the Yanks decided to break out the Stinger missile systems—as you know, a fire-and-forget weapon, heat-guided, fast as fuck with better range. Turned the war on its head. Anyway, I am going off on one of my daft tangents. Where was I?"

Before Bruce could answer, Frank said, "Yeah, Osama Bin Laden, he goes over there to join the aforementioned Azzam and begins to help the mujahideen with funds and machinery brought from his construction company. Then he starts to bring his own lads in, and despite what people say, he gets stuck in himself. Seen it."

"You've met him?"

"Briefly. Taller than you. Softly spoken—I think his English is better than he lets on, but his ***Terp*** does the talking. I wasn't there at the Battle of Jaji, but that lionised him. Cut a long story boring, he comes back, forms Al Qaeda and pisses off both the Saudi and Pakistani governments. Shit really hits the fan when the Gulf War kicks off. Osama goes to King Fahd and tells him not to accept US military assistance but to use him and his battle-hardened legion. The king asked how he would defend against Saddam's chemical and biological weapons. When

Osama answers '*With faith*,' the king promptly fucks him off and accepts the **kāfir** American's assistance. This riles up Osama no end—and he isn't shy in publicly spouting off against the king's support for the Oslo Accords. Excommunicated from Saudi and—allegedly—his own family."

    Bruce said, "So he's committed if nothing else."

    "He is something else," said Frank in mild admonishment. "From Sudan, he begins to get naughty—bombings, funding jihadis and that. But he's also building roads, investing in agriculture and doing the Robin Hood act by giving to the poor. Locals love the bloke. But the Americans put pressure on the Sudanese government, and they fucked him off last year. It's believed he's back in Afghanistan thinking up all kinds of heinous shit—and I reckon he has the means to do it."

    "How bad?"

    "I am not sure yet," said Frank. "We're going to see an… associate of mine to find out."

11

UKRAINE — KYIV — LATE EVENING

The air outside the Kyiv Central Officers' Club smelled faintly of wet stone and exhaust fumes.

Major Andrei Sokolova adjusted the collar of his overcoat in the cool evening. He descended the front steps with the casual authority of a man who had spent years navigating the currents of rank, politics and war.

The formal dinner had been the usual theatre: empty speeches and mutual back-patting amongst men who still wore their loyalty like medals from a forgotten war.

However, Director Rutko implored him to attend so that he could '...*make the Ukrainian top brass wet before you fuck them.*'

He was reaching for his car keys when he caught the movement.

A figure peeled from the darkness near the lot's edge, moving with an economy of motion, and the major recognised him from the photographs in his file.

Makar Gorokhov.

The myth of precociousness.

Sokolova's hand twitched near the pistol holstered under his coat, but the young man merely raised his palms in a casual gesture—neither threat nor surrender, just silent acknowledgement.

"Major," Makar said, his voice cutting clean through the brittle night air.

Sokolova squared his stance, scanning the lot

instinctively—no backup, no tail.
Just Makar. Alone, confident and more dangerous for it.

"Are you here to kill me, young Gorokhov?" Sokolova said quietly.

"You know you would not have seen my face if that was the case, sir."

Makar stopped a few feet away, his grey-blue eyes unreadable.

"Then what?"

"I know Bezmenov has been captured," he said. "And that you're heading the retrieval operation."

Sokolova's face didn't move.

Inside, however, calculations whirred like fast-moving gears.

"And?" he asked.

Makar's voice stayed low but steady enough to turn frost into steel.

"I stole the devices from Chernobyl."

There it was, spoken plainly beneath the indifferent glow of a broken streetlight.

Sokolova allowed a pause to stretch between them before answering. "Curious time for confession."

"Not confession," Makar said. "Clarification. Bezmenov told me it was sanctioned. That, given the deteriorating political situation, recovering those weapons from Ukrainian soil was… expedient."

Sokolova studied the younger man.

Lie? Half-truth?

In the collapsing chaos of the post-Soviet years, plausible enough.

"And you now seek absolution?"

Makar offered a rare smile. It was not warm.

"No, Major. I seek pragmatism."

From the inner fold of his jacket, he pulled three battered grey devices and placed them gently onto the hood of Sokolova's car.

"They're still transmitting. Four days at most. We prioritised endurance over precision."

Sokolova picked one up, weighing it in his palm.

"Terms?"

"You leave Ravil Yelchin and myself alone. No surveillance. No investigations."

A thin breath of steam escaped Sokolova's nose as he exhaled.

"And in return?"

"You recover the bombs," Makar said simply. "The right people know you saved Russia from this… vulnerability. And your career advances."

Sokolova's mouth twisted slightly. *Politically savvy, too.*

He understood how Russia worked: not through truth but through transactional silence.

"And what of you?" Sokolova asked. "With Bezmenov gone, you're a man without a leash now. You should come in."

Makar's expression barely shifted.

"I'm not interested in being put on a leash, Major."

"You'd rather run errands for a gangster?"

"I have my freedom, Major."

Sokolova's fingers tightened subtly on the GPS unit. His voice cooled.

"And if I renege on our agreement?"

Makar took a step closer, his frame casting a

longer shadow across the wet pavement.

"Then I suggest you send your best to find me," he said calmly. "And make sure they don't miss."

He smiled, a small, almost regretful thing.

And Sokolova appreciated the subtlety of the threat.

The young man standing in front of him might walk through Lubyanka's gates, through the marble corridors of Directorate headquarters, and bleed it dry before he went down.

Sokolova slipped the trackers into his pocket.

"You have a deal," he said.

Makar nodded once and then turned without ceremony, melting back into the night as quietly as he had arrived.

Sokolova stood alone in the parking lot, his reflection dim and fractured in the rain slick asphalt.

Above, the sodium streetlights buzzed and flickered, painting long, thin shadows across the ground—and across the future.

PRIVATE DINING ROOM — BUDAPEST — EVENING

The room looked as if it had been carved from the bones of an old Habsburg palace—ceiling high and vaulting, rosetted cornices browned by decades of cigar smoke. The wallpaper, once emerald silk, had faded to the pale green of old money. Two chandeliers—gilt, low-hanging, vaguely menacing—dripped crystals like teeth. A fireplace crackled beneath a marble mantle topped with Orthodox icons and brass figurines. No windows. Just the warm fug of lamb fat, perfume and quiet menace.

Frank Carlsmith sat beside Bruce McQuillan, both across from the infamous Semion Mogilevich, a bear of a man with jowls like overfed velvet and eyes that missed nothing. Mogilevich, the man who'd made a billion dollars vanish and reappear on the Toronto Stock Exchange like a magician with a taste for racketeering. He cut into a burger as if it were foie gras.

The ornament of a cathedral, made up of bullet casings of different sizes, formed the table's centrepiece.

Frank, loose and lean in a black sports coat, conversed with Semion in fast, sardonic Ukrainian. Bruce watched, surprised. Frank's fluency was effortless.

A silver tray between them held chargrilled lamb skewers slick with pomegranate glaze, bowls of buttery rice and pickled cabbage, and two bottles—one red, one brown, their labels in Cyrillic. Frank drank from a short tumbler of kvass while Bruce sipped slowly from a glass of Armenian brandy, both men having already picked their way through a shared plate of duck confit and now absently forking at roasted potatoes laced with dill.

Eventually, Frank looked Bruce's way. "Let's switch to English. I don't want to leave my protégé in the dark."

"Of course." Semion nodded. "What is a protégé?"

"It is like an apprentice."

Semion turned his gleaming knife upright on the table, then pointed at Bruce. "Apprentice? Like you are boss plumber, and you teach him how to plumb?"

Frank grinned. "That's the idea. I'm showing him how to stop leaks."

"Or start them," Semion said and took a long drink of red wine.

"Depending on the situation," said Frank.

Semion's voice lowered. "Frank, have you told your... protégé how we met?"

"I haven't."

Semion smiled, small and sharp.

"Two years ago, Frank pretends to be a plumber that is working in my restaurant. Just before my birthday dinner. He has his back turned to me with those headphones on," said Semion, animatedly cupping his ears. "I ask for his attention. He turns with a grenade in his hand—pin pulled."

"I was actually pretending to be an electrician that time," said Frank.

"Yes, of course," said Semion. "Frank then tells me that a rival... organisation is going to kill me at my birthday party—invited members! The Czech police raided the place. Thirty Bratva soldiers were arrested. I was not one of them because I was not there because of Frank."

The story impressed Bruce, more so because Frank hadn't told him it.

The Ukrainian Mafioso leant forward. For the first time, the humour left his face.

"I have some news. I do not believe it is good."

"Alright, I'll brace myself."

"Two weeks ago, an SVR colonel named Bezmenov reached out to a fixer named Viktor Szombati. Arranged a transfer of a weapons or explosives shipment to the towelheads from Saudi Arabia."

"With all due respect, Don Mogilevich, arms slipping off the back of Russian trucks to various nefarious entities isn't exactly unheard of," said Frank. "As much as I love coming here."

"This was not sanctioned. Bezmenov took his own life after being arrested trying to escape Russia," said Semion. "But not before this Al Qaeda paid forty million US dollars through Szombati, who transferred the shipment through a Romanian port."

Frank cursed under his breath and reached for his glass.

Bruce asked, "Where is Szombati?"

Semion shook his head. "I do not know of his movements these days. But I know someone who does. I will tell him you want to speak to him. I cannot force him to talk—but he owes me to take the meeting. Two days. Berlin. The rest is up to you."

Frank nodded. "We'll be there."

Semion finished his wine. "I told you, Frank. I pay my debts. And millions of dollars' worth of soviet bang-bangs in the hands of zealots? Bad for business. Bad for all of us."

Bruce sat back, absorbing the weight of it all. He pushed his half-finished lamb aside, suddenly full.

Semion clapped twice, then called out, "Dominik! Pryvedit' divchatok."

Frank nudged Bruce under the table.

"Don't refuse," he murmured. "Best not insult the host."

Bruce nodded, and the night turned another shade of strange.

A slow procession of women entered—

elegant, poised, groomed. But their eyes gave them away.

Seemingly to Bruce, despite their smiles, at least half had a certain vapidity in the eyes. He did not have a black-and-white view of prostitution; to his mind, it was context-dependent, despite the argument that it objectified women. If a woman had access to a full range of opportunities to climb the fiscal ladder without having to sell her body and chose to anyway, then he didn't see the real argument against it.

However, he had a feeling of uncertainty with these girls.

Semion clapped his hands and asked, "Frank, which is your choice?"

The Mancunian stood and addressed the girls, "You are all lovely. If I were twenty-five years younger, I would have asked for you all!"

A few of the girls giggled, and Frank continued, "I am an old man now, but I like a surprise, so without further ado."

With every word he uttered next, Frank would point to each girl consecutively, "Ip, dip, do, the cat's got flu, the dog's got chicken pox, and out goes you, with a dirty, dirty dish cloth round your neck, you do have it."

His finger landed on an angular blonde, who stood taller than the rest. She seemed genuinely enthused about being selected, albeit seemingly randomly.

"And you, young protégé? All the girls are clean."

Bruce asked, "Who has the best English? I like a bit of dirty talk."

"Ha," burst Semion. "Léa, take care of our

friend."

"Certainly," came the French-accented reply from the short-haired noirette with high cheekbones.

She held out her hand regally and said, "Come with me."

Bruce stood and felt her soft hand slip into his calloused one.

She walked him on the red carpeted, polished floor through a long corridor walled with various historical artworks. Léa stopped and opened the door to a room of peach and beige. The velvet-sheathed bed looked exceptionally soft and inviting.

Once inside, the French woman stepped back and reached for her gown's belt.

He said, "Stop. You're a beautiful woman, but sex with... sex for payment isn't my thing."

Her face fell into confusion. "You are not to pay."

"Someone is paying you."

"You think you are above sleeping with a whore?"

"It is not that. I will never know for sure that you want to or if you were enjoying it or not."

She raised her eyebrows. "You would not tell if any woman was enjoying it or not?"

"Well... there are ways to tell, but—"

"Then what do you want to do? I have no board games."

He nodded. "A massage?"

She smiled. "Yes, but we must take our clothes off."

"OK."

SBU HEADQUARTERS — KYIV — LATE MORNING

The hallway walls of the Security Service of Ukraine—SBU—were painted an indifferent bureaucratic cream, lit by flickering fluorescents overhead. Each step of Yuri Kozlov's boots on the polished terrazzo echoed faintly, reverberating through a silence more psychological than acoustic. He stood before a tall lacquered door of deep, reddish wood—its brass handle worn to dullness by years of tense palms—and knocked twice, firmly.

From the outside, the SBU headquarters could be mistaken for a neoclassical museum. The building's stacked exterior of indigo brick, smooth white stone and a navy blue tiled roof gave it a grandeur that defied the austerity inside. Inside, the corridors and stairwells bore the stark functionality of every post-Soviet institution: minimalist, utilitarian, unconcerned with comfort. The air smelled faintly of overused grape air freshener—cheap, cloying, artificial sweetness lingering in a space that otherwise reeked of paper, polish and power.

A young administrative clerk—nervous, uniformed and familiar—opened the door and silently stepped aside. Yuri entered.

Inside, the colonel's office was austere but expansive. A single large window behind a bank of vertical blinds cast diffused light over a desk broad enough to land a helicopter on.

Colonel Dmytro Hrytsenko sat at its centre in a high-backed brown leather chair, his uniform crisp, his back ramrod straight.

His white-streaked, iron-grey hair was cropped to regulation, and his slanted brows framed eyes that carried the distinct cold fire of those descended from Russia's far eastern borderlands. His presence radiated quiet command.

To his right sat a civilian, though only technically. The man's presence was weighted and purposeful. He wore a well-fitted navy blue cardigan over an eggshell collared shirt, framing a broad, square frame. His buzzed hair and neatly trimmed beard were peppered with silver, and his expression was unreadable but assessing. The eyes were flint.

The unoccupied chair facing the colonel felt oddly vulnerable, like an interrogation prop rather than furniture.

"Master Sergeant Kozlov," the colonel greeted without ceremony. "I trust you're well rested."

"I am, sir."

"Take a seat."

Yuri sat, although his body posture remained subtly braced. The other man spoke, voice precise and deliberate, his Russian dialect clear.

"Master Sergeant at thirty-two. That's rare. Fourteen years of service. Multiple successful operations."

Yuri tilted his head, tone flat. "The Ukrainian military values merit."

He could tell immediately from the man's dialect and manner: Russian. Civilian clothes aside, this was no ordinary guest. Likely SVR. And senior.

Hrytsenko confirmed it with a clipped edge. "Master Sergeant, this is Major Andrei Sokolova. Foreign Intelligence Service."

"Major," Yuri acknowledged with a short nod.

Despite the civilian attire, Sokolova looked more operative than an analyst—angular, physically capable and carrying the calm stillness that Yuri associated with men who'd walked through blood. There was nothing soft about the cardigan. It was part of the mask.

"First, I want to thank you," Sokolova began, "for your actions in saving Russian lives. Not only in your recent mission but throughout your career."

Yuri, who spoke a smooth blend of Ukrainian and Russian known as **surzhyk**, was no stranger to Russian voices. And yet, even after years of service alongside them, their tone—Sokolova's in particular—still grated.

"Thank you, Major."

"Thankfully, the issue over our supplying gas here has now been resolved. And despite our current… complexities," Sokolova continued, "Russians and Ukrainians are, and will always be, brothers of the Dnieper."

Before Yuri could respond, Hrytsenko interjected—perhaps sensing the tension.

"The major cannot commend you officially but felt it necessary to say so."

"In addition to issuing new orders," Yuri replied coolly.

Years ago, he wouldn't have dared. But his experience, combined with the shifting sands of Ukrainian-Russian relations, had stripped away the filter.

"You are perceptive," Sokolova said with something like approval. "And correct. But we have a serious problem."

"You mean Russia does."

"Any nation hit with a tactical nuclear device will have the most serious problem. Then, yes, Russia."

Yuri felt his heart kick once, then steady.

"Surely the Motherland has plenty of qualified operatives."

"We do. But not many with your experience with ***gryaznyye koleni***."

The Russian slur—"dirty kneelers"—rang bitterly in the air. Yuri didn't react.

"You mean the Chechens," he said flatly.

"And their Al Qaeda allies," said Sokolova. "Many of them met our soldiers in Afghanistan."

"That would've been Soviet soldiers, Major."

The colonel snapped, "Watch yourself, Master Sergeant."

Sokolova waved him off, seemingly more amused than offended.

"Let it be. He's earned his tone. And he's right to ask." Then to Yuri, "What I will say is this—your mission in Chechnya was not sanctioned by me. But we need your expertise now."

"You've come to secure my commitment before the details."

"Yes."

Yuri knew this was no more than a theatre play of him having a choice.

"You have it."

The colonel stood. "I have another matter to attend to, gentlemen."

When the door closed behind him, the air changed. Sokolova leant forward slightly.

"An SVR colonel by the name of Genrikh Bezmenov was arrested two days ago while attempting to flee the country."

"Why?"

"During the arms race with the Americans, we discovered that they were developing tactical nuclear devices small enough to be carried in a bag, satchel or—"

"A suitcase," said Yuri, finishing for him.

"Yes. Naturally, we developed our own," said Sokolova. "During the collapse of our empire, the decision was made to decommission these… security assets. Bezmenov was chosen to oversee the task."

"Oversaw one into his possession?"

Sokolova held up three fingers.

"Bezmenov possessed a rare patience. He waited, ascended the ranks, developed the contacts. Formulated his plan," said Sokolova with a hint of admiration. "Six years. When we arrested him, he believed he was going to defect. Turns out, he sold these suitcase atomic munitions to a Ramzi al-Wahishi, a high-level operational planner within Al

Qaeda. Reputably responsible for the planning of their truck bombing operation in Riyadh on American corporation buildings and a host of others."

"Did Bezmenov become ideologically captured by the enemy?" asked Yuri, playing the role of mourning the Soviet past.

Sokolova shook his head. "He thought he could literally sail off into the sunset with his millions and live the life of a king in Central America. A strange thing to observe, a man of such intelligence manifesting such a foolish idea."

"If he had escaped, he might have been seen as the cleverest man in the KGB."

"But he did not."

Yuri inclined his head in acceptance, and Sokolova continued, "We currently have the means of tracking the three units. It is intermittent, but we believe they are heading to the North Caucasus."

"To be used against us?" said Yuri, using the word 'us' instead of 'Russia'.

"It is a possibility," said the SVR. "But we do not believe so. Al Qaeda's main enemy has always been America. Still, the logistics of such an operation might mean that they select Europe or Israel, both of which they consider enemies of their backwards religion."

"Then why are they heading to the North Caucasus?"

"We believe they are to be held there until the time is right. What time that is, we do not know, but it would be catastrophic if Russian munitions of that magnitude detonated while our country is in such a state of... transition."

"So, why have you come all this way, major?"

"We believe al-Wahishi intends to hand the device to Ibn al-Khattab. They have had dealings with one another in the past."

That changed everything.

Sokolova continued, "Our intelligence suggests al-Khattab is somewhere in the vicinity of Grozny. We are yet uncertain where."

"You want me to recover the remaining bombs."

"Yes," said Sokolova. "We have a Spetsnaz team on standby. Some of the members are familiar to you from the war."

"What about Ibn al-Khattab?"

"Expendable."

Yuri took a breath. "Then I'm in."

"Good, we will leave together now."

12

WILHELM HOECK 1892 PUB — BERLIN — NIGHT

The interior of Wilhelm Hoeck 1892 felt suspended in time, a century-old Berlin institution steeped in varnished wood, brass fixtures and the perfume of slow decay. Panels of polished oak caught the low amber glow of hanging globe lamps, each one casting honeyed light that flickered across the walls like firelight in a cabin.

Every surface—from the bar top to the battered wood-panelled booths—gleamed with the careful wear of tradition.

Cigarette smoke curled lazily towards the ceiling in slow eddies, mingling with the murmur of German voices and the odd staccato of English slipping through. The air tasted of tobacco, hops and cooked meat.

Bruce McQuillan sat across from Frank Carlsmith, the two of them nursing cold, weighty tankards of Warsteiner. The beer beaded on the outside, dripping slowly like sweat down a boxer's back between rounds.

The older man had finished a course of *currywurst mit pommes*—sliced sausage with curry ketchup—while Bruce had a few bites of his beef burger left.

"You should take advantage of the local cuisine when you're abroad."

"I am," answered Bruce. "I haven't risked a burger in the UK since last year."

Frank guffawed, "Two cows in a field. One says to the other, 'You worried about this Mad Cow Disease?' The other says, 'Doesn't bother me… am a duck!'"

Bruce laughed with genuine mirth. "I'll remember that one."

"Every man has a few go-to jokes in his back pocket."

"And you warning Mogilevich of the police raid two years ago was your way of getting him into your back pocket?" asked Bruce, almost rhetorically.

"More to engineer a mutually beneficial relationship," said Frank. "You'll learn in time that it is the number one skillset in this business."

"I thought it was cultivating a lethal karate chop and seducing women."

Frank leant back, voice casual, lips curved around a grin. "I forgot to ask, how was your madam back in Budapest?"

Bruce gave a slow shrug. "She was a tidy lass."

"Yeah?" Frank asked, a mischievous glint in his eye. "You get the full treatment?"

Bruce, who believed lies weakened the soul, replied plainly, "I'm not a puritan, and I don't judge. I don't have a problem with that kind of prostitution, but I won't sleep with a girl unless I know she wants it. The girl gave me a full-body massage."

Frank raised an eyebrow, impressed. "I'm surprised. You stuck by your principles. She was a cracker, that lass."

Bruce smirked faintly. "Then, despite me telling her I wasn't after anything and that I was perfectly happy with the massage, she kept pushing. I had to give in, in the end."

A wide, knowing grin spread across Frank's face. "You manfully went through with it not to smash her dignity. If the Allies had allowed the vanquished German nation its dignity after World War I, there might not have been a World War II."

"Allowed an atmosphere of resentment to fester and be exploited," Bruce added.

Frank nodded, raising his tankard. "Exactly. But it's strange, isn't it? Germany and Japan lose the war, and three years later, they're economic phoenixes. Only the US beats them for GDP. These lot rule Europe, you know. Through the EU. Two of the trio who wrote the Maastricht Treaty?"

Bruce noted Frank made no effort to keep his voice down.

"I heard the Americans initiated both revivals," Bruce said.

"Yes—the Marshall Plan for the Jerries and the Dodge Plan for the Japs," Frank replied, taking a long sip of his beer. "The meek will inherit the earth."

"I wouldn't call the Germans or the Japanese meek."

"That's because you're thinking of the blitzkrieg Germans and the kamikaze Japanese. I'm talking about modern Germans tripping over themselves to apologise and the Japanese who've traded bushido for bureaucracy."

Bruce wasn't sure if he agreed. He'd heard that Japanese industries, particularly car manufacturing, had risen from the ashes using ***Kaizen***—a philosophy of continuous improvement driven from the factory floor up.

Instead, he said, "You think East and West Germany will always be divided?"

"Oh, of course. Like North and South England—but deeper. East will always vote right-wing. Can't trust the left after the commies. They're poorer, they're paid less, and they're seen as lazy. Meanwhile, West Germans get branded arrogant, sneaky gobshites."

Frank's gaze shifted to the entrance. "Speaking of which—here he is."

Bruce turned to see a man approaching—medium height, with a weak jawline and a hawkish nose. A bald dome gleamed beneath the lights, fringed by a half-ring of hair.

The man stopped stiffly. "One Bitburger," he said in a clipped Eastern European accent.

If Frank was annoyed by the abruptness, he didn't show it. Instead, he gestured towards Bruce. "Get Hans Gruber here a stein of Bitburger."

"My name is not "

"*Halt's Maul!*" Frank snapped, steel lacing his tone. "Your name is whatever I say it is. We don't want to know your real one, you unprofessional *Depp.*"

The German insult—twit—seemed to land hard. Hans froze like a gargoyle, rage stiffening his posture. Around them, the murmur of voices and clink of glasses never missed a beat.

Bruce rose, heading for the bar. He heard Frank hiss behind him, "Don't sit in his fucking seat. Fetch a chair."

The barmaids wore the revealing Bavarian-style costumes—either a permanent feature or a charming indulgence of the evening's theme. A blonde server greeted Bruce with a dazzling smile as he placed the order.

There was an easy grace in her movement, and Bruce's eyes lingered just a moment longer than they should have.

He remembered being gawky in school—bony, sharp-featured, invisible. But by the time his years in 3 PARA had slapped on and chiselled muscle into his frame, he'd discovered that women had begun to look at him differently. *The Magnet*, his mates called him back in Colchester. Always the one sent in to break the ice with groups of girls.

Returning to the table, he noted Hans had abandoned his arrogance. Bruce set the beer before him and resumed his seat. Hans took a sip, and Frank gave a nod towards the man's face.

"Where is Viktor Szombati?"

Hans did not speak for a moment.

"I do not have to tell you anything I do not want to."

"And you don't want to worry about Karin—the niece you call your daughter—falling off a Bavarian *Klettersteig* this summer. Or overdosing after the Spice Girls concert in Istanbul."

The Scot glanced sideways, watching as Hans's face drained of colour, like a man feeling a heart murmur for the first time.

Bruce hadn't known Frank had that leverage—*Did Semion tell him? He was talking to him by the time I left Léa's company. Or has he found that out another way?*

Hans looked at him, pleading. "Please don't hurt her."

"If you're not lying," said Frank, "you don't have to worry."

"He will be in Paris the day after tomorrow.

He has booked a table at the Le Coq de Minuit for that evening. That is all I know, I swear."

"If you warn him, I will know, and—"

"I will not!"

"Then you don't have anything to worry about," said Frank, draining his tankard with Bruce following suit. "We are leaving now. Stay here for ten minutes. The barmaid is watching you. She'll tell me."

Bruce knew that was a lie but reckoned Hans didn't.

Again, Bruce reminded himself that Frank had no reason to lie to him, too—all indications pointed to Frank genuinely wishing to mentor him, but he couldn't be sure.

Once outside, the Berlin night felt crisp against their skin. Traffic muttered past, and the streetlights cast long shadows on the wet pavement.

Bruce fell into step beside Frank. "So?"

"Viktor Szombati's protected from the average bad guy—not just by men with guns, but by the fear of what happens if he's touched," Frank said.

"So we can't reach him?"

"I said *average* bad guys," Frank replied, lighting a cigarette. "And I have a friend in Paris."

ON BOARD MIL MI-8 HELICOPTER — EN ROUTE TO STAGING AREA — EARLY AFTERNOON

The dull rhythmic thrum of the Mi-8's twin turboshaft engines filled the cabin with an omnipresent hum, broken only by the occasional metallic creak of the fuselage as the helicopter cut through the chill air above the southern Russian wilderness. The red interior lighting cast everything in a dusky glow—helmets, packs, crates of supplies—all vibrating subtly with each rotor beat. The seats were hard canvas, bolted to the frame in two tight rows facing inward, with a space in the middle filled by kitbags and the stench of cordite, fuel, and sweat soaked into the canvas.

Yuri Kozlov sat opposite Major Andrei Sokolova, both of them strapped in, bracing occasionally as the aircraft dipped and rocked in the updrafts skimming the foothills of the Caucasus. Sokolova leant forward slightly, his gloved hands clasped on his lap, his gaze steady.

"Tell the story," he said, his voice calm but unmistakably directive over the droning engine noise.

Yuri didn't move, eyes fixed on the blurred grey-green world beyond the tiny porthole.

"I'm sure you are very familiar with it."

"Sometimes details are lost," Sokolova said, unfazed. "In the travel from mouth to ear to pen to page."

Yuri looked at him then, one eyebrow barely raised.

"You know it is a long and unpleasant story."

"But not a boring one. Tell the story as you would to a trusted friend," Sokolova replied. "I will ask for any clarifications."

Yuri exhaled stale air and sat straighter.

"The unit I was seconded to scored several successful missions in taking Grozny."

"The *retaking*," corrected Sokolova. "And yes, not only was your unit recognised for its effectiveness during the house-to-house fighting, but your actions in defence of the Motherland in particular were praised, Master Sergeant."

Yuri said nothing for a moment. He knew what Sokolova was referring to. *The block clearance.* A row of buildings defended by members of the Ukrainian People's Self-Defence—nationalist volunteers fighting against the Russian advance.

The irony wasn't lost on him.

The moment he fully committed to that operation, without hesitation or objection, the Russians in his Spetsnaz unit had finally accepted him as one of their own.

"After we recaptured Grozny," Yuri resumed, "we were tasked with clearing out the guerrillas from the lowlands and mountainous areas. That proved to be decidedly more challenging."

"The terrorist rats knew the area better," muttered Sokolova.

Yuri ignored the slur.

"According to GRU intelligence, their mobile headquarters had settled in the southern mountains. Our unit was re-roled into a hunter-killer team. We hitched a ride with the 2nd Battalion from the 245th Motor Rifle Regiment. As the convoy passed near the town of Shatoy, we were hit."

He paused, eyes narrowing at the memory.

"The ambush point was textbook. A stream ravine on one side, dense forest on the other. Near-perfect kill zone."

Sokolova nodded solemnly. "They are rats—and rats are cunning. How did they initiate the attack?"

Yuri resisted the urge to scoff. Sokolova would have read the report in detail.

"They let the recon unit pass. They were well

ahead of the main convoy. Then the lead tank took a directional mine—immobilised. RPGs took out the rear APC and the command vehicle. Fixed the whole column in place. Then came the heavy machine guns and mortars."

His voice was level, almost dispassionate. But his eyes had darkened, remembering the chaos—the fire, the screaming, the smoke that clung to lungs and skin alike.

"Thirty vehicles. At least a hundred men. The official tally was fifty dead, but I was there. It was closer to double."

"And you were one of the survivors," said Sokolova.

"One of a dozen," Yuri confirmed.

The major shifted slightly, then said, "Captain Yashin's report goes into great detail about how you saved his life."

"I aided him."

Sokolova shook his head. "Nonsense. He was shot. Needed an amputation. He would not have made it out without you."

Yuri looked away. "I did what needed doing."

He didn't add that he'd done it as much for self-preservation as for heroism. If he'd come back as the only Ukrainian survivor, the suspicion alone might've seen him shot in the back on a future mission.

"You've seen the footage?" Sokolova asked, voice low now.

Yuri nodded—of course he had.

The infamous video.

Ibn al-Khattab, strutting through the wreckage, boots crunching over blackened bones and twisted steel, flanked by his lieutenants, rifles slung casually. Smiling for the camera. The footage had been copied, distributed and replayed in barracks across the former Soviet space.

Sokolova didn't press further. Instead, he looked out the porthole for a moment, then back.

"We'll be on the ground in less than an hour. Your team's already waiting at the staging area. You'll brief them at 1800. We move on al-Khattab's suspected coordinates as soon as we know."

Yuri gave a single nod. The rhythmic chop of the rotors above punctuated the silence that followed.

13

PARIS — MIDDAY

The lobby of the Hôtel Plaza Athénée shimmered like a stage set for the decadent twilight of empire.

High ceilings loomed overhead, draped in gold-leafed cornices, and the vast expanse of mirror-sheen marble flooring reflected the soft glimmer of crystal wall sconces and the gleam of red leather chairs.

Gilded pillars supported hanging baskets overflowing with fresh blossoms—orchids, lilies, sprays of hydrangea—each so perfectly arranged they seemed suspended in defiance of time.

Bruce McQuillan sat down, conscious of the expensive weight of his new suit—black, cleanly tailored, offset by a navy pocket square and a crisp, lighter blue shirt. Frank Carlsmith sat beside him, rakishly composed in a pinstriped blue jacket over a cream shirt, exuding the calm of a man born into uncomfortable places.

Around them, the murmur of voices in French, English, and the clink of crystal glasses mingled with the scent of polished wood, perfume and the faintest trace of cigar smoke.

As the revolving door spun gently, a woman stepped through, and Bruce had to consciously keep his admiration from his face.

Frank had described Anissa Rajah of the DGSE—but nothing in the briefing had prepared him for the striking elegance of her presence.

She moved like confidence incarnate: lilac

beret tilted at an angle over sleek, shoulder-length black hair, her pink tailored jacket and skirt flowing with each graceful stride. Caramel-toned skin shimmered under the lobby lights, pulled taut over high cheekbones and framed by dark almond-shaped eyes that didn't so much observe as assess.

The men stood in unison.

To Bruce's surprise, Anissa swept an arm around Frank's shoulder with casual intimacy, kissing his cheek lightly as she removed her beret.

"Thanks for insisting we meet at one of Paris's most expensive hotels, Anissa. Very under the radar," Frank said, deadpan.

In a stunning parody of Frank's dialect, she responded, "Alright, Frank, you've not 'ad to pay owt, so what's the mither? Like to treat ma pals, don't I?"

Frank rolled his eyes and gestured towards Bruce. "This is what happens when French women get obsessed with men from Manchester."

She tucked a strand of hair behind her ear and offered Bruce her hand.

Her voice changed as if flicking a switch, becoming an airy upper-class English lilt with a French finish. "I will be following Gary Barlow's solo career with earnest. Pity they had to break up."

Bruce shook her hand and replied evenly, "They say he is the talented one."

Her smile widened. Frank groaned.

"Jesus Christ."

"Anyway, Frank," Anissa said, slipping between tones like silk through fingers. "Who is this dark, tall and handsome? The British version of a Raven?"

Bruce gave a slight nod of acknowledgement,

noting the playful glint in her eye. He'd read about the KGB's famed 'swallows'—female agents trained to seduce men for secrets. The West had later discovered their rarer male counterparts: 'ravens'.

Frank drawled, "Regular James Bond, Action Man is our Bruce. Scottish and everything."

"Shall we go through?" she asked, already turning, the scent of jasmine trailing her like a whisper.

She led them down a corridor of decadent marble and velvet, briefly conferring with the maître d' before they were escorted into the main dining room—an opulent space of golden walls and glittering chandeliers, the carpet underfoot so pristine Bruce wondered how it hadn't been ruined by a thousand spilt wines.

Their circular table overlooked a manicured courtyard garden glowing under the sun.

Without consulting the others, Anissa ordered a bottle of Château Rougeval 1985 and a jug of mineral water.

"You seem to be in thought," she said to Bruce as they settled.

"I was just wondering just how much money the DGSE had to afford to wine and dine foreign agents like this," Bruce replied. "Albeit from a reputedly friendly nation."

Anissa smiled. "It is not the DGSE that has the money. It is I. My father left me an inheritance—I invested it in the French Riviera property boom and created the Galerie Lumière Noire."

Bruce murmured, "The Black Light Gallery."

"You can imagine how useful it is for French intelligence to know who the wealthy owners of the masterpieces I recover are."

"And the DGSE lets you keep the profits?" Bruce asked.

"They might want a cut, but the value of art is subjective. And where subjectivity rules, so too does laundering. I could take a shit in this ashtray, call it *La dualité du plaisir,* and some wealthy slave-to-status would buy it. So it is to their advantage that I keep my cover as a prosperous dealer."

Frank raised his glass, smirking at Bruce.

The waiter returned with the bottle and poured. Before they could even open the menus, Anissa turned to Bruce. "Do you have any allergies or foods you cannot stomach?"

He shook his head.

She handed the menus back. "Surprise us."

Frank leant in. "So, Anissa, the reason why I contacted you—"

She held up her hand, fingers pinched together. "You know better to talk business before eating, Frank."

"Are we Arabs now?" Frank shot back. "And you were just talking business with Bruce here. What is this—another man on the scene, and I'm out on my ear?"

"Playing the victim does not suit you, my sweet."

Bruce found the whole exchange oddly comforting. For a moment, the clandestine world of dead drops and intercepted transmissions receded.

Anissa turned to him. "Are you an art lover, Bruce?"

"I can't say I am."

"That is because you do not know its

purpose."

"It's to make you feel good to look at," Bruce replied, immediately realising how it might be interpreted.

Anissa's laugh was melodic. "Art can uplift the spirit, both collective and individual. In the distraction it offers from tragedy or banality, it restores our minds."

Frank raised an eyebrow. "That's how I felt watching Neil Buchanan make a giant rocking horse out of sawdust on *Art Attack*."

Bruce chuckled behind his hand as Anissa shook her head in mock dismay.

A small parade of waiters arrived, placing three pristine plates in front of them and filling the centre of the table with small, vibrant dishes. The waiter explained them at speed before vanishing with a bow.

Anissa locked eyes with Bruce. "Have you been to France before?"

"First time in Paris."

"Any surprises?"

"Parisians smoke more than Brits—Gauloises and Gitanes everywhere. And the driving seems… chaotically efficient. The lane markings seem to be just suggestions."

Frank snorted. "Yeh, I directed him onto the Place de l'Étoile roundabout to test his nerves."

Anissa arched a brow. "Did he pass?"

"He did alright, I suppose," said Frank.

Indeed, the Glaswegian could see why the twelve-exit roundabout that whipped around the Arc de Triomphe could be a terrifying spectacle to a non-native in the swarm of bumper-to-bumper, beeping, cursing Parisian traffic.

Bruce added, "The architecture didn't disappoint. More… evidence of dogs on the streets than I would have thought."

Frank uttered, "He's referring to the dog shit."

Anissa laughed. "Ah, the Parisian landmines."

Frank had earlier told Bruce that Parisians were more likely to discuss weighty topics, such as literature, politics and philosophy, in cafés in a way that would sound pretentious, perhaps even in London. Bruce, seeing an opportunity to educate himself further, hid his awkwardness by asking, "What are the social issues here at the moment?"

Anissa gave a small sigh. "Tensions. High unemployment, especially in the banlieue. Le Pen's National Front is gaining ground. Many ask, *What does it mean to be French?*' Strikes. Fractures. Unrest."

Frank raised his glass. "Sounds like most capital cities I've been to."

"Yes," Anissa said. "Quite."

She shifted tone. "So, Frank, to what do I owe this pleasure?"

Frank leant in. "First off, Anissa—it's you I wanted to speak to. Not the wider DGSE."

She tilted her head. "I knew this day would come. If I do whatever you're proposing, then we are equal, yes?"

"You mean even?"

"Yes, even."

"Yes."

"Go ahead, Frank."

"Viktor Szombati will be coming through Paris tomorrow. I want to have a chat with him."

"What do you wish to speak to him about?"

"What exactly did Al Qaeda pay forty million dollars to a now deceased SVR colonel for?"

A moment's silence and Anissa said quietly, "Monsieur Bin Laden certainly has ambition."

"Yes, he has," said Frank. "But now he might have the means. I need to speak with Viktor."

"You expect me to be a honey trap?"

"Are you offended?"

"Please, Frank," she said with a wave of her hand. "When have you ever seen me offended, despite your best efforts? I am simply… bored at the prospect."

Frank grinned. "A honey trap wouldn't work. Viktor loves a beautiful woman as much as the next man, but he's trained to anticipate it. We'll have to get… creative."

CHECHNYA — ARGUN — EVENING

The Lada Niva rattled along the ice-glinted road, its shocks long surrendered to the unforgiving terrain of the North Caucasus.

Ramzi al-Wahishi sat in the back seat, his long frame folded awkwardly, knees drawn high in the cramped space.

His gloved fingers rested loosely on a worn leather satchel beside him. Inside were false passports, a Quran wrapped in cloth, and a single photograph of the team he would ask to hide.

Outside, the day's dust had settled on the bramble-choked fields, the dry earth cracked and sun-bleached beneath it.

The town of Argun had long vanished behind

them, a smear of grey in the rear-view mirror. Before them lay the tree-shrouded foothills where Ibn al-Khattab made his camp—the Russians had spent years chasing the Chechen ghost in these woods.

Ramzi's breath fogged the window and smelled faintly of cardamom from the tea he'd consumed in Grozny.

The driver—a mute youth with a scar under one eye—glanced back occasionally, perhaps trying to understand what kind of man he ferried into the woods. Ramzi said nothing. Silence was a fortress. He had learnt that in Yemen, and again in Karachi.

He tugged the wool of his keffiyeh higher around his neck and leant slightly forward.

"How much longer?" he asked in Arabic.

The driver responded with a gesture: two fingers. *Two kilometres.*

The trees began to thicken, birch and pine pressing close to the road. Somewhere beyond them, Ibn al-Khattab waited—a man lionised across the jihadist world as a warrior, a tactician, a firebrand.

However, Ramzi knew better than to be seduced by myth. Al-Khattab was an emir with his own agenda. He seemingly burned with a localised hatred, fixated on Russians and their soldiers.

This was unusual as al-Khattab, like Ramzi, was an Arab, and though a few sources laid claim to his birthplace being Jordan, few disputed that his childhood and youth were spent in Saudi Arabia.

And everyone knew al-Khattab had left at seventeen to join the Islamic war effort against the Soviets over a decade ago.

Ramzi's war, however, definitely transcended borders.

Though Ramzi and al-Khattab had a few low-level business dealings through emissaries, this would be their first meeting.

They would agree on much, and yet perhaps on nothing at all.

He looked down at the scratched Raketa watch, steadily ticking, its Soviet origin a quiet irony. Time was always the enemy—and the ally.

He would need to make the warlord see the future through the eyes of a strategist.

And he would need to do it without appearing weak. Because in these hills, weakness was the last thing a man could afford.

The Lada stopped, and Ramzi stepped out into an eerie hush. The forest absorbed all noise—no distant gunfire, no engines, not even birdsong—just the crunch of dry grass beneath his boots.

The driver pointed towards a narrow trail disappearing into the pines. No further instructions. No escort.

Ramzi adjusted the strap of his satchel, tightened the knot of his keffiyeh, and began to walk.

The ancient forest surrounded him with indifference. Gnarled roots jutted like the bones of the earth, and the wind slid between the trees like a whisper of something watching.

For twenty minutes, he climbed, moving past felled logs and animal tracks, until he saw the sentry—silent, hooded, rifle across his chest. The man said nothing, merely turned and led the way.

Another five minutes, and the trees gave way to a small clearing, barely large enough for the canvas tents and the low, crackling fire. Men moved like shadows—matted hair, ragged beards, AKs slung across narrow shoulders. Their eyes followed Ramzi with a mix of curiosity and caution.

Arabs were not rare here, but they were seldom invited without purpose.

And then he saw him.

Ibn al-Khattab sat beneath a pine, cross-legged, the fire painting his face in flickering golds. He was younger than Ramzi expected—no older than thirty—but his presence carried weight.

Mane-like hair framed his strong features, and his hands, calloused and calm, rested atop a folded map. A rare Stechkin APS machine pistol lay on a sheepskin beside him.

He looked up as Ramzi approached.

"Ramzi al-Wahishi," al-Khattab said, rising. His Arabic bore the stamp of the Gulf, but his cadence had been reshaped by years in the mountains.

Ramzi offered his left hand—the black leather glove covered the stumps of fingers that Salafi Jihadists lost during the holy war in Afghanistan.

"Ibn al-Khattab. It is an honour."

Al-Khattab's grip was predictably firm. "You've come far. Your intentions must be important."

"They are—for all Muslims."

Al-Khattab let out a low laugh. "Very ambitious."

Ramzi steeled himself. "We should rejoice that the Prophet Muhammad had the ambition of ***Tawhid*** and ***Ummah***."

The wind seemed to peter out before al-Khattab gestured to a stump near the fire. "Sit. Speak your purpose."

They sat.

Ramzi opened the satchel, removed a thermos, and poured black tea into a tin cup before offering it. A test, perhaps. Al-Khattab accepted without hesitation.

"I need to hide a team," Ramzi said quietly. "Six men. Trained. Disciplined. They will need shelter. Perhaps for weeks."

Al-Khattab raised an eyebrow. "Why here?"

"Because this place is invisible," Ramzi said. "Because your network is trusted, and you are adept at being ghosts to the world."

A pause. The fire crackled.

"You are a very cunning man, brother al-Wahishi. Of course, I knew that before you came," said the Islamic warlord. "But why have you come to see the magician to make your men disappear?"

Ramzi met his eyes. "They will carry devices into the heart of the West."

"What kind?"

"Nuclear ones."

Al-Khattab blinked once. Slowly.

"You intend to burn cities?"

"No, they cannot destroy cities. Villages, perhaps," said Ramzi softly. "However, we have identified specific, strategic targets—the strikes will be measured and catastrophic. The Vatican City in Rome. New York's Wall Street. The London Financial District. Major US airports. All are options we need to study, but whatever the target chosen, the West will reel. Their economies will tremble. And our people will see we can strike as they have struck."

Al-Khattab exhaled, watching the smoke rise. "My war is with the Russians. With tanks and soldiers. A war of blood and soil. Despite your invoking of the final messenger, we have a differing opinion on how best to achieve a unified community under Allah."

"These devices," began Ramzi, "originate from Russia. And we will ensure the West knows that they are. This is what the Great Satan and Europe want—to keep a foot on the throat of their old enemy. Now that Russia is in the storm of rampant Oligarchic Capitalism, NATO wants a reason to scoop in the post-Soviet states. We will give them one. And the West will look for partners to undermine the weakened bear. They will turn to you, brother al-Khattab—just as they turned to us during *al-Jihād fī Afghānistān*. You will have helped free your country and perhaps the entire Caucasus."

Ramzi felt he might have overdone the pitch but hadn't wanted to leave anything off the table.

Al-Khattab said nothing for a long while. Then he leant forward, scooped a glowing ember with a stick and touched it to a rolled cigarette. He inhaled deeply.

"I will shelter your men," he said at last. "Forgive me, but we are not to simply wait to benefit from your grand plan. We need funds now—six million dollars for the shelter and protection of your men."

Ramzi knew he would have to feign reluctance or else face higher demands in the future.

"Brother Ibn al-Khattab, a million dollars for each man is too high. Even if we could provide that money, we could not pay immediately as—"

"Let us dispense with our Arabic need to haggle. This is not a negotiation. Six million is my price. Considering that you intend this to be the beginning of a world united under one Islamic rule, six million dollars is truly cheap."

Ramzi nodded, knowing the scourge of the Russians had choked any possibility of compromise between them—indeed, Khalid Sheikh Mohammed had permitted him to negotiate up to ten million.

"I will find a way to transfer the funds immediately through the usual channel."

"It amuses me that the seeds of their destruction will lie beneath their noses." Al-Khattab chuckled as they both stood. "As-salāmu ʿalaykum."

"Wa ʿalaykum as-salām," answered Ramzi before turning to walk back.

The wind returned as if on cue, sifting through the trees, carrying with it the faint scent of cedar and gun oil.

In the silence that followed, Ramzi felt the weight of their pact settle over the camp like snowfall.

Something had begun. Something irreversible.

14

LE COQ DE MINUIT — PARIS — EARLY EVENING

Viktor Szombati sat alone at a corner table draped in pale linen.

The chandeliers above cast a sheen across the crystal stemware and plates, which looked too delicate to eat from. Usually, he did not care for such pretentiousness, but given his final destination of Jakarta—a city where restaurants could not compete with the French capital—he decided to create a final memory of grand indulgence until he deemed it safe to return to Europe.

If he ever did return, with the money he had accumulated over the years, even if he lived another two decades, he could nestle in whatever luxury the Indonesian capital offered.

Indeed, he had very few active contemporaries with the difference between them being that they still needed to work.

A handful of years ago, Viktor had seriously contemplated retirement. In keeping with his expectation of staying home, he had a juvenile leopard shipped back to his mansion in Debrecen, a perk of the lawlessness in Hungary following the Soviet collapse.

However, it had escaped a few months later. He had been surprised to see that the Animal Control Officer looked around ten years older than himself.

After returning the feline predator, Viktor, thinking the older man financially consigned to work, had offered him a job creating and maintaining a private zoo.

The officer refused, stating that *'...retirement would kill me faster than a leopard could.'*

That had struck a chord with Viktor back then but now he had reached sixty, this might be a good time to bow out.

Le Coq de Minuit nestled discreetly in the 8th arrondissement, was the kind of restaurant that didn't need to advertise. It whispered wealth and silence—perfect for his current needs.

Viktor had read that when the French Revolution dismantled the aristocracy, it forced their private chefs—among the best in Europe—to open public restaurants. This democratised access to haute cuisine, professional cooking, and helped establish France's global reputation for fine dining.

His bespoke charcoal suit masked a Kevlar layer underneath. A blue smoke twirled from his cigarette. For several years now, he had refrained from smoking in restaurants, but this was Paris—
Everyone and their Toy Poodle smokes here.

One table over to his right sat Mikael, wiry, Nordic blades for cheekbones, sipping from a tall glass of water and occasionally glancing at the mirrored wall behind him. To the left, Dani, darker-skinned, Balkan, a limp as artificial as his French accent, picked absently at a crème brûlée, with half-lidded but focused eyes.

Both men battle-tested former soldiers, now security contractors, Szombati had paid them €60,000 apiece—half upfront, half if he left France breathing.

His appetite had diminished for a while since Constanța, but had returned in raging protest and he looked forward to ordering.

A soft clink of silverware interrupted his reverie. The waiter, no older than thirty, lean and overly polite, approached and addressed him in English as he slid a black and gold menu in front of him.

"Anything to drink, sir?"

"Château Margaux 1982. Bring the bottle."

Szombati's eyes lifted.

Ice blue met brown, and the waiter left.

Outside, the Seine hissed quietly in the warmth. Inside, the chandeliers flickered. And Viktor Szombati, who had brokered revolutions and vanished chemists, felt—for the first time in decades—*afraid*.

He knew what he had handed over in Romania. And if it went off—in London, in D.C., in Frankfurt—*everyone* would come looking.

And when they did, he would already be gone.

The waiter returned, set the glass in front of him and began to pour.

His heart dropped in tandem with the clinking spillage of the crimson liquid all over his lap.

Self-control strangled his roar into a venomous English hiss, "You fucking amateur. Fucking child."

He raised his hand to sink Mikael back into his seat.

"I… I apologise."

"Is your fucking apology worth more than fifty thousand Francs?"

"I am… I could—"

"Get the manager immediately."

The waiter bowed and scampered away like a

chastened Japanese geisha, leaving Viktor to drill stares into the other patrons' furtive glances.

The Hungarian calmed himself in the knowledge that his outburst had been augmented by the stress pressing on him.

Still, he thought, *He couldn't have spilt it more on me if he had tried.*

Dopamine feathered within him as she entered the dining room, the waiter gesturing towards his table.

Uttering an obvious dismissal, the waiter turned back into the kitchen like a dog that had disappointed its owner.

Gliding in long black-heeled strides, in a dress that folded at the hip like a blade drawn from silk, Viktor—usually a master at distinguishing ethnicities—couldn't be sure of hers.

He took in the burnished bronzed skin, as well as the black hair pinned in an elegant chignon, and made a guess of North African.

Viktor, realising he was still dabbing his crotch, immediately placed the soaked napkin on the table.

She stopped beside his table and looked down at him with dark, oval, unreadable eyes.

"Monsieur Szombati," she said in accented English with the faintest tilt of the head—no bow, no smile. Her voice was glass dipped in honey, neutral but rich. "My name is Anissa. This is my restaurant. It seems our waiter has had an accident."

Her restaurant? Not manager? he thought, looking at lady who appeared to be in her early thirties.

Not wishing to either cause more of a scene,

or to come across as pompous, he said, "Apologies to him on my behalf. I should not have sworn at—"

"Do not be ridiculous," she scolded, sending a pulse through him. "It is we who must apologise to you. This will be his last shift."

Seeing an opportunity to appear magnanimous, he said, "Please. That is not necessary."

Anissa continued as if not hearing him, "The good news is that of all the restaurants in the world, we have a dry cleaning service."

"As much as I appreciate the forward thinking," said Viktor, meaning it, "I am leaving Paris early tomorrow."

"You misunderstand me, monsieur, the service is immediate—it will take around an hour. Two at a maximum. You have not yet ordered your meal, which will naturally be at our expense."

He frowned, "I do not think it would be polite for me to dine in my underwear."

"A girl can dream," she said with an ego-energising smile. "But that is not necessary, we have a range of very nice suits in the back. Though perhaps none as tasteful as this."

The back of her fingers glided with electric contact on the upper sleeve.

He knew she probably gave this alternatively professional but flirtatious act to every inconvenienced male customer but Viktor did not care when one played the role this convincingly.

"One of my bodyguards will have to escort me."

With clasped hands, she turned for a moment, before her flashing eyes met his, "Make it the blond one. The other looks a little scary."

He smiled at her mocking wide eyes, "I will follow you through after I have spoken to them."

"Of course," she said, floating away.

Viktor beckoned Mikael over with two compressed fingers.

He concisely relayed Anissa's proposal to him.

On observing the mildly pained expression on the Scandinavian's face, he pointed out, "The authorities wouldn't need to scheme so elaborately—they would just arrest me publicly."

Mikael nodded his agreement with the assessment and the pair stood with Mikael leading to adroitly hide the stain.

Entering the door, Viktor noticed that Mikael's hand hovered by his hip.

Stainless steel and black chrome were the only two colours featured in the kitchen.

The barked orders and replies ping-ponging amongst the staff could be heard over the sizzle of meat hitting the grill, sputtering of oil, searing of onions caramelising and the bubbling of boiling water.

Anissa, stood at the far corner of a short corridor, held open a door to a more dimly lit area at a ninety-degree angle to the pantry door.

Viktor kept up with Mikael's marching stride.

As the Swede came within two steps, Anissa let go of the door such that Mikael had to palm it open to step in.

The instant he did, he lost his footing, windmilling his arms back for balance before tumbling in, the door swinging back like a trap door.

Viktor barely registered the sound of the

pantry opening as he rushed to the door.

A smack of muscular force caused him to gag on his own Adam's apple before yanking him back into a brawny torso.

The barrel of some sort of handgun rammed him beneath his chin.

The Hungarian recognised the accent to be British.

"When I say, you and I are going to walk forward into the room. We will have to be careful not to slip on the split oil like Mikael did. Understand?"

When he did not instantly reply, the grip on his throat squeezed purple into his face and he spluttered, "I understand."

"Good."

They stood there for a moment, and Viktor felt like a pig about to be butchered.

As if telepathic, the voice behind him stated, "Killing you would present problems we would rather not deal with. Believe it or not, we don't even want to keep you—you're just the broker, after all, Viktor. What we need is answers—and we will get them, one way or another."

The door opened to reveal Anissa, gripping a silenced MAC Mle 1950 semi-automatic pistol that looked ugly in her grasp.

His assailant's hand switched from his throat to the scruff of his collar, before frogmarching him over.

For some reason, Viktor noticed the cat litter spread just inside the door.

No black chrome in this cloakroom—just a white tiled floor, cedarwood lockers and a rack of jackets hanging at the back next to the exit.

Mikael sat against one of the lockers with cable ties biting his wrists and ankles together.

A stocky man, with a weathered face and a head of cropped grey with reddish undertones held a suppressed Heckler & Koch USP Compact Tactical pistol at Mikael's head.

"Now then, Mikael," said the man—another Britisher. "We are gonna take Viktor with us to ask questions. You should be able to get yourself out of those ties pretty sharpish. Later, I am going to make a call and if you have caused any aggro, Mikael, then the local police will be picking you both up. You might be OK, but your Serbian friend will be a different story. I believe Interpol will be pleased to see him. Or you both can fuck off without fuss, and live to protect some other scumbag."

Viktor could see the resignation in his guard's eyes and knew he was to be taken.

The blue Citroën Xantia's hydropneumatic suspension made its ride a little more comfortable over the cobbled Parisian streets.

Bruce doubted that Viktor Szombati, sat beside him in the back seats, would appreciate it.

A small blue leather Puma holdall rested on the SAS soldier's knee, his hand inside, gripping his modified and suppressed Browning Hi-Power, with its barrel facing Viktor's direction.

Frank drove and Anissa directed until they came to a stop outside a building that Bruce already knew didn't appear on any municipal registry.

At street level, it masqueraded as a shuttered boiler repair shop—chipped signage in flaking blue, graffiti tags sprayed over its steel gate.

Frank turned with the suppressor of his Heckler & Koch USP Compact Tactical pistol casting its menacing gaze on the Hungarian.

"Only run if you can run faster than a forty-five round."

Anissa and Frank alighted, with Bruce only following once Frank opened Viktor's door.

Creating a loose formation around their captive, they crossed the street to the blue and yellow door.

Anissa Raja unlocked it with a swipe card and an old-fashioned key.

Beyond the façade and down a narrow concrete staircase, behind a rusted fire door lay something altogether different.

The air inside was cool and stale. Fluorescent lights buzzed into life overhead, casting the room in clinical white.

The floor was tiled in grey ceramic. Drainage channels ran next to the walls. There were no windows.

"DGSE used this site during their war with the OAS," she said without turning around. "Back when no one asked questions about bodies and bleach."

Frank Carlsmith said, "Luckily for the DGSE, Detective Claude Lebel stopped the Jackal."

"Oh, so you do read?" she said, with an edge of teasing.

"Waiting is the true killer," said Frank. "Before I got into playing Tetris on a Gameboy."

For a brief moment, given the Mancunian's certain eccentricity, Bruce wondered if it was true before dismissing it.

Anissa walked to a metal locker in the corner and retrieved a first aid kit. She tossed it on the table, then leant against the wall, arms crossed.

"Go sit in the chair," said the Scotsman softly in Szombati's ear, "The one with the straps on the armrest obviously."

He gained compliance with a prod of the Hi-Power's suppressor into the Hungarian's back.

Bruce then placed the holdall on the same stainless surface as the first aid kit. Inside lay zip ties, gloves, a stun wand, a bottle of water, a folding knife, and two burner phones.

He noticed that even though Frank's USP compact pointed to the floor, the older man angled his approach to prevent Viktor potentially snatching it.

"Put your arms on the rests, Viktor, I need to secure you," said Frank, voice low but ironed flat.

"Are these theatrics necessary?" asked Viktor with the calmness of a man who had spent decades in a nerve-shredding profession.

Frank's eyebrows lifted. "How do I know?"

"You have brought me here to ask questions," said the international criminal fixer. "So ask them."

"What exactly got exchanged at the Port of Constanța?"

"First," announced Viktor. "What is the carrot for my truthful answers?"

No sooner had the words left his mouth, his nose cracked under Frank's jab.

A seal-like snort sneezed blood into Viktor's cupped hands.

"The pain does not escalate."

Szombati's hands left his claret-smeared face,

but he said nothing.

Anissa stepped forward now, her voice soft. "This does not need to get messy, Viktor. We are giving you a chance. We can keep this civilised."

The Frenchwoman gestured to the holdall.

"It is true that you can torture me," grimaced Viktor. "But it is also true that I can be the best liar in the world. You will not know what is true and what isn't."

"Don't be silly, Viktor," answered Frank. "We'd mix in questions that we do know the answers to with those we don't. We'll punish untruths with cutting off your fingers—you'll be begging to tell to us everything by the third digit."

"Or maybe the absence of my fingers will make me more determined that I should not have lost them for nothing."

As Frank went to answer, Bruce cut across his mentor with, "What do you want, Mister Szombati?"

The Hungarian's eyes met Bruce's. "I want a guarantee that I walk out of here free…without further harm."

"We cannot provide you a written guarantee," said Frank.

A few moments of silence, then Viktor said, "I see… This is not sanctioned."

"No."

"Well." Viktor smiled. "I will not tell—how can I? I believe Interpol have an interest in me."

"What's your point, Viktor?"

"I do not have allegiance to any organisation I dealt with on the matter. You understand that I am in Paris to collect my false identity documents before I leave Europe for my happy retirement. There is no reason we cannot all get what we wish."

"What do you suggest?" asked Frank. "Surely a verbal guarantee would not be sufficient?"

"Of course not," said Viktor. "But if my protection team are present, then whatever is in my brain is yours."

Frank laughed with seemingly genuine mirth. "Next you'll be asking for an orgy with the Spice Girls, Viktor. Bruce, bring the tools over."

"Wait," answered Bruce, ignoring Frank's baleful stare. "Did you see the address of this place, Viktor?"

"Yes."

"There are two mobile phones in here. You call your team and tell them the address. While we wait, you answer our questions. We don't wish to kill you if we don't have to—too many witnesses at the restaurant. And we do not know which bank holds your documents even if we did want to tell Interpol. Which we don't as you have accurately assessed—your snatching was unsanctioned."

Quiet cooled the room.

"That is acceptable."

Bruce looked at Frank, who looked at Anissa.

The DSGE agent nodded her approval and Bruce selected a phone and approached.

"English. No codes," he said before holding it out.

Bruce had read in *The Guardian* of a Nokia 9000 Communicator—a mobile phone released the previous year that had looked to Bruce like a handheld laptop.

One of its myriad of features was a loudspeaker and Bruce wished they had that now.

That said, Szombati spoke clearly and concisely without any unusual words or phrases.

He ended the call.

"What do you want to know?"

"What was exchanged?"

"At first, I thought they were large area weapons. Military grade—perhaps demolition charges of C-4 or Semtex."

"Why did you think that?"

Viktor shrugged, "These were not weapons and ammunition crates. Large drug shipments usually come out of the ports, not go in."

"What changed your mind?"

"He confirmed they were bombs but said 'the great Satan's sins of Hiroshima and Nagasaki have returned to punish them'."

"Who did?"

"Ramzi al Wahishi."

Frank said aloud, "One of Al Qaeda's key operations facilitators—second in that regard only to Khalid Sheikh Mohammed, his direct superior."

"This is wonderful," said Anissa, with assumingly faux-cheeriness. "Potential nuclear weapons in the hands of an organisation whose leaders are beginning to encourage the idea of suicide bombs—martyrdom operations as they call them. Seems like the 1983 suicide truck bombings in Beirut have left a mark on Osama Bin Laden and his friends."

Frank asked Viktor, "Did you identify anyone else with him?"

"He had several—most I do not know, except I recognised Adam Umar."

Anissa's whisper of "*Fils de pute*" filled the

room.

Though Bruce didn't ask, Frank answered his thought anyway, "Six foot three of Algerian, Islamic 'maim and pain'. Former Bosnian mujahideen and now Al Qaeda. During the Bosnian war, Adam liked to execute prisoners with blunt instruments rather than shooting them."

"Ammunition conservation maybe?" said Bruce rhetorically, eliciting a ghost of a smirk from Frank.

"Anyone else?"

"Yes," said Viktor. "I had one of my men take photographs with a high-powered telephoto lens—like the Paparazzi use to shoot Princess Diana, Madonna and Pamela Anderson. I use them for blackmail purposes you understand. I sent them to a man who knows of these things, if I do not—one of the gentlemen was Ali Barnawi. A nuclear physicist. Former Egyptian Islamic Jihad and a friend of Ayman al-Zawahiri."

Bruce hadn't heard quiet that loud before.

Though Frank spoke softly, his words cut through the air, "The rumoured Soviet manufactured so-called 'Suitcase Nukes'?"

"That was my conclusion."

"Which is when you decided that the best course of action would be to get out of Dodge?"

"Of Dodge?"

"Dodge City—don't worry, it's more an American thing," said Frank. "But in this instance, I meant out of Europe."

"It seems wise."

"I wonder if the Americans have decommissioned theirs," said Anissa. "But perhaps that is a question for another day."

Viktor coughed, "Do you have any other questions for me?"

"What about the original pick-up point. Who met you there?"

"No one," said the fixer. "But the container must have been on overwatch."

"I see," answered Frank. "I suppose it would be silly of me to ask if there is any other intelligence you can contribute?"

"No," said Szombati, "But if you have an address, I can send the original pictures."

Bruce watched Szombati stiffen as Frank reached into his pocket. However, his hand simply produced a notepad and a Parker Jotter pen.

He scribbled before tearing out the paper.

"Send them there, please."

Viktor warily took the slip, and Frank said, "We'll be on our way then."

When Viktor fidgeted, Frank said, "Don't fret, Viktor, a deal is a deal."

The trio packed up, exited and drove away just as the Hungarian's protection team roared in.

15

CHECHNYA — FOOTHILLS OUTSIDE OF GROZNY — DEAD OF NIGHT

The trees looked like skeletons in the dark.

Yuri Kozlov moved through them with every step calculated, every crunch underfoot absorbed by the soft roll of his weight. His breath coiled in the night air, but not a sound escaped his mouth. Neither the cold or heat was the enemy tonight—it was the wind that betrayed, the terrain that fatigued, and the minds of the weak that cracked before dawn.

He felt the stock of his suppressed AKS-74U snug against his chest as he shifted forward again.

Yuri had chosen the AKS-74U over the harder hitting AK-47 and the rangier AK-74 as, to his mind, if his ambush party was engaged at any sort of appreciable range, the mission would be a failure anyway.

The ultra-compact killer AKS-74U boasted more manoeuvrability and a faster draw than its two cousins, though Yuri understood the importance of allowing such highly skilled operators their own preference.

And this would be only the second mission where Russian Spetsnaz had operated weapon systems modified to have a torch attached—in this instance a Zenit-2 tactical light with red acetate film taped over the lens.

They were still two klicks out from the rough location of where the tracking signal had gone static before finally dying.

He halted, raising a gloved fist. Seven shadows behind him stopped immediately—seven Russian Spetsnaz operators, all hard men, well trained, with four not known to him beyond their brief call signs and dossiers.

He felt vaguely reassured in the knowledge that the other three had informed them of his soldiering prowess.

The ten-kilometre insertion march from the vehicle drop-off, behind a ridge, had been predictably arduous. Yuri had decided to come the 'long way' in, in a bid to mitigate the chance of being ambushed. However much the GRU insisted on the reliability of their human intelligence assets, the Ukrainian had learnt not to take any unnecessary chances.

Yuri crouched behind the thick trunk of a pine and scanned the slope below with a monocular. The thermal signatures of Ibn al-Khattab's camp flickered faintly between the trunks—small fires buried in pits, tents nestled against wind-swept ridges, patrols sluggishly pacing their perimeter. Eight… maybe nine hostiles. One of them might be the man himself: al-Khattab, the Saudi. The myth cloaked in Chechen legend and Wahhabist zeal the one whose name circulated in Moscow with the gravity of a coming storm.

A Mil Mi-8 "Hip" utility bird and a pair of Kamov Ka-50 "Black Shark" attack helicopters stood coiled, with engines growling eighty-five kilometres away in Khasavyurt, awaiting Yuri's unit's signal. The stipulation being that Yuri only call them in on either being drawn into a firefight with the enemy or upon the stealthy completion of their mission.

The Ukrainian knew that the likelihood of the

latter was negligible; the personal bodyguard of one of the Chechens' most infamous warlords boasted a mix of discipline, skill and paranoia, in addition to possessing more than a few technologically advanced items of equipment.

Due to political blowback if caught breaking the Khasavyurt Accord, the Ka-50s would travel on a southeast trajectory, possibly skimming the Chechen border, then diving into Argun valley terrain.

Seventeen minutes would be the quickest possible time from being called in.

Major Sokolova had been clear: '*You will bring back one alive. Preferably al-Khattab. Dead only if unavoidable.*'

And Yuri desperately wanted to succeed in that part of the mission. Not that he felt personally aggrieved regarding being caught in the great ambush at Yaryshmardy that Ibn al-Khattab had planned—but he felt professionally obligated to even the score.

That was the complication. Killing was simple. Capturing a man who knew the forest better than his own veins? That was a chess match. And tonight, Yuri had only seven pieces on the board. The rest would be timing and cold steel.

He turned to his second-in-command, a quiet but effective operator called Vladik, whom he had spent time with '**Restoring Constitutional Order**' here in Chechnya two years ago.

Yuri gave three short gestures—fan left, set overwatch, confirm positions. Vladik nodded and vanished into the trees with half the team—Volk-Two. Yuri's half-team of Volk-One became a phantom moving through bark and shadow.

Yuri checked his watch. 03:12 hours. As per

orders, no lights or radios had been allowed on the route in. Only the breathing of the forest and the distant howl of wolves.

One of the fires ahead flared briefly, casting the silhouette of a bearded man kneeling to adjust something—maybe tending a stove. The moment passed. Darkness swallowed them again.

This was it.

Yuri closed his eyes for a moment, drew in the night air, and exhaled through his nose.

He thought of Kyiv. Of the lies. Of a hundred men he'd killed in countries no one cared to remember.

He tapped twice on the frozen bark beside him.

Advance.

Whispers of confirmation after a crackle of static too faint for any of al Khattab's men to hear. In the dark, the unit moved with the precision of piano keys under a concert master's hands.

From their flanking positions, Vladik's half-team opened fire. Suppressed rifles issued muted coughs that cut through the night like venomous cobra spits. The first sentry collapsed with the sound of a potato sack tipping off a market stall. A second froze at the noise, weapon half-lifted—too late. He buckled backwards, arms flailing, his rifle clattering uselessly onto the hard-packed ground.

From within the camp came muffled shouting—Chechen and Arabic mingling in a confused chorus. Ill-dressed fighters emerged from half-collapsed tents, clutching rifles and bandoliers, eyes wide, minds disoriented from being wrenched from REM into this haunting, dark reality.

A flare of panic. A scuffle. One fighter screamed an oath and raised his weapon blindly towards the woods.

Yuri adjusted his stance and fired a controlled burst. The man dropped mid-curse.

The fire pits—half buried beneath makeshift shelters—flared again as a lit Molotov arced wildly, the bottle trailing fire, before shattering against a pine, engulfing the base in a hiss of enraged flame.

"Volk-Two-Alpha. This is Volk-actual. Call in the Gyrfalcons, over."

"Understood. Executing."

Yuri knew it to be likely that reinforcements from the nearby town of Argun would reach this warzone before the robot dragons came to save them.

The glow outlined a fighter's silhouette—bearded, tall, fast. He was running uphill into the forest, most likely towards reinforcements and a better firing position.

Yuri moved.

He cut through the trees in a half-crouch, breath tight in his chest. His feet kissed the twig strewn ground. The fleeing man's laboured breaths drew him closer—ragged, panicked, ignorant of the predator at his back.

The 5.45mm round Yuri fired destroyed the right knee, collapsing his prey.

The man moaned and twitched, alive but pain-wracked.

"Clear left!" Vladik's voice called, sharp and controlled. "Two down. One alive!"

Yuri exhaled through his nose. Sweat stung his eyes. He slung his rifle behind his hip, jammed a knee into the lumbar and roughly manipulated the fallen's wrists behind into pre-looped cable ties, securing them together.

His training and experience would allow him to track back.

The wood roared with a metallic spraying fury as PKM fire chewed through the underbrush like a buzz saw.

"Volk-One move to my position. Volk-Two hold. Maintain visual on Volk-One until we initiate a sweep."

Several confirmations sounded in his tactical headset.

The scattered line of Volk-Two returned fire with sharp, surgical bursts from behind mossy rock and half-frozen timber.

The Chechens pressed hard, with war-gifted willpower and discipline.

Somewhere in the trees, a rebel shouted in Chechen, half-prayer, half-battle cry.

Yuri Kozlov slid into a kneeling-supported position behind a tree, leaves crackling beneath him. He sucked in the cool oxygen, rising his chest under his webbing, in preparation to engage the chaos below. He raised his optics—a low-light monocular clamped to the side of his AKS-74U—and tracked the muzzle flashes flickering in the woodline two hundred metres out.

"Volk-Two, this is Actual. Sitrep." His voice was low, clipped, transmitted via throat mic.

Crackle. Then a hiss.

"Three contacts down. Two flanking east. One wounded."

Kozlov flicked his safety to full auto. "Copy. Hold. We're sweeping. Volk-One, ready?"

His headset crackled with three confirmations.

"Pairs. Left pair moves first. Execute."

Like wolves loosed from the ridge, Volk-One spilt from the high ground in a smooth, silent surge. Suppressed fire snapped through the trees—short, controlled as one pair move, with the roles alternating.

One of Kozlov's men, Pavlichenko, was first to engage, his AKS-74U rattling a pair of short bursts into the back of a Chechen fighter crouched behind a log. The man pitched forward without a sound.

Kozlov moved like liquid shadow, flanking right. He spotted another rebel—dirty parka, bearded, dragging a belt-fed RPK to reposition—and dropped him with a precise double tap. The man jerked, collapsing like a puppet with cut strings.

Volk-Two's lines steadied as pressure shifted. Kolesnik, manning the PKM, let loose a final blast of covering fire before slapping the weapon's smoking receiver. "They're pulling back!" he barked in Russian.

Kozlov didn't let up.

He moved fast, shoulders brushing fir branches as he advanced, rifle up, scanning. Another Chechen, younger, adrenaline-wild, broke from cover with a cry—an old Tokarev pistol in hand—Kozlov guessed he must have ditched his rifle. The Chechen barely raised it before Kozlov's 5.45mm round took him in the collarbone, folding him into the mud where the Ukrainian finished him with a single shot to the head.

"Volk-One, anchor left. Clear the rest."

Pavlichenko and Fedorov peeled wide through the brush, leapfrogging with silent coordination. Another body dropped. Then silence.

Smoke curled through the morning air, mixing with pine and cordite.

Kozlov lowered his rifle, breathing steady, his face expressionless. He keyed his comms again.

The faraway sounds of the ignition of engines told him not of the approach of reinforcements—but of the enemy escaping.

"Volk-Actual to all elements. Perimeter secure. One KIA, one WIA. Reorganise on my mark."

He looked towards the distant glint of aluminium—a cooking pot, maybe—half buried near a tent flap deeper in the valley. Al-Khattab's main camp lay where the vehicles were driving off.

This had just been the gatekeepers.

And the wolves were inside now.

Within two minutes the entire patrol had formed an outward facing protective circle around himself, Pavel—the patrol's medic, and Kirill who had taken one in the leg.

Yuri allowed Pavel a minute to tear at the combat trousers with scissors before he flushed the wound with water.

"Initial observation?"

"Flesh wound. Non-catastrophic. No need for tourniquet," replied Pavel, snapping off the dark amber glass ampoule and pouring the iodine in as Kirill growled with pain.

Yuri said, "Kirill, we have to clear further in. We must—"

"It is fine, **Komandir**, I can dress it myself," said Kirill stoically despite the burning he must have felt.

Yuri addressed the rest, "The main camp

seems to be fifty metres to my twelve o'clock. Reset into line abreast. Cover and move in pairs. Keep out of any structures until we've cleared outside."

The party did so with fast precision.

Though Yuri had considered the possibility of booby traps to be minimal due to the Chechens rush to escape, he couldn't discount it.

And he already knew al-Khattab would have escaped. If he hadn't and had been hit, they would never leave his corpse to the enemy anyway.

As they cleared through the main camp, one of the strewn figures dragged itself like a macabre zombie in a futile attempt to escape.

"Vladik, take over command."

"Yes, Volk-One," answered the Russian, directing the patrol to the perimeter as Yuri pinned the crawler with a knee and frisked him. After relieving him of a **Kindjal**—a traditional Caucasian Dagger, he rolled the man onto his back. Dark eyes blinked up at him, wide with disbelief.

"Where's al-Khattab?" Yuri asked in Russian.

The man spat blood. "You're too late."

Yuri drew his sidearm and pressed it to the man's thigh. "Try again."

"Wait, wait. I know where they are."

"Where what are?"

"The rest of the cases."

"Wha—where?"

"The pillbox. Over there," said the Chechen, flinging his hand in the direction of the smaller of the two octagonal concrete structures with slits two ***chyetvyerts'***—handspans—across and one up on each side.

A whistle blew low and long from across the

camp. Another signal from Vladik. They had secured the perimeter.

Yuri hauled the Chechen fighter to his feet, jamming the rare, ultra-secret PSS Silent Pistol into his ribs.

"Luckily, you're here to clear the bunker first."

Yuri then frog-marched the rebel over until the fighter violently baulked at the door.

"Grenade on a tripwire. Two mines inside."

"Pressure-plates?"

"What?"

"Do they explode if you step on them?"

"Yes."

The rest of the patrol dressed in, dead-checking the lain Chechen as the helicopters could be heard in the distance.

Yuri growled, "You go in alone and bring out what I need."

"Then what?"

"Then maybe you lay down and play dead—like you should have before."

"You are a liar. I will be in a Russian cell."

"Executing unarmed men is not my style, and we would prefer not to have to explain to the camp's commandant why we have returned from a live firing exercise with a dirty, bearded Chechen," said Yuri. "Besides, what choice do you have?"

The fighter nodded, seemingly in acceptance of the logic before asking, "Can I light a match?"

By way of reply, Yuri reached beneath the AKS-74U's barrel and shone red light into the Chechen's face.

"You will be able to see fine," said Yuri. And,

as a warning, "And I will see you fine."

He roughly spun the rebel around, who then took an exaggerated step over the trip wire.

The red light illuminated the chalky inside.

A trio of army-green footlockers lay at the far end—one had its lid open.

Though the floor seemed devoid of any markers of the mines, the way the Chechen resembled a pirate walking the plank convinced Yuri of their presence.

It occurred to him that if this Islamist were the martyrdom-type, this would be an appropriate time.

He trained his sights intently on the base of the Chechen's skull.

Yuri watched him lift the lids of the two that had been closed before gingerly lifting out what looked to be two oversized old cases.

As he turned, he approached Yuri like a servant presenting a sword to a medieval king.

The Ukrainian stepped back to allow the Chechen to set the cases to one side.

"And the other one," said Yuri, bracing himself for the response.

The Chechen's words confirmed his fears, as the helicopters dragged the wind over the area as they passed overhead.

"That is all of them."

"Lay down and put your wrists behind your back."

The Chechen sneered, "You said you would let me go."

"I said I would let you lay down and play dead," hissed Yuri. "The last thing I need is for you to grab one of your dead friends' weapons. Now turn around before I shoot you."

The rebel complied.

Vladik rushed up to Yuri, "We have to go."

Yuri nodded to the pair of cases, "The suitcase nukes. I need to check the other case."

Without waiting for a reply, Yuri entered and confirmed the footlocker's emptiness.

Coming back out, Vladik gripped the Chechen to haul him upright, and Yuri said, "Leave him."

"Alive?"

"He's unarmed."

"He's the enemy, and one that would not afford us the same courtesy," seethed Vladik, spinning his AK-74 onto the Chechen.

Yuri's gloved hand snatched the barrel upwards and hissed, "A true test of a man's honour is how he keeps it even in the face of those who have none."

Yuri's eyes cooled the fury that shone from his second-in-command, who bowed his head, "Of course."

"Grab a case. No amount of movement can trigger them. Let's go."

Just as Vladik hoisted the second case, the forest beyond the ridgeline erupted with sounds of multiple engines.

Trucks, maybe an old BRDM scout car, and boots thudding across frozen soil.

The Argun reinforcements.

Yuri turned his head towards the approaching storm, reading the rhythm of its movement like a terrifying old song.

"Contact incoming. We have three minutes—maximum."

"Signal them," Yuri ordered.

The signaller, Pavelchenko, had already dropped to one knee, antenna unfurling like a sword drawn in silence. His gloved hand tapped the encrypted code into the comms unit.

"Gyrfalcons, this is Volk-Actual. Fire support requested. Moving east, hot extract. Grid: Four-Bravo-Three-Seven."

The forest howled.

The patrol knifed back through the forest.

Yuri led the fighting withdrawal, eyes flicking between trees, his suppressed AKS-74U tucked close to his frame. The two suitcase nukes were passed off to Fedorov and Mikhailov—each moving with the reverence of a man carrying a god's heart in a briefcase.

Behind them, shadows moved—Chechen fighters, more than a dozen, maybe two, emboldened by numbers and vengeance. RPKs barked from a treeline to the west. Rounds chewed at bark and ice, spitting up white and brown in angry snarls.

"Contact west flank—twelve o'clock high!" Vladik shouted.

Yuri dropped to a knee and returned fire—controlled, precise bursts that stitched the wood line. Fedorov tossed a smoke grenade behind them, its hiss a ghost's exhale, obscuring their path of escape.

Then the sky roared.

The Gyrfalcons.

Two Ka-50 "Black Sharks" swept in low, their sleek frames slicing through the trees like mechanical phantoms. Rotor wash tore through pine as the gunships opened up—30mm cannons unleashing hell, tearing the ground apart with mechanical fury.

Rockets followed—S-8s thundering into enemy positions in fountains of flame and death.

Yuri's patrol emerged into the clearing just as the Mi-8 "Hip" utility helicopter flared in over the rise, side doors already open, crew waving them in.

"Go! Go!" he barked.

Volk-Two formed a staggered perimeter as the others loaded in, still firing—measured bursts into the encroaching darkness.

The patrol vaulted into the belly of the bird, two men dragging Kirill between them with another carrying the corpse of Igor on their shoulder. Yuri was the last aboard, slapping the fuselage as the "Hip" lifted—its skids scraping before they broke free.

The rotors screamed. The wind snapped like a whip across their faces as they gained altitude.

Then—a shriek.

Something brighter than fire sliced through the sky—a 9K32 Strela-2, launched from the woods. The SA-7 locked, trailing like a demon's tail, climbing fast.

Inside the chopper, breath stopped. Yuri's hand tightened on the edge of the bulkhead. Time folded.

The pilot saw it. The "Hip" rolled, banked hard left, flares bursting from its underbelly in a blossom of light and heat.

The missile bit the bait, spiralling wide—and detonated harmlessly above the treetops in a flash that bathed the valley in artificial noon.

Cheers broke out in the cabin—raw, visceral. Relief, however brief.

But Yuri didn't smile.

He turned, knelt beside the two cases, and stared at them. Army-green. Heavy with history. There should have been three.

He said nothing.

His gloved fingers rested on the cold steel.

Behind his eyes, he saw a city he hadn't chosen, a command he hadn't asked for, and a third nuclear ghost, still out there—crawling towards an uncertain future in someone else's hands.

The blades beat harder overhead, cutting sky and silence as the chopper banked southeast towards safety.

16

CHECHNYA — FOOTHILLS OUTSIDE OF GROZNY — EARLY MORNING

The cave was quiet, save for the occasional drip of condensation falling into shallow, stagnant pools. Smoke still lingered from the earlier fire, mingling with the stench of blood, sweat, and soot. The survivors had gathered around a dim lantern, less for its light and more to ward off the damp, their faces drawn and hollow, as if some essential part of them had been lost in the battle.

Zubayr al-Adel sat apart from them, close to the entrance, his silhouette hunched against the rock like a statue sculpted in patience and shadow. The AKM lay across his lap, fingers resting lightly near the trigger well.

He had not been given a weapon; instead he'd taken it from a Chechen gunned down by lethal ghosts in the dark.

He sensed the simmer of their collective distrust of him threatening to boil over in their harsh whispers and glances shot like arrows towards him.

Blood, not all his own, had dried into a rust-coloured pattern across his shoulder and forearm. He had not spoken since they had retreated.

When Ibn al-Khattab entered, conversation died immediately. The Chechen commander moved with the calm of a man untouched by panic. His long coat was dusted with ash, his boots silent against the stone. He carried no weapon—he didn't need one.

Al-Khattab stopped a few feet from Zubayr

and regarded him with what seemed to be something between scrutiny and respect.

"You saved Abdurrahman," he said quietly.

Zubayr nodded once and asked, "And the case?"

"Recovered. Hidden again."

Al-Khattab's eyes narrowed, as if searching for something unspoken in Zubayr's voice. Then he turned to the gathered fighters behind him.

"We must move," he said, louder now, his voice smooth as polished steel. "They have shown themselves to have broken the Khasavyurt Accord. We must alert Maskhadov."

Al-Khattab referred to the ceasefire agreement signed in Khasavyurt, Dagestan, by the Russian Federation's General Alexander Lebed and the Chief of Staff for the Chechen forces, Aslan Maskhadov."

A murmur rippled through the crowd. One of the older fighters, a man Zubayr knew to be Isa Khamzatovich Dzhabrailov—or Tsha-Kurkh, 'Isa the Fox', despite never being introduced to him—stood bandaged and bloodied.

"We have been here for almost half a year since our victory. It is only since these Arabs and their devices arrived that we have been attacked, my Kham," said Isa, using a Chechen word for leader. "And it is strange how this one is the only one alive."

Others nodded. The air thickened.

Before the boy could speak again, al-Khattab raised a hand. The silence that followed was immediate.

"I saw him fight, my friend," he said, low and firm. "I saw him drag Abdurrahman through fire. I saw him recover what the rest of them panicked in the face of—that is why they no longer breathe, but he does…"

He paused, letting the weight of his words settle.

"You want someone to blame?" he asked. "Blame those dead men. Or perhaps the man who brought them here. But do not blame a warrior who held the line while others broke."

There were no more protests.

Al-Khattab turned back to Zubayr, his tone softening. "Your operation is compromised," he said. "You can't trust your handlers."

Zubayr met his gaze. No defiance. No denial. Just grim acceptance.

"I know," he said. "That's why I go alone."

He glanced over his shoulder towards the mouth of the cave, where the grey light of early morning smeared the rocks in silver.

"Tell Ramzi I died," he added. "Say I was killed recovering the case."

Al-Khattab studied him for a long moment, then nodded. "I can get you out of the Caucasus," he said. "After that… you're on your own."

"Thank you, Emir," answered Zubayr, using an Islamist term that could mean both 'Commander' or 'Prince'.

Al-Khattab nodded before turning to his men, "Let the dead bury the dead."

Zubayr rose slowly, his joints stiff with fatigue and went to join the throng.

"No," said al-Khattab sternly. "You do not have time to waste here."

Before the Al Qaeda fighter could protest, al-

Khattab barked, "Ruslan."

A young fighter bounded to them, and al-Khattab ordered, "I decree that Zubayr al-Adel is to be given a protective guide through Abkhazia, into Turkey. Take as many or as few men as you need, Ruslan, but not one hair on his head will be harmed."

"I understand, Kham al-Khattab," said Ruslan. "I believe I would be best served taking him alone to lessen any eyes on us on our journey."

Zubayr understood that though Georgia provided unofficial support and sanctuary, by way of the Pankisi Gorge, the Russian FSB and GRU were active throughout the area.

"As you wish," said al-Khattab. "Ruslan will take you into the town for any provisions you might need."

As if reading his mind, Ruslan said, "We have rucksacks large enough for your supplies and… device. It might attract attention in Turkey but, by then, perhaps you won't need it."

"Necessity is the mother of invention," said Zubayr. "I know now why you won the war."

Zubayr lifted a scuffed satchel—its weight far exceeding its size—and slung it over one shoulder. He adjusted the scarf around his neck, picked up his rifle, and turned to face al-Khattab.

They exchanged no farewells, but Zubayr bowed his head in gratitude.

Al-Khattab turned to command his men.

Ruslan and Zubayr stepped into the silence of the highlands, leaving behind the flickering warmth of the cave.

CAFÉ MARGOT — RUE SAINT-DOMINIQUE —

LATE AFTERNOON — PARIS

The sky hung low over the Parisian rooftops, clouds smudging the horizon like smoke stains. Through the glass of Café Margot's terrace enclosure, the Eiffel Tower rose in the distance—majestic, indifferent. Bruce sat with his elbows on the iron table, the steam from his espresso curling past his face like smoke.

Frank sat opposite him, coat still draped over the back of his chair despite the spring chill, his eyes scanning the passing traffic with the faintest rhythm of a man who'd seen many cities.

To Bruce's left, Anissa Rajah stirred her coffee absently, gaze distant, jaw set with a grace that disguised tension.

The polished look of the DGSE officer belied the same frustration that was buzzing just beneath Bruce's skin.

Frank broke the silence first. "Nothing from London."

Bruce offered a slow nod. "Same with the DGSE?"

Anissa didn't look up from her cup. "No chatter. No secondary confirmation. And you know as well as I do… without that corroboration, they won't put forward resources."

Bruce looked down at the untouched glass of Perrier between them and said, "We're talking about a suitcase nuke."

Anissa's voice remained calm, but her grip on the teaspoon tightened. "Exactly. Which is why they won't gamble on a single tip. Every major service on this continent has been burned chasing red herrings. Dozens over the last decade. The policy is clear. No second source, no action."

Frank leant back and exhaled through his nose. "The whole damn thing was designed to stop panic missions, but now it's fucking us up for one that matters."

"What now then?" Bruce asked.

Frank answered without hesitation. "I've put word out through my old channels. If there's anything moving on the ground, we might get a lead."

Anissa lifted her gaze to meet his. "I've done the same. Marseille. Istanbul. A few in North Africa. But these things take time with those people."

Time might be the one thing we don't have, thought Bruce.

Frank finished his coffee, stood, and rolled his shoulders like a man limbering for the next blow. "All we can do now… is wait."

Anissa set down her cup. "And pray our sources get back to us before the radiation does."

Bruce sat a moment longer after they stood, his gaze drifting back to the skyline, to the tower that watched over Paris with its eternal, iron calm.

KYIV — SBU ALPHA HEADQUARTERS — 72 HOURS POST-EXTRACTION

The overhead fluorescents in the debriefing room flickered with a faint buzz, a tired rhythm matching the mood. The walls were blank but for a battered coat rack and a Soviet-era clock that seemed to tick louder than it should.

Not in Dmytro Hrytsenko's office this time.

The colonel and Major Andrei Sokolova stood to greet him before they all took a seat,

Hrytsenko directly opposite and Sokolova to his right flank as before.

Yuri knew that both the superior ranks would have read the collation of the after-action accounts from the surviving members of Volk Team.

Finally, Hrytsenko leant back in his leather chair and folded his arms, his thick neck bunching into his collar. "Master Sergeant Kozlov," he said in a tone devoid of irony, "you've completed your objective under challenging circumstances and recovered two of the devices. The casualties were regrettable but... not unexpected."

Yuri gave a nod. "Sir."

Sokolova's voice followed, smoother and colder. "The professionalism of your unit has been noted. Both by us, and—unofficially—by the GRU's operational command in Nalchik."

The major's expression didn't change, but something in his tone shifted—less polished now, more clinical.

"Still," he continued, "we would be negligent not to address the fact that your team was compromised earlier than anticipated. It resulted in a missed opportunity to secure the third RA-115S device."

Kozlov felt himself straighten. His voice came low and measured, like it had been packed in ice and unpacked piece by piece.

"With respect, Major, the GRU's intelligence assessment was not accurate. Their briefing claimed no more than a dozen hostiles in the area. We encountered close to thirty."

Sokolova didn't interrupt, so Yuri pressed on.

"They also placed the main camp half a

kilometre further down slope. In reality, al-Khattab's fighters had occupied high ground to the northwest. That position allowed them a clear approach vector to flank and retreat in force when the shooting started."

Yuri caught Hrytsenko's glance at Sokolova, but the major's face remained impassive. A long breath escaped the colonel's nostrils before he spoke.

"We've corroborated those claims with the rest of the patrol," he admitted. "Your observations are consistent."

Yuri didn't nod. He simply held their gaze, letting the silence do its work.

Then Sokolova shifted forward in his chair, interlacing his fingers.

"The third RA-115S…" he said slowly, "must not be spoken of. Not in your personal logs. Not in idle talk. Not to anyone."

His words settled on the atmosphere.

"There's every reason to believe the device is—how shall we put it—functionally obsolete. These systems were built decades ago. Their batteries degrade over time. Even the shaped charge mechanisms likely no longer align properly. Without the proper calibration, the fissile core is inert."

Yuri didn't want to enter the quagmire of pointing out if the devices were obsolete, then why did they risk such a dangerous and politically explosive mission?

Instead, he said nothing.

Sokolova went on. "But optics matter, Master Sergeant. If the wrong people learn that even one nuclear device is unaccounted for, the geopolitical consequences could be… inconvenient."

His pause was deliberate. Not quite a threat.

Yuri held the major's gaze for a beat longer than comfortable. "Understood."

"Good."

The Master Sergeant said, "I'd like to formally request leave. For restoration purposes."

He didn't want to point out that his operational frequency had been much higher than even the average Alpha Group operative.

He didn't have to, as Hrytsenko almost immediately said, "Approved. Two weeks, starting immediately."

Sokolova offered something almost like a smile. "You've earned it, Master Sergeant."

He stood, smoothed the fabric of his cardigan, and extended a hand that Yuri accepted out of habit more than respect.

"Your soldiering has been exemplary. Again."

Yuri released the handshake without reply.

Sokolova added, "And should we—by some miracle of tradecraft or divine providence—obtain a location on the third device, I imagine I'll find myself requesting your expertise again."

Yuri gave a faint, tired grin. "Wouldn't surprise me, major. These things have a habit of resurfacing."

He turned to go, boots quiet on the linoleum.

Behind him, the clock ticked on, steady and cold. Somewhere out there, an RA-115S waited—silent, sealed, and but waiting nonetheless.

17

SOUTH CHECHEN — EARLY EVENING

The evening heat in the Vedeno mountains settled on Ramzi al-Wahishi's skin like a damp, unwelcome hand—thick with sweat, grit, and the scent of pine and gun oil.

The Yemeni exhaled slowly as the wind hissed through the barren trees outside the compound. His gloved hand rested loosely on the worn leather arm of a folding chair, boots dusted with frost and mountain mud.

Across from him, beside a battered iron stove that hissed steam, sat Shamil Basayev—commander, warlord, lion of the resistance and now Deputy Prime Minister of the Chechen Republic of Ichkeria.

His eyes were steady, intelligent, and half-lidded with the weary patience of a man who had seen too many wars and fools.

On either side of the small room stood his fighters—stoic, rifle-armed men in mismatched camouflage and black *shemaghs*.

Ibn al-Khattab sat opposite Ramzi, relaxed in a chair as though this were a brotherly council and not the weighing of treachery.

Two of his men flanked him—faces carved from ice, knuckles calloused from years of dragging others into graves. Zuhayr ibn Salim, the taller of the two, had a jagged scar across his jaw that twisted whenever he smirked. The other remained motionless, a Kalashnikov balanced over his thighs like a loyal dog.

Ramzi had brought only Adam Umar, who stood behind him like a cliff face cast in human form, his eyes never leaving the Chechens. He was silent, unblinking, and Ramzi knew from long experience that violence needed only a flicker to erupt in this man.

Basayev cleared his throat.

"We are gathered, and I assume this is not a meeting of fellowship and nostalgia."

Ramzi leant forward, his voice low, smooth, yet threaded with steel.

"I demand answers. I arranged for substantial funds to ensure the protection of certain assets, and now those assets are gone. That is not acceptable."

Al-Khattab answered, with a sly edge to his voice, "I thought the money was also a gift for us to advance our Jihad against our imperialist, non-believing suppressors?"

Ramzi knew that al-Khattab said that for Basayev's benefit—the Deputy Prime Minister remained a Chechen nationalist.

However, al-Wahishi knew that the flame of pan-Islamism had begun to burn brighter within Basayev he knew because al-Wahishi had helped stoke the fires.

"The devices were the gifts from Allah to help achieve exactly that and our global Jihad. Our objectives are not mutually exclusive."

Al-Khattab met his eyes. His calmness was not the false serenity of a liar it was the maddening poise of a man with no fear of death—al-Wahishi knew he couldn't claim the same.

"We lived unbothered for months before you and your people arrived," Al-Khattab said. "Then ghosts in the trees, sky dragons and half my men are dead. Perhaps you should question your own security before mine."

"Are you suggesting I led them to you? That I sabotaged my own operation?" Ramzi asked, incredulous.

Al-Khattab shrugged. "Answer me this—how do men who live in caves, without phones, without radios, who bury their latrines and speak to no one, leak anything? We have no towers. No encryption. Your men brought that tech with them. Perhaps the leak came with your surveillance equipment. Or from the mouths of your young lions who still dream of Cairo nightclubs."

Ramzi could hear Adam Umar stirring behind him and sensed a subtle tightening of his jaw.

Al-Khattab went on, his tone biting. "Besides, do you think we orchestrated the destruction of our camp? The deaths of our fighters? For what purpose?"

"You failed," Ramzi snapped. "You failed, and the device is missing. I want the money returned."

Al-Khattab leant back, resting his elbows on the chair's arms. "Many of my men are dead. Men who protected *your* devices with their lives. Their blood was payment enough."

"Then we are at an impasse."

The temperature in the room dropped perceptibly. Adam's boot creaked faintly. One of al-Khattab's men shifted his rifle.

Basayev spoke before the air could be cleaved.

"You both make strong arguments," he said calmly. "And we all know how precious time is in these matters. But I would suggest restraint. We do not gain from turning our weapons inward."

Ramzi's eyes didn't leave al-Khattab's. "If this was a matter of pride, I would let it go. But this isn't about pride—it's about capability."

Al-Khattab tilted his head, and for the first time, the trace of a smile appeared on his lips.

"One of the devices *was* recovered."

Ramzi's breath caught for a fraction of a second. "Where?"

"With Zubayr al-Adel," al-Khattab replied.

That name pulled silence into the room.

Ramzi straightened. "He's alive?"

"He fought bravely. He saved one of my men. He retrieved the device when others hesitated. That's why he was spared. He asked to complete the mission alone. I granted it."

Ramzi's voice dropped. "I gave no such order. He has not been given a target package."

"Maybe he does not need one," al-Khattab said. "He understands what Al Qaeda is. He understands your objectives. He was handpicked for a reason, was he not?"

Ramzi inhaled through his nose. "Where is he now?"

"I cannot say. He is being escorted across Abkhazia. He will reach Turkey soon. After that, he is on his own."

"You thought it wise to gamble this mission—*this* mission—on a single man?"

"I'm trusting the only man who did not die or panic."

"Where will they cross?"

"How would I know? We are not in the habit

of crossing the Georgian border. My guide will perform his own map study and develop his own plan."

The Al Qaeda operational planner silently cursed; the Turkish-Georgian border ran over two hundred and seventy kilometres—there would not be enough Turkish militants to cover it even if they did answer the call.

Still, it would be worth disseminating Zubayr al-Adel's picture throughout the region.

Silence again. Ramzi drummed his fingers once on the arm of the chair, thinking.

Basayev spoke softly, "If this Zubayr succeeds, then your investment bears fruit. If he fails…"

"If he fails," Ramzi interjected, "I will expect at least some of the funds returned. That is business."

Al-Khattab nodded. "If the bomb does not detonate in the next month, we will speak again. And I will consider returning what we can spare."

The tension thinned, but the undercurrent remained. Ramzi rose slowly.

"Then we wait."

He didn't offer his hand, and neither did al-Khattab. Adam opened the door and waited for him to pass.

As they stepped into the bitter mountain wind, Ramzi prayed that his judgement in Zubayr remained correct.

Why has he not contacted me yet?

AUSTRIA — LATE AFTERNOON

The train sliced through the Austrian countryside, distant peaks hazy with heat, morning light casting the landscape in a warm, golden blur.

Inside the compartment, Bruce sat opposite Frank who seemed absorbed in a newspaper crossword.

The occasional tremble of track vibrations ran through the Scot's boots.

Bruce sipped from a paper cup of coffee, lukewarm and bitter.

When Frank straightened and rubbed his eyes, Bruce intercepted whatever inevitable question that was to come with, "What was Martin Dunn like on the mats?"

Frank smiled. "I am not just saying this, but that was a hard match that. I caught a couple of **Shidos** for being too defensive—it was only because he was non-stop attacking. Only won by **Yuko** after countering one of his throws with my own. To this day, I reckon I might have beaten Jacks for gold if our brackets had been swapped. Jacks had beaten us before, mind."

"Martin speaks highly of you," said Bruce. "Do you still follow judo, Frank?"

"Not as much now. Catch it on the telly when I can."

Bruce said, "I watched some of the Olympics last year. Old Jigoro Kano might be rolling in his grave."

"Why's that?"

"Double legs, fireman's carries," said Bruce. "Looked like bastardised wrestling at times."

Frank raised a brow. "If our trade teaches you anything, it's that adaptation's not the enemy, Bruce.

Japs from a hundred years ago didn't have to face former Soviet crossover athletes like the Georgian Khakhaleishvili or Russia's Islam Matsiev."

Bruce nodded, "The South Korean Jung Bu-Kyung won the silver. He cross-trains in traditional Korean wrestling."

"Yeh, it's called **Ssireum**," answered Frank to Bruce's mild surprise. "Still, it is what it is. Jigoro Kano's ghost shouldn't worry too much. The Japs will eventually get pissed off if they lose enough to leg-grabbing rugby tackles producing a low scoring **Koka**. They'll put pressure on the authorities saying judo is losing its identity and entertainment value. They might be right too."

"You ever been to Japan?" asked Bruce.

"Yeah," said Frank. "Met a beautiful girl out there. It was great but when it came to me breaking up with her, I had to drop the bomb twice."

When Bruce afforded him a smirk, Frank went back to his crossword, with the Scotsman staring out the window a while before opening a novel he picked up in Paris; *The Tunnel Rats* by Stephen Leather.

Bruce had read an article a few years before regarding a small group of U.S. and allied troops—primarily volunteers—who during the Vietnam War performed the infiltration and clearing out of the complex tunnel networks used by the Viet Cong and North Vietnamese Army.

Enemy combatants laying in ambush, booby traps, the claustrophobia-inducing narrowness of the tunnels, the poor air quality, as well as venomous snakes, tarantulas, scorpions and rats the size of cats, made it perhaps the most deadly and certainly the most terrifying taskings of the war.

Leather's first few paragraphs absorbed Bruce.

Frank interrupted his fictive dream murmuring a question without looking up from his crossword, "Americanism for a casual sports shoe? Begins with S, ends with—"

"Sneaker."

"Chuffing hellfire," said Frank, writing it in before looking at Bruce, "How do I know that an 'Unusual clergyman's tipple, one of refined taste' is Gourmand but my noggin can't get fucking sneaker."

"Has it bought me the right to know who we are going to meet?"

Frank leant back in his seat. "A Ukrainian I met years ago. In Romania, before the wall fell. We were both in different shadows, moving along the same wall—fuck me, am a poet, aren't I."

"It was, err… it was a good line," said Bruce.

"We met through an underground movement—*The Partisans of Europe*. Wanted the Communist regime to fuck off."

Bruce's eyes narrowed. "They still active? Even after the wall came down?"

"Kinda. Russia still has iron fingers around some of these Eastern bloc countries and certain people don't like it."

Bruce looked out the window. "Where are we meeting him?"

"Vienna. Trucking depot. Belongs to one of the Partisans' members."

SOUTHERN TURKEY — MID AFTERNOON

The road into Turkey had been stitched together in frayed back trails and cracked border roads, the kind that bore more goats than trucks, more ghosts than maps. Zubayr al-Adel, walked it with the type of fatigue that didn't show in his face, only in the calculated deliberation of his every step.

The trek from the Argun foothills to the Turkish border had been merciless—sleet-slick ridges, night crossings in silence, and sleeping beneath pine cover while GRU military recon planes like the Tu-22Ms skimmed the sky like vultures with cameras for eyes. Ruslan had peeled away a day before the crossing, his last words a muttered prayer and warning not needed: *'If they find you, they won't ask questions.'*

Zubayr crossed alone.

He had skirted Istanbul, aware that the city wasn't just a gateway but a cage of watchful eyes—Turkish intelligence, NATO liaison networks and the intelligence agency of his own nation. Better to blend in somewhere quieter. He moved south, hugging the Black Sea coast before doubling back inland to a nameless town between Samsun and Çorum, its train station cracked and sun-bleached, its faces unfamiliar and uninterested.

He carried no weapon now. The AKM was left buried near a Chechen riverbank, a ritual shedding of skin.

Over his shoulder clung a plain grey rucksack, which had been rolled within the much larger military olive one that saw him through the Caucasus hike.

His right hand held the old, battered suitcase within which lay the device—compact, silent, and heavy enough to remind him what he carried wasn't just metal and circuitry, but history on a trigger.

He had swapped his battle-worn clothes for the uniform of anonymity: denim jeans, a khaki jacket with stitched patches of Turkish military surplus, and a wool hat pulled low.

His beard was trimmed with a tourist's laziness. At a bus depot, he exchanged the substantial amount of roubles given to him in Argun for Turkish lira, careful to space the transactions, switching exchange booths and waiting hours between stops. A backpacker in no rush. A man between lives.

Now, in the stale quiet of a coin-fed phone booth, Zubayr fished a laminated card from his sock and dialled a memorised sequence routed through three exchanges. It rang once, then again. A pause. Then a click.

A familiar voice belonging to a man who knew Zubayr's real name of Elias Monroe.

Dry, Midwestern vowels warped through encryption static.

"Eli's Workshop." *Code phrase to confirm the handler is on the line.*

Zubayr replied, "Chevrolet Chevelle."

"What year?"

"1970." *Zubayr's date of birth.*

"What's the faults?" *Challenge phrase to verify he isn't compromised or under duress.*

"Suspension wear." *Confirmation he is neither.*

"Go ahead."

"I am in Turkey. Alone. I have one of them, including the trigger."

A beat. Then, the voice spoke with less certainty than usual. "We thought you were burned."

"Almost," he replied. "I need to know if we're still green."

He glanced outside. A boy selling sesame bread rolled past the booth, not looking twice.

The voice hesitated.

"We… haven't heard from the Old Man."

That stopped him. The Old Man—the architect of Operation BACKLASH, the mind behind every layer of Zubayr's legend—had never missed a check-in and never gone dark.

"How long?" Zubayr asked.

"Three days. We've tried everything. Cut-outs, voiceback, even the Riyadh team. Nothing. There's chatter he was on the Hill before he dropped off. We don't know what he said. If he said anything."

Zubayr closed his eyes briefly. Not in fear. In calibration.

"So the mission's aborted?"

"We don't know. Maybe we should delay. Just a few days."

He didn't hesitate.

"That's not possible."

"Why?"

Zubayr's voice went cold. Not sharp, not angry—just factual. Like reciting schematics.

"I have identified a target that will accomplish the Old Man's higher objective."

"What is it?"

"I do not wish to say at this moment."

A pause, and then, "OK."

"The window of opportunity is locked. Opens in ninety-six hours. Exfil slot closes seventy-two after that. I miss the window, we lose the opportunity for maximum impact, and this was all for nothing."

The line went quiet again, and then, "You're sure?"

Zubayr looked down at the suitcase. The weight of it was like a second pulse.

"This is Democracy's chance to spread further in the world," said Zubayr. "Besides, I didn't come this far just to come this far."

A breath on the other end. Not agreement—resignation.

"Copy that."

"Is there any chance you yourself have been compromised?"

"I have taken every precaution but the Old Man will sing eventually—everyone does."

"Understood—I will proceed as if you have been."

The handler sighed, "From this moment, you are Code Black. Zero support. You're on your own."

"Understood," he said. Then hung up.

The handler knew his real name—*Or maybe it's my birth name now*, thought Zubayr.

That man might be gone forever, replaced entirely by Zubayr al-Adel—a tool built for a single outcome.

He stepped out of the booth and into the Turkish afternoon. It was warm, the sun smearing the streets in honeyed gold. Children played soccer against a concrete wall. A dog barked in the distance.

And in the middle of it all, Zubayr walked unnoticed, carrying the change of history in his case.

18

VIENNA — AFTERNOON

The depot in the Austrian district of Favoriten squatted like a forgotten bunker, concrete walls streaked with age and graffiti. Bruce could smell rust and stale oil as they stepped inside. The building still echoed with a mechanical emptiness, as if it were waiting for the next war.

The Ukrainian stood in the corner outside what looked to be a row of bricked rooms—lean, upright, hands in the pockets of a grey coat that hung off his frame like a soldier's ghost. His eyes were sharp, winter blue and half-hooded.

"Frank," he said, stepping forward and clasping hands with Carlsmith. "It's good to see you—old boy."

"See you stole my pet name," said Frank before turning to Bruce. "Bruce, this is Yuri Kozlov."

Bruce extended a hand, "Good to meet you, Yuri."

The Ukrainian took it, shook once, then tilted his head.

"You wear that moustache with pride, I see?"

Bruce raised a brow thinking that the Ukrainian had put 'moustache' and 'Pride' together in a vague reference to homosexuality.

"Suppose so."

"Even I know that moustaches are a signature of the British Special Forces man. Maybe time to shave it?"

"Perhaps it is," admitted Bruce.

"Young man," Yuri said sharply, momentarily stiffening the back of the much taller Scot. Yuri and Frank harmonised, "There's no need to feel down."

Bruce grinned under the ribbing of the two older men.

It cooled after a few moments, along with Yuri's expression. "Frank… it's not good."

"I kinda guessed it wouldn't be since you dragged me out to Austria—how did you square being here with your top brass?"

"Even we are allowed *vidpustka*."

"Leave period."

"I am glad to hear your foreign language ear is still sharp, old man," smiled Yuri. "And they know I have an aunt in Slovakia. It was just a hop across the border."

He tilted his head towards the door and the Brits followed him inside.

Fluorescent tubes flickered overhead, casting a sickly yellow hue over cracked linoleum flooring and dust-caked filing cabinets. The walls were lined with peeling maps, faded shift rosters, and a rusting rotary phone dangled from its cord like a relic.

Bruce noticed a Würth wall calendar showing a topless, large-breasted blonde with an oversized drill, stuck on April 1995.

An ashtray overflowed beside a chipped mug.

Both Yuri and Frank simultaneously took out a pack of cigarettes; Yuri' a white pack with a red eagle logo with the name *Memphis Classic*, and Frank's a dark navy pack of *Gauloises Brunes*.

The two men, without a word, spoke, simultaneously offering and accepting a cigarette from the other's pack.

As they lit up, Bruce felt the same vague sense of being left out as he did during the 'Jungle Phase' of ***selection*** in Brunei watching the smokers—candidates and DS (Directing Staff) alike—congregate during rare and brief breaks by the river.

The pair smoked for a few moments before Frank said, "Alright, hit me with it."

Yuri replied, "The devices transferred by Szombati are RA-115Ss. What the Russians call atomic munition devices. They have a power of one kiloton. The blast will destroy everything within a five-hundred-metre radius if exploded in the open air."

The Ukrainian drew a circle with his fingers.

"What about the radiological fallout?"

Yuri said, "Thousands of metres."

"Kilometres," said Frank.

"Yes, kilometres," said Yuri, emphasising the 'o' more. "Ten days past, I led a mission into Chechnya for recovery of them. Held by Ibn al-Khattab."

"Ramzi al-Wahishi must have believed they would be safe there. Let the investigation calm before striking," said Frank. "Were you successful, Yuri?"

"We recover two—one is missing."

The last three words hung in the air with the smoke.

Frank asked, "How did they obtain the intel that they were there?"

Yuri shrugged. "It was the Russian SVR—not the GRU—who picked me. They did not tell me such things."

"If one remains at large," said Bruce, "then I would have assumed the SVR would keep up an operational tempo until they got it back?"

"That would be politically sensitive," answered Yuri. "One mission is a risk that can be hidden. More missions is to fire a second war before we are ready."

"So we are to wait until the Chechens use it?" asked Bruce.

"I do not know," said Yuri. "Now tell me what you know."

The Scot glanced at the Englishman, who took a drag and said, "An SVR agent, a colonel named Genrikh Bezmenov, is the original architect of all this. We have nothing concrete as yet, but he seems to have gone quiet since the start of the month."

"They have captured and interrogated him—and he broke."

"Seems so."

After a moment, Yuri spoke, "How did you know of Bezmenov?"

"We managed to… engineer a conversation with Viktor Szombati," said Frank.

"Is he… still capable of conversations?"

"We let him go with a bloody nose. That's it—scout's honour."

"Scout's honour. What is—"

"It just means I promise."

"So?" asked Yuri. "What now?"

"I am due to report back," Frank said. "I'll make the call but in the meantime, it looks like we'll have to stay here at least until the morning."

Bruce saw Yuri grin, "There is a beer festival that starts in two hours."

BAKU — AZERBAIJAN — AFTERNOON

The *Absheron Hotel* still carried the smell of Soviet ambition beneath its newer perfumes. Brass fixtures polished to an almost theatrical gleam, corridors lined with walnut panels too thin to be anything but cheap veneer. It was the kind of place where oil executives drank toasts with spies, and waiters were always listening.

Major Andrei Arkadievich Sokolova adjusted the cuffs of his jacket as he passed through the lobby, ignoring the glances from the concierge desk. He climbed the stairs himself—no need to announce his arrival by lift chime—and made his way to the mezzanine. The door at the far end was unmarked, but he knew it well.

The meeting room belonged to Rasim Dadashov, a former KGB handler turned Azerbaijani parliamentarian with a Rolodex deep enough to arrange peace between wolves.

Inside, the lights were dimmed. A low hum of refrigerated air. No waiters. No surveillance—at least none Rasim hadn't already neutralised.

Shamil Basayev sat at the far end of the table.

He looked almost unremarkable in civilian dress—dark jeans, a faded bomber jacket—but the man had a gravity all his own. The kind born from surviving landmines and planning mass hostage seizures. His beard was neatly combed, and his left leg sat stiffly, the prosthetic likely rubbing raw against the stump beneath.

Sokolova took his seat without ceremony. No handshake. No pleasantries.

Basayev spoke first.

"You violated Khasavyurt. Your people attacked al-Khattab's camp near Argun. We buried twelve men. Tell me, major—was that Moscow's idea of peace?"

Sokolova didn't flinch. He folded his hands before him on the table.

"If an operation occurred," he said coolly, "then it must have had justification."

Basayev's stare didn't blink. His voice sharpened.

"Justification? We signed your treaty. We honoured it. But you sent a death squad into the foothills to hunt your old ghosts."

Sokolova held his gaze. Beneath the table, he became aware of his pulse—not fast, but deep. Controlled, deliberate.

"If the operation was real," he said, "then someone believed a serious threat had surfaced."

Basayev leant back, reaching into his jacket. Sokolova's fingers twitched—just slightly—but no weapon came out. Only a worn photograph.

He slid it across the table.

"I assume you've heard the rumours," Basayev said. "Three RA 115S devices stolen from Ukraine. You lost track of them."

Sokolova took the photograph and studied it.

The face was young. Middle Eastern. Serious, intense. Handsome in the way zealots sometimes were—features carved sharp by belief.

"Zubayr al-Adel," Basayev said. "He has the device you seek in his possession."

A slow beat passed.

"Where is he now?" Sokolova asked.

Basayev's eyes narrowed slightly.

"He headed for Turkey. I do not know where he is now. He crossed through the hills near Batumi, through Adjara. He was guided through the forest line."

Sokolova slid the photo into his inner jacket pocket and allowed himself a breath. Not of relief—never that—but of clarity. Target acquired.

"If this intelligence is true," he said, "and we recover the device—then perhaps the Argun incident is best forgotten."

Basayev gave a faint nod.

"For now. But let me make this clear, Major. If your forces cross into Chechen territory again—if a single Russian boot tramples our soil—I will take this incident to the international stage. I will let the world know that your peace is just camouflage."

Sokolova stood, smoothing the lapels of his coat.

"This meeting never happened."

Basayev's prosthetic leg thudded softly as he shifted to stand.

"So long as your missiles stay sheathed, Major," he said, "neither will the war."

They didn't shake hands.

Before the SVR officer could turn, Basayev laughed, "Five years ago, I was present when Stanislav Yablokov of your GRU tried to sell them to us. The meeting was ambushed, and Chechen and Russian died alike. Some of my brothers-in-arms escaped, but I hid. And I watched another Russian officer execute a pleading Yablokov. Those bombs are a curse for Chechen and Russian alike."

Sokolova gave him a nod of agreement, as he processed what had just been said.

As he stepped out into the Baku night, the warm breeze off the Caspian did nothing to ease the chill behind his sternum. The photograph burned faintly in his pocket—Zubayr al-Adel. He had a name, a face, a path. Now the clock had started ticking.

For the world's sake, he hoped Zubayr did not succeed.

DGSE HEADQUARTERS — PARIS — LATE AFTERNOON

The air inside the briefing chamber was filtered, sterile, and faintly metallic. Outside, the Seine shimmered in a grey light as if suspended in time.

Anissa Rajah sat with legs crossed, her gloved fingers resting on the knee of her tailored black slacks, as an analyst droned through a bi-monthly roundup she was obligated to attend.

Five directorates made up the organisational structure of the DGSE: Administration, Technical, Strategy, Operations, and the one that Anissa recognised as not only the most painfully monotonous but also the most important—Intelligence.

This was an Intelligence meeting—the kind she loathed—bad coffee, clipped nods, and, due in no small part to the presence of Commandant Éric Chauvigny, layers of wholly unnecessarily pretentious technical jargon.

Meetings like this were possibly another reason she had made the wholly irresponsible decision to aid Frank and Bruce without informing her superiors.

The other agents in the room were a mix of

white-collar types—surveillance, cyber, and psychological profiling. No fieldwork visible in their collars or posture. Just suits, dossiers, and an unspoken reverence for hierarchy.

Then came a tremor.

"…taken by one of our human resources in Rise," said a field officer from the Istanbul liaison desk, scrolling through projected slides. "This one caught our eye—taken two weeks ago."

A grainy image flashed onto the screen. Five men in long coats moving along a market road. One in particular—a towering, heavy-set figure whose presence seemed to bend the space around him.

The field officer said. "Adam Umar. Confirmed. Walking six paces behind Ramzi al-Wahishi. No attempt to obscure identity."

The air changed.

A few murmurs.

Another slide. A closer shot of the group. Faces barely visible but postures telling. The kind of image Anissa had trained herself to read in a breath.

Raja said quietly, "Your human resource… are they embedded with Great Eastern Islamic Raiders' Front?"

The field officer looked at her cautiously and she guessed he was wondering how much to divulge.

"He is very low level. The Great Eastern Islamic Raiders' Front is primarily focused on Turkey and not France. However, we cultivated him for purposes of greasing the wheels of our relationship with the MiT."

He referred to Turkey's intelligence agency ***Millî İstihbarat Teşkilatı.***

Islamic extremism had long expanded from

their localities to become transnational, and with France possessing large immigrant Muslim populations from Algeria, Tunisia, and Morocco—fertile recruiting ground for radicals, and with groups like the GIA (Armed Islamic Group of Algeria), Al Qaeda, and Bosnian mujahideen veterans having at least a presence in both France and Turkey, a relationship had been formed—marred by a little suspicion on both sides, but a relationship nonetheless.

"Correct me if I am wrong, but during previous briefs, it's been stated that despite his high-position within Al Qaeda, Ramzi al-Wahishi usually travels with just a single bodyguard for the purposes of not drawing attention to himself," said Anissa.

"I believe that is correct."

"That there are several men with him, suggests there is an imminent and real threat on his life or the Islamic raiders were helping to train them. We know the lands in and around the tea fields have been used as holding areas for Al Qaeda missions."

"We are in the process of forwarding these to the Turks—somehow without compromising our source."

Anissa leant forward, voice precise.

"May I get copies of those photographs? I have a contact that may be able to identify the men without compromising the MiT or our relationship with them."

All heads imperceptibly turned, first to her and then in the direction of the commandant.

Anissa knew that the information she had provided over the years, in addition to some of the more hands-on operations she had conducted, had built substantial currency within the agency—substantial but not inexhaustible.

Commandant Chauvigny issued a nod and the field agent said, "Of course."

She walked the corridor alone afterwards, the photos folded into a leather case.

Outside, the Paris air was thick with noise and vehicle emissions.

Frank needed to see these.

Because what she hadn't said—couldn't say—was that she already knew what those men were training for. She knew *who* sold al-Wahishi the devices. She knew *where* the handoff took place.

She had sat in the meeting with the smoke of loyalty to Frank swirling around her.

Of course, she would tell her superiors, but not yet.

19

VIENNA — EARLY EVENING

The beer festival roared around them, a river of laughter, brass music, and the smell of grilled meat and sweet pastry clogging the cool Austrian air. Bruce had never seen anything quite like it—rows of benches under long white tents, the canvas ceilings bulging slightly with the noise, the air thick with cigarette smoke and the yeasty tang of freshly poured beer.

The waitresses, bustling between tables with arms full of sloshing steins, were dressed in the traditional Dirndl—tight-laced bodices that pushed generous cleavage upward, and full skirts that swayed with every quick step. Bruce wondered if large breasts had been a requirement for the job.

The men—old, young, clean-cut or scruffy—cheered them like returning war heroes every time they passed.

Bruce rubbed a hand over his upper lip, feeling the unfamiliar rasp of electric razor stubble. It felt oddly bald. Exposed.

Yuri elbowed him lightly in the ribs. "Even Freddie Mercury disappeared his moustache."

Bruce smiled, "Think he ditched it when he started singing with that opera bird."

Yuri threw his arms in the air and crowed, "Barcelona!"

The Scot admired how completely unbothered Yuri seemed by the glances.

Frank laughed, shaking his head. "Look at

him, Yuri. Looks bloody fourteen years old without it."

Bruce smirked and took a sip of his beer, but Yuri wasn't finished.

"Or maybe," Yuri said, nodding meaningfully towards a cluster of waitresses throwing glances their way, "it has made him more handsome."

Frank leant in. "Aye, it's no wonder they're looking—you're standing there six-two, built like a dark-haired Clint Eastwood in his Rawhide days. Meanwhile, Yuri and I here look like two Danny De Vitos."

"Speak for yourself, old man," said Yuri.

Bruce chuckled low in his throat. "I think you're exaggerating a tad."

Yuri snorted. "He is Sean Connery."

"Connery's from Edinburgh," Bruce said, shaking his head. "I'm Glasgow, there is a difference."

Yuri raised an eyebrow. "Explain this to me."

Bruce shrugged. "Glasgow's a real working city. Industrial, raw. Edinburgh's beautiful, aye, but it's more Anglified and… staged. Built to be admired. Glasgow's built to be lived in."

Yuri considered this like a man tasting wine for the first time. Then nodded approvingly.
"I like your city then."

Frank's hand shot to his hip, where the bulky Nokia mobile buzzed through his jacket pocket—a low, insistent vibration that he'd somehow gotten used to feeling without needing the ring tone.

"Excuse me, lads," he muttered, already stepping away into the noise.

Bruce watched him disappear between a

crowd of laughing men in lederhosen.

Yuri looked around and said almost to himself, "This is what I want for Ukraine."

Bruce frowned. "They don't have parties in Ukraine?"

"It is different. The Soviet-style festivals are more… official. Kupala Night and other such festivals are more in the country. In cities like Lviv or Kyiv, events like these are more underground. More for artists and students or powerful types," said Yuri, almost forlornly. "Besides, we drink mainly vodka."

"How likely to you think you'll see something like this in Ukraine?"

"Maybe not for a long time. Russia will stand again and will always see us as the younger brother. They can always interfere in Ukraine politics because they control gas. Remember how Freddie Mercury and Elton John married ladies despite liking men. What is that type of marriage?"

"A marriage of convenience?"

"Yes, yes, a marriage of convenience. That is what Ukraine and Russia have. The real trouble will come when Ukraine gives divorce papers."

"I like the analogy," said Bruce.

"Analogy?" asked Yuri.

"Aye. An analogy is when you explain one thing by comparing it to another—something more familiar," said Bruce before looking around and lowering his voice. "Like saying 'Finding a suitcase nuke in Europe is like finding a needle in a haystack'."

Yuri chuckled, "Thank you. I understand now."

Bruce saw Frank carve back through the throng before clapping him on the shoulder, "Get the beers in, **duty essence**."

"Duty essence?"

"It just means physically attractive."

Bruce decided not to point out that the waitresses would come around and serve them, instead said, "Same again?"

Yuri and Frank nodded, and Bruce pushed through the crowd towards the nearest bar station, sidestepping a group of drunken students singing what sounded like a German version of *'Country Roads'*.

The thought occurred to him how inappropriate it could be seen, their sitting in an Austrian beer festival with a rogue nuke on the loose.

He dismissed the thought. Maybe engaging in activities such as this not only provided a restoration in the face of the grind of such a high operational cadence but also reminded one what they were battling for.

When he returned balancing three enormous steins, Frank and Yuri were deep in the middle of a heated discussion, faces flushed more from passion than drink.

"I'm telling you," Frank was saying, stabbing a finger in the air, "the bloody Bundesliga isn't the second-best league. It's Bayern and then everyone else playing for second place. Even the Scottish League has two teams in contention, eh, Bruce."

Yuri held up a hand in protest. "Bayern is strong, but the Bundesliga has also Kaiserslautern! Dortmund! Very strong teams."

Bruce set the beers down with a heavy thunk.

Frank pointed at Yuri with mock outrage. "Yuri here might be the only man alive who can talk more shite than me when he gets going."

Yuri laughed, raising his stein in salute.

Bruce asked, "What's the best league then? You agree about that?"

"Yes," Yuri said, "Serie A is the best. No argument."

Frank nodded. "Stacked. AC Milan, Inter, Juventus."

He scowled slightly. "And I'll admit La Liga might be in second place. But Bundesliga over the Premier League? No. Can't do it."

Yuri shrugged, raising his beer to his lips.

"We shall see. This year's Champions League will settle it."

Bruce leant back, feeling the heat of the crowd, the music washing over them like a warm tide.

It dawned on him that his earlier suspicions regarding Frank's intentions towards him had faded; partially out of practicality—if Frank had wanted to drop him in it then it couldn't have been planned for a specific moment as the situation was constantly evolving.

For a moment, Bruce let himself enjoy the atmosphere—the ridiculousness, the noise, the camaraderie.

The world might be teetering towards chaos just beyond the festival tents, but for now, in this moment, they were just three men, drinking beer under the Austrian sky.

Frank said to him, "Take it steady ish. We have a meeting tomorrow morning."

ISTANBUL — BEYOĞLU DISTRICT — NIGHT

The hotel room smelled of old cigarettes and lemon-scented disinfectant. Zubayr al-Adel sat cross-legged on the parquet floor, his back against a chipped radiator that pulsed with unreliable heat.

The wallpaper, once white, was now the colour of damp parchment. Outside, the sounds of Istanbul hummed—horns, distant shouts, the cough of a diesel engine struggling uphill.

The suitcase—*the* suitcase—hid beneath the low bed behind him, components now wrapped in lead foil.

The maps, transit schedules, diplomatic schedules, flight manifests, and smuggling corridor reports spread around him in an ordered semi-circle. He had spent two days compiling this intelligence from old CIA-accessed data caches and some old contacts.

On being selected for Operation BACKLASH, Zubayr had been encouraged to cultivate his own contacts, false identities and he had been given two hundred thousand US dollars to deposit into drop boxes across Europe and the Middle East only known to him.

Fortunately, he had deposited thirty thousand US dollars and forged diplomatic courier documents in the Anadolu Birlik Bankası (Anatolian Unity Bank) that he picked up not long after crossing the border.

Zubayr pinched the bridge of his nose. His temples throbbed.

Twenty-one border checkpoints between here and Madrid, he thought in Arabic. He couldn't remember the exact time, but he now thought and dreamt more in Arabic than in his native American.

His eyes darted across a transit map of Southeastern Europe. *Fourteen of them with high-risk scans. Seven with NATO presence. Three with U.S. liaison agents.*

He traced the inked line he'd drawn earlier in the day—a jagged black route from Istanbul to Madrid, snaking like a surgical incision through unstable terrain: Bulgaria, Serbia, Croatia, Italy, France, Spain. It was the kind of route one planned for narcotics, not fissile material.

Too exposed. Too long. Too dirty.

But it was the only one.

He reached for a dossier beside him—a folded folder with taped edges. Inside: falsified papers. His new name: Omar Al-Fayez—a Jordanian engineer. Although the passport was obtained at his own initiative, the accompanying O-1 visa had been issued by Operation BACKLASH. He had just filled in the requisite name and details.

Not an identity Interpol would know.

Yet.

Zubayr exhaled through his nose and looked at the digital watch he wore on the inside of his wrist beneath his sleeve. 02:44.

He stood and walked to the window, parting the blinds just enough to scan the street below. No tail. No car sitting longer than ten minutes.

Still, his nerves were sharp as broken glass. He wasn't paranoid. Not in his line of work.

He was hunted now. By his own agency. Maybe by the Russians, too.

He turned back to the map and began marking the route with a red pen. Red for roads. Blue for waters. Green for cover.

Checkpoint alternatives. Vehicle switches. Safe houses. Neutral zones. Soft corridors.

He made notes in his own ciphered shorthand that only he could read.

He stared at the suitcase. The weapon inside wasn't just a bomb. It was a purpose. A lever to move the world. He never *actually* worked for Ramzi al-Wahishi—but that didn't mean he couldn't use him.

He folded the map carefully. Checked each exit strategy. Burned two old ID cards in the sink.

Somewhere between fear and clarity, he smiled.

Tomorrow, the road began.

HOTEL SACHER — VIENNA — MORNING

Bruce McQuillan woke to a pale shaft of Viennese sunlight slanting through the edges of the blackout curtains. The warmth on his face pulled him gently from sleep. He blinked, ran a palm across the stubble on his jaw, and slowly sat up, rolling his shoulders. The first thing he noticed—his hangover was barely a whisper.

He credited it to the litre and a half of water he'd downed before bed—his father's old parting advice from a thousand pub nights—and the fact Austrian and German beers weren't stuffed full of the chemical piss that passed for lager in Britain.

Swinging his legs off the bed, he sat for a moment and stretched. It came back to him: the laughter, the beer steins, the smoke curling into the air, Yuri's bad jokes and Frank's worse impressions.

And the women.

Frank and Yuri had each left with one—Bruce hadn't needed to ask. He'd seen it in the way they walked away, the half-grin of triumph from Frank and the offhand shrug from Yuri like he was collecting a debt.

Bruce had easily drawn the most attention that night—there had been no shortage of flirtatious eyes and incidental touches—but the idea of a one-night stand with someone whose name he'd forget by noon held no pull for him.

He wasn't some celibate monk or 'save yourself for marriage' puritan, but he felt a hollowness in encounters like that—an absence of meaning he could never quite ignore.

He pulled on his shirt and blazer, combed fingers through his hair, and checked the watch on his wrist. Seven minutes early. Good, he'd settle in the ambience before the others got there.

He took the glass off the door handle—a trick that might afford him a precious second or two, should someone attempt to creep into his room.

Downstairs in the hotel's breakfast room, the clink of cutlery and low murmur of German and English filled the refined silence. Bruce scanned the room. His gaze stopped when he saw her.

Anissa Rajah was seated near the far windows, her posture a sculpture of effortless control, one gloved hand resting on the handle of a delicate espresso cup.

She wore a black turtleneck under a fitted blazer, her dark hair drawn back but not tightly—just enough to reveal the sharp angles of her face. Her eyes met his before he could pretend not to stare.

"Bruce," she exclaimed, standing as he approached. She reached for his shoulders and kissed him on the cheek before playfully squinting. "What's different about you?"

"The pros to balding my lip outweighed the cons."

"You are still handsome." She smiled. "And thank you for being early."

He smiled back. "I was thirsty. Figured the coffee here would taste better than the instant upstairs."

She gestured for him to sit. "Frank is usually early for meetings too."

Bruce eased into the seat opposite her. "Frank might've got a little less sleep than me last night," he said dryly.

Anissa raised an eyebrow, something between amusement and faint disapproval on her lips. "And you? Left untouched despite your apparent charms?"

Bruce shrugged. "Strangers and one-night stands don't do much for me."

She gave him a look, and with a faint smirk said, "You're an unusually principled man for someone so inconveniently handsome."

Bruce laughed under his breath. "I am not sure about the principled part—not in this line of work."

Before she responded, the rhythmic thud of footsteps on carpeted stairs drew their attention.

Frank Carlsmith descended, shirt slightly untucked, hair combed only by the wind, followed by Yuri Kozlov, whose tailored jacket hung crookedly off one shoulder. Trailing behind them, two women—one brunette in a faux-leather jacket and boot—cut jeans, the other blonde, all in black with sleep still clinging to her eyes—offered short goodbyes before disappearing into the lobby.

Frank approached with a posture that seemed to teeter between sheepish and proud. "Morning, love," he said to Anissa.

Anissa replied, her tone cool but not unfriendly. "Though I see you've made friends. Again."

"Jealous?"

"Always, Frank, you know that."

Frank turned to Yuri. "This is Yuri—a friend of ours"

Bruce surmised either Anissa was familiar with the recently released film *Donnie Brasco*, or that Frank had briefed her on the phrase because she did not probe further.

Yuri offered a brief nod. "Ma'am."

"Anissa, please," she replied.

They ordered coffee, and as it arrived, Anissa's tone shifted. She set her bag on the table and drew out a slim leather folder, placing it down with deliberate care.

"I attended a meeting yesterday. A slide was presented… Something caught my eye."

She slid the folder open. Three grainy photographs were laid out.

Bruce leant forward, Yuri's eyes narrowing.

"Taken in Istanbul. Ramzi al-Wahishi, flanked by unknown men. This one here," she tapped a looming figure, "is Adam Umar. Confirmed. No attempt to disguise himself. The presence of others implies either training or a high-stakes mission in progress."

Bruce caught the subtle change in Frank's expression—the brief, arrested stillness. His jaw tensed, and he blinked once, slowly.

Bruce had not seen him like this.

Frank tapped the grainy photograph.

"I recognise him," he said, voice steady but low.

"Adam Umar?" she asked.

"No, this one," said Frank, pointing to a tall, wiry figure.

He sat back, fingers steepled in front of his mouth. He exhaled hard.

"He's CIA."

MAYFAIR — SECURE PRIVATE CLUB — LATE EVENING

The fire in the hearth flickered as if uncertain it should be burning at all. Books that no one would read lined the walls.

Miles Parker recognised the décor as homage to old Britain—walnut panelling, military portraits, the whiff of smoke-soaked leather.

Sir Andrew Maremount hadn't spoken since they'd entered, and that in itself was enough to keep Parker aware. The SIS chief had merely offered him a nod at the entrance, led him into the club through a back entrance, and now they were waiting.

Parker glanced at the whisky barrel wall clock. It was approaching midnight.

Maremount finally turned to him, voice hushed but clipped. "What you are about to hear never officially occurred. Not to the Cabinet Office. Not to Thames House. Not even to the Americans' own Oversight Committee. Understood?"

Parker nodded. "Yes, sir."

A tall man—though a few inches off Parker's height—entered through the side door. American. Mid fifties, still lean but with a build that suggested he once knew hardship. His mostly silver hair was swept back, and his stone face had deep lines carved in it. His eyes, pale and unreadable, flicked to Maremount and then rested on Parker.

"This is Deputy Director for Operations Harold R. Kellerman," said Maremount.

Parker recognised Kellerman as heading the clandestine service, responsible for HUMINT (human intelligence) and covert action globally.

Though Langley's Director, Deputy Director and even Associate Deputy Director of the CIA stood higher in the chain of command, Kellerman remained directly responsible for the edges of the ***Agency***'s blade.

"Call me Harry," the American said, offering Parker a firm grip. His accent was East Coast, possibly old Boston—tinged with the crispness of someone who'd long ago stopped trying to sound local anywhere.

"We're meeting like this," Kellerman began, settling into one of the leather chairs, "because something's happened. Or rather, something has already been put in motion. And because your man saw a face in a DGSE photo that he should never have recognised."

Parker leant forward slightly. "Then you've confirmed the man in the photo was—or is—CIA?"

"Embarrassingly, he may now be former CIA—the wider agency at least," Kellerman said grimly. "He is one of the more highly competent agents we have—or had."

Parker said, "He's gone dark?

"I do not believe in holding back when asking allies for help, so this version won't be as sanitised as it should be," Kellerman said, his chest noticeably rising. "This asset was trained and ran by a Colin Everhart. That name mean anything to you?"

"I've heard the name and rumours—nothing to substantiate them," said Maremount.

"Everman was born in 1929 in rural Kentucky. Joins the army at eighteen. Recruited into the fledgling CIA in 1951, after an exemplary performance in post-war Europe as an army intelligence officer. Multilingual and methodical, Everhart was deployed across Berlin, Tehran, Saigon, and Santiago through the most volatile decades of the Cold War."

"Sounds like he should be running Langley by now," said Maremount.

Kellerman sniffed, "Believe me, had The Old Man—as some of us call him—wanted my job, I would have voluntarily stepped aside."

"Then why don't we know his name on our side of the pond?"

Kellerman said, "Unlike many flamboyant field officers of the era, Everhart rarely left a trace. His operations shaped coups, sabotaged Soviet supply lines, and turned multiple KGB officers into double agents—all without his name appearing in a single internal memo. By the late 1970s, he had become a myth within Langley and a nightmare in Moscow's Lubyanka. As a result, Everhart was given a small unit and a black budget. Operation BACKLASH was meant to fight fire with fire. Disrupt Soviet operations, sabotage assets, seed dissent inside Warsaw Pact states, all off the books. He was damn good. His autonomy grew with each success. So did his budget. And over time, his leash vanished."

Parker raised an eyebrow. "No oversight?"

"Success has a way of buying you silence," Kellerman said. "And then the wall fell. The Bear stumbled. Most of us were celebrating. Everhart furiously pushed to go harder, stating this was our moment to kill the wounded animal. Said it would rise again. He had a bit of the Walter E. Kurtz about him. Most of us assumed he was acting out due to his sense of purpose being diminished."

Parker nodded grimly. "And then?"

"He threatens to resign to go private. Neither the Director nor the Deputy Director wants to lose such a valuable resource—who is still sharp as a tack—and instead widens his area of operations and increases his unit's budget a little. This seems to placate him—and remember, he's both a ghost and legend at Langley. I didn't even know for sure he existed until I took over operations."

"And here comes the plot twist," stated Maremount.

Kellerman nodded. "We only realised how far off-script he'd gone when we traced intel that connected a rogue asset to a suitcase nuke. And I mean the real thing—Soviet era. Compact, operational, unsanctioned."

"Everhart made a play for it?" asked Parker.

"That's correct. At first, we assumed that Everhart was simply trying to procure the weapon, but because it hadn't reached my ears, we pulled him in. Soon it was obvious by his evasiveness that that might not be his intention. His answers increasingly turned into rhetoric. Then I was forced to hold him before receiving the clearance to interrogate him. We were making progress—establishing that Everhart thought that if the bomb was to go off in the 'correct' place and circumstances, then the incident could be leveraged to take control of the former soviet bloc countries under the pretext of securing black market nuclear devices. He swallowed a cyanide cap hidden in a tooth before we could get the specific target."

After a moment of quiet, Parker asked, "Who was the man in the photograph that our agent recognised?"

"His real name is Elias Monroe. Highly trained and professional. Born in Arlington to an American mother and a Jordanian father who was a defected Ba'athist sympathiser turned informant. Orphaned at twelve. Raised under the CIA's Phoenix Foster Program, designed to cultivate deep-cover assets from mixed-nationality orphans. Colin Everhart got hold of Monroe not long after that. We are still trying to piece together much of what happens after but what isn't disputed is that he's integrated and apparently for a long time a highly thought of Jihadist fighter under the alias of Zubayr al-Adel. If Everhart was the architect, Zubayr—Monroe—is the executioner."

Parker said, "So he's the agent attempting to take possession of the device?"

Kellerman afforded him a brief shake of the head. "We think the handoff has already happened. Monroe is mobile. The device is live. We don't know where or when."

"Jesus Christ," exhaled Maremount. "So why tell us and not everyone else?"

"Because your people are already circling the periphery. The photographs from Istanbul confirm that. And because we cannot—*cannot*—inform the rest of the Five Eyes, not even GCHQ. The political fallout of admitting the CIA birthed a rogue element attempting to stage a nuclear false flag on European soil would tear the alliance apart. We need to take the device into our custody."

Parker considered this, his fingers laced together. "If we get the chance, will it not be prudent to have the device dismantled on site?"

Kellerman's smile thinned again. "If we find it, we'd prefer to recover it."

Parker refrained from asking why, hoping that Maremount would—he didn't.

Instead, the chief said, "If we help you, we want access to anything reasonably within your power to grant. I will also need a signed letter from you that my assets are to receive full immunity in their secondment to an agency mission."

"Agreed," Kellerman said. "And secrecy. If this goes public, it's not just the agency on the chopping block."

"Do not threaten me, Harry," bristled Maremount.

"Just stating, Andrew."

A moment of tension then Maremount rose. "Then it's done."

20

OUTSKIRTS OF SOFIA — BULGARIA — EVENING

The light began to die alongside Dmitri Chernov's patience.

He crouched beside the corroded frame of a chain-link fence behind an abandoned textile factory. Cigarette ends and bottle caps scattered the frozen ground along with a stiff-legged dog carcass he'd noticed an hour ago and tried to forget.

The stink of rusted iron and burnt diesel clung to the back of his throat.

Through a narrow break in the broken wall ahead, he could just see the rear lot of the *Motel Rila*. Eight rooms. Decayed signage.

A parking area lined with half-dead hedges and one grey Opel that hadn't moved all day. Zubayr had checked into Room 8 at 14:23.

A shoulder bag slung low on one side and a case held on the other.

Dmitri didn't blink when the call came through that morning. A tip from a source near Kapitan Andreevo—a lone Arab man with diplomatic courier papers and a face that half-matched the ghost he'd been ordered to keep a look out for.

The description went to Moscow, bounced all the way up to Major Andrei Sokolova, and a nine-word message came back to Dmitri.

"Confirm and track. Do not engage. Report when ready."

So Dmitri had tracked. Through bus depots, a tram transfer in Plovdiv, and a rented Lada that coughed smoke all the way to Sofia's outskirts. Zubayr moved like a cautious man—but not like one who knew he was being followed. And Dmitri was good. Better than most. He rotated angles, changed posture, and used shop windows instead of staring.

Now, the shadows had lengthened, and the motel remained quiet. No lights in the window. No silhouette behind the curtain. Dmitri's legs ached from crouching, but he didn't move. He watched.

And then—nothing.

The smell of motor oil and haze-thickened air. A silence that deepened.

Until the knife kissed his throat.

It pressed just below the hinge of his jaw—A killer's blade.

Dmitri's body froze. He tried to tilt his eyes without moving his head. He saw nothing. The man had come from nowhere.

A voice followed. Soft. Unhurried. The Russian was good. Not native, but precise.

"You should make your breath quieter—I can hear your fear on it."

Dmitri did not know what words to say, so remained still in an awkward huddle as the Grim Reaper loomed over them.

Zubayr broke the quiet with, "What were your orders?"

The blade didn't press harder, and it didn't have to.

"To track you," Dmitri managed, throat working. "Then report in when you went stationary."

"Have you?"

A pause before the blade's edge crept into his neck and he spluttered, "Yes."

"How long do I have? And do not lie for time—I will know."

Something about the stillness in his voice made Dmitri's blood ice-cold. He believed the man. He didn't want to die here. Not in Bulgaria. Not for a report that would be buried under six layers of red tape and deniability.

"I first called in this morning. They cannot be using any of the Bulgarian intelligence or services or else they would have been here by now," he said truthfully. "I would think the closest rendition teams will be stationed in Belarus or Crimea. If they were rolled out this morning, they could be very close."

Then the knife vanished like it had never been there.

Zubayr stepped around him, coat loose, and a smudge of road grime beneath his jaw. His eyes were dark. Not angry. Not cold. Just... *settled*.

Dmitri didn't move. Every instinct screamed to run, but his legs wouldn't dare.

Zubayr leant down, voice low. "You have to make a decision, Dmitri."

"What?"

"Are you more scared of what they might potentially do in the future?" said the Arab phantom.

"Or what I will definitely do to you now if you don't do everything I tell you."

OUTSKIRTS OF TIRANA — ALBANIA — RAMZI'S COMPOUND — NIGHT

The moon hung low behind the gaunt branches of the olive trees, casting fractured shadows across the tiled courtyard. The compound was quiet, cloaked in the hush of midnight vigilance.

On the far side stood the accommodation blocks holding over thirty men recruited from the post-Bosnia Islamic brigades, here for further training and loyal to Umar, and therefore himself.

Ramzi al-Wahishi sat cross-legged on a faded Persian carpet beneath a single brass lamp. The Quran lay open before him, though his eyes were not on the text.

They were on the smoke.

It curled upward from the half-burned clove cigarette in the brass tray beside him, forming shapes that moved and vanished, like men he had once trusted.

The air in the room was heavy—not from heat but from waiting.

Then the door burst open.

Adam Umar entered like a storm through the stone threshold, boots crunching over tile, one hand curled tight around a satellite phone.

His eyes burned. "It is him."

Ramzi rose and extended his hand. The phone, warm from Adam's grip, felt lighter than it should have—buoyed by hope.

He answered with no greeting. "It has been a long silence."

A pause. Then a voice crackled through, low and measured.

"The weather in Sofia is warmer than I expected."

Ramzi smiled faintly. Code confirmed.

"Then you must dress appropriately."

"I am… not many layers. But Moscow's eyes are on me—and soon the hands will be."

"How soon?"

"Storm might arrive tonight if I stay here. Maybe tomorrow. I did not want to call you. Not after… the kitchen fire. But I must now."

There was no plea in Zubayr's voice. Only necessity.

"Do you still have the cake?"

"Yes, it is with me."

"What are you calling me from?"

"A payphone I am bleeding money."

"Can you blind the eyes on you?"

"Yes."

Ramzi had to decide—it was highly unlikely the call was being monitored from either end.

"Prepare to receive coordinates."

"Ready."

"Latitude four-two point seven-four-three-six north, longitude two-three point one-zero-five-nine east. A wooded area near the Lozenska mountain foothills. Small heliport. Your brothers will get there in one hundred and twenty minutes," said Ramzi. "Will they have to wait? If so, how long?"

"No," said Zubayr. "I should arrive before them. I will wait by the heliport and reveal myself with my hands raised."

Ramzi said, "*Yusturuhā Rabbunā.*"—May God protect us.

The reply came back through, "*Lā ḥawla wa lā quwwata illā bi-llāh.*"—There is no power except with God.

The line went dead.

Ramzi exhaled and turned to Adam, who remained still.

"Mobilise your men," Ramzi said. "Take as many as the helicopter will allow. Those who have seen real fire. Be in the air within thirty minutes."

Adam's eyes narrowed, already calculating.

"Sofia?" he asked.

Ramzi nodded. "He is being hunted by the Russian dogs. Has eyes on him. He is unsure he can lose them, but wherever he goes, they will follow. Understand?"

"Of course, you are a genius to have us prepared for this **Qā'id**," said Adam, using the word for 'Commander'.

Adam stepped into motion, pulling on his coat, already barking instructions in Arabic to two fighters waiting beyond the hall.

They were less than fifteen minutes from the private airfield in Vlorë, built under the pretence of agricultural supply logistics. In truth, it had hosted more men and munitions in silence than any runway in the Balkans.

The local militia and intelligence assets were thankfully not always mutually exclusive, hence the money's ability to buy them access to a Mil Mi-17 transport helicopter currently logged as undergoing maintenance, and it's former **Forcat Ajrore Popullore**—Albanian Air Force—pilot.

The Mi-17 had a maximum range of between 450-500 kilometres and the flight over would be 350 kilometres. However, Ramzi's superior—Khalid Sheikh Mohammed—two years ago had leveraged the cooperation of a paramilitary group in the Skopje Region of North Macedonia with ex-Yugoslav hardware. Ramzi had already reached out to ensure they knew that a discreet refuel might happen in the coming weeks.

Ramzi would call them now.

The Mi-17 could also fit over twenty armed men.

He turned back to the lamp and closed the Quran.

He whispered, imbued with a sense of overwhelming gratitude, "**Al-ḥamdu li-llāh.**"—Praise be to God.

NEAR MINSK, BELARUS — MILITARY INSTALLATION HANGAR — LATE EVENING

The wind screamed against the hangar's corrugated metal shell like a beast caged too long. Inside, the noise was dulled to a low moan, but Yuri Kozlov felt it crawl along his spine all the same. He adjusted the strap on his chest rig, the nylon stiff from the hangar's artificial cold, and watched as vapour drifted from the mouths of his teammates—each of them suited, booted, and visibly coiled. They'd been on standby for hours, their gear lined up with parade-ground precision, eyes darting between the helicopter outside and the door through which their orders would arrive.

He had raced to get here. When the call came through, it wasn't a recall—it was a *pick-up order*. The helicopter had touched down in Slovakia, expecting him to already be there. He wasn't. He was on his way back from Austria.

One hour and twenty-seven minutes later, after burning every backroad between the Styrian highlands and the Slovak border, he'd vaulted into the bird with gear half-zipped and heart still pounding.

Now, standing once again beside Vladik and the rest of the team, he felt the edge creeping in. Not nerves. Never that. Just that *itch* in the back of the skull.

The door opened.

Major Andrei Sokolova entered like a glacier. He was dressed in that same unassuming civilian wear: a pea coat over a dark cardigan, slacks that looked almost civilian until you noticed the knife line creases. Steel blue eyes beneath greying brows.

Sokolova began without preamble. "We have intel on the possible location of the final RA-115S."

A murmur rustled through the men.

"It is at a small private airstrip near the foothills of Lozenska Mountain—southwest of Sofia. Our asset has confirmed Zubayr al-Adel in Sofia and is conducting a stand-off surveillance of him in real time now. Assume hostiles on site."

He paced once. Not for drama—Sokolova never wasted motion.

"You are to infiltrate. Secure the package. Any resistance is to be neutralised. All loss of life is acceptable. The success of the mission is *not* optional. Is that understood?"

Yuri felt the stillness in the air sharpen. There were no questions. Only nods.

"Dismissed. Wheels up in six minutes."

The team broke off, each man moving with the crispness of drilled instinct. Yuri's boots echoed off the concrete as he walked towards the chopper, the warmer air billowing under the hangar's partially open doors.

He reached beneath his gear for the secure satphone—a military-issue Motorola scrambler unit linked to a narrow-band satellite relay. With practiced fingers, he keyed in a string of prearranged digits on the hardened keypad. The signal was weak, the window brief—no more than a minute's handshake with the relay—but it was enough. There was no reply, and he didn't expect one.

Frank would understand.

The chopper's rotors were already spinning, the tail rotor humming like a devil's whisper. Yuri ducked low, following Vladik into the belly of the Mi-8. Once aboard, he settled into his usual seat, checked his rifle, then checked his mind.

Fucking rushed taskings, he thought, as the world outside blurred.

Rushed taskings meant missing pieces, sloppy plans and shouldering the blame for any failure as the narrative got rewritten by those more senior.

The least of his worries, he knew. Sokolova was correct—this was a nightmare come true.

A cold war relic, ticking towards a modern catastrophe.

He gripped the sling of his rifle as the chopper banked southeast.

Whatever waited near Lozenska would be destroyed without mercy.

21

CIA SUBSTATION — NEAR SKOPJE — NORTH MACEDONIA — LATE EVENING

Bruce looked at the text shown on the screen of the Nokia 2110 held by Frank's fingers.

No name. No frills. Just six characters, a time stamp, and a single asterisk at the end.

The two Brits stood beside the battered water boiler in the corner of the CIA's makeshift substation—a forgotten villa wrapped in fencing and half-swallowed by trees on the southern outskirts of Skopje.

The wind rattled the windowpanes.

Frank's cigarette hissed into the sink as he crossed the room towards the map on the wall—a satellite print pinned and curling at the edges. His finger landed just east of Sofia.

"The foothills. Lozenska Mountains."

"An old rural airstrip," said Bruce.

"Fuck me, you're smart you are," said Frank without sarcasm. "Probably is, isn't it."

"An infiltration or extraction," said Bruce. "Stands to reason whoever is helping him, is armed."

"Let's get our skates on," Frank muttered. "Grab what you need to *go kinetic*."

Bruce crossed into the narrow backroom—a supply space converted into an armoury, if you squinted and ignored the leaky radiator and exposed beams. The gear sat ready, like a Belgian Mal dying to be tasked.

He could hear Frank on the intercom alerting the pilot.

Already dressed in black fatigue trousers over thermal base layers, covered by the black assault jacket, Bruce's sidearm—a suppressed M1911A1 complete with a beaver grip and Novak sights—differed from the Browning Hi-Power and SIG Sauer P226 more typically used by the Regiment, but it had favour within *the Unit*—more commonly known as Delta Force—hence it being offered upon arrival.

Bruce had fired the M1911A1 extensively as part of his joining the Wing, as he knew Frank must have.

Ferocious and reliable, it went into a worn leather shoulder rig under the jacket.

Beside it, a Ka-Bar knife in a custom sheath.

The HK MP5SD waited in its foam-lined case; integrally suppressed, ideal for what this might be. Loaded, safety on, sling ready.

Frank, chest rig over a faded jacket, had the same sidearm but strapped on his thigh, and a Colt Car-15 with a Knight's Armament Company (KAC) QD suppressor.

Both men had their respective multi-tools on their belts; a Leatherman Super Tool for Frank, while Bruce had opted for a Gerber MP600.

Boots thumped across cold tiles. Every movement economical. No words wasted.

Outside, the King Air B200 sat in the open field they called an 'airstrip'—twin engines shrouded in frost, propellers tethered beneath canvas like sleeping vultures.

The pilot was already jogging towards the fuselage, zipping up his parka.

Though Frank would brief him on the possible hostile reception, the total lack of hesitancy spoke volumes.

Bruce climbed aboard, checking horizon visibility and weather conditions.

As the turbines spun up and the aircraft started its warmup sequence, Bruce looked at Frank, who was strapping in across from him.

The Scot controlled and lengthened his exhales.

Frank adjusted his shoulder rig and gave that dry, crooked grin.

The wheels lifted from the Balkan mud minutes later, the low hum of the twin-prop engines vibrating through the fuselage as they soared towards Bulgaria.

Both Bruce and Frank took out their respective rectangular plastic compacts and set about smearing their faces with the colours of green and brown with a little bit of black.

Once done, Bruce stared through the frosted window.

Somewhere below, a weapon that could erase a city block sat in a case.

NEAR LOZENSKA MOUNTAIN FOOTHILLS — ABANDONED AIRSTRIP — NIGHT

They approached from the south, through the treeline—no lights, no chatter, no errors.

The Mi-8 had dropped them five klicks out, as per Yuri's insistence. Too close and the engine noise would warn anyone with ears. Too far, and they'd lose the advantage of timed arrival. This was just right—long enough to stalk, short enough to hit their schedule.

Now, crouched at the edge of the forest, Yuri Kozlov scanned the airstrip through his monocular.

The abandoned tarmac stretched ahead—black, cracked, flanked by skeletal trees and framed by a distant concrete bunker. The disused radio mast leant like a rusted pike.

He let the listening-stop run a couple of minutes, then whispered into the throat mic of the R-159 VHF radio, "Volk-Two, hold perimeter. Volk-One, on me. Sweep the east side."

Vladik and his half-team shifted left, hugging the natural contours of the terrain. Pavelchenko and Mikhailov ghosted towards the treeline ahead. No words—only gloved hand signals, eyes scanning, barrels low but ready.

They were expecting to find Zubayr al-Adel—the man possessing a nuclear ghost in a case.

They knew what he looked like.

Yuri moved with a surgical silence up the embankment. Every footfall kissed the frost. Suppressed AKS-74U tight to his chest, his breath plumed only briefly before being swallowed by the dark.

Then came the signal.

A short double-click over comms—

Pavlichenko.

Yuri advanced quickly but controlled, stepping into the natural dip beside a toppled tree. Pavlichenko stood rigid, rifle fixed downward. He nodded once.

Beside the base of a pine, slumped a figure.
Not moving. Not breathing.
Not Zubayr.
Yuri crouched.
Slit throat—clean, fast. Still warm. Eyes glassy and open. No abrasions on the knuckles. No blood or skin beneath the nails.

A professional murder.

He glanced towards Vladik, who had just joined them. "Sweep out. Hold at twenty metres. No movement unless we call it."

Vladik gave a curt nod and melted into the brush stitched with sun-bleached leaves.

The surrounding forest erupted in a furious alien roar of gunfire.

Yuri let loose an unnecessary battle-scream of, "Volk-One: Contact."

Muzzle flashes lit the woods behind them in a horrifying fireworks display.

"Volk-Two! Fall back to the fall-back point Echo. Now!"

The crackle of acknowledgements came instantly.

Yuri didn't hesitate.

He swung his rifle up, sighting the treeline. Two shadows dropped—clean, surgical takedowns.

But more moved behind them.

Whoever was here had let them get close on purpose.

He keyed the throat mic again. "Volk-One, disengage and withdraw. We are compromised. I say again—ambush in progress."

A flurry of rounds peppered the pine behind them. Bark exploded like shrapnel.

Vladik slid in beside him, breath controlled, firing as he moved. "East flank breached. Three shooters, maybe more."

"Smoke," Yuri ordered.

Pavelchenko tossed it—thick white plumes began to hiss between them and the tree line.

As the Spetsnaz team peeled back through the woods in staggered bursts, the black firs swallowed them once again.

Yuri didn't look back—he knew they were numerically outmatched.

However, he knew that the adrenaline of being prey—not the noradrenaline of a predator—pumped in his veins now.

"Man down!" came the scream from his left.

Yuri held his position, firing at the unseen creeping death.

Pavelchenko shouted, "Got him. Moving."

Spetsnaz protocol dictated that the two closest men to the casualty grip him to extract. They would pull him back in bounds, setting the casualty down to put down suppressive fire for the other members to extract.

They would not leave a comrade behind. Not that they could anyway for unsanctioned missions in foreign countries.

Still the firing did not slow.

Yuri needed the team out of the killing zone as soon as possible.

They could not afford another casualty.
When another scream of "Man down!" scorched through the acrid air, he steeled his throat against the black fingers of panic.

The forest pulsed with muzzle flashes—red-gold bursts blinking through the darkness like the eyes of ***Shayṭān***.

Adam Umar moved forward through the trees like a prowling hunter, his rifle firm to shoulder, feet exact between roots and frost-packed leaves. His fighters—men who had seen fire in Bosnia, Chechnya, and darker corners still—pressed forward in a loose wedge behind him, shifting like shadows in the wake of violence.

He'd let them get close. Closer than most would dare. Watched them through slats in the brush, cold eyes beneath head-wraps, fingers steady on triggers.

The Slavic cyborgs had moved well—disciplined, precise—but they were still flesh, and flesh bled.

Umar's firing had detonated the ambush.

However, the others firing—like a Mexican wave of death—had taken a few precious moments building to a crescendo which he knew saved the Russians from immediate annihilation.

No matter—he liked hunting them down and could smell them now. Blood. Gun oil. The char of powder on pine.

Umar's eyes swept the darkness, scanning ahead for movement. The red-lensed torches were gone now. The enemy was in retreat—tactical, controlled, yes—but retreat all the same.

Three to one, he reckoned—his men held the number and now the high ground.

They should have been wiped out in the first few seconds. *Should have.* But they weren't.

A part of his mind, detached from the task of killing, admired them. The way the Russians had peeled back—covering, dragging their wounded, slipping between trees like wolves.

They would have been used to being the hunters.

But even wolves bled.

Ahead, a Slavic scream pierced the din. Not Arabic. Not English.

But Umar understood it perfectly.

"Man down," he murmured in English, smiling without warmth. The syllables needed no translation. The same tone in any language.

He could see them now—silhouettes between the trees, hard shapes bending, lifting, staggering. One dragging another.

Soon.

The next round of fire would tear them down.

He raised his rifle, sighting a fleeting shape.

Then—

Crack.

The flank erupted in gunfire.

Sharp, sudden. Close. Too close.

One of his men screamed. Another fell with a thump that cracked branches. The line staggered. Fire returned blindly into the dark, but the damage was done—their flank had been turned.

Umar pivoted behind a tree, instincts anchoring him in place.

"Enemy—right side!" he snapped, switching

to Arabic.

His men responded fast—spreading, shouting, some firing too high in panic. Years of war hadn't dulled their reflexes, but this was different.

The prey was biting back.

He dropped to one knee, tracking fire towards the flank, chewing the inside of his cheek.

We cannot afford losses. Not here. Not tonight, he thought.

He scanned quickly. Already two of his fighters were down. A third was limping, blood on his thigh. A fourth shouted for cover.

If this dragged out much longer, Bulgarian security forces would be all over the area—there would be no explaining thirty Arab fighters with AKs and a downed Russian team.

Extraction had a time limit.

He raised his voice again, clipped and cold. "Consolidate the centre line!"

His words stood as law.

He sighted again into the dark—this time not to kill, but to measure.

Whoever these Russians were, they would not go easy.

But Adam Umar had not survived Sarajevo, Grozny, and half the Balkans by relying on ease.

He gritted his teeth, raised his rifle, and pressed forward.

Frank Carlsmith lowered the monocular and blinked the frost from his lashes.

He and Bruce had landed at another airfield, the other side of Sofia, where a CIA asset—a policeman of all things—had given the two men with faces of war paint carrying weapons and equipment, to the edge of the forest where they hiked in.

The policeman had not said a word from the time he picked them up to leaving them—simply followed Frank's directions.

Now knelt behind a large tree, he could see through the tangle of pine and the lattice of swirling smoke enough to mark the players.

But no Zubayr yet.

The Russians were moving—tight, disciplined, in pairs. He recognised the precise adherence to the most basic infantry tactic in combat—no movement without covering fire.

But they bled.

Opposite them, pressing through the woods in broken files, came the jihadis. Not a rabble. They moved with the hard-edged intent of men who had fought together before. Their discipline wasn't Western, but it was effective. Swift and a semblance of coordination.

Frank clicked his teeth and muttered, "This is going to be a fuckin' 'mare."

Beside him, Bruce McQuillan adjusted the suppressor on his MP5SD. The younger man was quiet, his jaw set.

The Englishman couldn't help but think of the film *Braveheart*, released a couple of years ago, when he looked at Bruce, except the *cam-cream* constituted the Scot's war paint instead of the blue of **woad**.

Frank knew he was observing a rare composure.

The dark-haired Glaswegian met his eye. One short nod.

They moved.

Skirting low along the edge of a drainage ditch, boots soft on the dry grass, they closed the flank. Frank raised his suppressed Car-15, peered through the low-light optics, and picked his target.

Three fighters broke through the treeline ahead—AKs held tight, scanning for targets. Frank exhaled, squeezed—two dropped. The third turned and caught Bruce's burst to the chest before he could even scream.

Then hell woke.

The flank exploded. Flash, fire, crackling bursts of return gunfire. The enemy pivoted immediately—fast reflexes, battle-hardened minds.

Bruce moved ahead, veering behind a frozen log pile, and fired a three-round burst that stitched a shadow just beyond.

Bruce lifted a rock— half the size of a football—and heaved it to the right, into deeper brush. A second later, he raked a long burst to the left.

Two jihadis turned and opened fire on the decoy, revealing their positions.

Frank fell one with a chest shot, then put the other down with a tight snap to the throat.

He knew then that the Scot possessed the rare combination of being both game *and* switched-on.

A few soldiers, even decent ones, could allow themselves to become tentative with fright when the firing began. However, more, even some highly trained shooters, could get carried away and tunnel-visioned during a firefight.

The best maintained a birds-eye view of the battle terrain amid their aggression.

He watched Bruce push forward again, zigzagging from tree to tree, using the terrain like a craftsman used tools.

Still, the jihadis pressed. Determined and experienced.

A pair crept along the frozen streambed to their right—flankers. Another popped smoke ahead to cover a push. Discipline. Nerve.

They dragged the fire towards them now.

Good. That was the whole point. Pull them off the Russians. Let Kozlov regroup and fuck off.

The smell of heated lubricant mingled with the tang of carbonised residue—like a machine sweating under duress.

Frank dropped to a knee and laid down suppression. "Left!" he barked.

Bruce was already shifting, already sighting.

Rounds cracked past them, one skipping off the bark a foot from Frank's head. He dropped one fighter mid-run—caught him just below the ribs. The man twitched, folded.

Then, it shifted.

The pressure eased.

The enemy began to pull back—first slow, then decisive. Controlled retreat.

Frank squinted.

They're withdrawing, he thought.

Bruce crouched beside him, watching the shadows move.

Frank frowned. They still had the numbers. Maybe not total dominance, but certainly enough to swamp two men.

He was not sure if he thought it before Bruce said it.

"They can't leave any dead bodies here—and can only carry so many back."

Yuri Kozlov felt the situation deteriorating by the second.

Another enemy scream—raw and wet—ripped through the forest, somewhere behind the smoke and hail of fire.

However, Mikhailov had been hit. That made two down from an eight-man team.

Too many.

He pressed his back against the bark of a pine and inhaled sharply, forcing the night air to steady his thoughts.

The sharp bite of burnt gunpowder clung to his nose and tongue like scorched brass.

The forest had grown quiet, and Yuri knew that the enemy had decided to conserve ammunition and increase the speed of the trap closure.

"Volk-One," he muttered into the mic, "continue withdrawal. Regroup at the fall-back point Echo-Four. Now."

Vladik slid into cover beside him, his breath harsh, rifle still smoking. "Negative. We hold. We are not leaving you."

Yuri's head snapped around, eyes fierce beneath his sweat-slathered brow. "Do not be a fool, Vladik."

"We do not leave anyone remember," Vladik growled.

"You stay and you will sentence the rest to death." Yuri's voice was low but taut with authority. "You cannot carry two casualties, hold a rear guard, and fight off a numerically superior force. Not in this terrain."

Vladik's jaw clenched. "Then we die here together."

The Ukrainian thought of the words of the Second World War's most effective commander, Field Marshal Zhukov, *'It takes a brave man to be a coward in the Red Army'*.

"No," said Yuri. He placed a firm hand on Vladik's shoulder. "If they find my body, they find a Ukrainian. There will be no political blowback. No diplomatic incident. Any other member of this team will humiliate the Motherland."

Vladik shook his head, breathing hard through flared nostrils.

"This was a trap. The atomic munition device is still out there. Take the wounded. Take the rest. That is an order."

Silence.

Finally, Vladik muttered, "You are a splinter in the arse, Kozlov."

Yuri smirked faintly, then held out his hand. Vladik unhooked two full magazines from his belt and passed them over, followed by a grenade.

Vladik hesitated for just a moment longer, then reached out, grasping Yuri's shoulder tightly.

"Do not let them take you alive, my friend."

"I will not."

Vladik gave a tight nod, then turned and faded into the tree line, taking with him the last of Volk-One.

Yuri exhaled, slow and deliberate. He crouched low, checked his rifle, and glanced skyward through the canopy. Moonlight sifted through the branches, oblivious to the violence that crackled below.

He set the grenade close to hand. He risked a magazine change.

He had no illusions. He wasn't going to hold the line forever. Just long enough.

A rustle. A crunch.

He levelled the rifle towards the sound.

Nothing.

Then—

A voice cut through the cold like a blade.

English.

"Ramblers—dozen-one."

Yuri froze.

That code. He hadn't heard it in over a year. Not since—

He stood slowly, rifle still up but eyes scanning.

"Ramblers—dozen-one," came the voice again, closer this time.

He squinted through the frost-laced darkness, and then he saw him.

Frank Carlsmith.

Wrapped in black fatigues, rifle at low-ready, face grim but unmistakably familiar.

Yuri let out a breath that fogged the air between them. "Where have you been? Legs tired in old age?"

Frank smirked. "I have not been keeping up with my yoga."

Yuri lowered his rifle, just slightly. "What happened? To the enemy?"

"Thinned out. Seems they couldn't leave bodies either."

"Thank you, my old friend. I should go.

Where is—"

Yuri flinched at the sound of Bruce McQuillan's voice, "You don't have to go. You're a ghost now."

The Ukrainian just caught the rising of Carlsmith's eyebrows before he turned to the tall Scot.

"They did cut short my vacation."

22

SOUTHERN BULGARIA — NIGHT

The old Renault 4L groaned as it crawled along the pitted backroad, light rain pattering in haloes around its weak headlamps. Elias Monroe sat behind the wheel, gloved hands relaxed, shoulders still high from the fading surge of adrenaline. The radio hissed detuned static.

The heater was broken. So he breathed through his nose, slow and shallow. It kept the windows from fogging.

Outside, the Balkan Mountains loomed like frozen gods, silent and unpitying.

And far behind him—somewhere in the dark—a battle unfolded.

He thought he heard it then: the dull, distant thump of gunfire, like hollow bones striking ice. But maybe it was his mind playing tricks, still riding the residue of the kill.

The execution had been clinical. The shadow—the Russian—had barely made a sound as Elias slit his throat behind the pine tree. A precise motion, neck to spine, like gutting a fish.

He could have just escaped, but Monroe wanted the Russians to question every piece of intelligence they might receive in the future in order to slow them down.

And instead of killing the Russian asset in situ back in the town, Monroe decided that a dead body in the woods after a firefight would deflect any investigation away from his movements.

The case holding the RA-115S lay behind the passenger seat like a sleeping leopard. He had imagined several times it spontaneously going off—before he surmised that he'd be just as dead if a grenade went off in his vicinity as if a one-kiloton atomic device did.

And he'd reconciled himself that he would be ending the lives of thousands of non-combatants in addition to his primary targets.

However, he knew that American-led democracy was the world's only hope to halt the cancerous spread of radical Islamic ideology and to prevent any resurgence of Russian authoritarianism.

Though raised under the CIA's Phoenix Foster Programme, designed to cultivate deep-cover assets from mixed-nationality orphans, his handlers were not the ones to introduce him to the word of God—not directly at least.

Around a dozen years ago, when he had been fifteen, he discovered an old Gideon Bible amongst the array of books at the safe house in Phoenix. With no phone, internet or television, he had read it cover to cover.

The moral clarity of it resonated with him—especially the Old Testament.

His local foster liaison, a disillusioned Vietnam vet turned born-again Christian, introduced him to the Church in earnest.

Those lives would be sacrificed to the greater good. Their loved ones would suffer, but Abraham was willing to sacrifice his son, Isaac, in obedience to God.

He hadn't lingered.

Indeed, Elias did respect Osama Bin Laden.

The Saudi could have had a life of luxury in the West. It just meant that his, and the West's, sacrifice had to be greater.

The route from there had been mapped days ago. East through the foothills, then south-west to Blagoevgrad, avoiding motorways, avoiding towns. He would switch plates at a safe house outside Dupnitsa, discard his coat, and change to a corduroy jacket and carry a torn satchel.

His passport, forged in Brussels, bore the ink of legitimacy. He would keep his accent neutral and demeanour forgettable.

Elias reached into the glove compartment and pulled out the satellite phone the size of a small brick that he had taken off the Russian he murdered. It took a moment to catch signal. When it did, he input the number from memory.

It rang.

And rang.

Then it clicked.

"Zubayr." Ramzi al-Adel's voice was low, gravelled, but calm. Always calm.

"Ramzi. Thank you for Tirana's preparation."

"The misdirection worked. The Russians are bleeding in the forest."

"Then it bought me what I needed."

There was a pause. A long breath on the other end.

"You are continuing the mission?" Ramzi asked finally.

"Yes."

"Then I believe the time is now to give you the target."

Elias's silence was deliberate.

Then: "I already have the target."

There was steel beneath the softness.

"One that will achieve our aim?"

Elias's voice turned flint. "One that will turn whispers into war cries. That will force the Crusaders to reveal their intentions. One that cannot be ignored."

On the other end, Ramzi was silent. Then came the crackle of him shifting, perhaps pacing, wherever he was holed up.

"You were taught obedience," he said at last. "Not prophecy."

"I was taught secrecy," Elias replied, "and that even a whisper can be fatal. *'If you want to keep something hidden, keep it from your own tongue.'*"

He heard the frustrated sigh.

"You've read too much **Ghazali**."

"I will inform you when I have arrived. Until then, I ask for trust."

Ramzi's voice was tight. "You presume much."

"Perhaps. But I ask plainly: can I still rely on you if I call?"

There was a pause. Tension suspended like a blade between them.

"Yes," Ramzi said at last. "Call, and we will be there. But if you fail—"

"I won't."

Elias set the phone down and turned onto a more minor road, headlights cutting through the dark like a scalpel. Behind him, the embers of a dying ambush glowed in the night.

Ahead, history waited to be written in fire.

CIA SUBSTATION — NEAR SKOPJE — NORTH MACEDONIA — NIGHT

The rotors of the King Air B200 spun up with a low, growing whine as the aircraft sat idling on the warm tarmac. Night insects buzzed in the tall grass beyond the runway, and the air held the lingering heat of the day. Frank Carlsmith paced back towards the hatch, boots thudding softly, while Bruce McQuillan walked behind Yuri Kozlov.

The Russian was pale, his lips tight against the exhaustion, but he hadn't asked for help—not once.

As Frank climbed inside, the pilot craned his head to look back from his cockpit.

"Who is he?"

"His name is Yuri. He's—"

"I can't take a fuckin' Russian," exclaimed the pilot. "He hasn't been cleared."

"He's Ukrainian," said Frank, closing the distance without blinking. "And I know him outside of this."

"Well I don't know him. It's a company safe house for Christ's sake," the pilot snapped, adjusting his headset. "I am not flying an unknown in."

Frank leant forward, elbows resting casually against the cockpit frame. "If this bird isn't in the air in the next minute, all three of us will get off and you can fly back. But I guarantee your career with the Agency will end as soon as the wheels touch back down."

The pilot turned slowly, stared at Frank for a moment and then turned back. The rotor noise filled the moment.

Finally, the pilot sighed. "Buckle him in. He

doesn't speak English, right?"

"He's Glaswegian," said Frank, deadpan. "He'll understand if you speak slowly."

"No, I meant—"

"I know what you meant, you numpty." Frank smiled. "And to answer your question, yes I will lie and say the Ukrainian can't speak English."

The pilot muttered, "You Brits ougtha know that being cowboys is an American thing."

He turned back to the controls.

NEAR MINSK — SPETSNAZ FORWARD FIELD BASE

The rotor blades of the Mi-8 hadn't even fully slowed when the medical team surged forward, their white jackets flaring against the rotor wash like startled birds. Warm night air kicked up dust and dry grass as the rear hatch banged open and Vladik jumped down first, followed by two operators dragging the stretchers.

"Critical—shrapnel and blood loss!" one of the medics barked as they knelt beside the first man, already pulling shears and syringes from pouches. Oleg wore a mask of pallor but was alive. Leonid, on the second stretcher, coughed wetly just before the oxygen mask clamped over his face.

"Vitals are holding," another medic confirmed. "We can stabilise them."

Vladik stood back, panting clouds into the air, his face carved from frost and fatigue. The frozen blood of others splattered his slung rifle. Beside him, the rest of Volk-One and Volk-Two looked half-carved from stone—smoke-blackened, eyes hollow, post-adrenaline shaking just beginning to ripple through their limbs.

A junior officer shouted from the blast shelter entrance, "Command wants you, *now*."

Vladik nodded once and followed the man, boots slapping through slush and floodlight beams as the others fell in behind him. The door to the command bunker yawned open, and heat slammed into them like a wall.

Major Andrei Sokolova stood waiting.

He stood alone at the head of the briefing table, a steaming mug untouched beside him, his pea coat draped over the back of a chair. His slate-coloured cardigan gave no softness to the way his arms were folded.

The door closed behind the team.

Sokolova didn't waste a second.

"Where is Yuri?"

The silence in the room turned taut. Vladik stepped forward.

"Sir. We walked into an ambush. Well-coordinated. Militant fighters—likely Arab. Three to one ratio at least. We suffered two casualties. Yuri ordered us to fall back while he held the rear. He… he stayed behind so we could extract."

Sokolova's expression did not change, but his jaw worked ever so slightly.

"Was it clean?" he asked.

"He was still alive when I left," Vladik replied. "But he made it clear he had no intention of being taken."

A slow breath. Not quite a sigh.

"And the contact?" Sokolova asked, eyes narrowing.

Vladik met his gaze squarely. "We found him dead, sir. Throat cut—ear to ear. Left in the woods at the designated location."

For a beat, the only sound was the soft humming of the overhead fluorescents.

Sokolova's knuckles whitened against his bicep.

"So, the nuclear device," he said, voice like ice cracking, "is still out there."

"Yes, sir."

"And we still have no confirmed identity for the target."

"No, sir."

Sokolova didn't shout. He didn't slam the table or demand retribution. But Vladik thought the temperature dropped ten degrees.

The SVR major picked up his mug, sipped once, then placed it back down with care.

"Understood," he said. "I will notify Moscow. You and your men did well, Sergeant Vladik. You did your duty. Now go clean your weapons, eat, and sleep. I want all of you in debrief at zero-five-hundred."

Vladik nodded, saluted, and turned to leave. But as he reached the door, he paused.

"Sir."

Sokolova looked up.

"Yuri said—if they found his body, they'd find a Ukrainian. No political blowback."

Sokolova's face twitched, just once. Then he said, with grim finality, "He was always practical. Unfortunately, the contact was Russian, despite what his documentation might say."

Vladik left thinking he might rather be Yuri

now than the major.

23

CIA SUBSTATION — NEAR SKOPJE — EARLY MORNING

Early morning near Skopje, the villa's windows were fogged with the night's humidity, beads of condensation catching the first light. The trees surrounding the property stood motionless, their leaves heavy with dew and dust. Frank, Bruce, and Yuri stepped inside through the back entrance, the cool air of the tiled floor lingering on their boots, the faint hum of a ceiling fan doing little to cut through the sweat clinging to their gear. They didn't have to wait long.

The CIA station officer—mid-forties, high-and-tight haircut, brown wool jumper over a sidearm—strode in from the corridor with a clipboard in hand and a scowl already loaded.

"You brought him here?" he barked, eyes bouncing between Frank and Bruce before settling on Yuri. "Jesus Christ. He's not cleared."

Frank took off his gloves, clapped his hands once, and replied, "Then take it up with Kellerman."

"That's not how this works."

"Course it is," Frank said, settling against the wall. "Our friend here has even more of an interest in finding this atomic device."

The station officer gripped his clipboard. "So why bring—"

Bruce stepped forward, and despite keeping his voice calm but clear, Frank saw the look of intimidation flash on the station officer's face.

"There is a nuclear weapon out there due to go off in at a time and place unknown to us. Now, if the Agency can't provide more personnel, then we need all the help we can get."

The officer's mouth opened, then shut.

A beat.

The station officer turned and stalked towards the corridor, muttering as he went. Once the door had swung shut behind the American, Frank exclaimed, "Fuck me, you must have given 'im the same stare Tyson gave Bruno last year."

"Being a six-foot-two Glaswegian comes in handy at times."

"Aye, I *ken*."

"Ken is an east coast of Scotland term, but I'll let it lie."

"Thank you," said Frank, before removing a cigarette packet and turning to Yuri. "Gasping for *tab*."

SOUTHERN SERBIA — NIGHT

The Serbian border slipped behind Elias Monroe like a dream dissolving in smoke.

He had crossed just before midnight, along a shepherd's pass used more by Eurasian wolves than men, the heat clinging to his back like a wet shroud. His hands throbbed inside the gloves, slick with sweat and dust, every joint swollen from the climb—but he didn't complain. The discomfort reminded him he was still alive.

Tradecraft was a discipline of details. One frayed thread and the whole tapestry collapsed. He changed plates twice between Blagoevgrad and Pirot.

Slept in safe houses whose keys hadn't changed since the Tito years. Travelled roads that once bore Russian tanks and now shimmered beneath heat haze and the whine of cicadas.

Elias had picked up the identification documents for more than one alias that he had strategically hidden on his person, keeping one immediately to hand in case of being stopped.

This current one was a forged Serbian ID from the Federal Republic of Yugoslavia, listing him as a mining contractor

His new accent—a hybrid Arabic-Eastern Slavic concoction—might be curious but plausible in these regions of mixed decay.

He had walked the line between forgetting and remembering for so long that now, with the end in sight, it felt surreal.

For years he had been Zubayr but now felt the identity slipping the longer he remained out of the radical Islamist circle.

The town of Niš lay ahead. Beyond it, Kosovo, and from there, Montenegro or the Adriatic coast. And somewhere on that path, his final destination.

But the weight inside him grew heavier.

Not the bomb.

The choice.

Elias pulled the battered Renault into a derelict petrol station on the outskirts of town. The lights flickered above, moths battering against cracked bulbs. No attendant. Just a coin metre and the echoes of better days. He killed the engine and stepped out, scanning the lot. Empty.

He opened the boot and stared down at the

case. He had not opened it in three days.

He knew what waited inside. Compact. Mechanical. Sinister in its precision.

A weapon never used in an old war, carried now to begin a new one.

He rested his palm on the case. Not with reverence. But with the weary familiarity of a priest touching the altar before confession.

The pre-emption of a strategic horror in service of a bigger lie. Though he felt it in his marrow, he knew he would still act.

Because *inaction*, he told himself, was the greater sin.

Yet the verses wouldn't stop replaying in his mind.

"Thou shall not murder."

"Love your enemies, bless them that curse you."

"Whatever you did for the least of these brothers and sisters of mine, you did for me."

He gritted his teeth. Shook his head.

Scripture was not soft. The Old Testament burned with fire and righteousness. Abraham would have slit Isaac's throat had God not intervened. David had killed Goliath not with a sermon, but with a stone. God's justice was not always clean.

He looked skyward. The Balkan night bore no witness, only stars. And in their cold silence, he found neither permission nor reprieve.

I do this so that others don't have to, he thought. *If evil must be committed, let it fall to me. If there is judgement, let it come.*

He closed the boot.

Then, without fanfare, he slid back into the Renault and drove north towards Niš, wind howling against the chassis, the sound like a wailing choir made of steel and frost.

> The decision was made.
> Hell could wait.

CIA SUBSTATION — NEAR SKOPJE — MID-MORNING

The kettle clicked off with a hollow clunk.

Bruce poured the hot water into three mugs—two black and chipped at the rim, the third red, yellow, blue, white, with Cyrillic writing and a football crest Frank called out, "Give the Levski Sofia mug to Yuri."

The safe house was stone cold at the core, but the paraffin heater and tea gave it passable warmth. Outside, morning warmth shimmered across the forest, the trees standing tall and sun-bleached, their leaves whispering in the dry wind.

Yuri sat by the window, eyes trained on the treeline, the CIA folder open on his lap. Frank was half-reclined on the sagging sofa, boots resting on an old munitions crate, cigarette smoke curling like incense from the corner of his mouth.

Bruce handed out the mugs. "Ta," muttered Frank.

Yuri glanced over. "Ta?"

"Just means thank you," Frank said, flicking ash into a chipped saucer.

Bruce sat opposite, took a slow sip of the white coffee, and gave it a beat before speaking.

"Frank," he said evenly, "how did you know Zubayr—I mean Elias—was CIA?"

Frank didn't flinch. Just exhaled smoke

through his nose and smiled faintly. "Surprised it's taken this long for either of you to ask."

Bruce shrugged. "I figured if it was need-to-know, you'd tell us. Just chancing my arm now."

Frank leant forward, forearms on knees, tone shifting.

"Alright. Back in '93, I was in Amman—off-book, under a false Swiss passport. **The Firm** wanted someone inside the arms routes between Aqaba and the West Bank. During one of the meets, I clocked this lad going by the name Nader Fawzi El-Sharif. Claimed he was Libyan, educated in Alexandria, dealing ball bearings and modified circuit boards. Quiet type. Didn't seem to blink much."

Bruce narrowed his eyes. "Elias?"

Frank nodded. "Didn't know it then. We played each other for a few hours—small talk, drink offers, theological musings. He was soft-spoken, Qur'anic references dropped like punctuation. But it was rehearsed. Too clean. Then I noticed a tell—when one of the Jordanians used a tribal insult, he mistranslated it. Not because he didn't know it. Because he was thinking in English."

Yuri turned from the window. "He slipped?"

"For three seconds. And then he didn't," Frank said. "Wore a Traser watch with PX-issue scratching, same model I had from Kabul. He'd aged it deliberately. His hands were rough, calloused—but only at the fingertips, like someone simulating manual work."

Bruce folded his arms. "You confronted him?"

"No need. We parted as 'friends of necessity'. I made a call to my boss the next day. I suspected

Langley. When I went to inquire again, I got a stone wall of silence so high it cast shade. Once you have been in this game a while, you understand there are ways they tell you without telling you—vague references, codes and that. But this had a 'shut the fuck up, wipe it from your memory and never utter it to another soul' feel to it."

"So, not just a talented field officer?"

"No. Then I saw a picture of him again as part of a brief with ***The Footprint***," said Frank using the insider term for 'The Increment'. "It was him going under the name Zubayr al-Adel. Been working his way into the Wahishi networks since at least '92. Posing as a pan-Islamist engineer, helping cells with improvised detonators, surface-to-air rigging tricks. Smart enough to give value. Careful enough to avoid blame."

Yuri's voice was low, but steady. "He was part of Riyadh?"

Frank looked at him. "Orchestrated his own fake rescue during the chaos. Pulled two survivors out after the explosion—none of whom lived more than a week."

Bruce felt a chill settle that had nothing to do with the weather.

"He's not just embedded," Frank said. "He's revered. Walks and talks like a true believer and disappears like a jock when it's his round."

Bruce simply smiled at the jibe as he watched Yuri attempt to work it out.

His face turned serious as he let the information filter through. "Years of being undercover shows commitment. Which is'nae ideal now he's carrying a Soviet RA-115S with no clear target, no exit route."

Frank exhaled. "Of all the European intelligence agencies, only five have strong links to the CIA. SIS have more, but the Agency will want full control of who knows what. Besides, scanning CCTV footage will take time that we don't have, however many people they bring in to do it. We are reliant on one of their assets recognising him and calling it in, in time."

Yuri said, "It happened once with our contact."

"Yeh, the contact in the woods with a crocodile's yawn for a throat," said Frank. "Besides, lightning doesn't strike twice."

Bruce murmured, almost audibly and to himself, "Don't shoot where he is—shoot where he's going to be."

A moment's quiet.

"I get you," said Frank. "We better get to work then. Fuck all else to do. Not even a *Sun* newspaper—I haven't seen Melinda Messenger or Jo Guest's tits in ages."

"Your messenger and guest?" asked Yuri.

"No, for fuck's sake, Yuri. This is why we wear ear defenders on the range."

Bruce couldn't help grinning.

24

SERBIA — OUTSIDE NIŠ — ABANDONED GARAGE COMPOUND

The concrete reeked of old engine oil and sun-baked metal. Heat shimmered in from a broken window, cutting across the room in a shaft of light thick with drifting dust motes. Elias stood at the edge, back to the wall, arms crossed, eyes locked on the spread of maps, passport pages, and torn-out train schedules pinned under a rusted spanner.

He had not long finished shaving in the corner cubicle, using the dull edge of a Bic. The slight redness at his collarbones only helped sell the look: weary, overworked field engineer. The kind no one remembered.

He had four routes out.
Each one a gamble.
Each one, now, too slow.

Option one: overland to Hungary, then on to Spain through Austria or Italy. It had the advantage of stealth—existing support networks, a series of pre-paid safe houses in Győr and Trieste. But too many moving parts. A late train. A twitchy customs officer. A courier who got cold feet. One call to Interpol, and he'd vanish into a hole no one would dig him out of.

Option two: sea route through Albania—a freighter to Tunisia or Libya, then a land crossing into Morocco, followed by a ferry to Spain. An old Wahishi contact in Sfax could still arrange the vessel. But the summer heat brought storms too, and the Libyans had grown less patient with freelance

Islamists since the Benghazi sting. The timeline ballooned—ten days, minimum.

He didn't have ten.

Option three: the original plan—smuggled through Bulgaria, across multiple borders, hitching rides under tarps and in false compartments, changing papers every two days. He knew it. Trusted it. But it was built on too many unknowns. The sort of journey you made when the stakes were high, but the pressure wasn't yet lethal.

That window had closed.

His fingers drummed against his arm. There was only one play left.

He stepped over to the rucksack in the corner, unzipped the side pouch, and pulled out a battered leather wallet. Inside, crisp Deutsche Marks and French francs. Not dirty. Not clean. Old Muj money recycled through Gulf charities, now his.

France.

He'd avoided it for a reason. Too centralised. Too many surveillance cameras, too much SIGINT, and an internal intelligence service that liked to put its foot on the throat of the banlieue. But it also had a deep underbelly Algerian gangs, Syrian runners, a soft frontier in Marseille where things moved through unchecked if the right men were paid.

He could get into France. The Jordanian passport of Omar al-Fayez would pass casual inspection. And once there, he could disappear into the estates of Saint-Denis or the industrial sprawl of Lyon. One more nameless figure in a city already at war with itself.

He folded the map of Serbia, flicked his cigarette into the oil drum fire, and started repacking the rucksack. No more shadows. No more compartmentalised routes.

The safest option now was the one that moved fastest.

He zipped the bag, shouldered it, and checked the Browning tucked under his waistband. The flight left in six hours.

Part of his CIA training had involved memorising the level of professionalism of various international air and sea ports.

Serbia—not being in the EU or NATO aligned—had been known to be particularly lax in its security, to the point that a suitcase in a larger backpack in the luggage hold might not be scrutinised.

The time for clever had passed. Now it was time for bold.

LONDON — VAUXHALL CROSS — SIS CHIEF'S OFFICE

The red diode on the encrypted line blinked twice. Then twice again. Sir Andrew Maremount lifted the receiver, pressing it to his ear without speaking.

A moment of silence, broken only by the hum of fluorescent light.

Then a voice. "London Stone?"

Maremount stared out the window towards the black Thames. "Falling, but intact."

A pause. "Confirm voiceprint."

He gave the agreed phrase. "Still no cricket at Lords in winter."

A soft beep on the line. "Voiceprint confirmed," said the American voice. "This line is good for seven minutes."

"Plenty of time," Maremount replied. "Harry."

"Andrew."

They didn't speak for three seconds. Maremount allowed himself one sip of cooling Lapsang from a chipped porcelain cup.

"I want the face pushed out," he said.

Kellerman exhaled slowly through his nose. "You want to circulate the photo?"

"BOLO. All services. European theatre. SIS, BND, DGSE, possibly even the Italians if we need their ports."

Kellerman didn't respond immediately. When he did, his voice was lower. "That's a lot of eyes, Andrew."

"Too many eyes are better than no detonation."

"And if it does go off, and someone connects the BOLO to the agencies who pushed it out?" Kellerman asked. "You and I will be facing hearings that we won't survive."

"If we put it out now," said Maremount, rising from his chair and pacing slowly past the framed portrait of Queen Elizabeth, "we might stop it."

Kellerman's tone shifted. Just slightly. "Or... if it goes off, it might do what Everhart always imagined it could. Unify public will. Scare the post-Soviets back into economic vassalage. Hammer them Muslim zealots. NATO strengthened. Washington dominant—and by proxy, London. Moscow paralysed."

"You are playing with brimstone, Harry."

"And you're wearing gloves too white to handle this," Kellerman said. "Put out the BOLO if you want. Use SIS channels and contacts."

The line clicked dead.

Maremount placed the receiver down as if it were made of glass.

"Thoughts?" came a voice from the other side of the room.

The suited Parker stood near the map table. False hope showed on his features. *He'd learn.*

Maremount turned. "He wanted me to do it. He wanted to ensure if this ends in fire, it's our mistake."

Parker folded his arms. "And if we don't issue it, we risk missing him entirely."

"Or we find him too late," Maremount said. The rest of the European intelligence services leak it to the media that we desperately outed his picture just before it happened—then it becomes an SIS operation gone wrong. The CIA remains… adjacent. Deny, distract, deflect."

Parker looked towards the frosted window. "Christ. We're talking about a Soviet-era nuclear device in the hands of a rogue deep-cover asset. And we're negotiating accountability before it even detonates."

"Welcome to statecraft."

"And who's trying to stop it? Frank Carlsmith and whatever contacts he's built. The meagre few bloody DGSE or BND liaisons we can trust?"

Maremount sat down slowly. "Yes."

Parker exhaled. "It's absurd."

"It's necessary," Maremount said, quietly. "Because I cannot—will not—let this firm take the fall for Langley's sins."

A long pause.

Parker nodded once. "Then we'd best pray our people catch the ghost first."

Maremount looked at the red diode still blinking on the now-dead line.

And whispered, almost to himself: "And we best hope the target isn't on British soil."

ALBANIA — SKANDERBEG MOUNTAINS — 03:41

The room was dark but not silent. Outside, the creak of nocturnal insects drifted on the warm Balkan air. Inside, the glow from a desk lamp cast a golden aura over maps, passports, and stacks of tightly bundled U.S. dollars.

Ramzi al-Wahishi ended the call, the secure satellite phone still warm against his ear. He placed it face down on the desk and stared at nothing for a long moment, eyes unfocused, mind racing.

He tapped twice on the wooden tabletop.

"Adam," he called, not loudly.

The heavy door opened at once. Adam Umar stepped in, silent as ever. He had not been far. He rarely was.

"Sit."

Adam lowered himself onto the armless chair opposite. His face, as always, was unreadable.

Ramzi exhaled sharply, leaning forward, knuckles against his jaw.

"He's in France," he said. "They need to think he is staying there—wants the French chasing shadows."

"Qayid, may I speak freely?"

Ramzi nodded—Adam had earned that.

"Is the real target in Paris?"

"I do not know," said Ramzi, hiding his shame with, "I entrusted him to select the target himself in accordance with our global objective. I made this decision in the name of security."

Adam nodded once. "What do you and Allah require of me?"

"Set a decoy in Paris. Something that will draw the dogs—loud enough, violent enough. He said the name of the hotel himself. Saint-Rémy. There is a back-of-house laundry area with a narrow crawlspace, just wide enough to accommodate a person on hands and knees. It leads to an old post-war maintenance corridor—common in Haussmannian Paris. It leads to bookstore across the road."

"How does he know this?"

"He had some done reconnaissance work in Paris a few years ago," lied Ramzi—he did not want Adam to know that Zubayr held the power due to his possession of the bomb.

He had to trust him.

"Luckily he saw the ambushers in Lozenska mountain foothills and escaped before they saw him," said Adam, seemingly without any facetiousness.

"A testament to his skill," said Ramzi. "I want you to be there before nightfall."

He reached into the drawer beside him and laid out a laminated ID card, a brick cellphone, and two thick envelopes.

"You'll take Selim and Haddad. No phones except this one. You make a scene—civilian panic, tactical response, even DGSE attention if we time it right. But you vanish before contact. Understand?"

Adam didn't blink. "Understand."

Ramzi's mouth curled slightly. "And *akhi*, there is to be no loss of life on this one. For reasons I cannot explain. The deaths acceptable will be to you and your men—not preferable, but acceptable."

A long silence stretched between them. Adam reached forward and slid the envelopes and phone towards himself.

"Allah yusahhil," he murmured.

Ramzi nodded. "We do this for the bigger storm."

Adam stood and turned.

As he reached the doorway, Ramzi added, "Please try and escape. This is misdirection, not martyrdom. He only needs a day."

Adam didn't reply. He vanished into the corridor, no doubt already assembling the operation in his head.

Behind him, Ramzi finally stood and looked out over the Tirana skyline.

When Zubayr succeeded, the world would never be the same.

25

BELGRADE AIRPORT — DEPARTURES HALL — MORNING

The fluorescents buzzed overhead with a tired Balkan flicker. Elias could smell stale cigarettes and cold coffee.

Surčin Airport was half-modern, half-relic—new signage slapped over crumbling concrete, like lipstick on an old scar. The deep-cover spook stood in line at the check-in desk for Swissair Flight 238 to Zurich, his bag looped over one shoulder, with the Omar Al-Fayez passport in hand.

Two passengers ahead. The woman behind him reeked of wet wool. Somewhere down the concourse, a cleaner cursed under her breath while dragging a mop.

He scanned the layout.

Check-in desk: one agent, yawning.

Two airport police officers near the exit doors—local, bored.

No visible customs yet, no dogs. No Europol presence. That was good. If there were an alert, they'd be here. Or upstairs. Waiting.

The man ahead of him—over-packed, agitated—was arguing over a baggage fee. Elias let his breathing slow. It wasn't about faking calm. It was about being calm. He checked his watch: 05:02. Boarding was in forty-five minutes.

The agent waved him forward.

Elias placed his bag on the conveyor belt, which doubled as a weighing scale.

The agent looked up, "This is way over the weight. There is a hundred-dinar charge for every kilo you are over."

"Will Deutsche Marks be accepted?" asked Monroe, knowing full well that not only would they be accepted, they were preferred due to the hyperinflation of the dinar in the earlier part of the decade damaging the trust in them.

He spoke in French-accented English, just enough hesitation to back the illusion of a foreign student

"Yes."

Monroe pulled out dominations equating to fifteen-hundred Marks—way over the amount necessary.

"Keep the excess for the airport's funds—I never get around to exchanging them back."

The agent looked at him with a blank expression, which jolted Monroe's heart a little—*Maybe this was too blatant a move?*

"Passport, please."

He handed it over, his smile faint. Eyes down, respectful.

The agent flipped through the passport. Paused. Looked up.

"You've been to Algeria?"

"Yes. My father worked for Sonatrach. Oil work."

A nod. The agent looked again.

"Purpose of visit to Switzerland?"

"Transit," Elias said. "Connecting in Zurich. My uncle lives in Lyon. I have a family emergency. I will not stay longer than two weeks."

The man hesitated. Something caught his

attention on the screen. Elias could feel it—that slight change in energy. He kept his breathing steady. One hand relaxed on the bag strap.

"What are you studying?"

He blinked. "Mechanical engineering. Thermal systems."

The agent nodded slowly. Another flick of the passport. A longer pause.

Then he stamped it.

"Thank you for the… donation," he said, his smile washing relief through Monroe. "Gate 5. Security is straight through."

Elias thanked him and moved without hesitation.

He didn't rush. Didn't look back. Just let the current carry him forward, step by step, towards the international wing.

He passed through security—shoes off, coat open—no alarms. His bag wasn't flagged. He kept moving.

By the time he reached Gate 5, he allowed himself to breathe properly.

He'd made it.

For now.

CIA SUBSTATION — NEAR SKOPJE — EARLY AFTERNOON

The paraffin heater hummed like a dying generator. A map of Europe lay open across the table, corners pinned down by the now three empty mugs, and one of Frank's 5.56×45mm NATO magazines.

Red circles and black arrows spidered out

across Eastern Europe—Berlin, Budapest, Vienna, Sofia, Skopje. A scribbled question mark hovered over Prague.

Frank stood with one hand on the map, the other gripping a pencil like a scalpel. Bruce leant against the edge of the window, staring out into the black forest, lips pursed. Yuri sat cross-legged on the floor, flipping through a folder of intercepted signals reports, eyes flicking like a scanner.

Frank muttered, scratching his head. "He's got a working RA-115S. One kiloton. Clean yield. Small blast radius for a nuke, but big enough to incinerate everything in a five-hundred-metre radius. Two thousand dead in a built-up area, easy."

Bruce replied, "High impact, plausible deniability, and no smoking crater the size of a postcode."

Yuri looked up. "So where does he hit?"

Frank took a breath, then said flatly, "It's not just about destruction. It's about leverage."

Bruce turned. "They want to kill Al Qaeda in its infancy but also create the rationale for full NATO intervention across the former Soviet sphere. If a Soviet nuke goes off on European soil, especially blamed on a transnational Islamic network—"

"—then Washington gets a blank cheque," Frank finished. "Not just in operations. In narrative."

"He must know he should act quick," said Yuri. "The more land he has to pass over, the more borders to get through. I think Austria."

Frank tapped Vienna. "Originally, this made sense. Neutral ground. Cultural summit coming up. Media saturation. But they've tripled security. But I agree—a possible."

Frank turned the map slightly, tapping a new spot.

"Bratislava."

Bruce blinked. "Go on."

"Small enough to be penetrated. Border proximity to Austria, Hungary, and Ukraine. Strategic rail and road routes. The Slovak presidency is hosting a closed-door summit next week—OSCE observers, NATO liaisons, and a couple of Ukrainian defence officials. Enough high-value targets to justify a 'strike' from extremists."

Bruce narrowed his eyes. "Would it be high-profile enough?"

"Maybe not," Frank said, "but what if the real goal isn't the deaths—it's the documents. If Monroe's briefed, he'll know a classified treaty addendum is due to be signed there. One that outlines early contingency operations for Russian nuclear site security."

"And if that goes up in smoke…" Yuri began.

"Panic. Outrage. Permission to intervene. NATO moves in to 'protect the region'. Langley gets its claws into the post-Soviet mess. And no one asks where the suitcase nuke really came from."

A long silence fell between them.

Then Frank spoke, "We don't have a fucking clue, do we."

PARIS — ORLY AIRPORT — MID-MORNING

The wheels touched down with a subdued jolt, the fuselage humming like a tuning fork as the brakes hissed and grabbed.

Elias Monroe kept his chin tucked and eyes

still as the Airbus decelerated along the slick tarmac of Orly's southern runway. The overcast sky outside was the colour of ash. Unforgiving and grey—a rarity in a Parisian summer.

The flight from Belgrade had been long, indirect, and tense—shuffled through a connection in Thessaloniki with a layover that tested both his patience and legend. But no questions had been asked.

The Jordanian passport of Omar Al-Fayez passed inspection with nothing more than a routine glance. Just another Middle Eastern man, overworked and under-rested, arriving in the capital of Europe.

Just one border away.

The thought sat behind his eyes like an ember.

One kiloton. One clean flame. One historic correction.

His hands had started to shake slightly on the descent.

It landed and he disembarked without delay.

The airport's signage was charmingly outdated: yellowed boards with clattering flaps, the lettering mechanical and inefficient. The air inside was warm and stale. A child cried somewhere to his left. An elderly couple argued in low, musical French over a carry-on.

As he waited for the hold luggage to appear on the motorised carousel, Elias adjusted his watch. A Seiko automatic—no seconds hand, no luminosity, just the steady, barely audible, mechanical sweep of time beneath the glass. He'd tightened the strap and willed for his luggage to appear unmolested.

It did—like Cinderella to the ball.

He took it to a chair on the far side, opened it,

and reached in to feel the rectangular leather box.

Almost as if he did not trust his tactile sensors, he pulled it out to see it was the same case.

He drifted past the remaining passengers waiting for their baggage, his black duffel over one shoulder, his passport in his coat pocket, the case in one hand, and an eye always on the exit.

No customs check at this leg.

If he was going to be detained, it would be now—they'd be in civilian clothes, yes, but they would also be fit men between mid-twenties and mid-thirties, dotted around the area.

He couldn't see anything untoward.

Yet.

The man in the corner kiosk glanced twice at him.

A tickle at the base of the spine, but Elias dismissed it: *paranoia*. He reminded himself, *But paranoia was better than carelessness.*

The CIA asset stopped, seemingly aimless, by a vending machine. Inserted a coin. Bought a steaming *café noir* in a flimsy cup. He could throw it in a would-be arresting officer's face, run and maybe it would buy him some time—he knew it was silly; still, it was better than nothing.

When he resumed walking, he took a new angle to the exit. Shorter. Sharper.

If you're being followed, give them a chance to overplay.

Outside, the air clung warm to his sleeves. Paris smelled of hot pavement, diesel fumes, spilt espresso, and the faint sweetness of overripe fruit left out in the sun.

The city moved around him with beautiful, mechanical indifference.

Elias exhaled, fog clouding from his mouth like breath from a reactor.

They would have arrested him inside, where it could be contained. He had made it this far and would make it all the way. His professional gamble had paid off.

He was tight on time. But he would make it.

And God willing, the world would end and begin again—precisely where no one expected.

26

PARIS — 6TH ARRONDISSEMENT — MID-MORNING

The steam from Anissa's espresso curled towards the cracked skylight above her studio loft. Outside, the late morning Paris drizzle gave the cobblestones a slick shine, grey light filtering through like fogged glass. The soft strains of Érik Satie played from her record player.

She stood barefoot, a fine brush in hand, gently attending a watercolour painting of a photograph she had taken a week ago. Though Anissa had been painting for years and considered herself 'good', she hadn't been gifted by God—and this made her more appreciative of the more exquisite works she sold.

And she knew this type of pastime did her good—she wasn't often still, but the act of painting calmed her. It demanded precision, patience, and control.

On the side table, her Ericsson GH337 vibrated against a leather notebook—it had taken a while to convince her of the benefits of her carrying the gaudy walkie-talkie-looking gadget, though she loathed being tied into a contract. She reckoned that only one or two people in ten owned such a device but had been reliably informed that in ten years, that percentage would be reversed with only the very young and old not having one.

She wiped her hands on a linen cloth before picking it up.

"Oui?"

The voice on the other end was tentative but familiar. Male, mid-forties, Corsican accent softened by years behind a service counter.

"Mademoiselle Rajah… I think I've seen him. The man in the photo you gave me."

Her pulse didn't quicken. It never did. But her voice softened.

"Orly. Terminal Sud?" she asked before admonishing herself—*Of course, where else would he have seen him?*

"Yes, morning flight from Belgrade. He's clean shaven now and wearing a different coat. But I am sure it's him."

She moved to the window as if the sky itself would offer verification.

"You are certain?"

"He had a case."

He doesn't know for sure, thought Anissa. *But I can have the CCTV checked.*

"Merci, Claude. You have done well. I will make sure you are compensated."

There was a pause, then a warm chuckle on the line. "It is enough that you asked me to help. How about you let me take you—"

She ended the call, exhaled slowly, then immediately keyed in another number.

It rang twice.

Then: "Yes."

"It is your favourite French woman."

"Emmanuelle Béart? You have decided to take me up on my offer to tongue my balls?"

"Do not be so **grossier**. He might be here. I have an informant at Orly who says he is certain it was him. Clean shaven. Has a case."

Then Frank's voice dropped into that low, gravelly register reserved for operational mode.

"Jesus Christ."

"I will have to speak to my superiors now. Have the CCTV checked and put out an alert."

"Understood. We will be on our way."

Anissa hung up, tossed the phone on the divan, and reached for her coat. The canvas would have to wait.

The man in the photograph was no longer a ghost. He was flesh now—moving, breathing, closing the gap between obscurity and detonation.

In her city.

HÔTEL SAINT-RÉMY — 9TH ARRONDISSEMENT — PARIS — MID-MORNING

The entrance doors slammed shut behind them with a violence that made the receptionist flinch. Rain slicked the marble tiles, and the echo of boots was swallowed quickly by the velvet hush of the boutique hotel's muted décor.

Adam Umar led. Behind him came two men: Selim and Haddad—young, jumpy, filled with the kind of zeal that didn't ask questions. Both wore oversized coats concealing AK-74s and mock explosive belts. They were nervous. Adam was not.

"Silence," Adam commanded in French, stepping forward, raising his weapon without theatrics.

A woman at the concierge desk screamed. Adam's voice cut through it, calm but unrelenting.

"No one dies—unless they make it necessary."

He pointed towards the lounge.

"Everyone. There."

Within minutes, the staff and guests—sixteen in total—were assembled in the lobby. Adam counted: two Americans, one British couple, a journalist from Le Figaro, the rest French nationals.

He turned to Selim. "Begin the message."

Selim pulled out a small cassette recorder. He hit play.

A crackling voice emerged—heavily accented, deliberately clumsy:

"We are soldiers of the Iranian Revolutionary Cause. We demand the release of Brother Majid bin Safar from Guantanamo. Until then, no one leaves. This is justice."

It was fiction, top to bottom. There was no Majid bin Safar, no Iranian unit. Just the shadows Ramzi wove and Zubayr pulled through the fog.

CIA SUBSTATION — NEAR SKOPJE — MID-MORNING

Frank flipped down the Motorola StarTAC. The line had barely gone dead when he turned towards the others.

Yuri was hunched over the map again, rubbing his jaw with one hand, the other still flipping pages of the OSCE file. Bruce sat off to the side on a battered wooden chair, legs outstretched, expression unreadable.

Frank cleared his throat. "That was Anissa.

She's got a contact at Orly who swears blind our lad's just walked through Terminal Sud. Clean shaven. Carrying a case."

Yuri nodded, already shifting markers towards the western edge of the map. "So the target is Paris. Big capital, lots of people."

"Yeah," Frank muttered, lighting a cigarette. "That was my first thought too. Big fish. Global city. And it wouldn't be the first time jihadis planned to light up the Eiffel Tower."

He watched the smoke curl upward, then he realised Bruce hadn't reacted.

"Something?" Frank asked.

Bruce didn't look up right away. When he did, his eyes met Frank's squarely. Steady.

"Why would a man like Elias Monroe"—he used the real name purposefully—"risk flying into the *target country* on a commercial aircraft?"

Frank frowned. "Maybe he's compressed for time. Maybe the window changed."

Bruce shook his head. "You said how professional he was. If he had time to grow a beard, he had time to plan his route. And if Paris were the detonation site, he'd have crossed the border on foot or gone through Belgium by train. Not waltzed through an airport—not unless there was no other possible way."

Frank leant on the back of the chair. "So what's he doing in France then?"

Bruce looked at the map. Looked west. His eyes narrowed, and Frank knew something had clicked.

Bruce exhaled sharply through his nose, like someone who'd just remembered a punchline.

"Madrid," he said.

Frank blinked. "Madrid?"

Bruce tapped the date scrawled in the corner of the intercepted itinerary Yuri had annotated.

"The NATO Summit. Eighth to ninth July. Two days from now. That's why he has taken such a risk."

Yuri sat up straighter, hand hovering over the Balkans but not touching anything.

"The NATO-Ukraine Charter is to be signed there."

"Fuckin' Nora." Frank's mind caught up fast. "I remember talking to some of the higher up lads in our field on that side of the pond a few years ago. Barroom talk mind, but they weren't big fans of Clinton's administration wanting to authorise the declassification of certain Cold War operations—the MK Ultra stuff and that. And I know that not everyone liked his policies of what they saw as favouring Muslim Bosniaks during the Balkan War."

Bruce nodded once. "And if Elias hits it with a one-kiloton Soviet device? Small enough not to vapourise half the city, but surgical enough to wipe the summit off the map?"

Frank said, "Blair, Chirac, Solana. Plus the Czech, Polish, and Hungarian delegations. Accession talks. Like Yuri said, the NATO-Ukraine Charter. Jesus Christ, that's the whole fucking post-Cold War realignment in one room."

Yuri finished the thought. "Then the world blames Al Qaeda. NATO rolls into the former Eastern Bloc to secure all the other atomic cases that do not exist."

Frank dropped into a seat. He felt the weight

of it settle in his chest.

"That's *the* play."

Bruce's jaw flexed. "And we've got less than forty-eight hours to stop it."

Frank stubbed out the cigarette. "We need Anissa on the Madrid end. And I want that photo circulated to every unofficial eye we trust from Bordeaux to the fucking Balearics."

Yuri stood. "Russian Minister of Foreign Affairs—Yevgeny Primakov—will be there. I need to make a call."

And the room fell silent.

27

DGSE HEADQUARTERS — BOULEVARD MORTIER — PARIS — LATE MORNING

Anissa Rajah swept through the revolving doors of the DGSE's main operations centre, her ID badge clipped hastily to the outside of her trench coat. The usual air of subdued competence was gone. The building pulsed with an unfamiliar electricity—raised voices, clattering boots, the crackle of simultaneous phone lines and the blur of paper and plastic folders being passed between agents with far too much urgency.

She caught sight of a field officer she vaguely knew—a Corsican analyst named Savelli—striding past with three mobile radios on a lanyard and a look of controlled panic on his face.

"Qu'est-ce qui se passe?" she asked.

He didn't even slow down. "Hôtel Saint-Rémy, 9th arrondissement. Hostage situation. DGSI thinks it's Iranian."

Iranian?

She bolted towards the operations wing, weaving past civilian contractors and security, and spotted her immediate superior—Commandant Éric Chauvigny—emerging from a side room, flanked by two men from the counterintelligence desk.

"Commandant!" she called. "Sir, I believe Zubayr al-Adel may have entered via Orly. I—"

Chauvigny didn't even stop. "We're already on maximum response. Three armed men have taken over a hotel in the 9th. Iranian assets, we believe. Diplomats are staying in that building."

"But sir—Zubayr might be—"

"He's not a priority right now," Chauvigny barked. "And if he *is* here, then it's not a coincidence, is it?"

That brought her up short. He turned to her fully now, tapping the side of his head with two fingers.

"He'll be involved. Which means he'll show. Which means I'll see him at the goddamn hotel."

She opened her mouth to argue, but Chauvigny was already stabbing at his satellite phone. After a terse exchange, he glanced back.

"Go down to the Interior Ministry. They have set up an operations centre there and will be checking the airport's feeds for the last several days. You've got clearance for access Orly only. I cannot spare you anyone. That's all I can do for you with regards to this."

"Merci," Anissa replied, not taking his abrupt manner personally. He turned and was gone, a blur in the chaos.

She stood in the hallway for a moment, people rushing around her. Something didn't add up. If Elias were here, then a public siege would be completely off-pattern if what Frank said about him was true. He was subtle. Surgical.

Not theatrical.

That was it. The attack at the Hôtel Saint-Rémy was loud, messy, and politically provocative—everything Elias *avoided*.

She turned and started towards the carpool, her mind racing.

PLACE BEAUVAU — INTERIOR MINISTRY OPERATIONS CENTRE — EARLY AFTERNOON

Dozens of screens flickered with live feeds, aerial views of the hotel perimeter, and tactical overlays of central Paris. Phones rang constantly. On one wall: the words "SAINT-RÉMY – LEVEL 4 THREAT" in red across a projected situation board.

RAID's elite tactical unit had cordoned off three city blocks. Snipers were perched on neighbouring rooftops. Two armoured vans waited in the alley behind the hotel.

Inside the command centre, a DGSE counter-terror liaison snapped at a RAID commander.

"Where the fuck is the Iranian file we requested? Get Langley on a secure line!"

"No time!" barked another. "We just pulled surveillance from Gare du Nord—nothing. We also need everything from Orly and Charles de Gaulle to be checked. These bastards didn't walk in from Belgium!"

Anissa hovered in the corner, knowing herself to be redundant until the surveillance footage from Orly arrived.

She stood and left the room to make a call.

FSO HEADQUARTERS — KUNTSEVO DISTRICT — MOSCOW — EARLY AFTERNOON

The room was windowless, cooled by an ageing Soviet air-conditioning unit that hissed like a warning.

Major Andrei Arkadievich Sokolova stood

waiting as General Timur Mikhailovich Barinov entered—a bear of a man, barrel-chested and stony-faced, his FSO service uniform immaculate. His lapel bore the blue-and-gold insignia of the Presidential Security Directorate.

"Major," said Barinov, nodding as he sat at the plain oak table. "Your message said 'urgent'. That word has lost all meaning this week."

Sokolova slid a manila folder across the table. "An asset of mine will meet your Chief of Internal Security this evening. He will bring photographs. A potential bomber. NATO summit is the likely target."

Barinov opened the folder, revealing grainy surveillance shots of Zubayr al-Adel.

"Fucking **_Borodatye_**," Barinov sighed looking at the images, using the Russian military pejorative for Islamist, literally translated to 'Bearded Ones'. "We should inform the Spaniards. Cancel our participation. At least delay Primakov's speech."

"No," Sokolova said firmly. It was a tone rarely used with a man of Barinov's seniority, but one that the general did not interrupt.

"If we pull out now, the media of the world will ask why. And if that bomb detonates while we are absent—on Spanish soil, at a NATO summit—the narrative writes itself that we had foreknowledge. That we were complicit."

Barinov's fingers drummed once on the table. "And if it detonates while our Foreign Minister is sitting in the front row?"

"That is what I am trying to prevent." Sokolova leant in slightly. "To be clear, the President might be… politically aggrieved but not personally."

Barinov raised his eyebrows, "You have some

balls, Andrei, to say that out loud. Especially in this office."

Sokolova decided to remain quiet.

Eventually Barinov broke it with, "What do you need?"

"Can you increase the security numbers? Then we can have more of our men looking for the suspect."

"The summit protocols on delegation security are set—two officers per representative," said Barinov before rubbing his jaw. "I can bend it but a little."

Sokolova paused for only a second. "Could you receive a small number of… specialists. Not Russian. But aligned with our objectives. Quiet men. Capable men. Well, men and a woman."

"Your plan all along no doubt," said Barinov flatly.

Again, Sokolova did not answer.

Barinov considered for a long moment, then slowly nodded. "Send me their details—operational names only. I'll ensure they receive credentials under one of our auxiliary logistics firms."

"Thank you, general," answered Sokolova, but as he went to stand, Barinov gestured that he remain seated.

"I like you, Andrei," said the older man. "And your star is on the rise. However, the words 'friends' and 'allies' are two different meanings."

"I understand that it will be my head rolling on the floor should it go off."

HÔTEL SAINT-RÉMY — LOBBY — TWO

HOURS INTO THE SIEGE

Adam stood beside the windows, watching the flashing blue lights dance against the rain-slicked glass. He could feel the walls of French state security breathing down on them—he needed that pressure. It was part of the plan.

Selim whispered, "Why do we wait? We should send one more message. Fire the weapon. Let them know we are ready to die."

The back of Adam's hand collided with the youngster's cheek, skidding him to the floor.

The Bosnian War veteran growled, "We are not here to die. We are here to *mislead*. You die only when it ensures the lie lives longer."

Selim nodded, wide-eyed and gingerly stood before slinking away.

Adam knelt by the window. His hands—steady. His heartbeat—low. He watched the RAID perimeter adjusting every few minutes, recalibrating their assault vectors. They would storm the hotel within hours.

And when they did, Selim and Haddad would die in the crossfire. They wouldn't have a chance—Adam had taken out the firing pins of their AKs back in Tirana before he had summoned them. If it had not been explained to Adam why no one was to be killed, then he did not want the shame of telling the pair that.

He would drop his gear, and escape through the back-of-house laundry area with a tight crawlspace all the way to the bookstore across the road, before becoming another immigrant face, and vanishing.

He, not the men—they needed to slow the imminent raid.

He thought of Zubayr now.

He is the last clean weapon we have. The rest of us are already shadows.

If they succeeded, Western eyes would remain locked on Paris. If they failed, France might still turn inward to hunt Iranian ghosts.

Adam stood slowly, adjusted the cuffs of his jacket, and looked at the hostages—silent, trembling.

He had received teachings since joining '**The Base**', reasoning that because the civilians of the countries that oppressed Muslim democratically elected their leaders, then none of them were innocent in the global Jihad.

Despite this, he had to manufacture his hate for them—still, he did not feel sorry for them.

And they were the audience. And for the lie to work, they had to believe everything.

The lights flickered.

Adam inhaled once, deeply.

Let them come, he thought. *Let them waste their bullets on a play.*

28

SPAIN — NEAR ZARAGOZA — EVENING

The lights of the petrol station flickered in the warm Spanish night, casting long yellow shadows over the tarmac. Elias Monroe sat alone in the booth of an abandoned roadside phone box, his jacket clinging damply to his skin from the hours of travel. The French border now lay behind him—just—and with it the tightening noose of surveillance, helicopters, and checkpoints sparked by the chaos he had lit in Paris.

A few hours earlier, he had found a hardware store and bought his supplies, including a heavy-duty tool-carrying case.

He dialled the number from memory, eyes scanning the forecourt. Two rings.

"*Naam?*" came the voice. Ramzi al-Wahishi—measured, poised as always.

"I've made it through," Elias said.

A pause. Then Ramzi's voice again, quieter now.

"Good."

"Tell me, *Akhi*, why did you insist that there were to be no deaths in the distraction mission?"

Elias leant forward in the booth. *What harm could it do now?*

Still, he would have to speak in code, no sense in losing his professionalism while so close.

He lowered his voice despite his being alone. "Remember Mummar told Adam who had the most wins in Europe?"

During a break from one of Ramzi's

teachings, Adam had stated that AC Milan had won the most European titles only for Mummar to bravely correct him by stating it was Real Madrid.

Silence stretched between them.

"The top of the mountain?" Ramzi said, low.

Elias smiled at the wily Jihadist's code meaning *'The Summit'*.

"Yes. And if there is a slaughter, then one of the main mountaineers might stay behind. If he does, the hike might be delayed."

Elias meant that if the siege resulted in civilian deaths, then President Jacques Chirac might be forced to cancel his attendance. With France being one of the major NATO countries the entire event might be delayed.

Ramzi exhaled—resignation, perhaps, or admiration.

"I was right to select you."

"Allah guided us both," Elias replied. "I must go. The gap in the window is small but right now, it's open. Just enough."

There was silence again. Then: "*May God preserve you, Zubayr.*"

The line went dead.

Elias stepped out of the booth into the night, the hot wind of Aragon licking his face. He glanced once towards the distant south—towards Madrid—and began to walk.

NORTH FRENCH AIRSPACE — EVENING

The steady hum of the twin-engine turboprop filled the cabin of the unmarked private plane as it cut a clean line through the dusk. The seats were military grey leather, offering utility over comfort, and the narrow fuselage held only four passengers and a crate of gear.

Bruce felt glad to be out of the safe house. He'd had to hide his trepidation that his guess might be incorrect and felt grateful that Frank had backed his assessment.

The thought just occurred to Bruce, that if he was correct and they failed to stop it, he had effectively led them to their deaths.

Even as a sixteen-year-old he knew that in signing the **Attestation Form** he was signing his acceptance of the possibility of his death in service.

Felt different in that Catterick assembly hall than here, he mused.

However, he realised then he would not consider changing his position even if given the choice—If he could even save one innocent it would be worth it.

Frank sat near the rear, hunched over a field map of Madrid and the surrounding suburbs. His attention was elsewhere. Opposite him, Yuri leant back, his face pallid from the short captivity but eyes sharp. He sipped from a battered metal flask of black coffee Bruce had handed him before take-off.

A quiet kind of energy hummed between the three men.

Bruce turned as he felt the plane's nose dip ever so slightly to indicate the beginning of a descent.

Frank looked at his watch. "She'll be there. A strip this small doesn't get booked twice."

They touched down on crude tarmac barely long enough to qualify as a runway—somewhere east of Versailles, still outside the capital's surveillance net.

The sun had almost gone now, casting the airfield in a mixture of mist and amber glow.

Through the oval window, Bruce saw her before the engines even cut: Anissa Rajah, trench coat belted tight, a satchel slung across her shoulder, and a manila folder clutched to her chest. Two ground crew moved behind her, no doubt as beguiled as he pretended not to be.

The cargo door hissed open. Bruce stepped down first, his boots crunching on gravel.

"You look good with the…" she said, waving her hand over her lower face to indicate his stubble.

"I am glad I came to Europe to find my best look," Bruce replied.

Frank's head poked out behind him and bellowed, "Stop flirting you two-timing **_Half-price Helen_** and get on the plane."

As she complied, she asked Bruce, "Half-price Helen?"

"It's a compliment, as in you give people that feeling when they find out something is half-price."

Her expression suggested she was not convinced.

As soon as she boarded, Frank asked, "Got the prints?"

She handed the folder over.

Once they sat and buckled themselves in, Frank leafed through and handed out the still warm black-and-white photographs—telephoto shots of Elias taken from the Orly Airport security feed.

Bruce could tell instantly that despite the clean-shaven face, it was Elias.

"That's him," confirmed Frank.

Frank raised his voice above the hum of the

engines building up again as the plane pulled away from the crude airstrip, "What's the status on the hotel?"

Anissa pulled her collar back. "RAID's going in tonight. They have had visual confirmation of the gunmen, and all hostages are still alive. Negotiations stalled around twenty minutes ago. Intel says they are preparing to breach."

Bruce raised an eyebrow. "That'll tie up the DGSE for another twelve hours minimum."

"Longer," Anissa said. "They still think it is the doing of Tehran."

"He has got summat about him 'as our Elias," said Frank, glancing at Bruce with a grim look in his eye. "I wish he were on our side."

Bruce stared back. "I don't."

HÔTEL SAINT-RÉMY — SECOND FLOOR — NIGHT

Adam crouched just behind the stairwell, listening—feeling—the rhythm of state power about to bear down. The low hum of comms.

RAID was preparing to strike.

He had counted six hours since the initial perimeter was formed. Four teams, rotating overwatch. Snipers on the roofs across the street. He respected them. France had invested in its quiet killers.

But this was a stage.

Below, the hostages whimpered softly in the dimly lit lobby. Their fear hung in the air like perfume. The gunfire would come soon. But it would not come from him. He had ensured that.

Selim and Haddad sat by the hostages, fingers curled around AKs that would not fire. They still hadn't noticed. They never would.

May God forgive them when their time comes, Adam thought. *They believed they were martyrs. They will be symbols instead.*

Adam left his weapon and military attire in one of the staff cloakrooms in the rear and made his way over to the laundry area.

He had already identified and cut a large flap in the carpet to reveal the crawlspace entrance not long after they had contained and settled the hostages. He'd also taped the carpet flap to the top of the wood lid, so that when he replaced it back the carpet flap would return flat and hopefully not be seen.

He pulled his jacket tighter and attached the drawstring bag to his ankle—civilian clothes, forged identity papers, cash, and an old Paris Saint-Germain cap. All part of the shed skin he would leave here.

Sliding into it, he pulled his sweater over his mouth and nose against the dust. He used the ankle free of the bag to awkwardly fit the heavy lid back on with a dark inducing click.

He crawled into the black hard.

The sound of the RAID team breaching rolled through the foundations like an underground thunderclap.

The screams above came next, then French voices barking commands. A stun grenade popped, its echo muted down here.

Selim and Haddad would be dead within minutes. Probably less. He had positioned them to appear as if they were active shooters.

He pushed forward, forearms scraping against

the metal mesh and dirt. The crawlspace was tight, but it was enough. Old Paris—centuries deep—hid tunnels like arteries beneath its skin.

After six metres, the crawlspace joined a conduit maintenance trench. Concrete-lined, lit only by his breath and a dim chem-light wedged into a pipe collar. He twisted left, knees soaking in the pooled moisture as he slid past a corroded inspection valve, then up a sloped corridor once used for fibre-optic cabling.

At the junction, he stopped beside a bolted hatch. *Rue de Lille* was above—through the shuttered basement of an old bookstore that no longer paid rent. Though he had an adjustable spanner taken from a hotel's maintenance toolbox, he found he could twist the four bolts by hand before pushing the hatch open.

The hatch yawned open like a mouth, stale air pressing in. Adam climbed through, pulling the hatch closed behind him with a soft scrape. He did not breathe until it clicked shut.

He stood slowly in the cramped storeroom, careful not to trip on the debris—stacked crates, old shelving, a mummified mop in a bucket. Dust floated in his torchlight like fog.

His bag came off his ankle. He changed quickly: jeans, a zip hoodie, Adidas runners. Cap low over his eyes. He dropped the dusty sweater and latex gloves into a burn bag, zipped it, and shoved it behind a leaking boiler.

Up the stairs, through the side door, he stepped into the Rue de Lille, now eerily quiet.

Around the corner, lights danced across the façades of Saint-Rémy and the street beyond. Police vans, crowd barriers, camera crews. All eyes locked on the hotel's front.

No one watched the bookstore.

He walked west towards the Pont Royal, hands in pockets, head down. The first checkpoint was a civilian cordon—easy enough to pass. He moved like someone who had been evacuated. Confused. Damp. Anonymous.

Ten minutes later, he was on Line 1 of the Métro, carriage half full, eyes on the floor.

By the time RAID called clear on the second floor, Adam Umar was already hundreds of metres away.

29

MADRID, PALACIO MUNICIPAL DE CONGRESOS, OUTSKIRTS OF MAIN SECURITY ZONE — EARLY MORNING

The air in the early morning was dry and tinged with dust kicked up by service vans pulling away from the rear of the conference centre. Sunrise crept up pale over the horizon, casting long blue shadows behind the delivery trucks and security trailers flanking the building's loading bay.

Elias Monroe watched from behind a row of hedges, cap pulled low, clipboard in hand, lanyard hook already clipped to his belt in anticipation.

A short man in his twenties exited through the rear gate, scratching his stubbled jaw and lighting a cigarette. His fluorescent orange contractor vest hung loose over his frame, and his ID badge swayed against his chest—*Technico de Sonido, Grupo Estrella*. The man looked like half of Madrid's youth—dark eyes, short-cropped hair, a forgettable face. That was the point.

Elias fell in beside him as they both neared the pavement. "¿Turno largo?" he asked in casual Spanish.

"Doce horas," the man groaned, exhaling smoke. "Nada funciona. Puto aire acondicionado se cayó otra vez."

Elias laughed, walked parallel for a few steps, nodded sympathetically—and then, as the man reached into his bag for his lighter, Elias's left hand slipped the lanyard from his neck in one clean motion. A tug. A step. Gone. The contractor barely blinked.

"Bueno, suerte con eso," Elias said, tapping his own pocket as if checking for something. He veered off into a side street, tossing a quiet "Hasta luego."

By the time the man realised his pass was gone, he'd be home or passed out in a Metro seat—no way he returns to report it missing, not until his next shift, which would be tomorrow.

Fifteen minutes later, Elias stood in line behind two sleepy AV techs and a woman wheeling a box of lighting equipment near the service entrance of section B2. His posture was relaxed, the lanyard around his neck now bore a slightly modified photo—his own face, glossier than the original, trimmed and laminated with a heated press between the ID card and the holder.

The security guard glanced briefly at the pass, barely looking up from his clipboard. No metal detectors here—this entrance was for loading gear, not guarding heads of state.

Elias gave a grunt of recognition, nodding towards the techs ahead of him. "AV team. Sound check."

The guard waved them all through.

And just like that, he was in.

In forty-eight hours, the leaders of NATO—including Yevgeny Primakov—would be standing less than two hundred metres from where he now walked.

And all Elias needed… was thirty quiet seconds, and a bag no one thought to scan.

PRIVATE JET — DESCENT INTO MADRID —

MORNING

The sun burst over the Sierra de Guadarrama as Bruce stared out the oval window. Beneath sprawled Madrid—amber-hued rooftops and modernist curves blending under the morning haze.

Below, a man prepared himself to commit the unthinkable.

Frank sat opposite him, cross-legged, thumbing a dossier of floor plans. Yuri simply stared out the window. Anissa leafed through a packet of grainy surveillance stills—Elias Monroe at Orly Airport, the sharpness just enough to show the hard-set jaw and predator's gait.

They landed and the quartet alighted not unlike soldiers from a Chinook, except for Anissa who surreally strode at speed without looking hurried.

They got into the black Mercedes G-Wagon waiting on the tarmac, flanked by two local Policía Nacional outriders. No introductions. No ceremony. Just nods. They were already running late.

PALACIO MUNICIPAL DE CONGRESOS — SERVICE LEVEL ACCESS TUNNEL

Elias Monroe crouched behind a stack of cleaning supplies in the dim-lit rear corridor beneath the Palacio Municipal de Congresos. Sweat glistened on his brow, not from nerves, but the residual heat of the Spanish afternoon trapped in the concrete underbelly of Madrid's pride and joy.

He glanced at his watch. There must be a security shift rotation soon. The rear staff entrance—

through which vendors and caterers filtered in like ghosts—was lightly manned this time of day, particularly while summit preparations remained logistical. No ministers yet. No press. Just electricians, stage riggers, and contractors walking around with purpose and too many badges.

He pulled the contractor's lanyard from his jacket and slipped it over his neck. The photo was a close-enough match—a civilian lack of attention to detail would take care of the rest.

He moved.

Through the service door, past the cleaners' break room, and up a flight of steel stairs. A custodian nodded absently, distracted by the cigarette trembling between his lips.

One floor up. First checkpoint's just a desk, no scanner.

Elias walked past with the tired shuffle of a man doing overtime he didn't want. His tool-carrying case hung from his left shoulder. Inside it was the RA-115S suitcase nuke, split into two parts. The core and its activation mechanism were housed separately in padded compartments. Crude-looking from the outside. That was the trick. No one looks twice at old tools in the hands of working men.

He turned down a hallway marked *Auditorio Principal / Instalaciones Técnicas*. His eyes scanned the junction. Power panels. HVAC access. Cameras—yes—but none pointed towards the ventilation shaft. That was where he would leave it. Inside the service duct that ran beneath the main auditorium's stage.

The plan was simple. Plant the weapon. Activate the remote trigger. Disappear to a safe position six hundred metres away, across the

Manzanares River, to his room's balcony at the Hotel Río Imperial.

The four-star hotel was mostly empty of the journalists, contractors, or foreign dignitaries' staff it had housed the evening before—they now swarmed the summit's complex and would leave straight from there—so it was easy to book a room with the view he required as many contractors would be leaving now the structural works had been signed off.

He could press the trigger from his coat pocket and vanish before the echo hit the windows.

But first, he had to plant it. He ducked into the ventilation alcove, knelt beside a loose panel, and unscrewed it.

No radiation portal monitors or handheld Geiger counters would be deployed without credible intelligence. Monroe surmised that the Russians might not even guess this to be his target, let alone that one of their nukes was on the loose.

And if he was right, French and American counterintelligence were still preoccupied with the Paris false flag. Ramzi's play had bought him time.

He slid the power unit into place inside the vent and fixed the radio-receiving trigger mechanism.

The red light coming on momentarily transfixed him like observing a dragon opening its eye.

He snapped himself out of it and wrapped more magnetic foil lining around the body to deaden any residual signature ensuring none of the foil touched the receiver.

This weapon had been designed for undetectability anyway. *That was why the Soviets built it.*

As he replaced the grille and wiped down

every surface he'd touched, he felt no fear. Only gravity. History tilted towards him like an unstable structure, waiting for the last stone.

If the summit proceeded uninterrupted, ideally the bomb would go off during the *closing address*, while world leaders shook hands and cameras flashed.

However, it going off any time after the arrival of the representatives would be good enough.

He stood, collected his toolbox, and whispered a single phrase in Arabic.

"Al-Naṣr min khilāl al-taḍlīl."—*Victory through misdirection.*

Then Elias Monroe walked out the way he came, vanishing into the mosaic of Madrid's afternoon bustle, unseen, unheard, forgotten.

30

NATO SUMMIT COMPLEX — SECURITY OUTER PERIMETER — 11:46

Steel, glass, concrete. Power disguised as architecture. Bruce took it in at a glance—the kind of modern fortress built not for war, but for image. Flags flapped in the breeze like polite lies. The Manzanares glinted nearby, indifferent to politics or bombs.

Too much glass, Bruce thought. *Too many angles. Too many bodies with no idea what could be walking among them.*

Frank seemed to echo his sentiments with, "It's like a fucking super-sized, steroid-injected, **Crystal Maze** but no Richard O'Brien to give us a steer."

Security stood like androids in the sun—hard-eyed, well-drilled, but ultimately passive. Sniffer dogs, retina scans, metal detectors. Layers upon layers. All of it meaningless if the threat had already stepped through.

A figure emerged near the perimeter. Compact, dense with muscle—face like a man who still boxed for discipline, not nostalgia. Black suit, silver star lapel. Colonel Pavel Taranov.

Bruce had never met him, but didn't need to. The way he moved screamed military with old-school Soviet edges.

His eyes flicked to them and narrowed.
Then he saw Yuri.
Recognition.
Stiffened shoulders. A nod. Then he stepped

forward.

"Yuri Kozlov," Taranov said.

Yuri nodded and answered in English. "Colonel. We need your help."

Bruce stayed just behind Frank, watching the dance unfold. Taranov gestured them towards the shade behind a column. Out of direct sight, just enough to talk but not enough to hide.

Anissa passed the photographs across. Elias's face. Bruce watched Taranov's reaction. Nothing. Frank had ordered them to refer to Elias by his original deep-cover alias.

Yuri handled the talking. "The man's name is Zubayr al-Adel. We believe he entered France through Orly on false documentation. If he's here—it's with a tactical nuclear device. Soviet era. RA-115S."

Bruce could feel Anissa's tension beside him. Frank said nothing, jaw clenched.

"I heard that they detained General Bezmenov and he fed them this story," said Taranov, not even blinking. "If true, I wonder why the summit has not been cancelled?"

"Political sensitivities," Yuri said with a hint of an edge. "But the Foreign Minister's attendance is one of the reasons we have permission from General Barinov."

"And you are well-versed in the political sensitivities of our nation... Master Sergeant."

"I am sure my knowledge is child-like when matched against yours," answered Yuri.

Bruce admired the Ukrainian's self-control—he knew that Yuri hated Russia's neo-colonial attitude towards his nation.

And hidden in the more obvious concerns, the signing of the NATO-Ukraine Charter would be a major triumph for Yuri, and all his years fighting for Ukrainian independence from Russia.

But the Ukrainian also seemed to know how to 'play the game', which was important when the stakes involved lives.

Taranov's face remained unreadable, but his voice softened a fraction. "Today is sensitive for Russia. Minister Primakov is expected to deliver a framework for cooperation regarding NATO expansion. His presence must project… poise."

Taranov's hand dipped into his inner jacket. Four laminated passes. He held them out like they cost more than gold.

"These are valid until five minutes before thirteen hundred hours. The opening address will take place at 13:00 hours. After that, the complex is fully locked down. No exceptions."

The realisation hit Bruce, "That is when he will detonate."

He could tell by their looks that Frank, Yuri and Anissa agreed with his assessment, but Taranov did not.

The Russian simply said, "Search fast."

Bruce stepped in. His voice was even, calm. "When do we meet the men who are helping us?"

The SAS soldier's stomach lurched at the general's next words.

"They remain on task. Protection of the Minister. Zubayr's image is already with them. That's the extent of what I can offer."

"You're leaving this to four people," said Frank with a dry scoff. "So, we've got not much more than an hour to find a case in a city's worth of corridors."

Bruce met his eyes. No hostility. Just cold certainty.

"I'm following orders," Taranov replied. "You're lucky you have a window at all." He looked directly at Bruce. "You'll get a thirty-minute grace period before the full lockdown begins. Use it well."

The general marched off, and the three circled Frank, who said, "We'll have to split in pairs. Bruce and Anissa, take the service corridors and back entrances. Yuri and I will search the delegation lounges and main halls—we're looking for him and it. We regroup in an hour at the western entrance."

The inside was pure modern bureaucracy—glass, chrome, and corridors that all looked the same. The kind of place where danger could wear a lanyard and a smile.

They split—Bruce with Anissa towards the service elevators, Frank and Yuri cutting towards logistics and infrastructure.

Bruce's hand brushed the pass around his neck. Temporary. Like them.

The air was already beginning to thicken with bodies—aides, journalists, diplomats, administrators. All talking, moving, unaware.

Bruce quickened his pace.

The clock had started.

Somewhere in this polished labyrinth, Elias was waiting.

Or maybe he wasn't, thought Bruce grimly.

HOTEL RÍO IMPERIAL — 11.56 A.M.

Elias Monroe stood motionless behind the sheer curtain of his eleventh-floor hotel room, eyes locked on the summit complex sprawled across the Manzanares like a steel crown. Flags danced in the summer air. The dignitaries had begun to arrive—black cars, motorcades, murmurs of cameras flashing from the far boulevard.

He turned away from the window and stared at the small, innocuous black box resting on the table. The detonation trigger.

It looked like nothing—two inches of matte plastic and copper. But it held the weight of revelation.

He laid a careful hand beside it, but didn't touch. He hadn't since placing it down.

The Ring, he thought. *Tolkien's cursed ring. The more one held it, the more one wanted to use it.*

And like the One Ring, this device could summon fire over the cities of men.

He clenched his jaw, resisting the itch to pick it up again. He still had time. It had to be when all the players were seated, the summit in full theatre. Anything earlier would rob it of its purpose.

Though the hotel lay outside the immediate blast radius of the bomb exploding in its current concrete surrounding, he knew the initial radiation fallout could reach up to a kilometre. However, the fallout wouldn't begin for at least several minutes post-blast and he would be far away by then.

He had opened the windows to prevent further interference of the signal and to mitigate the glass shattering. He would also duck his face and close his eyes to stop flash blindness.

His burner phone vibrated.

He snapped it open, knowing it could only be one person.

He answered with a hiss of frustration. "Yes."

Ramzi's calm, textured voice came down the line. "I have useful news."

Elias stepped away from the window. "Go on."

"Adam Umar is en route to you."

Elias stopped breathing for a moment. "What?"

"I have instructed him to support your endgame."

"He could draw attention. We are so close, and this risks the entire operation," said Elias making an almost inhuman effort to contain his exasperation and anger.

"He may be useful in another way now," Ramzi said, seemingly unbothered. "He is no longer viable to me as an asset. His name is stained. But *you*, Zubayr… you still have clean hands. You still wear your face without history."

Elias turned sharply and glanced at the detonation trigger but said nothing. Ramzi's words lingered.

"If the world sees Umar's corpse," Ramzi continued, "they will not go looking for another ghost. Let the lion take the blame for the serpent's bite."

Elias felt the fire drain slowly from his chest, replaced by a cold, clear logic. *If Umar's name is burned, then mine remains. If mine remains… I can return.*

"Perhaps…" he said softly, "perhaps Allah is giving me another chance. Perhaps this fire will purify the field. And I will remain… to sow what's next."

The silence stretched.

Elias exhaled. "I'm ten floors above the river, northeast quarter. Room 1103. Pass it to him. The trigger will be pressed within one hour at most. Whether he is here or not."

Ramzi hesitated. "He said he would call from a payphone when ready. He may be closer than you think."

Elias looked at the trigger again, like a king staring at a crown he was afraid to wear.

"I'll be ready," he said. "But I won't hesitate. He has sixty minutes."

He killed the call. Set the phone down. Walked back to the window and watched the slow procession of dignitaries filtering through the gates.

The clock ticked.

And the Ring still waited.

SUMMIT COMPLEX — WESTERN ENTRANCE — 12:49

Frank wiped the sweat from his brow with the inside of his wrist. The sun had broken through the clouds now, smearing its heat across the glass façade of the complex. A group of security aides passed by, heads down, lanyards bouncing against their chests. None of them knew they were all standing on a knife's edge.

He turned to the others—Anissa looked exhausted, her usually sharp features drawn tight with tension. Yuri looked at him. Bruce had his eyes fixed on the river.

Frank followed his gaze.

Across the Manzanares, rising like a quiet observer, stood the *Hotel Río Imperial*. Clean white

balconies, a rooftop restaurant, panoramic views—
he'd noticed it earlier but written it off. Now, seeing
Bruce stare at it with a calculating look piqued his
curiosity.

Frank stepped towards him.

"What is it?"

Bruce didn't answer straight away. His voice,
when it came, was low.

"You should go up there, Frank."

Frank blinked. "What is it?"

"You could see half the summit from up
there," said Bruce, pointing with his chin. "But it's
just outside the initial blast radius. Take one of the
photographs—maybe a receptionist has clocked
him."

Frank's gaze narrowed. He turned, looked
back at the hotel, then at Bruce. The logic was
frighteningly sound. He still had his mind on
Zubayr—an Islamist fanatic who might martyr
himself in the operation, and not Elias—a cold
professional who might not.

And Frank understood why Bruce suggested
he go—*he's afraid if the bomb goes off, he'll be the one who
survives.*

"I am the team leader," Frank said quietly.
"You go."

Bruce didn't move. Frank had known men
like him before, not many but a few—brilliant,
principled, and bone-stupid when it came to self-
worth.

Frank gave a tight grin.

"I know you don't want to be the bastard
looking down while we're vaporised."

Bruce opened his mouth, but Frank waved a

hand.

"But you'll spot something I'd miss. You're the younger and more of a *racing snake*. Besides you've got more years to offer. Just promise me that if it does go off you get the bastards back."

Bruce finally met his eyes. Frank gave him a firm nod, and after a second's pause, Bruce turned and took off at a sprint, weaving through the checkpoint without a backwards glance.

Frank turned back to the others.

Yuri grunted. "So what now?"

"We've got twenty minutes," Frank said. "We are just looking for the case—or something like it now. Especially, any panels or gratings that can be removed with a manual tool."

Anissa nodded, tucking her hair behind one ear. "I'll take the kitchens."

"I will return to the utility entrances," Yuri said.

Frank nodded. "Good. We move. And if we spot him, we don't wait. We'll deal with the fallout afterwards."

They scattered again, the knot in Frank's chest winding tighter.

31

HOTEL RÍO IMPERIAL — RECEPTION — 12:55 PM

Bruce burst through the glass double doors, boots striking marble like gunfire. The polished floor blurred under him as he skidded to a halt at the reception desk. Sweat streamed down his spine, shirt clinging to him beneath the jacket. The dash—well over a kilometre uphill in a wide arc to stay out of Elias's eyeline—had redlined his cardiovascular capacity.

Behind the desk, the receptionist—a young woman in a burgundy waistcoat and crisp white shirt—jerked upright, startled by his sudden arrival. Her hand hovered near the phone, and for a split second, he wondered if she was about to press an alarm.

Bruce planted both palms on the counter, breath tight in his chest.

"Do you speak English?"

The woman nodded, eyes wide. "Yes—yes, I do."

With a snap, he pulled out the lanyard and flashed the access pass to the complex. To prevent her scrutinising the ID, he slammed a black-and-white photograph onto the desk—Elias Monroe, mid-stride, grainy but clear.

"Plain clothes police," Bruce snapped. "This man is wanted in connection with a major incident. He is extremely dangerous. I need to know *right now*—has he checked in here?"

The receptionist blinked. Her fingers, trembling slightly, moved to the guest log—a bound ledger, the pages thick and tabbed by date.

Bruce's gaze twitched towards the brass-plated elevator doors just ten metres away. One of them chimed softly as it descended.

She flipped back through the morning entries, lips moving as she read under her breath. Bruce leant forward, his knuckles whitening on the edge of the desk.

"Is he here?" he barked despite himself, his voice like a whip crack.

The receptionist's brow furrowed. She hesitated.

Bruce felt time grinding down around him like teeth.

HOTEL RÍO IMPERIAL — ROOM 614

Elias sat at the table near the balcony window, the tactical detonator resting before him like a coiled serpent. His fingers, usually precise and unshakeable, hovered above it with the reverence of a priest before the sacrament. The whole of Madrid glistened beyond the glass—flags fluttering atop the summit complex, guards stiffening with each passing second.

His physiology was changing—a heightened state, honed over years in deep cover. His vision had narrowed, focus sharp as a blade. His heart thudded not with fear but with clarity. The moment was coming. The hour ordained. A just strike, not for vengeance but for history.

He closed his eyes, breathing deeply. One

breath in. Hold. One breath out. Hold.

His lips moved silently, thanking God, but not in Arabic as had been habitual for years. His prayer invoked strength in accepting fate. *If today is my end, let it count.*

The American noticed the tight pressure that had settled in his bladder. He ignored it at first. A minor signal. *Damn coffee. Not now.* Then, another more urgent pulse. He hissed, annoyed. Not out of discomfort but the irritating practicality of it.

He would need to move swiftly after detonation—he'd mapped every step, every corridor, every second. There would be no time to urinate when the chaos broke.

With a reluctant glance at the detonator, he muttered, "It'll still be there in sixty seconds".

He stepped into the en-suite bathroom.

As the flush echoed behind him and he dried his hands with mechanical calm, a sound reached his ears.

A subtle creak. A footstep? A whisper of pressure on carpet.

He froze.

No alarm bells rang in his mind—not yet. Hotels had noise. Guests. Staff. And perhaps Umar had arrived early. Elias looked to the door, considered calling out, but dismissed the thought. No surprises. No visibility.

Probably nothing.

The moment shattered with a loud crack. The door splintered open with a thunderous blow. Wood shattered, hinges tore loose. The frame caved inward, and a man filled the space—shoulders broad, face tight with resolve, hair the colour of coal, eyes like winter steel. His jaw defined, his clothes dark and practical.

Not a hotel guest. Not Umar. Not French. Not Spanish.

The stranger had the calm of someone who'd done this before, a storm walking upright.

You're too late, Elias thought—but didn't say.

The human personification of a Grey Wolf leapt at him as Elias dove for the detonator.

Bruce's boot splintered the door open. He surged into the room, eyes locking onto Elias lunging for the device on the table.

Bruce tackled him mid-dive, their bodies colliding with a thud. The detonator skidded across the table, teetering on the edge but remaining in place.

They crashed to the floor, a tangle of limbs and intent. Bruce recognised the fluidity in the man's movements—trained, precise.

Before the Scot could cinch his arms around the thrashing legs, he felt his hair snatched in a fistful as Elias straightened his arm and violently twisted and scooted away.

Though Bruce managed to block the boot sole ramming towards his face, it shunted him enough to allow Elias the room to bolt to his feet a fraction of a second before him.

In addition to his years of judo, Bruce had done some inter-battalion boxing back in 3 Para. In the regiment, **_Jap Slapping_** referred to any unarmed combat training, and by the time Bruce got there, a system named Goshinkwai was being taught. It originated in South Wales, combining elements of traditional Japanese jiu jitsu and judo.

He guessed the skillset of his opponent to be more diverse, and his opponent didn't need to beat Bruce; he just needed to reach the detonator.

A desk lamp flew at Bruce like an enraged bat.

He parried it with his right forearm, as he shot a jab with his left.

An elbow caught him in the solar plexus as Elias whipped around him.

The judoka's foot shot out in a panicked hurdler's stretch, catching Elias's mid-stride to topple him forwards.

Bruce saw the mistake—saw that he would be victorious.

Elias, instead of spinning to his back, attempted to stand.

Bruce seized the opportunity like a leopard on an antelope, rifling in a ***hadaka jime***—rear naked choke, ensuring a steadily increasing squeeze as opposed to ripping it on.

Elias's fingers clawed for his eyes as Bruce clamped them shut. Then he gripped his ears.

He should be out by now. Bruce grimaced, feeling the blood rivulet from the seam where the ear met his head.

Mercifully, the grip transferred to digging for purchase on his fingers and wrists.

Gradually, his resistance waned, and his movements slowed.

The gurgling, choking snore and the relaxing of Elias's fingers signified his passing over to unconsciousness.

Bruce released his grip and rose, breathing heavily, and turned towards the detonator.

Adam Umar moved like a shadow in trainers, a ghost up the back stairwell of the Río Imperial. He'd ditched the weapons back in the Hôtel Saint-Rémy in Paris. In his escape, he surmised that if he were picked up afterwards, it would be best not to have anything incriminating on him.

He wished he hadn't now—if he had been arrested, they would have had enough evidence against him to bury him beneath a prison anyway.

At the top of the stairs, he heard it.

A dull crash.

His eyes shot down the corridor.

A door—Room 614—already splintered.

And then: scuffling. Sharp, fast. Breathing. Strained. Bodies colliding. Furniture shifting.

Someone's found him.

Umar's pace quickened, closing the distance in seconds. The door hung crooked in its frame, kicked in. Beyond it, the sound of fists and feet—a fight between killers.

Umar didn't hesitate.

He entered just in time to see Zubayr sprawled unconscious on the carpet.

Above him was a broad-shouldered man in dark clothing, breath heaving, blood dripping from his ear, one knee rising from the floor.

A silent rage in Umar's chest pistoned him forward, driving a shoulder into the man's back like a freight train, sending him crashing. The enemy rolled, head tucked against a curved arm, like he'd been thrown before. Combat muscle memory. Trained.

The dark-haired man landed on one knee and turned fast. Ready.

The two men locked eyes—soldier to soldier.

Umar read it all in that single glance. This wasn't law enforcement. This wasn't security. This was a government-sponsored killer.

Still, Umar knew that Allah had placed him here in this exact moment to rescue the mission.

He stepped forward, fists loose, breathing steady.

He wasn't armed. He didn't need to be.

32

**PALACIO MUNICIPAL DE CONGRESOS —
TECHNICAL HALLWAY — 12.58**

Frank Carlsmith slowed as they passed the last of the backstage service doors. He glanced once over his shoulder—habit, nothing more—before his eyes drifted towards the ventilation shaft halfway down the corridor wall.

It was just another panel among dozens they'd passed that day, nondescript and harmless. But a cold marble grew at the base of his neck. He stopped.

"Hold on."

Yuri and Anissa halted two steps ahead.

Frank turned back to the duct and stared. It was too convenient. Shielded from the cameras. Largely overlooked. No airflow. A dead space. *If I were him*, he thought, *this is where I'd put it.*

"I'll try this one," Frank said quietly, crouching in front of the vent.

Anissa stepped closer. "You think he used the duct?"

"Yeah," Frank replied, already fishing out his Leatherman Super Tool on his belt. "I don't just think it—I'd bet my pension."

He flicked open the screwdriver head and set it to the first rusted screw.

Yuri knelt beside him, watching with the impassive calm of a soldier under orders.

Frank paused and looked at him, something unreadable flickering in his eyes.

"This is my last play," said Frank as he

gestured down the hall. "Go find Bruce."

Yuri didn't argue.

He nodded once and disappeared at a jog down the corridor.

Frank got to work.

One screw off. He pocketed it.

Second screw—

"¡Oiga! ¡Alto ahí!"

The bark came from behind.

Frank turned to see three Russian security officers in blue jackets and black utility belts approaching at speed, their boots loud against the tile.

The lead one—a stocky officer with a shaved head and too much authority in his stride—snatched a glance at Anissa, then fixed his eyes on Frank.

"You are not authorised to tamper with infrastructure. This is a secure venue."

Frank stood, slow and deliberate, hands away from his body.

"Colonel Taranov authorised this search," said Frank, holding the temporary pass.

"Colonel Taranov authorised it to a time ending minutes ago. You have disregarded this."

"I just need," he said, pointing to the panel, "two more minutes. It is wor—"

Anissa hissed in French-tinged English. "The colonel must have told you we are looking for a fucking atomic device here at the summit, not documents relating to Watergate."

The officer ignored her, stepping closer to Frank, tension in his stance.

Frank kept his voice measured. "Listen to me. I'm not trying to undermine your authority. But if there's something behind this panel and we walk away from it, everyone here dies today. And hundreds of others, eventually, from radiation poisoning. Is it worth just two minutes longer?"

The Russian officer's eyes didn't waver. Nor did Frank's.

Behind them, the vent remained untouched—two screws loose, two still holding.

The officer glanced at his subordinates, then back at Frank.

HOTEL RÍO IMPERIAL — ROOM 614

Bruce had rolled with the hammer blow to his back, tucked and turned, muscles obeying on instinct. Came up on one knee, fists raised.

Adam Umar stood there—thick arms, square jaw, eyes like polished onyx. Quiet rage radiated off him like heat from asphalt. No weapon.

Bruce didn't wait.

He stepped in fast with a jab-cross combination, the first striking the man's cheek, the second barely brushing past as Umar pivoted, absorbing the blows like a plastic wall. A short, sharp, expertly placed blow burst the wind from Bruce's lungs.

Bruce stumbled back, hands raised, sucked in a breath, then launched forward with an ***Osoto Gari***, aiming to reap the outside of Umar's leg.

The Algerian blocked it with the brutal simplicity of a headbutt.

Lights exploded behind Bruce's eyes.

He staggered sideways, blood running now from somewhere near the brow. Umar kept coming—disciplined, no flair. A professional. One-two to the body. Clinch. Knee to the thigh. Another.

The Scot knew then that, despite his own physicality, training, and being taller, Umar possessed the advantages of weight and even raw strength.

Bruce twisted, trying to break the grip, snuck his right arm inside and latched onto the belt line, feinting a backwards sweep but spinning into a modified ***Harai goshi***—hip throw on his adversary's push back.

Umar resisted, but Bruce, instinctively adhering to ***Kuzushi***—breaking balance—had his centre of gravity beneath Umar and wrenched to topple him over his hip. Both men crashed to the floor again.

This wasn't combat anymore. It was survival.

Bruce, sideways on top of Umar's muscled chest, wrapped his opponent's head and locked a ***Kesa-gatame*** with such pressure it blew a grimace onto Umar's face.

He punched with his free hand, anticipating snatching Umar's arm when it came up to defend.

However, the Bosnian War veteran hand had snaked around his head, and a finger dove into the inside of his cheek before wrenching.

McQuillan instantly let go of the hold and spun his head with the pull, a split second before his lips could tear. Both men scrambled to their feet.

Umar was already advancing Terminator-like.

Bruce drove a low front kick aiming for the knee but catching the shin, then surged forward with an elbow to the jaw.

Umar's head snapped sideways, but his hand grabbed Bruce's collar and yanked him forward into another headbutt, this one deeper, bone-on-bone.

Bruce bit his tongue. Blood filled his mouth.

His pride seared. *That's two Glasgow kisses he's caught you with.*

They grappled again—forearms locked, torsos heaving. Bruce pulled him forward, timing the pull back before using his weight and a **Kouchi Gari**—inner foot sweep—to drive Umar into the desk, reaching and scrabbling for—anything.

His hand found the iron.

He brought it upward, smashing the flat metal into Umar's temple with a dull *crack*. Umar staggered, blinked, and Bruce hit him again, with more leverage.

The big man finally dropped. Knees first—another smash—then face-first into the carpet.

Bruce collapsed against the wall, breath ragged, vision swimming.

A noise behind him. Soft. Sharp. Like breath returning to a throat.

No!

He turned just in time to see Elias Monroe's eyes open. Bloodless lips curled into a smile as his fingers—shaking but certain—stretched across the floor to snatch up the fallen detonator.

Bruce lunged—

Click.

And everything froze.

33

INT. HOTEL RÍO IMPERIAL — ROOM 614

Click.

Click.

Click.

Elias walked backwards towards the shattered balcony doors, thumb flicking the detonator with an outstretched arm and deliberate malice. His face showed no panic—just calculation. When the third click yielded no apocalypse, he turned to look out across Madrid, flags still fluttering peacefully above the summit complex.

Bruce surged to his feet.

Elias turned back, paused and hurled the detonator straight at Bruce's head as he sprinted forward.

Instinct took over.

Bruce just barely caught it, hands cradling it like a live grenade. But in doing so, he missed Elias, who slipped past, shoulder brushing Bruce's arm, before bolting out the door like a strange moggy out the cat flap when the owner appeared.

Bruce gave chase on thrashed legs, pulse hammering and vision swimming.

He didn't chase far.

He had the detonator now. Elias might win another encounter and if he got hold of it again maybe he'd run it closer to the summit and could activate it.

He remembered in 'the Det' one of the more experienced guys telling him not to lose the war for the sake of winning a battle.

He turned back into the room and knelt by Umar.

Two fingers pressed to the neck. Pulse—weak, but present.

Bruce considered finishing him.

No time.

He holstered the detonator deep in his coat pocket and left the room, his body a patchwork of pain, but nothing felt broken.

Bruised, bloodied, and exhausted, but in one piece.

He walked the corridor and descended carefully, hand brushing the wall, alert for traps. Elias was the type to leave something waiting.

The hotel was oddly quiet now.

On the second floor, a maid stared at him with wide eyes and stepped aside. He didn't acknowledge her.

Sunlight struck his eyes like a slap. He blinked, adjusting, still half-expecting gunfire or pursuit.

Then—a car.

Unmarked, dust-smudged.

It pulled up fast.

He stepped back, already considering his options. The back door flung open.

"Bruce!" Anissa's voice. Urgent.

She sat in the rear, hair pulled back, eyes sharp.

The front windows were down—Frank was driving, Yuri in the passenger seat.

Bruce slid in, body aching. "Elias is gone. Umar's unconscious in the room. I've got the detonator."

"Fucking top work," said Frank, not even looking back. "We found the suitcase nuke three minutes ago. I detached the radio receiver."

Bruce exhaled. "And they just let you drive off with it?"

"I wrapped my watch around the receiver—told the Russian security boys it was on a timer. They gave us the car to get it as far away as possible—we'll have to swap vehicles soon."

Bruce nodded. "What now?"

Frank's jaw tightened. "We go dark. Until I figure out the lay of the land. See who's playing what."

Bruce looked down at the detonator in his hand. "And the bomb?"

Frank glanced at him in the rear-view mirror. "I am not sure yet."

A moment.

Bruce said, "I've got an idea about that."

And they sped off, disappearing into the backstreets of Madrid.

34

SIS HEADQUARTERS — SIR ANDREW MAREMOUNT'S OFFICE — NIGHT

The room smelled faintly of old wood polish and the dried leaves of Maremount's Lapsang tea. A night wind hissed against the windows high above the Thames, the kind that set London's night skyline shimmering and sharp. Parker stood just inside the room, hands clasped behind his back, watching the transatlantic tension boil.

Harold Kellerman wasn't just angry. He was coiled, like an old viper, jaw set tight beneath silver-streaked stubble. The Deputy Director of Operations didn't bother with pleasantries.

"Where is it?" he asked. "The RA-115S. Where. Is. It."

Parker met his stare. "It's been returned to the Russians."

Silence. Then—

"You did what?" Kellerman said, voice rising half an octave. "You handed them a tactical atomic device?"

Parker kept his tone measured. "We didn't exactly have a display booth at the Madrid summit. Gaining access without triggering global panic meant liaising with the Russians. Once our time window elapsed, they insisted on oversight."

Kellerman's face darkened. "So, let me understand—you gave a nuclear weapon back to a corrupt, unstable, increasingly adversarial regime because of... manners?"

Maremount, sitting behind his desk, raised one hand, but said nothing.

Parker continued, unfazed. "Before the handover, my asset rendered it inert. He removed the radio receiver module. Without it, it can't be remotely detonated."

Kellerman scoffed. "That's supposed to reassure me?"

Maremount interjected, voice calm but hard-edged. "Over one hundred RA-115S units were reputedly manufactured. The notion that handing back one inert specimen shifts the global balance is absurd. What matters is that the summit didn't end in nuclear ash."

Kellerman turned towards him. "I want to speak with your asset. Whoever his handler—he acted under my operation. I assume you haven't forgotten that this was a CIA mission? Our safe house, weapons and transport."

"And our assets," said Maremount, leaning back in his chair and steepling his fingers. "We saw the mission as simply to prevent the detonation of a nuclear weapon by terrorists—successfully completed. That makes it a shared victory. We thought you came to make a toast."

"Your asset brought a foreign player onto the safe house without authorisation."

"Wood for the trees comes to mind."

Parker noticed the slight twitch in Kellerman's jaw—the tell of a man used to giving orders and receiving deference, not being reined in by allies.

But this was Maremount's office, and the old man didn't blink.

Parker could see it all too clearly now.

Kellerman had wanted the device. Wanted it whole, intact, and quiet. Not for safety. For leverage. But he couldn't admit that—not here, not in this room.

The room settled into a brittle silence. Kellerman adjusted his cuffs, eyes moving from Parker to Maremount and back.

Maremount stood. "Perhaps, Harold, your energies would be better spent tracking down the man who made this necessary in the first place. Elias Monroe—a rogue CIA agent."

Kellerman held his stare a moment longer, then nodded—once, curtly.

Without another word, he turned and left.

Parker watched the door close behind him, the tension leaving the room like smoke from an open window.

Maremount said. "We don't owe them contrition for saving lives."

Parker didn't respond. He just stood there, the image of Elias Monroe still burned behind his eyes.

He hoped—God help him—that the man hadn't vanished entirely.

NICOSIA, CYPRUS — PRIVATE TERRACE — EVENING

The coffee had long since gone cold, untouched between them.

Major Andrei Sokolova sat at the shaded terrace table of a rented villa on the outskirts of Nicosia, his expression unreadable.

A distant breeze stirred the bougainvillea

vines. Across from him, Commandant Éric Chauvigny exhaled slowly, arms crossed with a French arrogance. To his right, the strikingly attractive Anissa Rajah looked less composed—alert, defensive, like a field operative suddenly thrust into politics.

The Russian admired the realism of her act.

Sokolova, speaking mainly in French with a smattering of their second shared language of English, fixed his cold blue-grey gaze on her. "You were one of the four granted access to the summit complex by Russian security. I've seen the internal coordination logs myself."

"Yes?" said Anissa with a hint of frown. "There has never been a denial of that."

"Then where is it?"

"Monsieur Carlsmith decided to keep it in his custody once it had been rendered inert. He kindly deposited me outside the French embassy. As far as I knew, he was returning to the summit to pass it over to the Russian security officers who loaned them a vehicle."

"A vehicle loaned under the untruth that Mister Carlsmith and his team were going to drive it as far away from the summit as possible due to the detonation being under a timer. Except the RA-115S never has, nor could it ever have been retrofitted with a timer. And the said vehicle was eventually found around one hundred kilometres away in Cuenca."

"I was not to know of intricacies of the atomic munition's engineering—I am an art dealer. And to repeat, what happened to it and the vehicle was not within my power once deposited outside the embassy."

"Convenient," Sokolova said softly, the syllables surgical.

Chauvigny stirred. "This is beginning to sound like an interrogation that perhaps you should be putting certain Russian engineers through—if still alive. Or certainly those charged with the security of these illegal munitions. Perhaps if they were not guarded so carelessly, then the hostage siege in Paris would never have occurred."

Sokolova knew the concept of limiting the damage of a defeat. He adjusted the cuffs of his cardigan slowly and stood.

"I thank you both for your candour." His voice was smooth. "And your hospitality."

Chauvigny gave a polite nod, dismissing him like a waiter clearing plates. Anissa rose to shake his hand and he left the villa.

The sun dipped low as Sokolova walked alone through the quiet Cypriot backstreets, the soft thrum of distant prayer calls echoing through the alleyways.

He'd parked the rental—a grey Peugeot 406—two blocks away, a standard counter-surveillance protocol.

They had the bomb—probably the Brits or, Lord preserve him, the Americans.

He wouldn't survive this politically—General Barinov had already redundantly educated him on that.

They would bury him in some administrative gulag within the Ministry of Emergency Situations—overseeing nuclear decontamination charts and pretending to matter—if he was lucky.

He turned the final corner. The car sat where he left it. No disturbance.

He reached for the keys in his coat pocket.
Click.
The unmistakable mechanical snap of a handgun's hammer cocking.

"Turn around. Slowly. Hands where I can see them."

The voice was Scottish—working-class, clipped. Western Central Belt, Sokolova assessed.

He turned.

The man standing behind him was tall, broad-shouldered, lean with tension. Dark hair and steely grey eyes. Plaster resting over the top crease of the right ear.

That he was a professional was obvious.

He kept the pistol—a compact Browning Hi-Power—partially concealed within his jacket. Sokolova obeyed.

"Open the boot—the ***bagazhnik***," the man said.

Sokolova did so—his heartrate rocketing.

Inside lay the RA-115S. The Soviet-era device was secured with foam blocks, the radio receiver detached. Still intact. Still salvageable.

"We've removed the radio receiver module so it can't 'hear' the detonator's signal even if reattached," the man said. "The detonator is in your glovebox."

Sokolova turned his head slightly. "You returned it?"

The man shrugged. "It's yours—I'm a bit too old for finders keepers."

Sokolova almost smiled before murmuring to himself aloud, still in English, "How am I supposed to explain this?"

The man gave him a look. "Maybe you say you cultivated a British asset who tracked it down. Played the long game. Pulled off a coup that'll make your bosses sweat with admiration."

Sokolova tilted his head. *My career saved—enhanced even*, he thought.

"And what do you want in return?"

"Upon your arrival back, you will write a formal report on how instrumental Master Sergeant Yuri Kozlov has been in the retrieval of this device. His career should rise in tandem with yours."

"We are two differe—"

"Spare me. Everyone in our business knows how much influence the SVR has within the Ukrainian intelligence and political spheres. I hear you're a man of honour—as much as you can be in our game—and this is the price you pay for the gift we've given you."

There was a silence. Then Sokolova said, "What would the codename for the British asset be?"

"That's up to you," the man said. "Just don't make it too cheesy."

Sokolova looked at the case, then back at the man.

"Opekun."

The man raised an eyebrow. "What's that mean?"

"The Guardian."

The Brit gave the faintest smile, then turned and vanished into the Nicosia darkness.

EPILOGUE

SEVEN MONTHS LATER

LISBON — ALFAMA DISTRICT — SMALL BAR — EVENING

The glass of amarguinha caught the last of the sun through the shuttered window. Elias Monroe—now known as Dr. Yusuf Khouri—watched the golden light flicker across the polished bar. He wore linen, loose at the collar, and had let his beard grow to frame a face that had forgotten how to look young.

Portugal had proven fertile for anonymity. Tourists came and went. The city's steep hills and fado cafés distracted the curious, and his work—consulting on outdated nuclear plant designs—was enough to keep him legitimate on paper.

He wasn't sure when he sensed the presence behind him. It wasn't footsteps—those had been swallowed by the low music and murmured conversation. It was more like a weight in the air. A change in current.

He turned slowly.

Carl Frankson—probably not his real name—stood there, and he instantly remembered Amman.

Same hazel-green eyes. Same creased-leather face. A little greyer and therefore a little less ginger.

He looked like a man who had spent the past months climbing out of ash.

Elias's throat dried slightly. He had to assume the Englishman was armed.

"Mind if I sit?" Carl asked casually, already

pulling out the chair.

Elias gave a slight nod. *If he were here to kill me, it wouldn't be across a cocktail menu.*

The Brit's grin twitched. "You like that almond piss you're supping? Or is it part of the cover?"

"Is being a narrow-minded Brit part of your cover?"

"Touché, Doctor Khouri."

With almost comic timing, a waitress appeared to slide two more amarguinhas in front of them both.

Carl thanked her before taking a sip. "Not bad. A smooth, nutty tang."

Elias stayed silent. Watching.

The Brit leant forward. "Relax. The only person who knows you're here is sitting across from you now."

Elias's jaw tightened. "Why are you here?"

"I am not here to kill, kidnap or even blackmail you, though I'd have every right to any of those after what you tried to do."

"Then what?"

"I am here to offer you an opportunity. Like I said, I won't grass on you if you say no."

"Grass?"

"I won't rat you out."

Elias didn't speak for a few moments before asking, "Opportunity for what?"

Carl's eyes didn't blink. "Your skillset's going to waste, mate. I can see it in your eyes—just over half a year and you're already bored. And you can't go back to the CIA. You're radioactive to them now. No pun intended."

Elias leant forward. "Do not be vague."

Carl smiled. "But Ramzi's still out there. He'll want to make another move. Al Qaeda's teeth are growing bigger and sharper, and they've not forgotten the brilliant Zubayr al-Adel. According to their books, you're still him. Revered. Untouched. Prime for resurrection."

"Zubayr al-Adel failed in his mission."

"No, Adam Umar betrayed you—that's the story a dead man cannot refute. You have spent the last half year trying to determine if Ramzi al-Wahishi sold you out. You have decided he did not."

Elias's eyes dropped to the base of his glass. He thought of the weight he still carried. Of the cross tucked behind a stitched seam in his jacket. Of the lies he once lived with such discipline they nearly became truth.

Elias asked, "Do you believe in God?"

"Without being melodramatic, I have felt the hand of God, yes."

"When was the first time?"

The question seemed to surprise the Brit. After a moment, he answered, "Around fifteen years ago I was in Afghanistan. I was confronted by a boy no older than eleven with an AK47. It was dark and there had been some cross tribal shenanigans in the area. He pointed it directly at me and fired."

"Stoppage?"

"No. The selector had rusted on auto. Kid couldn't control the recoil. I ran up to him and smacked him," said the Englishman. "But let me tell ya, when the bullets singed my beautiful red locks, there wasn't a doubt in my mind—nor is there now—that God played a part in that."

Elias did not speak.

"I'll leave it with you, chief," Carl said as he stood. "I'll be in the *O Cais Velho*, seeing how Coulthard gets on in the European Grand Prix. If you don't rock up before the end of the race, then I'll take it as a no."

The Brit clapped him on the shoulder and left.

Elias stared at the empty seat, the air still holding the scent of worn leather and London aftershave.

And he didn't realise his hand had drifted to the rosary beads tucked in his jacket's lining.

AUTHOR'S REQUEST

Please leave a review of Genesis of Opekun

As a self-published author, Amazon reviews are vital in me getting my work to as many readers as possible.

Your review means I can continue to write the series for you.

Thank you so much.

Quentin Black

Genesis of Opekun
Review

GLOSSARY

Amadán — Irish Gaelic for fool or idiot.

Akhi — Arabic for 'my brother'.

Art Attack — a British kids' television show revolving around art that began in 1990.

Attestation Paper — the form used to swear one's allegiance to the crown and embark on a military career with the UK armed forces.

Aum Shinrikyo — A Japanese religious and doomsday cult responsible for the Tokyo subway sarin attack in 1995.

Banlieue — suburbs of large cities, often economically challenged with diverse communities.

(The) Base — Al Qaeda's literal

translation, as in 'The Base of Jihad'.

Beour — Irish slang for an attractive girl or woman.

The Bill — a British police television drama series, at its most popular in the late eighties to mid-nineties.

Bloody Sunday — thirteen Catholics were shot dead and several others injured during a civil rights demonstration on the 30th of January 1972 in Derry, Northern Ireland.

Brass — slang for money in northern England.

Brew — a term used in the British Army and Royal Air Force to describe a tea or coffee.

(the) Circus — a nickname for MI6 deriving from John le Carré fiction novels.

Crow — a term for an inexperienced soldier deriving from a World War I parlance of **C**ombat **R**ecruit **o**f **W**ar.

Crow Culture — a system of mentorship and maintenance of a unit's pecking order, which includes the assignment of subservient taskings to the more junior servicemen and women. Almost everyone is someone's Crow with the only person within HM Forces is the King or Queen themselves.

The Crystal Maze — a British game show popular in the first half of the 90s, set in a labyrinth.

Dacha — Russian term for a second, usually holiday, home in the countryside.

Deservice and reservice kit — clean, tidy, fix clothing and equipment to ensure readiness for operational taskings.

Dickers— refers to enemy spotters or informants of British forces. More commonly used during operations in Northern Ireland.

Glasnost — roughly translated to 'transparency' or 'openness' with regards to political discourse. Popularised by the Soviet Union leader Mikhail Gorbachev back in the eighties.

FARC — (Fuerzas Armadas Revolucionarias de Colombia) Revolutionary Armed Forces of Colombia. A Marxist-Leninist guerilla group.

The Firm — an informal insider term for the British Secret Intelligence Service.

FSB — the FSB is Russia's main domestic intelligence and security agency responsible for counterintelligence, counterterrorism, border security, and surveillance within Russia and former Soviet states.

Galley — the kitchen/canteen of a ship or aircraft.

Ghazali — means 'philosopher' after the eleventh-century Sunni Muslim scholar Al-Ghazali.

Ghillie suit — a full-body garment used for camouflage.

Gralloching — the removal of hunted game's internal organs to prevent the potential contamination of the meat.

Grossier — French word for coarse, crude, vulgar.

GRU — the foreign military intelligence agency of the General Staff of the Armed Forces of the Russian

Federation. Though now named Main Directorate of the General Staff of the Armed Forces of the Russian Federation, it is still commonly referred to as its soviet predecessor the GRU.

Half-price Helen — a good-natured (usually) north of England term for a loose woman.

Kāfir — Arabic term for 'non-believers'.

Ken — east coast of Scotland slang for 'know'.

Keffiyeh — traditional Arab headdress.

(Go) Kinetic — to fight, usually with firearms.

Klettersteig — German for 'climbing trail'. Iron cables are bolted to the mountainside with which the climbers secure themselves to with karabiners and rope.

Koka — prior to being removed in 2009, the Koka was the lowest score in judo, given when throw results in the opponent landing on his or her side, buttocks, or thigh. Also if you could hold the opponent down for ten-fourteen seconds.

Julie Andrews — a term to describe that one likes their tea or coffee with milk but no sugar— white nun. Not, as some think, with 'Just a spoonful of sugar'.

Mither — Northern English slang for 'bother'.

(The) Office — an old Russian colloquialism for the KGB, and therefore by extension the SVR.

Omerta — criminal code of silence.

Over-the-river — the Headquarters of SIS in Vauxhall Cross and MI5's Thames House in Millbank are on opposite banks of the River Thames.

Owt — Northern English slang for 'anything'.

(the) Stickies — in 1969, the original Irish Republican Army divided into two groups: the Official IRA and the Provisional IRA. Though both sought the unification of Ireland, one of the main dividers between the two groups was that the Official IRA believed that the reunification could not be attained until a peace between the Catholic minority and Protestant majority of Northern Ireland had been established.

Panda — slang for regular police cars due to their colour scheme.

Quiet tour — British military euphemism for covert work, especially in Northern Ireland or overseas.

Racing Snake — old British military slang for an excellent runner.

Red Notice — Interpol's list identifying fugitives wanted for capture or extradition. Includes descriptions of the said individuals.

Restoring Constitutional Order — how the Russian Government termed the First Chechen War prior to the Second.

Ripping ma knitting — Scottish slang for someone annoying you.

Salfords — Mancunian rhythming slang for 'socks' as in 'Salford Docks'.

SBS — Special Boat Service; one of the United Kingdom's two (or three depending on who you ask) Special Forces units, with the other being the

SAS (and SRR depending on who you ask).

Selection — the process to screen and train recruits for the United Kingdom Special Forces.

Shaytān — Islamic Devil.

Shemaghs — square scarf traditionally worn in the Middle East in protection against dust, wind, andor sunburn.

Shchur — Ukrainian for Rat.

Shido — Penalty given in judo for minor infringements.

Simunition — Simulated ammunition—essentially paintballs though wax pellets can be used.

SIS — the Secret Intelligence Service—universally referred to in intelligence circles as **SIS** and colloquially as **MI6**—

is Britain's external intelligence agency, responsible for gathering, analysing, and acting upon intelligence related to foreign threats.

SNCO — Senior Non-Commissioned Officer.

Solntsevo Group — a Russian organised crime syndicate.

Stein — around one litre, almost two pints.

The Regiment — a nickname for Britain's Special Air Service.

Tab — term for cigarette used in certain parts of northern England.

Tawhid — an Arabic term for the worship of one God.

Terp — interpreter.

The Troubles — A violent, ethno-nationalist conflict in Northern Ireland that lasted from the late 1960s to 1998. It involved republican paramilitaries (mainly Catholic, seeking unification with the Republic of Ireland), loyalist paramilitaries (mainly Protestant, wanting to remain part of the UK), and British state forces. The conflict caused over 3,500 deaths and ended with the Good Friday Agreement.

The Wing — an abbreviation and nickname for the SAS's Revolutionary Warfare Wing. This was later co-joined with a small equivalent detachment from the SBS (Special Boat Service) to be formalised into 'E-Squadron'. The common misconception is that it is also known as 'The Increment'; however, 'The Increment' is the detachment that performs specific operations for SIS.

Tom — slang word in the Parachute Regiment for a soldier holding the rank of private, and therefore they are usually, though not always, young and inexperienced.

Tout — originally used in England and Ireland within horse racing circles to describe in-the-know tipsters. The term morphed during The Troubles to describe informants for the RUC and/or British Security Services.

Thawb — traditional Arab male gown.

Ummah — an Arabic term and core Islamic theme of a unified community.

Ushankas — a furry hat that the Russians commonly wear against the cold.

Vor v zakone — Russian term meaning 'Thief-in-law', a loose comparison to being a 'made guy' in the Italian mafia.

What it is, right — north-west English

phrase that precedes an explanation. Can be swapped out for the term **'the thing is, right…'**

Woad — a flowering plant native to parts of Europe used for war paint by Pictish warriors and for dying cloth.

Yuko — a minor score in judo.

ABOUT THE AUTHOR

FOLLOW ME

Follow me on Amazon to be informed of new releases and my latest updates.

Quentin Black is a former Royal Marine corporal with a decade of service in the Corps. This includes an operational tour of Afghanistan and an advisory mission in Iraq.

AUTHOR'S NOTE

Join my exclusive readers clubs for information on new books, deals, and free content in addition to my sporadic reviews on certain books, films, and TV series I might have enjoyed.

Plus, you'll be immediately sent a **FREE** copy of the novella *An Outlaw's Reprieve.*

Remember, before you groan, 'Why do I always have to give my email with these things?!' you can always unsubscribe, and you'll still have a free book. So, just click below on the following link.

Free Book

Any written reviews would be greatly appreciated. If you have spotted a mistake, I would like you to let me know so I can improve reader experience. Either way, contact me on my email below.

Email me

Or you can follow me on social media here:

IN THE CONNOR REED SERIES

The Bootneck

How far would you go for a man who gave you a second chance in life?

Bruce McQuillan leads a black operations unit only known to a handful of men.

A sinister plot involving the Russian Bratva and one of the most powerful men within the British Security Services threatens to engulf the Isles.

Could a criminal with an impulse for sadism be the only man McQuillan can trust?

Lessons In Blood

When the ruling class commoditise the organs of the desperate, who will stop them?

When Darren O'Reilly's daughter is found murdered with her kidney extracted, he refuses to believe the police's explanation. His quest for the truth reaches the ears of Bruce McQuillan, the leader of the shadowy Chameleon Project.

As a conspiracy of seismic proportions begins to reveal itself, Bruce realises he needs a man of exceptional skill and ruthlessness.

He needs Connor Reed.

Ares' Thirst

Can one man stop World War III?

When a British aid worker disappears in Crimea, the UK Government wants her back—quickly and quietly.

And Machiavellian figures are fuelling the flames of Islamic hatred towards Russia. With 'the dark edge of the world' controlled by some of the most cunning, ruthless and powerful criminals on Earth, McQuillan knows he needs to send a wolf amongst the wolves before the match of global war is struck across the rough land of Ukraine.

Northern Wars

The Ryder crime family are now at war… on three fronts.

After ruthlessly dethroning his uncle, Connor Reed must now defend the family against the circling sharks of rival criminal enterprises.

Meanwhile, Bruce McQuillan, leader of a black operations unit named The Chameleon Project, has learnt that one of the world's most brutal and influential mafias are targeting the UK pre-BREXIT.

Counterpart

Can Connor Reed survive his deadliest mission yet?

Bruce McQuillan's plan to light the torch of war between two of the world's most powerful and ruthless mafias has been ignited.

Can his favoured agent, Connor Reed, fan the flames without being engulfed by them?

Especially as a man every bit his equal stands on the other side.

An Outlaw's Reprieve

"When there is no enemy within, the enemies outside cannot hurt you."

Reed, a leader within his own outlaw family, delights in an opportunity to punish a thug preying on the vulnerable.

However, with his target high within a rival criminal organisation, can Reed exact retribution without dragging his relatives into a bloody war?

The Puppet Master

For the first time in history, humanity has the capacity to destroy the world.

When a British scientist leads a highly proficient Japanese engineering team in unlocking the secrets to the biosphere's survival, some will stop at nothing to see the fledging technology disappear.

In the Land of the Rising Sun, can Bruce McQuillan protect the new scientific applications from the most powerful entities on Earth?

And can his favoured agent Connor Reed defeat the deadliest adversary he has ever faced?

A King's Gambit

Can the Ryder clan defeat a more ruthless organisation that dwarfs them in size and finance?

When the **dark hands of a blood feud** between Irish criminal organisations begin to choke civilians and strategies to halt the evil fail, fear grips law enforcement in the United Kingdom, the Republic of Ireland and continental Europe.

When this war ensnares the Ryder clan, Connor finds himself with the choice between trusting the skill and mental fortitude of untested family members, along with the motives of his enemy's enemy…

Or the complete **annihilation of his family.**

The Devil's Nemesis

Connor Reed owes a lethal debt.

A year on from a brutal **encounter with Irish mobsters**, *the Ryder clan have solidified their standing as one of the UK's most efficient outlaw organisations.*

However, when Carlo Andaloro calls in a favour, Connor Reed has no choice but to travel to Canada to face its most **savagely cruel** *crime lords.*

As the black operations agent gets closer, he discovers a plan **to flood Canada's cities with death.**

And the intent lays higher than **anyone could imagine.**

Armageddon Games

Can Bruce McQuillan unravel a web of deception and prevent a global inferno?

The fires of war burn in the Middle East and along the Ukrainian-Russian border.

When the notoriously guarded Israelis request the British black operations maestro Bruce McQuillan examine the security failings of the Simchat Torah Massacre, he senses his entanglement in a deadly spider's web.

The question is— **Who has spun it?**

A flame ignites to draw the world's superpowers into a confrontation of **holocaustic consequences.**

It is up to McQuillan and his premier agent, Connor Reed, to put it out.

Printed in Dunstable, United Kingdom